LEGACY *of* TRIL

BOOK ONE:

Soulbound

HEATHER BREWER

LEGACY of TRIL

BOOK ONE:

Soulbound

DIAL BOOKS

· an imprint of Penguin Group (USA) Inc. ·

DIAL BOOKS

A division of Penguin Group USA Inc.

Published by The Penguin Group

Penguin Group (USA) Inc., 375 Hudson Street, New York, NY 10014, U.S.A. * Penguin Group (Canada), 90 Eglinton Avenue East, Suite 700, Toronto, Ontario, Canada M4P 2Y3 (a division of Pearson Penguin Canada Inc.) * Penguin Books Ltd, 80 Strand, London WC2R 0RL, England * Penguin Ireland, 25 St. Stephen's Green, Dublin 2, Ireland (a division of Penguin Books Ltd) * Penguin Group (Australia), 250 Camberwell Road, Camberwell, Victoria 3124, Australia (a division of Pearson Australia Group Pty Ltd) * Penguin Books India Pvt Ltd, 11 Community Centre, Panchsheel Park, New Delhi—110 017, India * Penguin Group (NZ), 67 Apollo Drive, Rosedale, Auckland 0632, New Zealand (a division of Pearson New Zealand Ltd) * Penguin Books (South Africa) (Pty) Ltd, 24 Sturdee Avenue, Rosebank, Johannesburg 2196, South Africa * Penguin Books Ltd, Registered Offices: 80 Strand, London WC2R 0RL, England

Library of Congress Cataloging-in-Publication Data

Brewer, Heather.

Soulbound / by Heather Brewer.

p. cm.—(The legacy of Tril; [1])

Summary: Seventeen-year-old Kaya, a Healer who wants to learn to fight, must attend Shadow Academy where fighting by Healers is outlawed, and so she asks two young men to train her in secret, leading to a choice that will change their lives forever.

ISBN 978-0-8037-3723-5 (hardcover)

[1. Fantasy—Fiction. 2. Healers—Fiction. 3. Soldiers—Fiction. 4. Boarding schools—Fiction. 5. Schools—Fiction.] I. Title.

PZ7.B75695Blo 2012 [Fic]—dc23

2011035025

Designed by Jason Henry

Text set in Itc Berkeley Oldstyle

Printed in the U.S.A.

1 3 5 7 9 10 8 6 4 2

For my daughter, Alexandria—
one of the strongest girls I know.

ACKNOWLEDGMENTS

Not many authors make it a point to thank Penguins and Minions, but without them—my amazing team at Penguin Young Readers and my incredible Minion Horde—I would not be where I am today. Thank you, all of you, for being so supportive and for believing in me.

There are many people who I owe huge thanks to, Penguins and Minions aside. First off, my editor, Liz Waniewski, who continues to surprise me with her brilliant insight, and my fabulous agent, Michael Bourret, who is always available with excellent advice. I'm beyond thrilled and totally honored to call you both my friends. Here's to the future, and to many new worlds in the Heather Brewer universe.

I also need to thank my sister, Dawn Vanniman, who makes me feel normal and loved and so, so grateful that I have her in my life. And my amazing mother-in-law, Gwen Kelley, whom I want to be like when I eventually (maybe) grow up. You are the most amazing women I know.

Last, but never least, I want to thank my family. Paul, Jacob, and Alexandria—you guys rock my world in ways that no one else ever has. You get my weirdness. You support my innate love of the macabre. And you put up with my crazy writing schedule. I love you all so much. Thank you for everything that you do.

LEGACY *of* TRIL

BOOK ONE:

Soulbound

One

*T*he sharp edge of the paper sliced into my thumb and I sat up with a jerk. "Fak!"

Blood blossomed from the cut and I tossed my book to the ground, shoving my thumb in my mouth and sucking on it to make the bleeding stop. I should have known that I'd give myself a paper cut. I'd just picked up the book from the bookbinder this morning, so its pages were still crisp, not well worn like those in the books that lined the shelves of my bedroom.

"What would your mother say if she heard you cursing like that, Kaya?" As he ducked under the moss that was draping from the tree branches above and made his way along the water's edge, my father smiled at me. In his left hand was a net full of freshly caught fish. He held it up proudly. "Dinner. I hope I didn't scare you."

Shaking my head at his subtle attempt at humor— he'd always been able to sneak up on me without much effort, ever since I could remember—I brushed the grass from my leggings and stood, clutching the book in my hand. "Scare me? I actually heard you coming. First time for everything, I suppose."

"I made certain you did. Walk back with me? I want to talk with you about tonight." He didn't wait for an answer. I knew he wouldn't. My father was a take-charge kind of person. Not cruel or demanding, but a natural leader. When he said something, people were meant to listen, and they did, for the most part. Maybe it was because he was a Barron, and people—even the Unskilled people of Kessler who had no idea what Barrons even were—just sensed that they were supposed to follow his lead. My mother was a Barron as well. Sometimes I wished that I was like them, but then I'd push that wish away. After all, there was no sense in wishing for what one could never possibly have. My parents had been born Barrons, and I . . . well . . . I had not.

The walk back to our cabin was filled with light breezes, birdsong, and the occasional animal darting into the woods as my father and I navigated our way down the riverbank. Wet sounds of water lapping against river rock distracted me some from the conversation I knew was coming, but not even nature's song was enough to drown out the usual argument. My father slowed his steps so that I could keep pace with him, and looked at me from the corner of his eye. I always knew when he was looking at me—especially when he was doing so in that oppressive parenting kind of way. "Kaya," he began, his tone ever so calm, "you know your mother and I trust you completely."

Sighing heavily, I rolled my eyes. "I'm not going to be out late. Besides, I'll be with Avery. You love Avery."

The corner of his mouth lifted in a small smile. "I wouldn't be doing my job as your father if I didn't lecture you at least a little before such a big night."

He pulled a large, leafy branch to the side and I stepped through, spotting our cabin right in front of me. My father had built this place when my mother was pregnant with me. They slept under the stars until it was time for me to enter the world. The night my mother went into labor was their—our—first night in the cabin. It was small (sometimes too small) and damp (sometimes too damp), but it was home, and I always felt a wave of comfort wash over me at the sight of it. "It's not like I've spent every Harvest Festival out wreaking havoc. It's the same thing every year. Avery and I will wander the festival grounds for a few hours, eating everything in sight and playing some of the games of chance. Then Avery will fall madly in love with some boy and we'll end up stalking him the rest of the night, until I stumble into our cabin the next morning, bored and exhausted."

"Sounds like a good time." My mother peeked out from behind one of the wet sheets that was hanging on the clothesline beside our cabin. She was smiling, which told me that the usual events had transpired. Father had told her he was going to talk to me about how to behave at Harvest Festival, and mother told him not to bother, I'd be fine. By the look in Father's eyes, he knew that Mother was right, but he still worried, as fathers tend to do. He also knew he'd been defeated.

He shook his head at both of us and wagged a finger in my direction. "No boys."

Groaning, I said, "I'm not the one stalking boys. It's Avery."

But my father was not to be deterred. *"No boys."*

I shot my mother a look. "Does he ever listen to anyone?"

"Not since I can remember." My mother chuckled.

As she moved through the cabin's back door, she threw a glance at me over her left shoulder. "Avery stopped by a while ago to let us know the festival grounds are all set up. She says it's even bigger than last year, which is believable, considering how many funds the trade brought in over the summer. The farmer's market is open now, so you girls could head over anytime."

I waited for her to say what she always said to me on the day of the Harvest Festival—she and my father were so predictable. When she didn't continue, I couldn't help but be surprised. Maybe this year was different. Maybe this year, she'd finally learned to trust that I wouldn't do something incredibly stupid and risk exposing Barrons and Healers everywhere to the Unskilled.

She threw me another glance before turning toward the stairs that led up to our sleeping quarters. "And Kaya . . . don't say anything about you-know-what, okay? Even to Avery. All it takes is for one person to overhear a word they don't understand to unravel everything we've worked for."

I knew what she was talking about, of course. The fact that they were Barrons. The fact that a whole society of Barrons and Healers existed apart from what we called the Unskilled, or normal folks like the villagers of Kessler. We lived here, sure. But none of the villagers knew that my parents were Barrons, or that I was a Healer. And I knew that if I uttered the word *Barron* in public that I could undo eight centuries of keeping those worlds apart. I just didn't like being reminded every time I stepped out our front door.

Plus, there was that other thing. The fact that my parents had coupled, and it was against the law for two Barrons to become romantically entangled. One Barron to one Healer—that was the law. And my parents had broken that law. I didn't much see a problem with it, but apparently the Barron-run Zettai Council did. And they were in charge of just about everything.

"I'm not going to say anything. Do I ever say anything?" I could hear the distinct snap of sarcasm in my tone and immediately reeled my attitude back in. The last thing I wanted was to get grounded on the night of Harvest Festival.

My father was standing behind me at the sink, working the water pump. The metal squeaked as he pressed the handle down, and a moment later, fresh spring water splashed into the basin. I could hear him rinsing his canteen, and though I knew he wasn't looking at me, I could also tell that he was very aware of my every move, like a hunter. Sometimes that aspect of both of my parents set my nerves on edge. They were fast, strong, and had heightened senses beyond anyone I knew. I'd gone hunting with him before, but only once.

I was just ten years old when my father had taken me deep into the woods to show me how to hunt. Nothing vicious, he'd sworn. Just a Raik or two, or maybe a Khaw. Raiks were easy to track, after all. Their furry bodies kept so low to the ground that a trail was simple to spot. And Khaws hardly ever flew away when people approached. Both were delicious, and besides, he wanted me to learn.

And learn I had. Just as we'd crested a hill, my father spotted a Khaw on a nearby branch. He unsheathed his katana and whipped the blade forward, beheading the creature with skill and precision. Its blood flew through the air, speckling my cheeks.

I'd cried the entire walk home, and my father had never taken me hunting again.

After that, we stuck to fishing.

His tone was far warmer than I'd expected it to be,

considering how snotty I'd just been to my mother. "We just want to make sure you don't forget, Kaya. You're seventeen now, and a Healer, which means the Zettai Council's likely been searching for you for five years. They don't take Soulbound announcements lightly, even if your parents are fugitives. If they find you, you know what that means for our family."

Of course I knew what it would mean. How could I ever forget something so horrible? "It means I'll be shuffled off to some life I never wanted, and you and Mom will be punished for your crime."

"*Killed*, Kaya." His eyes snapped to me then, and mine to his, his dark eyes burning with a sincerity that he needed to drive home. "Not just punished. We'll be *killed* for falling in love. So you see how important it is that you never slip up and say anything to anyone about Barrons and Healers, yes?"

"Of course I do." The word *killed* rang through my mind over and over again. I dropped my attention to a knot in the wood floor, worried that my father might not understand why I hated the pressure they put on me to keep their—our—secret. "I just don't understand why you don't trust me not to say anything."

"We do trust you. Your mother just worries. Plus, she's feeling a little out of sorts lately. Her seventeenth year was the year her Soulbound Healer was killed. I think your birthday has reminded her of what it felt like to experience that loss." He'd dropped his tone to a near-whisper, perhaps not wanting my mother to overhear our conversation. I couldn't blame him. My mother hardly spoke of her Soulbound Healer. I wasn't even entirely sure if her Healer had been a man or a woman. "She was heartbroken. Soulbroken. Nothing can truly heal someone after a loss like that."

Soulbroken—that sounded awful. I couldn't imagine what it must feel like to lose a part of yourself in that way. My parents had explained to me years before that I had a Soulbound Barron, but I couldn't imagine it hurting to lose someone I'd never met before, and likely never would. "What about you? You lost your Healer in the Battle at Wood's Cross, right? Don't you miss her?"

Something in his eyes shifted then, revealing a haunted, broken man behind the usual strong facade. Seeing this weakness frightened me far more than the precision he'd used to kill during our hunting session when I was a child. My father never showed weakness. Largely because he didn't contain any. I'd thought so, anyway, until now. "Deeply. I miss Sharyn deeply. But I know she'd be happy that your mother and I fell in love. She'd want this life for me. Minus the threat of the Zettai Council, that is."

My heart welled up so big that it felt like it was choking me. This was a side of my father that I had not seen. He'd mentioned his Healer before, but only in passing, and only in the lightest of tones. Stepping closer, I hugged him, and whispered the only words that came to mind. "I'm so sorry you lost her. It must have been awful."

He squeezed me, just a little too tightly, and then held me at arm's length and forced a smile. "It was. It still is, and always will be. But today isn't a day for sadness and regret. It's a day of gratitude for all that we have."

A hard knock on the front door stole the moment away, and I was strangely grateful for it. It was unsettling to view my father as a person with real feelings, real weaknesses. He was the glue that held my universe together. The last thing I needed was for that glue to come . . . well . . . unglued.

Her impatience getting the best of her, Avery opened the door and poked her head inside. "Kaya? Come on! We're missing everything."

By *everything*, I could only assume, based on past experience, that she was referring to the freshly baked waffle bowls filled with mounds of fresh berries and dusted with powdered sugar, and the promise of harmless flirtation with one of the Bowery boys, who happened to belong to the most gorgeous gene pool imaginable in all of Tril. As much as I was dreading witnessing yet another failed harvest romance on Avery's part, I was certainly looking forward to a berry bowl or two, and the celebratory atmosphere that the Harvest Festival brought with it every year. I hurried out the door, a grin on my face, and echoing after me was my father's stern reminder, "No boys, Kaya!"

Avery and I raced all the way to the crossroads, where traffic—both on foot and in wagons of various sizes and styles—had picked up considerably. My lungs burning, I steadied myself with my hand on Avery's shoulder and slowed my breathing, watching the people as they poured into Kessler's main street, which wasn't a street so much as it was a wide, dirt road down the center of the village. I'd never thought much about how ill constructed our village was until my father had taken me to Howe, where the streets, while dirt, were smooth and even, the structures solid, the roofs freshly thatched. I was still proud to call Kessler my home after that, but traveling definitely helped to point out its flaws. Still, I loved it here.

Once we crested the small hill, to a full view of the Harvest Festival, I heard Avery suck in her breath. The dirt street was lined with tall, lit torches, which were wrapped in elaborate corn-husk bows. Lining the crowded street were carts filled with all manner of food and drink, and at the far end of the street, in what we referred to as the town center, were the various games of chance that had attracted people from three villages over. Avery's favorite was always the axe-throwing booth.

But not because she was particularly gifted at throwing axes.

Grinning and squinting into the setting sun, she tugged my sleeve, pulling me forward down the street. "He's here."

I rolled my eyes, but let myself be pulled toward the town center. Standing at the axe-throwing booth was a tall boy, lean and very tan. His disheveled blond hair stuck up this way and that, and when he saw us coming—or rather, when he saw Avery—his lips split into the happiest of grins. He waved, and Avery waved back with an enthusiasm that I envied. So far, no boy had ever made me that excited to see him. And every year since we were seven, Micah had come to work the Harvest Festival from the other side of the continent of Kokoro, and every time, he'd made Avery smile as if she were looking at the stars.

As we passed the food carts, my stomach rumbled, but it practically screamed when we were next to the cart with sugar-coated fried breadcake. I tried to tell Avery that I was going to stop and grab a bite, but she was so focused on Micah that she hurried ahead, leaving me to my own devices. Camra, who'd taught my mother how to sew when I was a baby and had since been a regular visitor to our cabin, was working the breadcake cart. I flashed her a smile and dug in my pocket for three trinks—my father had given me plenty of coins the night before—but Camra shook her head. "Your money's no good here, Kaya girl."

Louis Bowery whined from behind me, "What about my money, Camra?"

Camra handed me a large breadcake and shook her head at Louis. "Your money's just fine. That'll be three trinks, if you're hungry."

Camra didn't much care for Louis—not many of the townsfolk did. He and his brothers were known to be troublemakers of the worst kind, the kind that wouldn't confess to anything that they'd done, no matter how small. I didn't much enjoy his or his brothers' company either, but Avery had a mild crush on both Decker and Vadin Bowery, so I went along with her just to keep her from getting in too much trouble. With a nod of thanks and a polite shrug at Louis, I turned away from the corner and bit into the soft, warm breadcake and relished the sweetness as the sugar melted on my tongue. After my second bite, I sensed something in the revelry around me change. Then I heard it, high-pitched and in the distance. Someone was screaming.

Two

There is a stark difference between a scream of joy and a scream of terror. Something in its pitch shakes you to the core when you hear a terrified scream, and my core was trembling. Who was screaming? What was happening? I turned around, trying to locate the source of panic, but was nearly knocked over by Louis. His face was white and drawn, and just as I opened my mouth to ask him what had frightened him, he mumbled something unintelligible through trembling lips and took off toward the north woods.

Someone screamed again, this time so loud that it hurt my ears. The crowd pushed toward me as people rushed to flee whatever it was that was causing such fear, but I fought against the tide of running feet, pressing my way against them, toward whatever had instilled such terror in my neighbors. Bodies slammed up against me. I was surrounded by wide, frightened eyes. It was as if no one could see anyone else, just different routes of escape from whatever was behind them. Friends climbed over friends. Fathers ran ahead, leaving their children behind. And through it all, my heart slammed against my ribs in a terrified rhythm. But I pushed forward anyway, determined to see the source of all this fear with my own eyes, and help stop it if I could.

The crowd's movement was dizzying, and after a moment, I lost my direction. People were running everywhere, and I was spinning around, uncertain where to turn. My foot slipped on something slick, and I steadied myself, regaining my balance. Then I looked down.

The toe of my shoe was tipped in burgundy. The ground beneath it held a puddle of something wet and dark. I inhaled slowly, forcing air into my reluctant lungs. Blood. There was blood on my shoe, on the ground. Which meant that someone or something was hurt.

The puddle at my feet branched out and I followed the bloody trail through the crowd, my heart racing, my nerves so ramped up that I was shaking. I pushed past a woman dressed all in blue, who was sobbing uncontrollably, and stopped dead in my tracks.

Avery was lying on the ground, covered in blood. The moment I saw her, my heart stopped completely.

It took me a second to notice Micah lying over her, bloody and limp, his eyes staring lifelessly into the crowd. Avery cradled his head against her chest, tears drawing lines down her dirty cheeks. A large, mouth-shaped wound had left Micah's neck mutilated. Something had attacked and killed him. But it hadn't been able to take more than a bite. On the ground beside Avery lay a large, bloodied rock. Avery had apparently bashed the thing over the head a few times to stop it from eating Micah completely.

I ran over to her, shoving my way past the thinning crowd, and dropped to my knees beside her in shock. "Oh, Avery, I'm so sorry. What happened? What . . . what did this?"

Avery's sobs grew louder, but they were drowned out by a terrible screeching noise. I stared up into the tree-tops, where the noise was coming from, but couldn't make out anything in the darkness. The torches that lined the street cast a warm glow over the village, but outside of the flames' range, the darkness was intensi-fied. It was as if the darkness itself was crying out and hungry for nothing but the villagers of Kessler.

Then something large and heavy dropped down from the treetops, landing with surprising grace just feet in front of me. It stood on all fours, but towered over me, its black, soulless eyes staring me down. Its skin was blue and scaly, as if the creature had been born with its own defensive armor. And its breath smelled foul, like rotten meat and blood, metallic and sour. The smell of it, even at a distance, sent the threat of vomit to the back of my throat. Snorting, it turned its head slightly, peering around me to Avery.

A word flitted through my mind, and chasing after it was denial. I'd heard rumors, fairy tales that no one really believed, about monsters that lurked in the treetops up in the mountains where the villagers didn't dare travel. And my parents had told me stories about the beasts—stories that insisted that these monsters were real. But I didn't believe them. I thought my father was teasing me, or that maybe they were just trying to keep me from climbing the mountains unguarded. But standing directly in front of me, growling, a long strand of spittle hanging from the corner of its mouth, was a Graplar.

One thing raced across my thoughts as I stood there staring at it, shaking with fear.

Graplars eat people.

In a moment of panic, certain that the beast was about to lurch forward and attack Avery, I waved my arms and shouted, hoping to distract it. Just as my shouts left my throat, I heard my father shout as well, only his was a word, and the word was *No!*

The creature lunged at me, opening its mouth wide. As it snapped its jaw closed, I jumped back. Its teeth closed over the fabric of my shirt and I yanked away, scrambling backward, hoping that Avery had the good sense to run while the thing was distracted. As it threw its head forward again, gnashing its teeth at me, I stumbled, tripping over Micah's corpse. Avery had wiggled herself free and stood. Our eyes met for a brief moment before she turned toward the woods and took off in a sprint. It was then that I heard my father calling out again, his voice full of warning. "Don't run! Don't move! It attracts them!"

The beast leaped over me, charging after Avery, and seconds later, my father was jumping over me as well, chasing it down, katana in hand. I hurried to stand, and ignoring the blood and dirt that was sticking my clothes to my skin, I ran after him, after Avery, after the monster that had attacked our small town. In the distance, beyond the edge of the firelight, I heard rustling, then grunting, then a heavy, meaty thump. As I reached the edge of the light, I saw my father emerge from the darkness, the front of his shirt spattered with blood, dragging the Graplar's head behind him. He dropped it to the ground, shaking his head, his brow troubled. As he returned his katana to the sheath on his back, I breathed a sigh of relief. My muscles relaxed. My father had saved us, all but the boy. We were so fortunate. I wondered how far Avery had gotten, or whether she was still running away from the beast. Hugging my father tightly, I said, "Thank you. Thank you for killing it. I'm sorry I didn't believe you. I'd better go get Avery and tell her it's dead."

As I stepped forward to move past him, my father put his hand out, gripping my shoulder. He looked down at the stains on his shirt before his dark, troubled eyes found mine. After a moment of confusion, my heart shattered into a million pieces. He didn't have to say the words for me to understand what had happened. The monster had gotten to Avery before he could. It was Avery's blood on his shirt—an image that would forever haunt me. My best friend was dead, and all because I hadn't known how to stop the creature from attacking her.

As tears welled in my eyes, my world swirled around me in the muted colors of night. Sounds blended until all I heard was silence. I was certain I was falling, but the last thing I remembered was my father's arms lifting me from the ground and carrying me away from the monster that had killed my friend. Then everything went black.

"Let her rest, Patrick. She's been through a lot." My parents' voices drifted through the cabin in hushed tones—ones not quiet enough for me to fully ignore. I lay in bed, still stunned, still feeling numb. The moon was casting shadows of trees on my wall. I stared at the dancing branch shadows, not thinking anything, trying not to feel, most certainly not letting the image of Avery's blood into my haunted thoughts.

My father's voice broke in then, full of warm determination. "And she's about to be faced with worse, Ellen. We have to get her up, get her moving around, and prepare her for what's coming."

"How do we prepare her for that, exactly? We don't really know what's in store for her."

"We know this much. She has no idea what to expect right now, and delaying that information isn't helping her."

There was a long silence before my mother replied. "Okay. Wake her. But be gentle."

Heavy footfalls approached my door. As each one sounded out into the night, my heart beat heavy and solid in my chest. Finally the door to my bedroom swung open and my father spoke, the warmth that had been in his tone just a moment before replaced by something I very much needed—strength. "Kaya. Come downstairs. Your mother and I need to talk to you."

He was right, and I knew it, but still it took me a moment to sit up and swing my legs over the edge of my bed. It took me a moment longer to stand. Every movement I made felt like I was swimming through murky waters. Slowly, I made my way downstairs to the dining room, where my parents were waiting with looks of trepidation on their faces. I looked back and forth between them. "Something's happened. What is it?"

Sitting in front of my mother on the table was a stack

of folded rice papers. Clinging to the outer paper was the burgundy ribbon and broken wax seal that had held them all together. "This was delivered by messenger late yesterday. It's for you. You'll have to pardon us for reading it. When we saw who it was from, we couldn't resist."

After a moment—one where the air grew heavy between us—she slid the small stack across the table to me. On the outside sheet was scribbled my name and address. In the upper left-hand corner was a swirling script which simply read Zettai Council. My heart stopped at seeing those words. Mostly, because hearing from the Zettai Council when your parents were fugitives was probably the worst thing that could ever happen, next to losing your best friend to a horrible monster's insatiable appetite. I hesitated with the letter in my hand, not wanting to unfold the paper, hoping that avoiding doing so might erase the words within its well-worn creases. As if sensing my hesitancy, my mother closed her hand over mine and met my eyes with a teary smile. She'd likely intended for her actions to comfort me, but seeing my strong Barron mother brought to tears by the presence of a letter from the Zettai Council had the opposite effect. It meant that we all knew what was about to happen. It meant that everything was about to change: for me, for my parents, for our family. And nothing would be the same ever again.

With a breath so deep it made my lungs ache, I unfolded the paper and smoothed out its creases, taking my time to do so. At last, I read the thickly scripted words at the top of the page.

By Order of the Noble and Honorable Zettai Council

Below that, in smaller and thinner letters, were two paragraphs. My eyes scanned them at first, hoping to find a word like "pardoned" or "excused," but nothing lay on that page but my deepest fears. The first paragraph was written as part of the order, but the second seemed to be a personal note. As I read the first paragraph, my vision blurred with tears.

It is with our deepest pride and pleasure to announce that Kaya Oshiro has been granted admission to Shadow Academy, to join in the grand position of studying alongside some of Tril's greatest Healers. As pursuant to Article 9 of the Loyalty Act, Kaya Oshiro must report to the Academy within three days' time of receiving this official notification. If Kaya fails to report in the time allotted, please know that proper measures will be taken to ensure her attendance at this prestigious educational institution. Congratulations to Kaya and her family on what we know will be the beginnings of a fruitful future.

As upsetting as the first paragraph had been to read, it was nothing compared to the second, which was written in an elegant, swirling script.

Dear Kaya,

We at Shadow Academy look forward to you joining our ranks as a student Healer. It is with deepest regrets that I must inform you that the Barron to whom you were Soulbound has perished. A new Barron has been selected for you, however, and you will be Bound to him shortly after your arrival. Please give my regards to your parents—indeed, it has been many years since their presence has graced Skilled society. It would be a shame if anything were to happen to them. I look forward to meeting you in three days' time.

Sincerely,

Osamu Quill

Headmaster, Shadow Academy

I read the paragraph over again before setting the letter on the table. My mother had given up on dabbing her eyes with her sleeve and buried her face in my father's shoulder. The headmaster's letter had sounded every bit as proper and polite as it needed to pass for something dignified to the untrained eye, but my parents and I knew to read between the lines. They knew where we were now. And if I didn't join the cause and learn my part in this unending war, the Zettai Council would send someone to murder my parents, for committing the crime of coupling and abandoning their stations.

And my Barron. My Barron had died. The fact hit me in the chest like a thousand stones, paining me to my core.

I hadn't known the Barron I was Soulbound to. How could I? My parents had eloped to Kessler before I was born, leaving everything about Skilled society behind. But somewhere in Tril, the very moment that I had been born, another child had been born. We took our first breath together. Our hearts had beaten together for the first time. Our first cries echoed out into the world at the same exact moment. We were Soulbound, as all Healers and Barrons are when they are born. But now my Barron was dead, and though I never knew him—and it was a him, a boy, I don't know how I knew that, but I did—my soul ached to know that he was gone, before I'd ever had the chance to look him in the eye.

Before I could stand, my father grabbed my hand and spoke, his voice burning with fury over the entire situation. "We can run, Kaya. You don't have to go. We can leave everything behind tonight and run for our lives."

Gently, I pulled my hand from his and met his gaze, shaking my head slowly. I loved him for saying what he had, but I knew that any choice we'd had had been erased, and any chance we'd had of remaining out of the watchful eye of the Zettai Council had been stolen away the moment that the rumors of the Graplar attack on Kessler reached the council chambers. Because an Unskilled wouldn't know to behead the beast, and certainly wouldn't have done so with a katana—such weapons were only ever used by Barrons, and every single one of them capable of taking down a Graplar in a single swipe, like the one my father possessed, was forged at Starlight Academy. There was no doubt in their minds. They had found my parents—had found me—and if I didn't attend Shadow Academy, my parents lives were forfeited. Really, as twisted as it seemed, the Zettai Council had been lenient by allowing my parents to live at all. They could have simply smashed in the door, killed my Barron parents, and taken me away, kicking and screaming. But they hadn't. Maybe because they knew that my parents were some of the best trained fighters of their day and it wouldn't be an easy task. Or maybe it was because they'd rather catch flies with honey than with ass-kicking vinegar. We'd likely never know. But I did know one thing. Avery had died because I didn't know how to stop the Graplar from attacking. And as sweet as my father was to spar with me in the clearing behind our cabin, I knew that he'd been playacting, and would never really teach me how to fight. The only way I was going to learn to protect anyone from those horrid beasts was to train at length. And Shadow Academy was going to provide me with just that. I didn't want to go. I needed to go—to protect my parents, and to protect myself.

I knew what it meant, leaving home and entering the Academy. My parents had told me all about the hundred-year-old war, and how once you entered a school for training, the war became your way of life. I also realized that by returning to that lifestyle, I was virtually undoing everything my parents had fought for to give me a normal, peaceful existence. But I couldn't, in good conscience, let anyone else lose a friend to the insatiable hunger of a Graplar. Avery would want me to go. Avery would tell me it was the right thing to do.

As I pressed my lips to my father's brow in a kiss, my mother's tears turned into body-racking sobs. I kissed her forehead too, suppressing my own tears—after all, there would be another time to cry, maybe one when I was alone, away from my parents, and my tears would cause them no further grief—and went upstairs to my room to pack.

Three

*I*f I ever found Maddox, I was going to kill him. Granted, all I knew of him was his name and the fact that he was supposed to pick me up from the trailhead three hours ago, but that was enough to place blame on him for the predicament I was in. After waiting for what seemed like forever, I'd gripped the note from the headmaster in my hand and trudged up the hill, dragging my trunk behind me. After all, how hard could locating Shadow Academy possibly be? It was supposed to be this giant school with an enormous wall around it. Should be fairly easy to spot, considering there were no other buildings around—just miles and miles of forest. Little did I know that an hour later, the beaten path I was on would abruptly end, and I'd be dragging my trunk through the prickly underbrush, over roots, dead leaves, rocks, and every insect known to man. I hadn't broken down and cried—I prided myself on that—not even when a rogue branch had slapped me across the face, scraping my cheek. But my stomach was rumbling and my muscles had just about enough of wandering through the woods as the sun began its descent. It was time to eat, time to rest, time to find Shadow Academy already and just be done walking for about a billion years.

And kill Maddox. Can't forget that.

Shadow Academy was certainly living up to its name, as I couldn't see it anywhere, despite the crudely drawn map on the headmaster's letter. My father had checked and double-checked the map, assuring me that if I stayed true to the dotted line, I couldn't go wrong. "Wait at the trailhead," he'd told me. "Your guard will collect you there. Don't get impatient and start wandering the woods alone."

But my father hadn't been counting on my guard forgetting all about me, leaving me alone in near-dark with no food.

It hadn't occurred to me that it was an odd thing for the headmaster to give me a map when he was sending a guard to meet me at the trailhead where the wagon had dropped me off. Not until Maddox had forgotten me. Then it all made sense, and I was starting to think that maybe this was the norm for Maddox. But then, my mind needed something to think about, someone to blame, while I made my way up the pathless hill. Might as well be that.

I leaned forward, digging my shoes into the soft earth as I climbed. For the hundredth time, my trunk got caught on an exposed root and I had to wrench it free. My shoulder screamed with pain, but I pulled harder. With a loud snap the root gave way, sending me flying. I landed hard right in the middle of a mud puddle.

Slowly, I thought to myself. That's how Maddox would die. Slowly.

Standing and wiping the mud from my face, I opened and closed my hand to stretch the muscles and get the blood flowing and then rested for a few minutes on top of my trunk. The woods around me were thick with roughthorn trees, and the forest floor was covered with leaves. There weren't many prickly bushes and weeds, but what were there had found me with ease. It was going to take hours to remove all the woody thorns from my legs. A slight breeze rustled the treetops and several leaves showered down on me. The woods smelled crisp, like fall, even though summer had just begun to fade. It wasn't entirely unpleasant. But I was tired and, as my stomach insisted on reminding me with its gurgles and grumbles, I hadn't eaten anything since lunch, almost seven hours ago.

A sound reached my ears, one that sent a chill through me. Had it been a screech, like the one I'd heard the night that I'd lost my best friend to a monster's hunger? Or was I imagining things? Exhaustion did funny things to a person's imagination, so I wasn't at all certain that I could trust my senses. I listened for a moment longer, but when I heard nothing but the usual forest noises, I reached down, gripping the trunk's handle, and turned to continue my trek up the hill. But then I froze in place, unable to even unleash the scream that was building in my throat. I couldn't breathe, couldn't move, couldn't even blink, taken over by instant terror.

All I saw were teeth. Hundreds of large, sharp, glistening teeth—row after row after row of them—attached to an enormous, animalistic mouth. Just inches from my face and terrifyingly familiar.

"Don't move. Don't make a sound any louder than a whisper." A man's voice to my left—confident, commanding. I was enormously relieved to hear his voice—at least I wouldn't die alone. It was easy to follow his instructions, as my muscles had forgotten the basic concept of movement and, at the moment, I wasn't sure that I had ever possessed the power of speech. Besides, he sounded like he knew what he was talking about—he was giving advice that mirrored my father's, after all.

I hoped he did, anyway. For both our sakes.

I swallowed my screams and was careful not to move, though my body shook against my will. So much for priding myself on bravery. I wondered if Avery had seen the beast's teeth closing in on her, or if she'd been attacked from behind, ripped away from life without so much as a warning. She must have been terrified. Keeping my voice a breath on the wind, I said, "I've seen one of these before. It's a—"

The name escaped me momentarily, largely because a long strand of drool had begun stretching from the creature's mouth to the forest floor.

His voice was just as soft, his breathing calm and even. "It's a Graplar, and only half as dumb as it looks."

The beast growled under its breath, as if it couldn't quite understand what he'd said, but knew it was insulting.

A Graplar. Of course.

I inhaled and at once I was hit by the rancid, foul breath of the beast before me. It was all I could do not to gag. I had to close my eyes for a moment to stop seeing those horrible teeth, so I'd stop imagining what it must have been like for Avery in her final moments. A shiver crawled up my spine and I resisted the urge to bolt. Something deep inside of me said that he was absolutely right, and that moving right now would be a huge mistake.

Opening my eyes again, I hoped against hope that the thing would be gone. But it wasn't. I squeaked, "Why hasn't it attacked us?"

"Graplars thrive on movement. They love the hunt. It's waiting for us to run." His voice was stern, but calm, like he'd faced these things a hundred times before. Oddly, there was a modicum of respect for the beast in his tone.

My heart was beating in a crazy panic, but I willed it to steady, to slow. Freaking out would not help at a time like this. In a hopeful, trembling whisper, I asked, "If we stay still, will it go away?"

"No. It'll just kill us slower to punish us for not running." It was twisted, but I was pretty sure I heard a smile in his statement. Bemusement. Maybe he thought facing hideous creatures like Graplars every day was just business as usual, but I didn't find it even remotely entertaining.

"So what do we do?" I knew what my father would have done. He would have grabbed his katana and chased after the beast, not coming back until his clothes were sticky with its blood. And when he did return, his eyes would be alight with a strange fire—one that would simultaneously terrify me and make me very proud. But I wasn't my father.

"If you want to live, I suggest you do exactly what I tell you, without question. Understand?"

I nodded slowly, wishing I could turn my head even slightly so that I could glimpse the man I'd just agreed to take orders from. The Graplar emitted a low growl, as if chastising me for even thinking about moving any farther.

"On my signal, run north, toward Shadow Academy."

I was still nodding—as slowly as I could manage—when I said, "Question."

"I thought I said no questions."

"This one's kind of important."

He released an irritated sigh, which elicited a grunt from the monster that was eyeballing me. "Fine. What is it?"

"Which way's north?"

"To your right. Past that big tree and straight up the hill." He paused, letting his instructions sink in. "Are you ready?"

My mouth went horribly dry as I slowly shoved the headmaster's letter in my pocket and braced myself to run. Then I blinked and whispered frantically, "Wait . . . I thought you said running was bad!"

"GO!"

A split second before I could move, the man started to run in the opposite direction he'd told me to go. I guessed he was trying to lure the creature away long enough for me to escape. So I dropped my trunk and took off as fast as I could, slipping on the leaves under my feet. Once I had solid ground under my shoes, I bolted up the hill, leaving both the man and the monster behind.

The Graplar didn't follow him for long.

The ground behind me pounded as the monster made chase after me, the horrible, hungry sound of its breath panting on my heels. My heart was beating so fast I thought it might explode right out of my chest, but I picked up the pace, running faster than I ever had before. Fear gripped me, driving me forward, but I knew it was just a matter of time before the beast got me, that I was just delaying the inevitable. Once it tired of the chase, or if I slowed down even a little bit, that Graplar was going to grab me by the ankle and drag me off to wherever it preferred to chew its dinner. Or maybe it wouldn't drag me anywhere. Maybe it'd gnaw the meat from my bones right here.

Against my better judgment, I stole a glance over my shoulder. Its beady, black, soulless eyes stared at me intently as it licked its razor-sharp teeth—all three, ugly, Kaya-chomping rows of them. I flung my arm back, flailing a wild punch into the air. My fist connected uselessly and I kept running.

I picked up speed, remembering what my dad had taught me about fighting something bigger and stronger than you: if you can't hurt them, outrun them. The sounds of its movement quickened. I felt hot breath on my back, and flecks of spittle—oh God, it was drooling again—spattering against my arms and the back of my shirt. Up ahead of me one fallen tree leaned against another, leaving a triangle of space beneath it. Moving as fast as I could, I fell back and drew one leg under the other, sliding forward. I ducked under the tree and the Graplar leaped overhead. As it flew through the air, watching me more than it was watching where it was going, I dug my foot into the earth and brought myself to standing on the other side. The Graplar turned its head midair, its cold, beady eyes focused on my every move. It was just starting to wrench its body around when it slammed into a large oak. With a high-pitched squeal it fell to the ground disoriented, shaking its head.

With newly bought time, I took off again, my heart drumming in my ears. Sudden, unexpected confidence surged through me. I was going to make it. I was going to beat this thing. My dad would be proud.

The toe of my shoe found a root and I lurched forward. Down I went, my newfound confidence disappearing in a puff, squeezing my eyes tight as I fell, not wanting to be witness to the monster's mouth closing over me. I was dead, DEAD if that thing got a hold of me with those enormous jaws and monstrous teeth. Flipping over, I scrambled up the hill in a blind crabwalk, trying to delay what I knew was coming. The beast's hot, terrible breath was on my face. It stank like rotting meat and spoiled vegetables.

The thing squealed and I clamped my hands over my ears but couldn't block out the sound. It shook me to the core—its battle cry, no doubt. The last thing I'd hear before I died.

Something slick and wet spattered my cheeks and I let out a scream. Drool. Oh God, it was drooling on me, ready to devour me whole, its razor-sharp teeth closing in . . .

"You can open your eyes now. It's dead." The stranger's voice again. Calm, cool, collected. As if this was an everyday occurrence.

It took a moment for his words to sink in, but when they did, I opened my eyes. Well, one eye really. The left one. And only halfway. But as soon as I realized he'd taken the Graplar down, I opened both wide. The immense monster was lying no more than three feet from me. Most of it was, anyway. Its head was in the brush several feet to my left. I looked at my savior, who was slipping a katana into the sheath on his back. His silver hair was stuck to his forehead and cheek, held in place by thick, red blood. "It should have known better than to travel alone. For that matter, so should you."

My hero was dressed in black from head to toe. His pants clung tightly to his legs; his jacket donned patches of armor. He had short, silver hair and dark eyes. His skin was sun kissed, but just barely, and his figure was lean and strong. He was clearly a fighter. And even in the growing darkness, I could see that he was beautiful.

I swallowed hard. "Are you . . . Maddox?"

I immediately rethought my plans to kill him.

The corner of his mouth twitched slightly as he helped me to stand. After a moment, he said, "No. I'm not Maddox."

There was clearly offense in his demeanor, and I wasn't exactly sure what I had done to spark it. I was about to ask when he said, "It's not safe here. You should get to the south gate before we have anymore unwelcome guests. Graplars like the night life, if you know what I mean."

A small smile touched his lips then, as if even he couldn't resist his own charms. I probably would've smiled too, if he hadn't just told me that the danger wasn't over yet. I wiped at my face, which was still sticky. As I pulled my hand away, I noticed my palm was covered in red. It hadn't been saliva that spattered me, but blood. Gross. But it could have been worse. It could have been mine. Still shaking, I said, "I don't even know your name."

His smile wilted and I felt sorry I'd said anything. I dropped my gaze and noticed the crimson slash on the left side of his chest. "Oh, you're hurt."

Instinctively, I reached out my hand to pull the fabric away from the wound. His hand closed tightly over my wrist and our eyes locked. I relaxed, pulling my hand away, but he held fast.

It took me a few seconds to find my voice again. "I was only trying to help."

After a moment he let go, pushing until I staggered backward, as if he wanted nothing further to do with me. When he spoke, his voice was filled with venom. "I said, go, Kaya."

Distrusting, I slanted my eyes. "How do you know my name?"

"What part of 'it's not safe' are you having trouble understanding?"

My eyebrows came together in a glare. "You don't have to be so rude."

"Listen, damn it. I don't have time to play twenty questions with you." His eyes slanted too, like he was trying to outglare me or something . . . which he was succeeding in doing. "Go."

I was about to ask him just what the hell his problem was, when there was a loud screech in the trees just down the hill from where we stood. It was followed by growling.

My heart stopped. Oh no. Not another Graplar. I looked around, but saw nothing. When I found his eyes again, all I could do was blink, terrified.

He looked at me as he withdrew his katana and growled, "Go! Up the hill! NOW!"

I took off as fast as I could run. Never mind my trunk with all of my belongings. Never mind the wounded stranger who'd saved my life. I was told to run, and my instincts told me to do so. My heart hammered against my ribs, and I cursed myself for being so afraid, but still I ran, and I didn't look back.

four

My chest was burning, and it felt like if I kept up the pace I was running at, my lungs were either going to cave in or explode. But I couldn't stop. The screeching sounds of the Graplar echoed after me in the forest, bringing to mind poor Avery, so I ran, half staggering, until I came to an immense metal door, flanked by what seemed like miles of stone wall. The stones that made up the wall were round and most of them were covered in a lush, green moss, reminding me of the rocks along the Kessler River back home. Vines drew crooked lines up the wall in several spots. I moved to the door and, just as I was debating whether or not I should knock, a small window slid open, and a voice spoke from the other side. "Papers."

When I spoke, my voice sounded harsh and raw—more like a mudfrog's than my own. I croaked, "Excuse me?"

The bodiless voice sighed. "I need to see your papers."

I searched my memory, but drew a blank. My mind was lost in a haze of adrenaline, fear, and exhaustion. "What papers?"

The voice blew out an agitated snort and said, "Do you have a letter from the headmaster?"

"Oh," I said, feeling more than a little stupid. "Yeah. I do. Right here."

Pulling the crumpled parchment from my pocket, I smoothed it out and slid it through the small barred window.

At first, nothing happened. The only sound around me was that of the woods. Birds chirped. Something rustled in the distance. Just as I was beginning to wonder if he was ever going to let me in, the enormous door slid open and the guard waved me inside. He was dressed in clothing similar to that of the stranger in the woods, but his clothing seemed more structured, as if his position as a gate guard required more protection. His voice softened to something resembling concern. "Where's your guard, Kaya?"

With a grateful sigh, I crossed the border and the door clanged shut behind me. The sound normally would have made me jump, but at the moment, I was relieved to have a giant, thick wall between me and drooling, hungry monsters. It was just as dark on this side of the wall, but I could make out lit torches along a beaten path that led to a large building in the distance.

There had to be more to the campus, but the darkness in this part of the Kokoro continent was unreal—heavy and unforgiving. I cast a weary glance at the guard who'd questioned me. "Who, Maddox?"

The look on his face said that he was familiar with the name, and that that wasn't necessarily a good thing. I shook my head. "Believe me, when I find Maddox, he'll be the one who needs a bodyguard."

His eyes grew wide, which made the tiny creases on his forehead more noticeable. "You mean you made it all the way from the trailhead alone?"

"Pretty much."

The guard groaned and swore under his breath. "That little—be assured that the headmaster will handle Maddox's punishment swiftly."

"Whatever. I'm just glad to be here finally. I was almost eaten by a Graplar."

Several of the surrounding guards took a sudden interest in our conversation. Their raised eyebrows and surprised glances told me without words what the guard in front of me soon confirmed. "You're very lucky to be alive, miss."

I nodded, suddenly in need of a long nap. Who knew tromping through the woods and facing death could be so exhausting?

"Are you injured?"

I blinked at him, confused, but then I spied my hand,

which was covered with dried blood. My face must have looked terrible. "No. It's not my blood."

He nodded in understanding and asked, "How many Graplars were there?"

"One. And then another one showed up after the first one was dead."

"And how did a *Healer* manage to take down two Graplars?" He grew quiet for a moment, somehow disturbed by the very idea that I could be anything more than a damsel in distress. Oh yeah, I was loving this place already. Not even in town a full day and I'd already had a near-death experience, and now I was being looked down on by the doorman.

I thought for a minute, the image of my silver-haired hero filling my mind. It left a bittersweet taste in my mouth. What was that guy's problem anyway? All I tried to do was take a look at his wound, to help him. It seemed only fair after he saved my life. Was it some Barron thing? Ugh. I would never understand Barrons—not even after being raised by two of them. "There was a . . . man. A young man. He killed it before it could get to me. He told me to run when we heard the second one coming."

The guard furrowed his brow, then pulled back his sleeve, revealing a mark on his skin, which looked suspiciously like a tattoo. But it wasn't a tattoo—it was his Trace, the mark of a Barron. His was a black crescent, which meant that his Soulbound Healer had died. I'd seen my parents' Traces a thousand times before—both black. My parents had said that Traces were silver when they were born and turned red once they'd spent time with their Soulbound Healer. I'd never seen a red one before, and couldn't help but wonder what it would be like to see one on someone whose Healer was still with them. Jolting me out of my thoughts, he said, "Did he have a Trace? Like this one here? Did you see one of these anywhere on his body?"

I shook my head. "No. But he had silver hair."

He sighed, looking over his shoulder at another guard. "Better go find him. I'm sure the headmaster will want to hear what really happened."

I tensed, insulted. Apparently my word wasn't good enough.

Turning back to me, he said, "Let's get you something to eat. And . . . you want to clean up a bit before meeting the headmaster?"

The last sentence came out awkwardly, as if he were not used to dealing with the female persuasion much. "That would be nice."

He led me inside one of the turrets in the wall by the gate. The room was clearly fashioned to be a soldiers' break room, but at the moment the chairs surrounding the small table beckoned to me as the greatest comfort. I sat and the guard, whose name I hadn't learned—how strange that everyone seemed to know my name, but never offered their own—rummaged through some baskets on the counter and carried what he'd found over to the table that I was leaning my weary head on. He dropped a large wedge of cheese, half a loaf of bread, and three apples in front of me. I looked up at him—what did he think I was, a starving army? As if puzzled by my stare, he furrowed his brow again. Then he pulled a dagger from his side, stabbing it into the wood of the table. He smiled proudly. "For the cheese."

I smiled weakly, but gratefully, in return. "Can I just have some water, please? To wash up with?"

He stood there for a moment. Then in a flash, he'd moved to the fireplace in the corner and removed the kettle, pouring some of the boiling water into a bowl. He grabbed a jug from the floor and poured in cool water as well, testing it with his fingers until the temperature seemed right. After a short search, he placed a towel and washcloth on the counter, next to the bowl. I thanked him on his way out the door, both for the water and for privacy.

Washing my face and hands, I turned the water in the bowl a rust color. Then I picked as much of the broken bits of twigs and weeds from my clothes as I could. From what I glanced in the water's reflection, my hair was tangled, so I did my best to comb it out with my fingers, but it was fairly hopeless. I was going to have to face facts: I was going meet the headmaster with messy hair and scraped palms. My clothes were covered with blood and mud, but there was nothing I could do about that now. I tidied up as best as I could, and munched on an apple until the guard came back. By the light in his eyes, he seemed really pleased that I'd eaten at least some of what he'd brought me. "If you're ready now, Headmaster Quill would very much like to meet you."

I was less enthusiastic about that meeting than I was sure he was. Mostly because the headmaster struck me as a really charming guy. If by "really charming guy," one meant "total dek."

The guard nodded and opened the door wider, ducking out of the way. A short, squat man waddled into the room, concern creasing his forehead. Headmaster Quill, I presumed. He didn't appear nearly as threatening as his letter had implied. He had a balding head and small, square spectacles perched on the end of his nose. He looked way too much like an old, chubby bookbinder and not at all like the tyrant my imagination had dreamed up. "My dear girl, are you all right? Raden told me that you were attacked by a Graplar. You must be terrified."

Shrugging, I tried to play it off, like it was no big deal. Just a giant blue monster that tried to eat me. I can handle it. Didn't run away screaming or anything. "I was, but now I'm just glad to be here. And I don't know if it matters, but there were two."

His eyes widened immediately, disbelief obviously filling his features. Apparently, nobody here thought I was remotely capable of taking care of myself. "Two? How on earth did you manage to escape?"

I shrugged again. I was so tired; I really didn't feel like going over this again. All I wanted was a soft bed to sleep in. Maybe some hot-pepper chocolate. And a book to lose myself in.

The door swung open and in walked my silver-haired hero, dragging my trunk behind him. In the light I got a better look at him. His lips were pressed together in a thin, determined line. His eyes sparkled and his skin was flushed—it was easy to see how much he enjoyed the thrill of the kill. Despite my irritation at his reaction to me, I couldn't help but confirm my former thinking—this man was utterly beautiful. Almost too pretty to be real.

The front of his shirt was now covered in blood, and I was betting that only a little of it belonged to the Graplar. He dropped my trunk on the floor and said, "I can answer that for you, Headmaster."

Headmaster Quill darted his squinty eyes to the newcomer and sighed. "Ah. Of course. Meet me in my office in fifteen minutes for a debriefing, if you would."

With a nod, my savior turned and walked back out the door, without so much as a glance in my general direction. My stomach shriveled a little, and I couldn't help but wonder if I'd done something wrong.

The headmaster was quiet for a long while and, just as I'd become convinced that he was never going to speak again, he said, "Well, it's a good thing he found you when he did, or we wouldn't be having this conversation."

He said it was a good thing, but his tone, his eyes, his posture—everything, really—said that it wasn't. Though I had no idea what could be so bad about having a skilled fighter pop out of nowhere to save me from being something's midnight snack. Maybe my hero wasn't allowed outside the walls. Or maybe he'd been up to no good. Whatever it was, I was grateful for his presence. Even if the headmaster wasn't.

"Now, Kaya, if you're ready, I'll escort you to the dormitory." He nodded toward the door and after a moment, cleared his throat. The kindness in his eyes shifted and for a second, I saw the man behind the polite exterior, the man who'd written to me and threatened my parents' lives if I didn't comply.

A guard held the door open for us, but said nothing. I reached for my trunk, but the headmaster shook his head. "I'll have it brought to your room."

He stepped outside and I followed, wondering briefly if I would ever set foot outside that wall again. The walk across campus was cool and dark. Not to mention utterly silent. Several windows of what appeared to be dorm buildings were lit up, but the grounds were empty. As if to explain, the headmaster said, "Curfew has passed."

As I moved deeper inside the surrounding outer wall, it felt like every step I took was farther away from my parents, further away from my old life. And no matter how much it hurt, I couldn't stop my feet from moving forward. In order to protect them, in order to do whatever I could to help stop another Graplar attack on Kessler from destroying any more innocent lives, I had to leave everything, including them, behind.

"I want to thank you for coming to Shadow Academy, Kaya."

Thank me. Because I was clearly doing him a big favor by trying to protect my parents. It wasn't like I had much choice in the matter, but . . . whatever.

"Your parents were wise to send you."

Remembering their anguished faces as the wagon had pulled away from our cabin, I met the headmaster's gaze and said, "I would do anything for them."

He nodded, his eyes darkening some, as if I didn't have a choice in the matter. And I didn't. Not really. "Tell me, Kaya. How much have your parents taught you about the war?"

"Some," I lied. In truth, they hadn't really spoken openly about the war until the letter arrived, and even then, they only muttered a few sketchy details. What I did know was that they didn't much care about whatever the squabble was between the Barrons and whoever they were at war with. So it really was no surprise that I had little idea what the headmaster was flapping his jaws about as we crossed the campus grounds.

"Your parents are skilled Barrons. They both fought

valiantly in the first battle at Wood's Cross. It was a shame to lose them." He paused then, and it was a pause full of meaning. We kept walking, and when I fell behind by a few steps, I noticed a red crescent moon on the back of the headmaster's neck, peeking out of his collar. His Soulbound Healer, it seemed, was alive and well.

My parents had been loyal to the cause. They'd fought valiantly in the war. But after losing their Soulbound Healers, they'd fallen in love, and chose that love over the war, and over what had been expected of them as Barrons. It was the right thing to do, despite what the headmaster might think. He could pause all he wanted to, look at me however he liked, but it didn't change the fact that he and the Zettai Council were condemning my parents for all the wrong reasons.

"But what's important now is that their union produced a Healer." He looked hesitant for a moment, as if the subject of me being a Healer were a sensitive one. Sensitive, or unfortunate, I couldn't tell which. "You see, Kaya, we are in the midst of a terrible war. A war brought to us by King Darrek and his damned Graplars. He has an immense army on his side, oh yes, but the prevailing threat is that he's trained his Graplars to rid our population of Healers. He believes that by doing so, he can lessen our Barron numbers. Darrek may be completely mad, but he is also crafty in the most dangerous way."

I had no idea who or what Darrek was, but my throat dried instantly and I backpedaled, sputtering. "Rid . . .

you mean those *things* are specifically hunting Healers?"

He nodded slowly. "It's really quite the dilemma."

My eyes snapped back to him at his casual tone. He spoke of it like someone had just spilled milk on the floor and there were no clean rags to speak of—not at all like those monsters were seeking out Healers . . . Healers like *me* . . . and killing them. And apparently that wasn't a big deal. Just a minor annoyance, really.

"Barrons, as you surely know, are able to withstand more blows and pain than any Unskilled person could ever imagine."

Oh, I knew, all right. I'd watched my dad sew his own stitches without as much as a wince. I saw my mom set a broken bone with a stream of curse words, but a surgeon's touch. The pain hadn't even made her flinch. Barrons were tough. Me, I almost pass out when I get a splinter.

The expression on the headmaster's face changed slightly, as if he knew what I was thinking. "But they are not immortal. With the aid of their Healer and through the blessing of their bond, Barrons can be healed from any wound that they endure, even brought back from the brink of death in a matter of moments. And this is why Healers are being exterminated. Because only through you and your kind can Barrons go on fighting the Graplars and Darrek's armies. You're a threat to his greedy plans to dominate all of Tril, because through Healers, Barrons have the power to stop him."

I pictured my parents fighting for a cause they didn't believe in, watching as those they were Soulbound to had perished. I snapped, "Why should they go on fighting? I mean, if they don't want to . . ."

The headmaster sighed, as if he were losing his patience with me already. A shame—I hadn't even gotten around to telling him how I really felt about this whole mess. About leaving my family and friends, about being forced into attending a school that supported a war I could give a fak about. But something told me he wasn't the least bit curious about those things.

"This is not a history class, Kaya. I tell you these things so that you will see what a blessing it is to have you here. Of the three training academies, Shadow Academy has been hit hardest by Darrek's efforts. As such, we have the highest population of Bound couples, and the lowest population of Soulbound couples. Your Barron is anxiously awaiting your arrival. Study well, and practice your skills, because he will need you to survive."

Great. No pressure or anything. Clearing my throat, I looked down at my hands for a moment. "So, when will I meet this Barron I'm supposed to be Bound to?"

"*Your* Barron."

No. Not *my* Barron. Not the Barron I was Soulbound to. Not the Barron I had been born to heal. He'd died several months ago. I knew, because the headmaster had said so in his letter to me. It hurt. Without reason or sense, it hurt, like a piece of my soul had just withered into dust.

I'd known I was Soulbound, of course—my parents had explained to me at a very young age that all Healers and Barrons were born attached to another, that I was Soulbound to someone, somewhere, and that eventually we would find our way to one another. Nothing could stop that. The bond was too great to resist. But their explanations hadn't meant very much to me until I read the headmaster's words: "It is with deepest regrets that I must inform you that the Barron to whom you were Soulbound has perished."

I was completely heartbroken that I never had the chance to meet him. He was my Barron, and it broke my heart to lose him.

So . . . no, the Barron I'd been assigned to wasn't *my* Barron. He was just someone who was supposed to fill the space that *my* Barron had filled, but couldn't anymore.

"Soon. Tomorrow, after we meet to discuss the academy's expectations of you. Say, ten o'clock in the morning, my office? Your guard, Maddox, will show you the way."

With a snort, I said, "Yeah, Maddox has done a great job so far."

Without a word, perhaps suspecting that I was baiting him for an argument—which I totally was—he led me to the largest building and opened the door, then directed me up two flights of stairs. "The second door on the right, please."

I reached the door and paused. The headmaster passed me, and knocked on the third door. As if he were too anxious to wait, he knocked heavily a second time. The door opened to reveal a rather petite brunette girl with sheared short hair and the bluest eyes that I had ever seen. The headmaster's relatively pleasant demeanor wavered and he hissed, "Maddox, have you forgotten something?"

Maddox flicked her eyes to me—*her* eyes! Maddox was a girl? Why didn't anyone tell me?—and groaned. "Fak, I forgot."

I felt bad for her at first. Then I remembered the Graplar and didn't feel as bad. Still, I shrugged and offered up a small smile. "It's all right. No harm done."

"Tomorrow night, while Kaya is sleeping, you will assist the south gate guards in their patrols. Perhaps it will strengthen your memory." The headmaster clapped his hands together eagerly. "Now . . . is he here?"

"Yes, Headmaster." Maddox opened the door wide and stepped back.

A voice from within took on a concerned tone, like the speaker was worried a Graplar might have devoured me whole. At least somebody seemed to care. "Is she—"

"Yes, yes, she's fine. I simply wanted to remind you

of our appointment tomorrow morning . . . and of Protocol, of course."

A pause. "Of course."

Maddox stepped out into the hall. I heard the door close slowly just as the headmaster was turning back to face me. His voice was almost singsongy, like he was trying desperately to keep my entrance into this school as pleasant as possible. It was nauseating. "There we are. I'll leave you in Maddox's most capable hands. Good night. I'll see you in the morning."

I rolled my eyes, but doubted he saw before turning and leaving me alone in the hall with my inept guard.

Maddox crossed her arms in front of her and looked at me, sizing me up. Without her saying anything at all, I got the feeling she wasn't enormously happy about being assigned as my guard. At the moment I was too tired to care.

I couldn't help but notice the small crescent, about the size of a coin, on the back of her hand. Her Trace. It was black.

With a sigh, she opened another door and gestured for me to go inside. "After you, Princess."

I stepped inside without a word, too exhausted to argue with her over why I wasn't even close to being a "princess." After all, princesses were loved and adored by all, and those were two things that were decidedly missing from my present company. Oh yeah, and princesses also had bodyguards who would lay down their lives for them, and I was pretty sure that those guards never forgot them at some trailhead.

The room—my room, I assumed—was small, but tasteful. A large bed dominated the center of the space, and it was covered with a fluffy down comforter, encased in rich green velvet. Luxurious tapestry drapes outlined the window. A small desk sat near the door, a pile of books on its surface. My quarters were lovely, but I wanted very much to hate them, because they weren't home.

Maddox opened a door that connected to the next room. She seemed in a hurry, as if she couldn't wait to be away from me. The feeling was mutual. "This is the parlor, where I spend each evening. It's also the room that connects your room and your Barron's living quarters. If you need anything, don't ask."

She shut the door behind her so fast I almost didn't have time to register that she'd gone. Great. Not only did I have a full-time guard . . . she hated me.

Yawning, I pulled back the covers, content to sleep in my bloodstained, mud-caked travel clothes. I climbed into bed and felt my sore muscles scream their gratitude. I didn't have time to think about how much I missed my parents, or meeting the Barron tomorrow. The moment my head hit the pillow, I was out.

five

I woke in a puddle of drool, with crease lines from the sheets pressing into my cheek. The details of my dreams grew fuzzy as I awoke from heavy sleep, but left me shaken and homesick in the worst way, and there was nothing I could do about it. According to what my father had said as he lifted my trunk onto the wagon, the only time during the school year that I could see my parents was during midsummer break, when they were allowed to visit the school grounds. It would be an entire year before I'd see them again and, given their current state of popularity among the current administration, I wasn't even sure if I'd get to see them then. My heart sank.

After watching my walls turn pink, then gold with the sunrise, I slid out of bed with my usual morning grace and stubbed my big toe on my trunk, which had been placed at the foot of the massive bed during the night. Apparently, I'd been so out of it that I hadn't even noticed the mysterious delivery person. Swearing loudly, I threw open the trunk's lid and grabbed a purple shirt and black leggings, and a handful of other things I'd need to make myself presentable.

Crossing the bedroom, still grumping about my sore toe, I opened one of the three doors along the inner wall, looking for the washroom, but instead found what looked like a walk-in closet and dressing area.

Dressing area? Seriously, who needed an entire room to get dressed in?

Remembering Maddox's "princess" remark, I couldn't help but wonder if all Healers were like that—spoiled and pampered. It was possible. But then it wasn't like I knew many Healers. Just one actually. Myself.

After I gawked at the size of the closet for a bit—fak, it was almost as big as my bedroom back home—I eventually found the bathroom and headed through my morning routine.

I was meeting the Barron today. Sorry, "my" Barron. It wouldn't do to have the headmaster hear me refer to him as "the" Barron, or I'd have to suffer the consequence.

Something told me I'd be suffering a lot of consequences during my time here.

Fantastic. I'd have bet some serious coin that he'd be everything my stress-filled thoughts had made him out to be. Ugly as sin. Bossy. Egotistical. Bratty rich kid.

After all, that was just the way my luck seemed to be going lately.

I took a long look at myself in the mirror. There was no way this occasion called for casual attire, but that's just what it was getting. You can't steal a girl away from her life and imprison her in some weird place where Graplars are the norm and expect her hair to look flawless. Besides, I was tired. And homesick. And hungry.

As I was brushing some powder on my nose, a light knock came on the only door I hadn't opened. With a deep breath, I opened it to Maddox. She didn't say anything, only stood there looking irritated that I hadn't turned out to be just a bad dream. I waited, but when she didn't speak, I said, "Can I help you?"

"How nice of you to get all dressed up for the occasion, Princess. It's not every day that you get to meet your Barron." I didn't speak, only sneered in her general direction. She rolled her eyes some and said, "You're due to meet with the headmaster in a half hour. If you want breakfast, we have to leave now."

Though I was sorely tempted to stick to my room for the remainder of my time here, I sighed, resolving myself to the inevitable. "Let me grab some shoes."

After digging around in my trunk for some clean shoes, I slipped them on my feet and threw Maddox a glance. "So . . . what? You're like my bodyguard or something?"

Maddox sighed, doing her best to appear exasperated. "I swear. Healers get dumber every generation."

She turned her attention away from whatever omnipotent force she was talking to on the ceiling and back to me. "It's my job as your guard to make sure you get fed and don't miss your classes, *and* escort you around campus, *and* act as chaperone when you and your Barron are together. For an entire year, while you get adjusted to life at the academy. So call it what you want: bodyguard, babysitter, whatever. When all is said and done I'm stuck with you."

My eyebrow twitched in irritation. It was sounding like, other than the time I spent in my room, I was never going to be alone here. For someone who greatly values her alone time, this was a tragedy waiting to happen. I stood up and folded my arms in front of me. We were going to hash this out before we did anything else. "Do you have a problem with me or something, Maddox? Because I'm not the one who peed on your pancakes, all right? I'm not any happier than you to be in this situation."

She stepped closer, trying to eye me down. Tiny freckles dotted her small nose. It had to be a challenge to come off as intimidating with cute little freckles on your nose, but somehow, Maddox pulled it off. "I have a problem with Healers in general. I'd try explaining it to you, but I'm not sure you'd hear me way up there on your pedestal."

It felt like I'd been punched in the chest. "And just exactly what do you mean by that?"

Maddox rolled her eyes so far up into her head that they almost disappeared entirely. "C'mon, Princess, I've been here for a while now. You're not the first Healer that I've had to babysit. And every one of them has been the same. Why should I expect you to be any different?"

My jaw clenched until it ached. How could she judge me so harshly before she even got to know me? "Well, I've never met another Healer, so I can't speak for them. You could be right. But I'm not a snob."

"Never met another Healer?" Her eyes widened, a peculiar smirk melting the bitter purse from her lips. "How could you have never met another Healer? What part of Tril are you from?"

My defenses went up. From what my parents had told me, most of the Skilled lived among the Skilled their entire lives. The fact that I knew so little about how things worked in this part of the world meant I was an easy target for anyone who wanted to make my life here more difficult, which so far seemed to be everybody. I hesitantly replied, "Kokoro. The village of Kessler, near the river."

For a moment, she didn't respond at all. Then Maddox did what I was beginning to suspect was the impossible. She smiled. "No kidding?"

"Yeah, why?"

"So, you grew up around the Unskilled, not in one of these prissy boarding schools, huh?" The left corner of her mouth was raised slightly higher than the right, giving her smile a slight crook.

I couldn't help but wonder where this was going, exactly. "So? Do you have a problem with Kessler?"

"Nah. I spent a summer in Kessler when I was eight. It was gorgeous. We stayed at this cabin and my dad and I went fishing. It was so much fun."

That was enough to give me pause. For one, according to what my parents had explained to me, unless it was to trade tools or barter for food and supplies, Barrons and Healers didn't tend to interact with the Unskilled. It was just socially unacceptable, for some stupid reason. As a result, the Unskilled had no idea that people like Barrons and Healers even possessed the skills they did. And for two, they sure as hell didn't vacation among them. That's how my parents had managed to stay hidden for so long, because they could always count on those certain sects of society staying separate. "Wait. How is that even possible? Kessler is—"

"An Unskilled village?" Maddox nodded. "Come on, let's go get some breakfast and I'll tell you all about it."

Once my shoes were tied, Maddox led me into the hall, which was relatively empty, and then downstairs, which wasn't. She strode forward through the sea of students without effort, throwing a glance over her shoulder every few steps to make certain I hadn't wandered off. At the end of that hall stood a set of immense carved wooden doors, which were standing wide open. Delicious, warm, breakfast-y smells of cinnamon rolls, pancakes, sausage, and bacon beckoned from within. My stomach rumbled.

Inside was a huge room with stone walls and wooden rafters. Tables and groupings of chairs were scattered all over the room, most of them occupied. At the far end was a cafeteria line. Maddox led me to an empty table in the corner and went to grab some food. If she brought me a cinnamon roll, I was totally going to rethink that whole not liking her thing.

During her brief absence, I took the time to survey the room. Less than half of the students were dressed in white soft-soled shoes, white cotton leggings and matching tops that wrapped around the front and tied closed at the waist. They must have been Healers. The other half—I guessed they were Barrons—dressed in black cotton pants that clung gently to their legs, black, loose-fitting, wrap shirts, and soft-soled black shoes. The Barrons with longer hair wore their hair tied back with leather thongs, but the Healers didn't, for some strange reason.

I noticed that everyone was sitting in small groups. Boys with girls, girls with boys, boys with boys, girls with girls. Some were Barrons and Healers, some

Healers and guards, some small groupings of Healers, Barrons, and guards. But none, it looked to me, were sitting alone. Like I was.

I bit the inside of my cheek and sighed. I was also the only one without a uniform.

My parents hadn't told me very much about the academy—just that the training sessions had been the best part. I wasn't exactly a force to be reckoned with, but I was adept enough to take down my father once or twice while we were goofing off in the backyard, to everyone's surprise including my own. I was looking forward to proving myself. But just because I was born a Healer didn't mean I wouldn't have to fight for my life on the battlefield.

As I continued my examination of the crowd, I noticed a flash of silver hair three tables over. Even though he was facing away from me, I'd have recognized that hair anywhere. I smiled, recalling the way that he'd saved me from that horrible monster in the woods. Then I frowned at the memory of his weird departure. Why had he looked so irritated with me? Was my company really that bad? Hmm . . . Maybe I had bad breath. Or maybe he just hated Healers. Almost as though he could sense my presence, he stiffened. Then he stood and disappeared into the crowd with his tray.

Maddox returned with a tray for me, piled with a variety of things. I looked over the mountain of oatmeal, muffins, toast, scrambled eggs, bacon, fried ham, banana, grapes, orange juice, and milk she'd brought and said, "You're joking right? There's no way I can eat all of this."

Maddox shrugged. "Well, I didn't know what you'd like. So I brought you what I usually eat for breakfast."

Looking at her lean figure, I raised an eyebrow. There was enough food on my tray to feed three people. I had wondered if my parents' appetites had been a fluke or if all Barrons ate that much. I was about to ask when Maddox confirmed it.

She shook her head. "I always forget that you Healers require many fewer calories than us."

"Are you hungry? I'd hate to throw most of this away."

Maddox shook her head again, rolling her eyes some at my lack of common knowledge. "A guard can't eat while they have a charge. It's Protocol. I'll eat while you're in class."

"Protocol." I rolled the word over on my tongue. It tasted bitter. "Something tells me I'm not going to like that word very much. What is it?"

She raised her left eyebrow sharply. "Your parents never taught you Protocol?"

When I shook my head, she said, "Protocol is a strict set of societal rules, put in place by the Zettai Council. It basically governs how people are suppose to react in certain situations."

Biting the inside of my cheek slightly, I said, "I see. And what happens when you break Protocol?"

"Depends on whether you get caught." Maddox winked and let out a chuckle. Something told me she could give a fak about following the Zettai Council's rules. I liked that about her. "It also depends on what you did and who saw you do it, and how old you are. From what I hear, adults can be punished with anything varying from paying a simple fine to the Zettai Council, to something as drastic as death. For minor infractions, students get extra duties. For something major, you can get sent on some pretty harsh patrols or your family can be fined. Or worse."

Worse. I had a feeling I knew exactly what "worse" would be in my case. I sighed. "Well at least sit down or something. You're making me nervous hovering over the table like that."

But the look on her face said it all. "Let me guess. Protocol?"

Maddox grinned. "You're catching on, Princess. But we can talk. You probably have questions. I can probably answer them."

Chewing on a bit of bacon, I swallowed and said, "So how is it a Barron vacations with the Unskilled anyway?"

Maddox looked longingly at a slice of French toast. It had to be ridiculously hard to only eat when your ward was in class or sleeping. How often could that be? Just a few hours during the day, and a few at night? No wonder they ate such huge portions. My father had been known to eat most of a whole ham in one sitting, and my mother never appeared to gain an ounce, despite the mounds of bread she'd consume over dinner. Whereas my pants got tight if I so much as glanced at dessert.

Pulling her attention from the food on my tray, she said, "My parents went AWOL after I was born, and raised me just outside of Drago. I didn't know any Barrons or Healers besides them until I moved here two years ago. What about you?"

Drago. I knew Drago. It was right down the river from Kessler. My mom used to take me shopping there. They had a killer pub. Best sandwiches this side of Tril. As far as I knew, anyway. I'd never traveled to Kaito or Haruko, and had only barely seen an eighth of the continent of Kokoro. My father had promised to take me to some of the northern villages of Haruko someday. But apparently that—along with the rest of my life—was on hold now. Maybe forever. Strike that—probably forever.

The thought of my parents stole my hunger away and I returned a half-eaten slice of bacon to my plate. "About the same. Did the headmaster threaten your parents too?"

Maddox stiffened, that hard, cold look returning to her eyes. But I could tell it wasn't for me. "Not exactly."

A momentary, uncomfortable silence settled between us. It was all I could do to break it. "We don't have to talk about it, if you don't want to."

She plucked a grape from my tray and, with a glance

around to make sure no one was watching, popped it into her mouth and chewed quickly. "My dad was a Barron; Mom was a Healer. Thanks to my dad's exemplary war record, they were allowed to retire early. Only they didn't want to raise me where my only future would be spent on the battlefield, so we moved to Drago. When I was fourteen, a group of Barron guards knocked on our door and told my dad that I would have to come to Shadow Academy and train to fight. My parents resisted. My dad had been out of practice for a bit too long and the Barrons were fresh out of training and very fit. It wasn't even a contest."

I furrowed my brow. The Barrons claimed to be fighting against tyranny, but something told me they needed to look the definition of it up again. "What happened?"

"The guards killed my father, imprisoned my mother, and brought me here." Maddox shrugged casually, but I could see the pain in her expression. I thought I knew pain, being forced away from my family and home, but there was nothing like watching one of your parents murdered by the very people you were being forced to live and work among. "I never saw her again. She died two months ago."

"Oh . . ." It was all I could manage to say for a moment, as the horror of her loss sank in. As discreetly as I could manage, I passed her a handful of grapes. She nodded thankfully, both for the food and for not hugging her and making a scene. "Where's your Healer?"

"My Soulbound Healer died at birth." She shrugged again, but this time it was far less painful. "So my parents pretty much died for nothing. The war will go on just fine without me. It's not like I can fight without a Healer. Without a Healer I couldn't quickly recover from any wounds I might receive. It'd be suicide."

Furrowing my brow, I said, "Could they put you on the battlefield anyway? Without a Healer?"

Her eyes darkened some, and I saw how much the subject bothered her. "Technically, yes. They don't do it often. Unbound Barrons generally are assigned Healer guard duties, though a few get stuck with gate guard duties—normally inside the wall, but outside as well. The truth is, the safest place I could be right now is following you around campus."

Maddox had been through so much pain, so much loss. No wonder she seemed so hard. "Will you get a new Healer?"

Maddox shrugged and popped another grape into her mouth. "Not likely. See, there aren't really enough Healers to go around, so there's this list they put our names on. If your family is part of high society or they donate a lot of money to the school, your name gets moved to the top. Then there are people like me, who they put on the list just for show, when we all know it's never gonna happen. But then, it's not like I'm anxious to hit the battlefield. Of course, I could do with some companionship . . ."

Companionship. So I wasn't just expected to heal the Barron I would be Bound to. I was supposed to be his steady girlfriend too. Good-bye, romance and freedom of choice. Hello, Shadow Academy. I swallowed the bit of muffin I'd been chewing. It didn't go down easily. I looked over the crowd once again. "Are all Bound and Soulbound couples . . . you know, *couples*?"

The silver-haired man returned to his table, his tray once again full. Only this time, he sat on the opposite side, facing me. But he didn't look at me. Not once.

I picked up another piece of bacon and chewed it thoughtfully.

"No, but some of them are. About half, I'd guess. The Soulbound couples share a pretty intense relationship, sometimes romantic, sometimes a really close friendship. It's said they're like soul mates or something. And Bound couples . . . well, sometimes their bond is strong, but never as strong as the Soulbound and sometimes . . . sometimes there's no connection at all." She nodded a few tables over to a girl with honey blond hair and long legs. Next to her stood a pale, redheaded boy who watched the girl's every move as if it were a ballet. I guessed him to be her Healer. "Take Melanie, for example. David, her Healer, thinks she walks on water, but she barely notices his existence."

I was about to ask who the guy with silver hair was, when Maddox swore under her breath at the clock on the wall. "You're due at the headmaster's office in five minutes, we need to go now."

I stood and tried to pick up my tray, but Maddox shot me a look that said my picking up after myself would break some kind of Protocol and get her in big trouble, so I let her take care of it. I was beginning to understand why she thought all Healers were snobs. Apparently, the rules regarded Healers as delicate flowers that needed to be taken care of. Some Healers were probably all right with that, but I wasn't.

Maddox had just returned to my table when Melanie stood and sashayed over to us, a small group right on her heels. I could feel Maddox's muscles tensing beside me.

"So," Melanie said, tossing her perfectly sculpted curls over her shoulder. "You're the new girl, huh? Let me guess. You're a Healer."

Maddox spoke, her tone irritated. "Melanie—"

"Maddox, if I need a sitter, I'll call you. Hush." She had barely thrown Maddox a glance, and then turned her attention on me. Something spiteful was lurking in her eyes. "So?"

It was clear she hated Healers. It was written all over her face, and in the way she completely disregarded the boy next to her. I shrugged. "So . . . yes. I'm a Healer."

"I knew it. There's a certain look to the lower life-forms." She groaned, and rolled her eyes for her audience. Something told me that Melanie always had an audience. "What a shame. This school needs more people who can fight and less walking bandages."

I growled under my breath. "You want a fight? Throw a punch and I'll give you a few wounds that no kind of bandage will fix."

Melanie laughed, leaning closer. "Ooh, I'm scared . . ."

Maddox tugged my sleeve. "Come on, Kaya . . . the headmaster's waiting."

I eyed Melanie down, but she didn't flinch, and to what I'm sure was her utter surprise, neither did I. I turned and followed Maddox out the door.

"All right, fak Protocol. That was brilliant. I don't think I've ever seen anybody stand up to Melanie, let alone a Healer." Maddox leaned over and hugged my shoulders as we walked down the hall. "You and I are officially friends, Princess."

Maddox was really pretty nice once she let her defenses down.

We reached the headmaster's office with a minute to spare. At Maddox's knock, the headmaster called, "Enter, and be known."

Maddox swung open the door and breathed a reminder. "I'll be waiting for you after your meeting."

The headmaster looked up as I stepped over the threshold and smiled. "Ah, yes, Kaya. How did you sleep? Did you have breakfast?"

Nodding, I took a seat in one of the chairs opposite

his desk. "I slept okay, and Maddox made sure I ate."

"Maddox is a fine guard." He eyed me for a moment, his jovial expression cracking for a moment. "Though she needs a bit of discipline. It's not customary to share details of punishments with students, but as containing the details is such an enormous challenge in a school full of teenagers, I suppose it doesn't hurt to share that Maddox will have extra duties to make up for failing to collect you yesterday."

"I'm sure it just slipped her mind. You don't have to—"

"But I do, and I have. I don't enjoy doling out punishments, but do so swiftly when needed. Now . . . onto business." He opened the top drawer of his desk and withdrew a small black book, then slid it across the desktop. "This guidebook should greatly help your understanding of what will and will not be tolerated here at Shadow Academy. Please commit the rules to memory and follow them. I would hate to see you pulling extra duties alongside your guard."

There it was again, his honey facade slipping just long enough to see the man he really was beneath.

Without missing a beat, he opened another drawer and withdrew a slip of paper, which he handed across the desk to me. "Here is your schedule. Absences are not allowed without the permission of one of the Master Healers who run the hospital wing or an instructor. Tardiness will result in suitable punishment, given by an instructor or myself. You will be issued six sets of uniforms later today and will be required to remain in uniform every day except for special occasions. Laundry will be collected every Friday evening. Just place your bag in the hall and we'll take care of everything."

I looked over my schedule:

HEALING 101

AN INTRODUCTION TO PROTOCOL

ANATOMY OF WAR

BOTANICAL MEDICINE

Not one class having anything to do with training. I frowned. "When do I learn how to fight?"

"Pardon?"

"When do I learn how to fight?"

As if summoning up all the patience he could muster, he took a deep breath and said, "Healers do not train for battle."

My jaw hit the floor. Was he crazy? There was no way I was going to face another Graplar without knowing how to take the thing down, or at least delay its inevitable chomping of my midsection. "How am I supposed to defend myself?"

"It is your Barron's duty to ensure your safety on the battlefield." His tone was light, but condescending, as if he were speaking to a three-year-old.

Great. So now I was expected to be a damsel in distress? I didn't think so. Quickly reorganizing my approach, I said, "But what if he gets hurt and I need to get to him?"

The headmaster's mood slipped from condescending to really, really irritated. His face turned beet red, and I was pretty sure he was either having a heart attack or preparing for his eyeballs to explode. "Kaya, I understand that you were not raised in the tradition of Healers, but I would suggest that you embrace your calling very soon or else Shadow Academy will prove to be a very difficult place to live. Healers *do not* train for battle. End of discussion."

Frowning, I sat back in my seat. I'd say it was sexist, but as all Healers weren't girls, maybe it was healerist? It was annoying, anyway. I bet that I could kick a Graplar or two's butt with the proper combat training.

"Now . . . as to your Barron . . ."

I sank down in my seat, my blood boiling.

"Trayton is very important to our cause at the front. Before his mother's passing, his father, Cedric, was probably the finest Barron to ever grace the battlefield, and it stands to reason that Trayton will follow in his father's genetic footsteps. It is crucial that a Barron of his potential caliber receive the utmost care and attention. And what with Cedric's generous donations to the academy . . ."

I rolled my eyes, but only slightly. So not only was "my" Barron the all-star favorite around here, but he was a rich snob whose daddy had to pay his way to the front of the line.

"It was a terrible tragedy when Trayton's Healer perished. It has been a long and arduous search for a fitting replacement, and, like it or not, you, Kaya, are that fit."

Sighing, I was ready to hate Trayton, ready to despise him without ever having laid eyes on the pretentious, muscle-bound daddy's boy. I parted my lips to ask when he would get here, but my words were interrupted by a knock on the door.

"Enter, and be known."

The door opened to reveal a young man with shoulder-length black hair and smooth, pale skin. He was tall, thin, muscular, and lovely. Nothing at all like I'd expected. When his incredible eyes met mine, he seemed to relax. His lips curled into a smile, and mine naturally followed. He silently mouthed hello, and I felt myself smile against my will. I wasn't supposed to like him. He was a spoiled, bratty rich kid who wasn't giving me a choice of who I was supposed to spend the rest of my life with. He was probably dumber than a pile of rocks and incredibly dull to boot. And—I held his gaze, feeling my angry resolve melt away—he was the Barron, the man I'd come to be Bound to. He had to be.

And if he wasn't, I'd demand a recount.

*T*he headmaster turned back to me, his face once again a normal flesh color, looking as proud as a father would of his most prized son. "Kaya, it is my honor to introduce you to the Barron to whom you will be Bound tomorrow morning. One of our finest students, and the son of a personal friend, I present to you . . . Trayton."

I started, blinking in dizzy confusion. Tomorrow? That was so soon. *Too* soon. There was no way I was ready to be Bound to someone else for the rest of my life beginning tomorrow. I fidgeted uncomfortably, hoping I heard him wrong, but knowing that I hadn't.

Trayton stepped into the room, his cheeks flushing pink for a moment, as if he were uncomfortable with receiving praise. Then he moved toward me and held his hand out, bowing his head. His words were soft, gentle, coaxing. "If I may . . ."

His voice was instantly familiar to me, like a song I'd once heard long ago, but forgotten. He was the person the headmaster had been speaking to at the dorms last night. The one who sounded so concerned about me.

At first I wasn't exactly sure what he was doing. Then, with a mental forehead smack, I hesitantly placed my hand in his and relished his smooth, warm skin. He tilted his head up, meeting my eyes. A smile danced on his lips and he shook his head some, as if berating himself. Maybe he was chastising himself for being too kind, too familiar, too warm too soon. Maybe he was punishing himself for breaking some stupid Protocol rule that I wasn't even aware of. Regardless, his eyes were sparkling. He said, "It's my pleasure to make your acquaintance, Kaya."

When he spoke my name, he drew it out in a near-whisper, as if savoring the taste of it on his tongue. He gave my hand a slight squeeze and stood once again.

The headmaster clapped his hands together. "Wonderful. Just wonderful! An excellent match, I can tell."

My smile faltered some at the reminder that I wasn't being given a choice in who I spent my life with. Not that Trayton wasn't nice—and gorgeous—but I really hated that my entire life's path had been decided for me.

Tomorrow loomed over me: dark, oppressive. I would be Bound, like it or not.

Bound.

What a scary word.

As the headmaster droned on about something called "proper procedure," Trayton nodded and answered when he was expected to. The headmaster stood and began pacing slowly around the room as he spoke. Daring a glance at me, Trayton smiled and mouthed "It's nice to meet you."

I smiled back, mouthing, "You too."

He leaned closer and pointed to his eyes as he silently said, "You have pretty eyes." His skin flushed pink, and I found myself utterly charmed by him, despite my reservations.

He had pretty eyes too—slate gray and dazzling. I was in the middle of mouthing "thank you," when my imagination wondered what color eyes the boy I was Soulbound to had had. I settled back in my seat, admonishing myself. It didn't matter, anyway. That boy was dead. And I would soon be Bound to Trayton.

The headmaster's voice broke in. "Trayton? Are you paying attention?"

Trayton's eyes widened and, caught, we both shot the headmaster a look. Trayton stumbled. "I . . . of course. You were saying?"

The headmaster slanted his eyes. "A few rules to remember. First, you two will not be allowed to be alone together for one year following your binding ceremony. This will allow you time to adjust to your new arrangement. Maddox will accompany you at all times. When she can't, a suitable chaperone will be arranged. Also, school policy dictates that there will be no . . . ah, er, well . . . I should say . . . no touching with the ah . . . uhm . . . nudity . . ."

My face flushed with embarrassed heat. When I glanced over, I could see that Trayton's face was just as flushed as mine felt at the mention of sex. Trayton very calmly said, "I think we know what you mean, Headmaster."

The headmaster took a moment to straighten some papers on his desk that didn't really require straightening. It took him a moment to speak again. "Yes. Well. None of that."

"Ever?" I squeaked, then immediately recoiled. Great. Trayton was going to think I was some kind of boy-obsessed girl, like Avery. "I mean . . . not that I . . ."

Trayton blushed a deeper shade of red.

The headmaster took on that sarcastic, snotty tone that I was beginning to understand was business as usual for him, at least in conversations with me. "Not while you are students here."

"About that . . . how long do I have to stay here?" I had expected him to reply with the standard four-year answer that most upper schools in Kokoro fell under. The upper school in Kessler had been a four-year institution. I had no reason to expect any different here.

"You will attend Shadow Academy until it is determined that you are ready for what awaits you in this war, be that two years or twenty."

With the schedule clenched in my fist, I shook it in disgust, my voice suddenly rising in anger. I didn't want to be here, didn't want to be part of their stupid war. Especially since it seemed like Healers might as well be walking around with a big target on their chest. "And what about math and science? What about training and self-defense? Why won't I be learning those? Do you have any idea how important those subjects are?"

He looked down his long nose at me. "You will learn all that you, as a Healer, are required to learn."

"Well, it's a damn good thing I didn't grow up around you people. It'd be a wonder that I could even read and write." My hands were shaking. Trayton shot me a concerned glance, but didn't speak. I was betting he was an absolute rule follower.

The headmaster sighed, annoyed with my interruption. "I grow very tired of your impertinence, young lady. I realize that you are not thrilled about being here. I assure you that if your participation in this war were not extremely necessary, we would have left you to lead your life among the Unskilled. We here at Shadow Academy do not make it a habit of bringing people in against their will. It tends to not go as smoothly as we would like, as I'm sure you're aware. However, while you are here, you will follow our rules and you will do as you're told. If you choose to make this a difficult experience, I can assure you that it is not only you and I who will experience these difficulties."

The threat was veiled enough that I wasn't sure if Trayton picked up on it, but I knew exactly what he meant. Get in line or my parents would be the ones to suffer.

When he spoke again, it was to Trayton and Trayton alone. After all, I was just a Healer. I had no business interjecting my opinion in a Barron-to-Barron conversation. The arrogance amazed me. My parents were both Barrons, but neither had ever treated me the way I was being treated now. Maybe it wasn't a Barron thing after all. Maybe it was an arrogant dek thing. "Now back to business. Kaya must never be allowed to wander the grounds alone. I don't have to tell you why. Please make certain this isn't a problem—we can't risk the loss of another Healer. Also, as you well know, Trayton, curfew is nine o'clock in the evening. Now . . . I believe you're both due for your next course. Should you require anything at all, please don't hesitate to stop by my office. If you'll excuse me . . ."

Trayton held open the door and I exited with him close behind. When the door closed after us, we were surrounded by a hush. For a long time, Trayton and I simply exchanged uncomfortable smiles. He turned his head briefly to look over at Maddox, to make certain we hadn't been left entirely alone, and I spied the edge of the marking on the right side of his neck. Clearing my throat, and trying like hell to let go of all of the anger I was feeling for Headmaster Quill, I said, "Your Trace . . . can I see it?"

"Of course." He drew back his hair and I took a closer look. A small black crescent, lovely against his pale skin.

I reached out to touch it, then caught myself and pulled my hand back. My cheeks felt warm again, but this time, it was a pleasant warmth. Trayton smiled, flicking his eyes in the direction of Maddox. I guessed he was suggesting that touching his Trace before we were Bound was a no-no and nodded. "I'm supposed to be in some stupid Healer class in about twenty minutes."

He sighed, but averted his eyes, as if he wasn't sure what he should say to me. "I'm supposed to be training as of ten minutes ago."

I caught his gaze and smiled. "Well, aren't we a pair?"

The corners of his mouth lifted and I swear, I almost melted into a puddle of goo right there. He turned to walk away, but paused midstep, as if wrestling with something in his mind. Then he turned back to me. "Do you like books?"

My mind drifted back to my bedroom in the cabin. Stacks and stacks of well-worn, well-read, well-loved books lined my walls. The memory brought a smile to my face. "Love them. Well, good ones. Why?"

"I want to show you something after dinner tonight, I mean . . . if you'd like." He smiled sheepishly, revealing a small dimple just to the left of his mouth.

I could hardly contain my grin. "I'd love to."

"Good. I want to take you to my favorite place on campus." He nodded and moved down the hall and out the door. I watched every step.

Maddox snickered. "Oh man."

Her words shook me from my apparent trance. "What?"

"Flirt much? You just met the guy, for fak's sake."

Already, she could see right through me. "I wasn't flirting! I was . . . talking."

"Yeah, sure you were." She walked past me and started down the hall. "C'mon, Princess."

This time when she called me by the nickname she'd given me, it sounded different—more like a sarcastic quip than an insulting dig.

And I *was* flirting. I couldn't help it. Trayton was hot as could be, sweet like honey, and had that clever shyness that I found irresistible. Any girl in her right mind would have flirted with him.

By the time we got outside, Trayton was already gone. "Headmaster Quill wants me to give you a quick tour of the campus before your first class. That is . . . if you're done drooling over Trayton for the moment."

I smiled, suddenly feeling lighter than I had all day. "For the moment."

Maddox raised a sharp eyebrow in my direction. "Is that all it takes to make you relax, a pretty face? You were awfully tense before your meeting with the head-master."

"It's not like that. I'm just . . ." What was I doing? It wasn't like I wanted to be here and the fact that Trayton was super nice and really good looking was making that all better. Tension returned to my muscles. "I don't know what I'm doing."

Maddox gave my shoulder a comforting squeeze. Her eyes were full of sympathy. "You're flirting with a great guy. No crime in that. Trayton is about the nicest boy on campus. Cutest too, I think."

After a moment, I offered her a smile. Maddox was all right.

The campus was several acres long, a rectangle of lush, green grounds, spotted with various buildings and trees. Moving north, we walked alongside the dorm building that contained my room and the dining hall. Once we cleared the building, Maddox pointed out its twin, which sat parallel and to the east. Beyond the dorms was a field and in the far-off area to the east were gardens and a small, shabby cottage. To the west of my dorm stood a wide open area that Maddox referred to as the courtyard. On the courtyard's edge, facing my dorm, was another cottage, this one well cared for. Most of the courtyard was green, but a smaller area—the one right between the cottage and dorm—was paved with flag-stones and home to a large fountain. Maddox pointed out two large L-shaped buildings near the north gate that were home to classes, and she explained that there were more dormitories to the far west just for the guards.

Just west of the courtyard cottage was another open field, with two sets of bleachers bookending it. Probably forty students filled the stands, and two men were sparring at the center of the field. I nodded to the area. "Is that where the Barrons train?"

Maddox nodded. "Want to take a closer look? We still have a few minutes before your first class."

We walked over and stood on the side of the field, close enough to see, but far enough away that we wouldn't interrupt class. All the Barrons were dressed in what I had thought was training gear—turns out, I was right. And all of them, the boys and the girls, wore protective face masks. All but one.

At the center of the field stood two men. One with long black hair, who I recognized immediately. Trayton looked strong and sure, his movements calculated. The other man, the one who wasn't wearing a face mask, the only one with short hair, just long enough that it brushed the collar of his shirt. Short, silver hair.

My hero.

Biting my bottom lip, I hesitantly asked Maddox, "Who is that?"

"That . . ." —she sighed— " . . . would be Darius. He's the best teacher on campus when it comes to fighting. If anyone knows how to handle a katana, it's him."

It wasn't hard to see that though they were roughly the same age, Darius was clearly the more skilled combatant. From across the field, Darius turned his eyes toward me, his skin flushing, and flipped Trayton over, putting him down hard on the ground. Without even pausing to take a breath, he shouted, "You, out of my training area!"

Somebody was in trouble, for sure. I glanced around the outskirts of the field, but couldn't even guess who he was yelling at. It was only when he crossed the field in an angry stride right toward Maddox and me that I realized it was us. He locked eyes with Maddox and jabbed a thumb in my direction. "I don't want her near my training area, Maddox. Get her out of here."

Me? He wanted me to leave? I couldn't believe what I was hearing! I hadn't done anything to him. My heart thudded in my chest, and I narrowed my eyes in disgust. "Y'know, if you're going to talk about me like I'm some kind of plague, you might as well do it directly. I'm standing right here."

He looked at me, a fire burning like hot coals in his eyes, and then directed his attention back to Maddox. "Now."

Maddox grabbed me by the sleeve, dutifully trying to lead me away from the field. "Kaya, we should—"

Shaking her off, I stepped toward Darius, but he didn't budge. "Why do you want me to leave?"

His eyes were alight with anger, his shoulders tense.

He was fuming, and I had no idea why. "I will not have some *Healer* standing around gawking at my class, distracting my students."

Shaking my head, I lost my cool completely. "The only one who seems to be distracted is *you*!"

No one made a sound. Even Maddox seemed to stop breathing.

Darius lowered his voice to a growling whisper. He was standing so close, his breath was warm on my cheek. "Extra duties for you tonight, in the rose garden. That's on the opposite side of the campus, just so you know. As far away as you can be from me and still be at the academy."

My jaw hit the ground. "But—"

He turned his eyes to Maddox. "See to it she gets there after her final class of the day."

Before I could say anything else, Maddox dragged me away from the training area and we headed toward one of the L-shaped buildings.

I ranted the entire way. "What the hell is that guy's problem?"

Maddox sighed. "Darius is . . . temperamental."

"Not exactly a good quality for a Barron, is it?"

Maddox opened the door and we moved inside, keeping our voices respectfully low, as classes were already in session. "Oh, he's no Barron. Darius is an Unskilled. One of the few who knows just about all there is to know about the war. He's also one of the best fighting teachers available. He can even put Barrons down, something that's almost unheard of. An Unskilled against a Barron? Normally, there's no question who'd win. But Darius is pretty amazing."

I snorted, still fuming over the way he'd emphasized *Healer*, like I was a thing rather than a person. "Yeah, an amazing dek."

"Yeah, well . . . Listen, I'll be here when you get done, okay?" Maddox opened a classroom door and smiled. "Good luck."

With a deep breath, I stepped inside the classroom, trying to put Darius out of my thoughts. The room might have passed for any normal classroom outside Shadow Academy. Three rows of three tables each filled the room, with a large slate board at the front of the classroom, two small buckets of chalk rock sitting on the floor in front of it. There were about twenty students inside, both male and female, though most were girls. And, as expected, all Healers, not a single Trace in sight. The woman standing at the front of the class wore a bitter, pinched expression as she noticed my entrance. "You are late."

I unfolded my schedule, as if it alone gave me reason for not being here on time. According to the clock, I was. But maybe she meant I was late for being early. "My name is Kaya. I'm supposed to be—"

"Kaya," she snapped, and I took a step back.

"Yes . . . ma'am?"

"You will address me as Instructor Baak." She picked up a sponge and started wiping the already smudged words from the board on the wall, already dismissing me like I was no more than some annoying fly buzzing around her head. "For your tardiness you will have extra duties tonight after your final class."

I swallowed hard, shuffled my feet, and wished that everyone in the class would stop staring at me. "But I already have extra duties tonight."

That got her attention. She whipped her head back around and gave me the evil eye, staring as if she were trying to read the small print on my forehead that labeled me a troublemaker. "Tomorrow then. I'll give your guard the details. Now take your seat."

Great. My first day and I already had two days of extra duties to look forward to. I was on a roll.

I slid into the nearest empty seat, at a table next to a boy who kept making moon eyes at the mousy-looking girl next to him. Barrons weren't allowed to couple up with other Barrons, and the same went for Healers, as far as I knew. It was kind of odd to see a Healer openly gawking at another Healer like that, but I shrugged and tried to pay attention to the instructor lady's lecture on the importance of being a Healer.

"Barrons have been fighting for lifetimes to keep the Graplars at bay. Both to bring an end to this century-long war and to preserve our way of life—something that would be impossible if not for the aid of Healers.

After all, for as long as Healers continue to heal their Barrons, the Barrons will remain healthy and strong, fit for the battlefront. Small wounds, of course, can be healed with the smallest touch. Larger wounds require a longer touch. A Healer can bring a Barron back from the brink of death on the battlefield. Almost always."

I didn't question the *almost* part, though I very much wanted to. Instead, I groaned a bit. No pressure, Kaya, just know that whether or not Trayton lives or dies is all on you.

The instructor's head snapped in my direction. "Something you care to add, Kaya?"

She hated me already, and I had only just taken my seat for the first time. "I'm afraid I'm not much of a nurse. Seriously, I can't even keep a bandage from falling off. How am I supposed to save my Barron's life on the battlefield?"

She pursed her lips so tightly that it looked like she'd had lemons for breakfast. "Self-doubt is the mark of an amateur."

Without waiting for a response, she turned back to the board and continued her lecture.

That didn't exactly answer my question, but . . . whatever. I slumped down in my chair and tried to stay awake—and quiet—until class let out.

After another forty-five minutes of Instructor Baak droning on about what a gift it was to be a Barron, and what a duty it was to be a Healer, class finally, mercifully ended. Maddox was waiting right outside as promised. Several guards were milling about, waiting for their Healers too. "How'd it go?"

I sighed heavily. "I think Instructor Baak hates me."

"Don't worry about it. From what I understand, she hates everyone."

"Great. At least I'm fitting in." We both laughed as we walked toward my next class.

CHAPTER

Seven

With just minutes left in my Anatomy of War class, I stared at the door, willing time to speed up so that I could escape the dull hell that was Mr. Ross's lecture.

"In fact, the very reason that our training schools exist lies solely in the hands of King Darrek. Without war, we would have no reason to train Barrons with katana skills or Healers in the art of healing. The katana training is especially important here at Shadow Academy, as our reputation precedes us all across Tril as the leading educational authority on the matter—just as Darkmoon Academy is known for their Healer training and Starlight Academy is known for their weapons craftsmanship." He took a breath and I thought that the sound of it would go on forever—that horrible, wheezing, nasally noise. It was mind-numbing. Glancing around the room, I wasn't the only one who thought so.

"We have been at war for approximately one hundred years, but no one can explain why King Darrek has failed to age in that time. Our scholars can offer no explanation to Darrek's abnormal youth, but it is important to remember that everything that lives is mortal, including Darrek. Which brings us to your homework assignment." The entire class groaned, but I knew that the very mention of homework meant the doldrums of class time was about to come to an end. Even freedom had a foreboding kind of ring to it. Mr. Ross took a breath and said, "I want you each to write a thousand-word essay on your personal theory as to why Darrek remains youthful after more than a century of living, due tomorrow."

At long last, Mr. Ross bid us good-bye as the class poured out the door. Maddox was waiting for me outside, looking sympathetic, but bemused. I shook my head at her, exhausted. "Why didn't you warn me the classes would be so boring?"

"All I know of Healer classes is what I've heard from the rumor pool. Is it really that bad?"

"It's worse."

Maddox walked me across campus to the rose garden, which was way off on the unpopulated side of academy grounds. Far away from the training grounds, just as Darius promised.

At the far side of the rose gardens, which seemed to stretch on forever—who needed that many roses, anyway?—sat a large greenhouse and beside that a small, wooden shack that looked like it had seen better days. An old man was washing each pane of glass in the greenhouse with the care and precision of someone who firmly believed that what he was doing was very important. Maddox patted me on the back. "That's Mr. Gareth. Don't worry; he's much nicer than Instructor Baak. Have fun. I'll be back in a few hours."

She walked away, and I couldn't help but think about how much it bothered me that she couldn't just hang around while I worked. I could have used the company. But then, I was kind of pouting about having extra duties. Thank you, Darius.

Mr. Gareth must have had a sixth sense about someone entering the gardens, because the moment I set foot on the nearest row, he turned and waved me over. He was an old man, that much was clear from a distance, but what wasn't clear was just how old. He hurried down the ladder as if he were in his thirties, but the wrinkles and crazy eyebrows said he was closer to his seventies, maybe eighties. I smiled politely as I approached and was about to say hello, when he pointed to the shed. "Everything you'll need to prune and fertilize the roses is in there, miss. I'm afraid we don't have any gloves lying around, but you look like you can handle a few pokes. Start at the south end, work your way north, row by row. Remove any dead leaves you find and prune any rogue stems—those go in the leaf bags on the other side of the shed. And don't forget to mulch the roots."

I stared at him for a moment, trying to process all of his instructions. I opened my mouth, but nothing came out, so I closed it again and wondered quietly why "we" were all out of gloves if "we" were going to have "our" hands in thorny bushes all day. Mr. Gareth simply smiled and pointed again to the shed. "Go on. Get started."

The old shed looked exactly the same on the inside as my imagination had conjured up. Dozens of shelves lined the walls, all filled with various gardening instruments. There was barely room to step inside, thanks to all the spare pots taking up residence on the floor. There wasn't a single glove in sight, but there were bags of mulch and some pruning shears, so with a deep sigh, I gathered my supplies and got to work.

There was a lot to be said about pruning rosebushes, and every one of those things could be spelled with three letters. Two hours of pruning back thorny bushes, mulching the roots, and removing dead leaves had left my hands bloody and sore, with bits of thorn stuck here and there on the tips of my fingers. I brushed a stray hair from my eyes with the back of my hand and sighed with relief to see Maddox approaching from the west side of campus. I looked to Mr. Gareth and he gave me the nod to get out of here and back to the dorms. I could hardly wait to sink into a hot bath. My stomach rumbled loudly, reminding me that food would be a good idea too.

The sun had begun to set and if I hadn't been in pain and seriously ticked off at Darius's attitude—not to mention flabbergasted at why I was being punished in the first place—I would have taken in the beautiful scenery around me. But all I wanted, all I really wanted, was for Maddox to walk me back to my room, so I could eat, bathe, and sleep.

Maddox picked a leaf from my hair and shook her head. "You look awful."

That's what I needed to hear. "Thanks."

"You should at least pick the dead leaves off and maybe wash your hands and face before you see Trayton."

My eyes went wide. Trayton! I had totally forgotten we had plans tonight. I looked down. My hands were covered with dirt. My clothes were stained with mulch and grass. I could only imagine what my face and hair must have looked like. Like some crazy forest woman, I was sure.

Maddox smirked. "You look great. I'm sure Trayton absolutely goes for that lost-in-the-woods-for-a-week look."

"Do we have time to stop by my room, so I can clean up and change?"

"No, but let me put it this way. If he's attracted to you looking like this, he's a keeper."

We hurried to the courtyard, and my heart sank to find it empty. I had really been looking forward to getting to know Trayton . . . even if I had totally forgotten about our plans. Maddox eyed me quietly for a moment, and then said, "The plus side is that he won't see your hair."

I got the feeling Maddox didn't have many friends.

Combing my hair back with my fingers and fixing my ponytail, I sighed. "Well, at least I can get something to eat."

"The dining hall is closed."

My day couldn't get much worse at this point. I was being Bound forever tomorrow morning to a boy I hadn't even had a five-minute conversation with. My teachers hated me. I was forced to work in that horrible rose garden all because Darius—what? Didn't like my presence? And now, I couldn't even get a measly ham sandwich. Topping it off with how much I missed my parents, I found myself fighting back tears.

"There you are." A voice from behind me. Warm and vaguely familiar. I swallowed my tears and turned around. Trayton crossed the flagstone and held out a leather satchel. "I grabbed you some food. Figured you might be hungry."

A smile curled my lips. It was touching in that he-wouldn't-let-me-starve way.

Before I could say anything, I noticed movement out of the corner of my eye. I turned to see Darius crossing the courtyard toward the small cottage there. When he saw Maddox, Trayton, and me, his steps slowed. He hunched his shoulders up and growled. "It's a half hour until curfew. I'd hate to have to dole out more extra duties today."

But something told me he wouldn't hate it at all. His tone sounded almost eager.

Trayton didn't look worried. Maybe he'd never had the luxury of an afternoon spent weeding the garden before. My palms were still stinging. With a small smile, Trayton said, "In that case, we'd better hurry."

He took off at a run and I bolted after him, forgetting the pain in my knees and palms, breathless as we ran across campus. I threw a glance over my shoulder to Darius, who wasn't bothering to watch after us.

Trayton and I ran across the commons and finally, in a fit of laughter, reached a large, round building. Trayton opened the door and a man inside said, "Trayton, I'm just closing up."

"Please. My Healer is here and she loves to read. Fifteen minutes, no more. I promise."

The man sighed, as if he were powerless to refuse Trayton's whim. "All right. Fifteen. But lock up on your way out."

The man dropped a second set of keys on the desk and walked out, and Trayton turned to my guard. I was the only one still trying to catch my breath from our sprint. "Maddox, may we have a moment?"

"Alone?" Maddox's defenses were up. I could tell by the way she slanted her eyes. "You're seriously asking me to break Protocol after I just got my head handed to me by the headmaster this morning?"

Trayton smiled and I could see what a charmer he was. "Come on, Maddox. We're supposed to be Bound tomorrow and we haven't even had a short, private conversation. We won't do anything, just talk. I give you my word. We won't even touch."

Maddox flicked her eyes to me, then back to Trayton, and groaned. "I don't know."

"I'll owe you one. Seriously."

"By *one* do you mean a new head? Because if we get caught, mine's getting bitten off." Maddox folded her arms in front of her, tapping her foot as she mulled over his offer. Finally, she sighed in exasperation and threw her arms up. "Fine. But you owe me big-time. Don't forget it. I'll be right outside. No touching. Not until after your binding tomorrow."

Trayton reached inside for the light switch. I was no way near prepared for what was coming.

A giant, golden chandelier hung from the ceiling, dripping with crystals. It cast a warm glow over the entire room. Rich, ornate rugs covered the hardwood floors. And if it weren't for the obvious, I would have doubted that I was in a library at all. The walls were covered with immense, dark bookcases, each lined with hundreds and hundreds of books, their spines soft and faded with age. More shelves stood like a maze in the middle of the room, and through it was a smattering of cozy chairs and small tables topped with lamps which spilled soft light into the darkened maze. To the right of the front desk a spiral staircase wound its way to a loft area—the steps were marble and wide, which led me to believe the library often had droves of students eager to make the climb to what awaited them above.

Trayton stepped forward slowly, as if asking my permission with his hesitancy. I met his eyes, so dark, so full of questioning. He looked so fragile, like he'd been hurt before. The last thing I wanted was to be responsible for causing Trayton any pain. I smiled and followed him inside.

His eyes instantly brightened. "Come on. It's upstairs."

We climbed the stairs at a moderate pace, and I marveled at how beautiful the library was. The ceiling was an immense glass dome, something I hadn't noticed from downstairs. As we climbed higher, I noticed that some of the glass ceiling panels were stained glass, miniature portraits among crystalline squares.

Once upstairs, I saw what drew the attention of so many students, the purpose of the stairs being so wide, and the reason that the handrail was careworn. An enormous fireplace commanded the far end of the room. In front of it were several velvet sofas. Large, fluffy pillows and cushions lay here and there, as if students were quite comfortable sitting on the floor. And then, a dreamer's room come true. Whereas the bookshelves downstairs were filled with textbooks and works of academia, the shelves up here, though much smaller, were overflowing with hundreds of works of fiction, as far as the eye could see. In the corner was another bookcase, this one filled with sketchbooks and tumblers stuffed with drawing implements. An enormous tapestry that seemed to trace the war's history stood guard between the restroom doors at the back of the loft, and I was instantly transported back home. Back to where I read a new book every week, just for fun. Back to where my father sketched and my mother did her needlepoint.

My chest ached. I missed them so much.

Trayton said, "By the look on your face, I'm guessing you like it. We call this place the loft. It's probably the most interesting place to hang out on campus. But . . . it's not what I brought you here to see."

He released my hand and my palm tingled as it cooled in his absence. I plucked a book from the shelf and flipped through it, reveling in this moment of normalcy. "This library is incredible."

Trayton was fiddling with something on the wall behind the tapestry. "Just wait. It gets better."

There was a clicking sound and a section of the wall beside the fireplace swung open. Inside was another set of stairs, this one narrow and made of bare wood. I dropped the book on the nearest shelf and looked with wonder at Trayton. "A secret room?"

He grinned. "I told you I wanted to show you my favorite place. Go on up."

Unable to resist the unknown, I stepped into the narrow corridor and slowly made my way up the steps, which creaked as I ascended. Trayton stepped in behind me and closed the hidden door, leaving us cloaked in shadows. My eyes adjusted after a moment and I kept moving upward, not knowing what awaited me above. I could feel Trayton close behind me in the darkness, and I knew without asking that he would catch me if I fell, that he would never lead me anywhere where I would be in danger. But even if danger found us, he'd protect me. I slowed my steps, and in a breathy voice, Trayton said, "Is something wrong?"

Smiling in the darkness, but suddenly hesitant, I said, "Why aren't we supposed to be alone together, exactly?"

He was quiet for a long time, and as I turned around on my step to face him, I caught his sweet breath on my cheek. His voice was hushed, and our bodies intimately close in the small space. "Tradition, mostly. I . . . it's not like I'm going to hurt you or anything, Kaya. I just . . . wanted to show you that not everything about Shadow Academy is terrible."

I didn't know what to say. I hadn't thought it was so apparently obvious that I'd resolved myself to hating everything about the academy. After a moment, I turned around again and continued up the stairs. At the top of the steps was a small, round room with dust-covered boxes and larger items covered with dusty sheets. I moved forward, wondering why Trayton would bring me here. He stepped to my left and whispered, "Look up, Kaya."

I raised my eyes to the ceiling and discovered that it was also a glass dome, though much smaller than that of the main library. This one didn't have any stained glass, but it was perfectly clear. Thousands of stars twinkled above us, and I gasped at the sight of them. Moonlight filtered through the clear panels, lighting the room in a cool bluish tint. I marveled at the perfect view of the star-speckled sky until I heard Trayton moving something behind me. When I turned, he was uncovering what looked like a velvet chaise. He sat down and leaned back, looking up at the stars. After a moment, I sat beside him. "What is all this stuff?"

I opened the satchel he'd brought me and munched on grapes, soft cheese, warm bread, and roasted chicken while he explained. "I think it's an old storage room. No one but me knows about it, so I really don't have anyone to ask. Of course, now *you* know, but I don't suppose you have any idea what it was used for, hmm?"

I laughed and finished my dinner while watching the stars twinkle. After a while, I could feel Trayton's eyes on me. I met his gaze. His close proximity both elated me and made me nervous at the same time. What was I doing in a room alone with a boy that I hardly knew? My dad would have a heart attack if he knew. Clearing my throat, I asked the only thing that I could think to ask him. "Do you want to be Bound to me, Trayton?"

Trayton leaned forward, elbows on his knees. His soft hair fell forward, hiding his face like a curtain. After a long silence, he said, "Did you know the one you were Soulbound to?"

"Don't change the subject."

"I'm not." He lifted his head to look at me. The curtain drew back, revealing his pale, handsome face. "Did you?"

I debated for several seconds what to tell him and finally settled on the absolute truth.

"No. But when I learned he'd died, I felt . . . broken. I didn't leave my room. I was just so sad." I shook my head. "It sounds crazy, but I can't explain what it felt like to lose him . . . and I don't know why I felt that way over a total stranger. I've never talked about it until now."

He watched me for a moment, and I couldn't tell if he was gauging my sanity level or empathizing with my loss. When he spoke, his voice sounded gruff, as if he were on the verge of tears. "Now imagine having known him, having been there to hold him when he cried, having held him and kissed him and dreamed of a life together. Imagine how much bigger the pain of that loss would have been if you had counted on him always being there for you, if you had loved him before you lost him."

A tear escaped his eye and rolled down his cheek, glistening in the light of the moon.

It was all I could do to keep our promise to Maddox, to not reach out and wipe his tear away, to offer him whatever comfort I could. "Oh, Trayton . . . I'm so sorry."

"When Samantha—my Healer—died, I sank into a deep depression. After her funeral, I wouldn't leave my parents' home to return to the academy, wouldn't even receive any visitors. I was broken and nobody could fix me. After a month, my father brought me into his office and told me that he had offered the headmaster a substantial amount of money as a show of gratitude for treating our family so well. But I knew what he meant. It was a bribe to move my name to the top of the list of those who were waiting for Healers." He clenched his jaw. "I hated him. And when I learned your name, I hated you too."

He took a deep breath and wiped his tears away, something I couldn't do. "But the hate, the reluctance, the fear went away with time. And now, I'm just hopeful that maybe we'll find even a small part of the happiness, the closeness that Samantha and I shared."

He met my eyes then and his became warm, all tears gone, all sorrow tucked neatly at the back of his mind. It had to be unbearable to live with that kind of pain.

"You'll never replace her, but if I had to choose some-one to stand by my side, I can't think of anyone more fitting than you. So . . . yes. Yes, I do want to be Bound to you, Kaya. But something tells me you don't feel the same way."

I nodded, not wanting to lie. Trayton deserved better than that. "Up until this evening, I would have said that you were right. I mean, I was threatened away from my home, forced into training for a war I don't have any-thing to do with, and given no choice of who I'll spend the rest of my life with. It's awful."

I fell silent.

After several minutes, Trayton cleared his throat, as if preparing for the worst, and said, "And now?"

"Now I'm not so sure. Now I'm wondering what to-morrow will be like. Now I'm . . ." I dropped my eyes to the floor. "Now I'm curious about what it will be like to be Bound to you."

When I looked back at Trayton, he was smiling.

"We should get going before Maddox has a heart at-tack."

I chuckled. "Should you walk out shirtless, just to make her wonder what we were doing?"

"I like the way you think. But I think we've caused her enough stress for one evening." He smirked as we made our way out of the room and down the grand stair-case. After a pause, he said, "Maybe tomorrow."

Trayton locked the door and we stepped outside. The

sky had grown overcast with clouds—gray puffs against the black nighttime sky as an unexpected storm rolled in. Lightning flashed, lighting up the night. Suddenly, the sky opened up and rain poured down on us in sheets. I lifted my face, closing my eyes, enjoying the cool water on my skin. After a moment, I looked at Trayton, who was smiling at me. "Promise me that you'll always be so open with me, Trayton, that you won't change once we're Bound."

Trayton leaned close and my heart was completely still. My rational mind knew that he was a virtual stranger to me, but I comforted myself with the fact that he was also a completely gorgeous, highly kissable stranger. His lips were incredibly close to mine, and I could feel his whisper on my skin. "I promise."

A cough, almost indistinguishable from the rain, gave his actions a pause. Maddox spoke from several yards away. She didn't sound happy. "Three minutes until curfew, you two."

Trayton frowned. "It takes at least five minutes to walk back to our quarters."

"What's the matter, Trayton? Out of breath?" I grinned, egging him on.

His grin returned. "Maybe if you'd stop stealing it away . . ."

Maddox practically shouted. "Two minutes! I suggest you run."

We took off running through the rain and reached the

door of our dorm building dripping wet and breathless, with about ten seconds to spare. Trayton didn't leave my side the entire time. He smiled brightly. "Thank you, Kaya. I haven't had this much fun in a long time. Maybe we could talk more tomorrow, go for a walk after our binding?"

"I'd love that." I meant it. I wanted to spend time with Trayton. I wanted to get to know him. Even if the idea of being Bound forever with no choice did leave me a little nauseated and a lot terked off.

Trayton had just reached for the door when the head-master opened it from the other side. "Ah, just the man I wanted to see. Trayton, if you would accompany me to my office. We have a few things to discuss before tomorrow's festivities."

"Of course, Headmaster." He threw me a smile and departed with the headmaster, leaving Maddox and me alone.

Maddox grumbled. "There better not have been any touching, Kaya."

"No touching. Promise." A light caught my eye and I turned my head. The upstairs window of the cabin was open. Darius was standing in the window, his shirt partially undone, leaning on the frame with both hands. Something in his expression looked haunted, sad. Then suddenly, his jaw tensed and anger returned to his eyes. He slammed the shutters closed.

I jumped at the sound of it.

Maddox shook her head. "What is his problem?"

But the answer seemed obvious. It was me. And I had no idea why.

Yanking open the door to my dorm, I huffed inside with Maddox right behind me.

Eight

I woke early, just as the sun's light had pierced the window glass, to the scent of roses. Light, airy, beautiful roses. A dozen of them—in rich, glorious red—were sitting in a vase atop the table near the door, a small piece of parchment tucked neatly between their leaves. Slipping out from under my down-filled covers, I plucked the note from the bouquet. In swirling, elegant script, it read simply *Yours, T*. A smile touched my lips then and I couldn't help but wonder just how Trayton had managed to get the flowers past Maddox. After all, he owed her after our alone time. Did his charms know no bounds? I rummaged in my trunk for something to wear. Something comfortable, with maybe a hint of pretty. I still didn't have a uniform, but I wagered that the headmaster would insist on it soon. Especially once . . .

Something in my chest clenched my heart.

. . . once Trayton and I were Bound. Which happened to be in about an hour.

I'd forgotten. I'd completely forgotten that I was about to be forever Bound to a boy I hardly knew.

Dragging my feet, I slowly made my way into my washroom, bathed and got ready—my thoughts never far from Trayton and what our binding meant exactly. It meant that there would be no other boys for me. It meant that we were an item, in a way, and that I had no choice but to go through with it if I truly valued my parents' lives. It meant that I had better suck it up and stop moping, because there was no other choice in the matter.

In short, it meant that I was royally fakked.

After running a comb through my freshly dried hair, I checked my reflection in the mirror, pausing when I heard hushed voices from the other room.

"Is she awake?" Trayton. Even though we'd hardly spoken, I would have known that voice anywhere.

Maddox's voice followed with a hint of harshness. "Yes, but I'm not letting you in. You know the rules, Trayton. And I'm not breaking them for you again."

"You do know that we're due at the temple in a half hour."

Maddox's voice took on a more formal tone. Something in it suggested it wasn't the first time the two of them had butted heads. "I'm well aware of that fact, *Barron*."

When I opened the door, the looks on their faces

were priceless—a mingling of surprise and embarrassment. I forced a smile, despite the sick feeling that was churning in my stomach. "Good morning."

Trayton brightened. Maddox cleared her throat, and grumbled, "Are you up for breakfast, Princess?"

My stomach clenched at the thought of food, threatening to cramp. Nerves, I supposed. "I don't really feel like eating."

The corner of Maddox's mouth lifted in a smirk. I was sure she was looking at Trayton with her peripheral vision. "Nauseous, huh?"

Trayton ignored her jibe and stepped closer, careful not to touch me. "Did you like your flowers?"

For an all too brief moment, my tension waned, and my smile didn't feel as false, as forced. "I love them. Thank you."

"Are you okay?" He flicked a nervous glance about the room before returning his eyes to me. "About . . . about today, I mean."

"Fine. I'm fine." But I wasn't fine. I wasn't even in the same hemisphere as fine. My legs were wobbly and my heart was racing. I felt sick to my stomach and so very sad. All I could think about were my mom and dad and how my binding would save them from the wrath of the Barrons, from the twisted, vengeful actions of the headmaster.

I stepped back, my thoughts shadowed, my eyes on the floor. It wasn't Trayton's fault. None of it was. But that didn't change the fact that I was being forced into this.

Without saying a word, Maddox crossed my room to the door that led to the hall. She opened it and caught my eye, a fierce protectiveness washing over her features.

Maddox got it. Maddox knew exactly what was going on and exactly how fakked up it was.

That lightened my mood some, but it still didn't change things.

Silently, like monks on a journey to someone's funeral, the three of us made our way across campus to a small stone building near the north gate. Trayton took the initiative and knocked on the wooden door using the large iron knocker. None of us spoke.

After several seconds, the door opened to reveal a tall man with stark black hair and a pointed black beard. He was dressed in navy blue robes that hung to the floor, a hood on his back. Though there was no familiarity in Trayton's eyes, the man barked, "Trayton, come inside. Bring Kaya with you. The guard remains outside."

The strange man disappeared inside once again and Maddox met my eyes. "I'll be right here, okay? You need me, you scream."

Nodding, I fought back a chuckle at how serious we were all acting, like I was going to my death or something instead of being Bound to a really sweet, really good-looking guy like Trayton. "Should I scream anything in particular, or will wordless noise attract your attention?"

Maddox grinned. "Depends on what they're serving in the dining hall, but you might try yelling help."

That brought a smile to my face—but it faded quickly once I laid eyes on Trayton, who looked like he'd just had his heart stomped on. I didn't have to say anything to Maddox; she took a few steps back to give us some space. Then I met Trayton's eyes and said, "I'm sorry. It's just that I'm still getting used to this whole arrangement. It's . . . it's not easy."

"You think it's easy for me?" His eyes were full of hurt. Somehow, I'd forgotten that Trayton didn't have much of a choice in this either.

"No. I don't, Trayton."

He was quiet for a while, before lightening his tone, the corners of his lips curling into that irresistible shy-boy smile. "We could always run. Fight off the gate guards, climb the north gate, take off for parts unseen."

I nodded sagely. "Not to mention become a Graplar's midday snack. That is, if we survive the Barron hunting parties."

He shrugged, a chuckle escaping his lips. "It's an option."

And that's when my stress level dropped. Because even though this was a no-choice situation, even though we barely knew one another, we were in this together. Until the bitter end. A smile touched my lips and I reached for the door. "Come on, Trayton. Let's get started on that whole forever thing already."

The sadness left his eyes then, and it was replaced by something that resembled what I was feeling. Then he smiled too, and together we walked forward, entering the temple of our own accord.

The inside of the small building was lined with wood stained so dark it looked like night. For a moment, my vision wavered, as if the adjustment from the outside morning sun to the stark blackness of the temple were too much to bear. But they adjusted after a moment and Trayton and I moved forward. He looked around in wonder, which made me think that not many people were allowed to enter this place—maybe only those who were being Bound.

Candles lit our short walk to the center of the room, where the black-haired nameless man was waiting. Behind him, at the far end of the room, was a long altar, covered with a plain white cloth, atop which were an incense censer, an open, ancient-looking book, and a black dagger. In front of the man was the most bizarre piece of furniture I had ever encountered. All black leather and dark wood, it appeared to be a chair of the worst sort, with leather straps and silver buckles that screamed containment. My eyes found Trayton's—he looked as worried as I felt. My imagination was flooded with horrible visions of what was to come, but before

I could get too carried away, the man with the pointed beard spoke.

"Trayton, if you will take your place in the chair, please, we can begin."

Trayton straightened his shoulders, and after casting me a less than convincing reassuring glance, he sat down, matching up his arms and legs with the strange bends of the chair. By the time he was settled, he looked fine, like he wasn't at all worried about what was about to occur.

The man moved around Trayton then, strapping his limbs in tightly. With each tug, Trayton looked a little less confident. When the man drew a thick leather strap across his stomach and buckled it snugly, Trayton released a small sigh, as if resigning himself to his fate.

I could only watch. And wonder.

Our ceremony master turned to the book on the table and began reading from it in a strange singsong tone, chanting words that I didn't understand from a language I didn't know. He raised up the lit censer and swung it toward the back corners of the room, then moved around to the front corners and swung it toward them, chanting all the while. Returning to Trayton, he swung the censer over him three times, then once over me. I tried catching Trayton's eye, to silently reassure him or even just raise my eyebrows at the weird chanting, but Trayton's eyes were closed, as if he were concentrating, or maybe falling asleep. When I looked back at the ceremony master, he was returning the censer to its spot on the altar. He picked up the dagger and turned to Trayton.

My heart raced at the horrible thoughts running through my mind.

Late last night, Maddox had shared the rumors with me about what a binding included. She'd spoken of daggers. She'd spoken of pain. She'd spoken of blood.

I moved forward, protectively standing between Trayton and the man who hadn't even shared his name with us. Parting my lips, I readied barbs on my tongue.

But then I felt the soft brush of Trayton's fingers on mine. I looked back at him and he whispered, "It's okay, Kaya. Trust me."

Tearing my gaze from the ceremony master, I searched Trayton's eyes, finally relenting to his will and stepping out of the way. But rules be damned, I squeezed his hand in mine, refusing to let him go through whatever was coming without me by his side.

The ceremony master moved closer, clutching the blade in his hand, and all I could do was hold my breath and squeeze Trayton's hand even harder. The man chanted, raising the dagger, while his chants became louder. Repeating words over and over again that I couldn't understand, he brought the weapon down. It sliced through the flesh of Trayton's biceps, and Trayton groaned but held fast. His fingers were crushing my hand for a moment, but after taking some quick, shallow breaths, he relaxed again and met my eyes.

What I saw in his expression was nothing short of a nightmare—confirmation that the worst of this experience wasn't over.

The smoke from the incense was drying my throat. It smelled sweet, but tasted rancid, and felt as if it were burning my lungs away. I held back my urge to cough, but it wasn't easy. Blood gushed from Trayton's open wound, dripping onto the floor. To my astonishment, the man cut Trayton again, this time across his thigh. Trayton—despite his tough-guy Barron training—howled in pain as the blade cut deeply into his leg. His face blanched and I gasped, glaring at the ceremony master, ready to snatch the dagger from his cruel hands. But before I could, he returned the weapon to its spot on the altar. Trayton's blood stained the white cloth.

The man turned back to me, silent now, and moved my right hand to the cut on Trayton's arm and my left to the one on his thigh. Then he started chanting again, this time loudly and more meaningful than ever before. Worried tears welled in my eyes, and all I could do was whisper to Trayton that it would be okay, somehow it would be okay.

My palms grew warm and a strange tingling crawled up my arms—as if tiny bolts of lightning were making their way slowly through my veins. Despite the sound of chanting and the noise of my coughing, which

I could no longer hold back, I noticed something had changed. That steady drip, drip, drip of Trayton's blood on the dark wood floor had ceased. Something else, too. The blood on my palms had grown sticky, no longer fresh. Marveling, I looked down at Trayton's wounds, and they were gone. Completely healed. As if he'd never been injured at all.

Pulling my hands back with a gasp, I looked from Trayton's drying blood to Trayton himself, who weakly smiled up at me, something like relief flitting across his expression.

We'd done it. We'd been Bound. I'd healed Trayton with only a touch of my hand.

My fingers trembled slightly. Even though I knew that I was a Healer, even though I'd heard my entire life that I was capable of this act, I was filled with shock. I'd healed him. Just by pressing my hands to his wounds.

The ceremony master remained all business as he gathered his tools. "You can wash the blood away in the basin near the door. There are clean rags there as well."

I helped Trayton with the leather straps and washed my hands in the basin of warm water before empty-ing the basin out the front door—pausing a moment to breathe in some fresh air—and refilling it with the pitcher from atop the table. After dunking one of the rags into the clean water, I moved back to Trayton, who was sitting up and marveling at his lack of injuries. I handed him the moist cloth and watched as he wiped as much of the blood away as he could. His clothes were stained, and the holes in the fabric were gaping. His uniform was ruined, but that seemed to be of little consequence. Trayton stood and turned to the man who'd caused him such horrendous pain with hardly an introduction. "Thank you, Elder Barron."

The man nodded and turned back to his cleaning duties.

With a smile, Trayton gestured toward the door and I led the way, relieved that he was all right, but still very shaken about the bizarre ritual.

As we stepped outside, Trayton's hand found mine and squeezed. A peculiar warmth spread through my hand and up my arm—a wonderful tingling sensation. I glanced at Trayton—at my Barron—and couldn't help but grin. Trayton was blushing and grinning too. I squeezed his hand back, a surge of excited hope filling my soul. A connection was there—a real, strong, certain connection, like nothing we'd ever shared before.

For the first time since setting foot on academy grounds, I found myself ready and anxious for what the future might bring.

I'd expected Maddox to be waiting for us when we got outside, but she was nowhere to be found. She'd been replaced, momentarily, by a quiet, standoffish guard whose name I didn't have a chance to catch before Trayton pulled me in the direction of the rose gardens. After a while, we passed the gardens and then we walked east along the perimeter wall. For the first hundred yards, neither of us spoke a word. Our nameless shadow hung back, always present, but not invading our moment semi-alone together. After all, we weren't allowed to be alone together for the first year of our bond. By the time we reached the rose gardens, I'd grown used to the feel of Trayton's hand in mine. It felt right. Like two puzzle pieces that fit perfectly against one another.

The scent of roses reached my nose and I watched the flowers as we walked in comfortable silence, keeping my eyes away from the enormous stone wall. The wall was a heavy, unbearable symbol. It meant to protect us from all that lurked outside of it, but all I could think was that it was keeping me inside, away from my parents, away from the life I had known and loved. The wall was oppressive and symbolized everything that the headmaster stood for. It was here to control me, here to keep me in my place. I hated it with every fiber of my being.

Trayton's steps slowed as we reached the midpoint of the rose garden. "The roses look especially lovely, don't you think? Mr. Gareth must be working overtime."

I didn't say what I was thinking—that Mr. Gareth wasn't the only one hard at work on the roses; that I and who knows how many other delinquents had been busy grooming the blooms to the magnificence they were now, all because we'd stepped out of line in this way or that. Instead, I made a sound that sounded vaguely like "mm-hmm" and tried like hell to ignore the wall, even though it was barely three feet to my right.

Trayton stopped short. "You're awfully quiet. Is everything okay?"

I shook my head, wanting to put him at ease. It wasn't his fault I was distracted. It was the headmaster's. And the wall's. "Everything's fine. I just—"

A sound thundered through the wall and my entire body jolted. I'd know that high-pitched shriek anywhere, but recognized it mostly from my nightmares. Accompanying its sound was a flash of enormous teeth in my twisted imagination.

Trayton squeezed my hand, drawing my attention for the moment. "Hey. It's okay. They can't get through the wall. As long as you're inside, you're safe. And when you aren't, I'll protect you."

His words should have been comforting to me, but while they might have been well intended, they sounded too similar to what the headmaster had said—I wasn't allowed to learn how to defend myself. I was expected to behave like a damsel in distress and just wait for my Barron savior to protect me. My cheeks flushed warm as I pulled my hand away from Trayton's, but my palm cooled instantly, as did my demeanor. "I can protect myself."

Doubt filled Trayton's eyes, but to his credit, he didn't give voice to it. He turned to the wall and gazed up at it for a moment before looking back at me. "Their cries are unnerving, but you shouldn't let it worry you. There are worse things in the world."

Worse than Graplars? I somehow doubted that.

To my left came the sound of feet moving over grass, and I turned my head to see Instructor Baak leaving one of the rows of rosebushes, a straw basket, piled high with red and pink blooms, looped over her arm. She nodded a hello to Trayton, but didn't even look my way. A small part of me was grateful. Better to be invisible than the object of her disgust. After she'd gone, I shook my head, hoping to ease the strange tension that was now between Trayton and me. "That woman hates me."

"She doesn't hate you. She's just been through some rough times." Trayton plucked a leaf from one of the many vines that had grown over the wall and tossed it carelessly on the ground as he turned and continued his—once our—trek along the perimeter. After a heartbeat, I followed, knowing that I'd ruined our moment, even if I had done so for a very good reason. Something told me that while Trayton was sweet, he was also used to things going exactly as he planned. I kept my thoughts to myself for the moment and quickened my pace so that we were once again walking side by side, though our hands didn't touch.

As if I'd voiced my curiosity, he said, "Instructor Baak lost her daughter at the second battle of Wood's Cross. It must have been pretty brutal, as there was an inquiry and shortly after, the records of the event were sealed.

That's when she came to Shadow Academy to teach. They say she couldn't face the battlefield after that. Her heart just wasn't in it. So you shouldn't be too quick to judge someone."

Stinging from his obvious snap, I slowed my steps and bit back the words that were building up in my mind. "If you don't mind, I think I'll head back to the dorms and get a head start on this paper that Mr. Ross assigned."

Trayton hung his head, sighing. When he met my eyes, he looked remorseful. "I'm sorry, Kaya. I just wanted today to be perfect and I'm fakking it up fabulously. Can you forgive me?"

He hadn't done anything that awful, so I nodded and smiled. "Of course I do. But I do have that paper to finish."

"I'll walk you back and you can get started. Then maybe later you'd go to a party with me?" He smiled sheepishly and once again, I found myself entangled in his charm. It was a wonder that any girl could resist him.

Smiling, I said, "Sounds fun."

"Great." He clapped his hands together once in satisfaction. "I'll pick you up at eight and we'll head over to Melanie's."

My heart all but stopped before it sank into my stomach. "Melanie's?"

"It's her party." He shrugged casually, obviously blissfully unaware that Melanie and I weren't exactly the best of friends.

Breathing out a sigh, I took another step forward, trying desperately to ignore what my evening would be like. "Wonderful."

I was sure it would be anything but.

Let's just get this over with."

Maddox wasn't exactly what I'd refer to as excited about the prospect of attending a party hosted by Melanie—neither was I—but Trayton had asked me to go, and she could've been at least a little more supportive. The last thing in the world I wanted was to hang out in Melanie's dorm room with a bunch of people I didn't know, especially if Maddox was going to be complaining about it all night.

She opened the door to the hall, where Trayton was waiting. He was still wearing his school uniform, as was expected by the headmaster's rules, but something about the way the light hit him made it seem different, more casual. It took me a moment to speak. "You look nice."

Immediately after the words had left my lips, I wanted to reach out and snatch them from the air between us. Nice? I sounded like his grandmother, rather than the girl he was Bound to. I should have said something impressive like "debonair." But no. "Nice" was all I had.

The corners of his mouth lifted into a pleased smile, his cheeks blushing somewhat. "Thank you. You look lovely."

Maddox snorted. Not because she didn't like the way I looked or anything. But because it had taken me exactly three hours and twenty-three minutes to stop complaining about my school uniform. Not that there was anything wrong with the white wrap top and roomy white leggings. But I would have given anything for some color options. Back home, I'd helped my mother dye bolts of fabric with various flowers. The smell filled the cabin and had forced my father outside on more than one occasion, but the vibrant colors that were a result of our efforts were stunning. I missed wearing my own clothes already. I missed wearing pretty colors. They reminded me of freedom and joy, rather than rules and institution.

Maddox said that she didn't understand girls, even if she was one.

She also didn't understand why we had to go to Melanie's party, but that much I did understand. If I had said no, it wouldn't have been fair to Trayton, who obviously felt obligated to go. And there was no way I was leaving him alone with Melanie. Not that I didn't trust him. I just didn't trust her. Not any farther than I could throw her—which probably wouldn't be very far at all.

Melanie's room was down our hallway, up two flights, and then a long walk to the midpoint of the building. And every step I took closer to it sent my nerves jumping up another notch. Trayton must have noticed, because he reached over when we were only ten steps from her door and gave my hand a comforting squeeze. I smiled at him, or tried, anyway, and turned my attention back to Maddox, who was asking me with her eyes if I was sure about this and if I was ready to face the in-crowd. My answer was no, but I nodded in spite of myself.

Maddox raised her fist and knocked on the door. It seemed a simple enough gesture, something she'd done a dozen times since I'd been at Shadow Academy, but the fact that it was Melanie's door changed the sound of it, somehow. Her knock echoed into the hallway. Heavy. Ominous.

I swear, if Trayton hadn't been holding my hand, I'd have turned and bolted.

But before I could plan my masterful escape, which likely would have involved some arm flailing and girlish screams, the door opened to Melanie's parlor, revealing a tall, thin, statuesque girl with flaxen curls and stunning green eyes. She looked less than impressed as her eyes moved over Maddox and myself, but when her gaze fell on Trayton, she brightened considerably. "Trayton! Mel said you'd be coming. Mel! Your guest has arrived!"

From across the relatively crowded room, Melanie sashayed, her curves commanding the attention of every male present.

Well. Thankfully not *every* male.

Trayton smiled reassuringly at me. As Melanie approached the door, Trayton gently coaxed me inside. Melanie was all smiles. She hugged Trayton, planting a light kiss on his cheek. "I'm so glad you came. Can I get you something to drink? Carly smuggled in some artesian wine. It's fabulous."

There was a distinct moment when Melanie noticed me. It was the exact same moment that she noticed my hand was holding Trayton's. Choking back what looked like an equal mixture of disgust and disdain, she said, "Your . . . friends . . . can have some too, of course."

A smile settled on Trayton's lips then. It was definitely proud, and almost smug. "You remember Kaya, Melanie."

"Of course." She grimaced, forcing an unreal smile. "The Healer you're going to be Bound to."

"As a matter of fact, we're here on a mission of celebration." Trayton gave my hand another squeeze. "You see, Kaya and I were Bound this morning."

Shadows covered her mood then, and if my eyes hadn't been locked on Trayton, wondering if he'd lost his mind completely, I would have likely noticed the dark, ominous-looking clouds rolling in overhead. Probably accompanied by purple lightning streaking across the sky.

Then, suddenly, strangely perky, Maddox pushed past us and said, "I'll just go get us all drinks so we can toast to the happy union."

I couldn't escape the feeling that I was about to die. It was getting hot in there, or maybe it was just the fire shooting from Melanie's eyes into my soul.

By the time Maddox had returned, I'd had to slip my hand from Trayton's and wipe the sweat on my leggings. Maddox struggled a bit with carrying four full glasses, but she managed well enough, shoving the first into Melanie's hand. Once we all had glasses, Melanie seemed to swallow an enormous, bitter lump that had been occupying her throat and said, "To happy unions."

Trayton raised his glass just as Melanie had been about to drink and said, "To Kaya, and to being Bound."

Maddox beamed. "Hear, hear!"

I sipped mine quietly—the wine tasted almost too sweet, like candy that had spoiled somehow. Melanie set her glass on a nearby table, untouched.

Trayton drained his glass like a pro, but I had no idea how he could stomach the stuff. I wasn't the only one. Maddox retched and set her glass beside Melanie's. After another polite sip, I set mine by hers and looked around. The small parlor was packed with people, and from the noise coming from each of the bedrooms—Melanie's and her Healer's—those rooms were full too.

Melanie put on what I was sure was her most charming smile and looped her arm around Trayton's, practically dragging him into the next room, her bedroom. After exchanging glances with Maddox, we followed them inside. As expected, several people were sitting on the bed and several more were standing in small groups, chatting. One couple was swaying sloppily near the bathroom door. Another couple near the closet looked as if they were trying to swallow one another. Trayton was already chatting with a fellow Barron—a boy—and trying to ignore Melanie, who kept pushing her way into the conversation. The music was obnoxiously loud and made my head ache slightly, so I pinched the bridge of my nose and wished that time would move forward faster, so I could go back to my room. But no way was I leaving Trayton here. Not in Melanie's greedy, well-manicured claws.

"You hate her, right?" Maddox was smiling at me. She nodded toward Melanie, who had thrown her head back and laughed harder than was necessary for the joke Trayton had just told.

I eyed her hand on his arm for a moment before answering. "I don't hate her. I just wish she'd stop pawing at Trayton for a second. I mean . . . does she have no respect for personal space?"

"Not where Trayton is concerned."

"They have a history?" I would have turned to face Maddox, to get a reading on her emotions, but my eyes were transfixed by Melanie's fingers, which were lightly edging their way up Trayton's arm. When they reached his biceps—his strong, rather sexy-looking biceps—they squeezed and continued their trek north, toward his neck.

I had never considered myself the jealous type, but the sight of her fingertips grazing lightly against the skin on the back of his neck was filling me with an angry heat that threatened to boil over if she didn't stop touching him soon.

Trayton brushed her hand away like she was an annoying sucker fly and continued his conversation with the other Barron. It was enough to quell my jealousy for the moment.

Maddox said, "I wouldn't say that they have a history, but that Melanie does. She's always had a thing for him, from what I hear. Since they were just kids. And she completely despised Samantha, his original Healer, from day one."

After I flashed her a questioning look, she shrugged. "What? Guards talk."

A couple passed by, laughing and clinging to one another. After they'd gone, I said, "Mind sharing?"

Melanie was pouting a little, but still sitting so close to Trayton that it was clear she was trying to send a message to the room about who he was there to see—a message I was certain that Trayton wasn't aware of.

"When Samantha died, she made a move. But I guess Trayton didn't react well to her timing. Some say he didn't react well to her disregard of Protocol about

Barrons and Barrons coupling up, but I think it was more than that." Maddox was watching them too, looking only mildly concerned. "I think that Trayton can see through her physical beauty to the ugly thing she is under the surface. And I don't think he likes her much at all."

A boy walked by with two bottles in his hands. Maddox snatched one and removed the cork. She took a swig and made a face before handing the bottle back to him.

Melanie's hand squeezed Trayton's arm and my eyes narrowed a bit. "If that's true, why come to her parties? Why hang out with her at all and be nice to her in public? Why not just avoid her?"

Maddox shrugged. "Because they were friends when they were kids. Their parents are still friends. There's an unspoken obligation there. Besides . . . he may not want to date her for whatever reason, but they're still friends, in a messed up kinda way, for whatever messed up kinda reason. People get weirdly loyal to their friends. Even if their friends are terrible people."

Turning my attention away from Melanie for the moment, I looked at Maddox. In many ways, she reminded me of Avery. Only tougher. And far less boy crazy. Far less anything crazy. "Who are you loyal to, Maddox?"

"You. Because you're probably the worst Healer I've ever met." She smiled, and I couldn't help but wonder whether she'd had too much of whatever was in that bottle. "And Trayton. Because he was nice to me once, and I'll never forget it."

Her eyes took on a strange glaze then, and I could tell that her thoughts were far away from this time and place. I was so tempted to ask her about Trayton being nice to her, but the look in her eye said that that information was only available on a need-to-know basis, and while I was high on her trust list, I did not need to know. Not yet, anyway.

"Kaya!" Trayton shouted across the crowded room, a smile on his lips, gesturing with his hand for me to come join the conversation. Melanie's hand was still on his arm, but the expression on her face was one of a dog that's been kicked into submission. I was betting she'd keep her fingers off of Trayton's neck for the duration of the evening—which I was hoping would be very short.

Maddox smirked. "You go on ahead. I'm going to try to find some food and maybe something decent to drink. You want anything?"

Shaking my head, I worked my way through the crowd to Trayton, who patted his knee. I hesitated, then shook my head. No matter the strong feelings I had for Trayton the instant we were Bound, I didn't think we'd quite reached the sit-on-my-knee portion of our relationship. Trayton looked disappointed, but hid it well enough in front of his friends. He turned to the Barron beside him and said, "Luke, this is Kaya, my Healer. Kaya, Luke studies with me under Darius."

A cold shock ran through my veins at the mention of Darius's name. Just when my thoughts had finally had a moment's peace not thinking about the silver-haired boy and why he seemed to loathe every fiber of my being, there he was again. I managed to smile at Luke. "Nice to meet you, Luke. Have you and Trayton known one another for long?"

Luke smiled, revealing dimples. His blond, wavy hair was tied back in a thong, and his eyes were intensely blue. "Pretty much since we were born. Our parents are close."

Trayton was beaming. "Luke always got us into trouble growing up."

Luke gave him a light shove. "Hey, swimming in Harper's Pond was your idea."

"But that trip to Cartertown—"

"Okay, you win." Luke laughed openly, his smile spreading to his eyes, but it didn't last. Abruptly, his features dropped as his eyes fell on something across the room. He leaned forward and muttered under his breath to Trayton. "Looks like the party's over. For us anyway."

Trayton followed Luke's eyes before chuckling and standing. I turned to see who had caused this ripple in the party atmosphere and felt a jolt go through me.

Darius looked serious as ever as his eyes scanned the room. When he found Trayton, he crossed the room with purpose. It was as if I weren't even in the same room as everyone else. The party—and its apparent end, if Luke was to be believed—was happening all around me, but I wasn't a part of it. I was merely a bystander.

That is, until Darius's eyes found mine. There was a fire in his gaze, and one not born of anger or bitterness. Darius looked alive, and he pulled everyone—me included—into that excitement with hardly a glance. I tore my gaze away from him, remembering how awful he'd been treating me, and looked over at Trayton, who was looking at Darius expectantly, and whose expression also contained that same bright, wild excitement. Darius said, "A dead youngling has been found just outside the north gate, and no one knows where its parents are. Searching for a possibly angry Graplar mother is too much for the inner patrol to handle, so it's on us, Trayton. Are you ready? Luke, you're coming too, along with fifteen of your best. You decide who. Let's have some fun."

Trayton stood, almost anxiously. He flitted a quick glance my way. When he spoke, though, it was to Darius. "Should we bring our Healers?"

Darius tensed. It was only slight, but to me it seemed so jarring, so obvious. Maybe because I knew that he wasn't my biggest fan. Maybe it was because we hadn't exactly had the greatest beginning. But he tensed and I saw it. I could almost feel him looking at me with his peripheral vision. "No. No Healers."

This time it was Luke who tensed, but far more noticeably. "No Healers? But . . . we're going outside the gates. What if something happens?"

"If you get injured, I'll drag your wounded body back inside the gate." A smile, both cruel and bemused, touched his lips as his words came out in a challenge. "What's the matter, Luke? Afraid to face a few overgrown pups without your nursemaid?"

The Barrons in the room grew utterly silent. These were more than a few overgrown pups. They were Graplars. One bite could mean death.

But no one was about to argue that with Darius.

Trayton stood. It was clear that no one but him would or could dare say anything in question to Darius's orders. "Does the headmaster know something that we don't? Why else would he order us outside the wall without our Healers?"

Darius pressed his lips tightly together for a moment before speaking. "The headmaster doesn't know. This is my order. No Healers."

"But, Darius." Trayton grabbed him by the shoulder and lowered his voice, but if he were hoping to keep the conversation between them, it was a lost cause. All eyes and ears in the room were on the two of them. Still, Trayton spoke his next words out of concern, and in the quietest of tones. "It's against Protocol to leave our Healers behind without the express instruction of Headmaster Quill."

Darius swept his eyes across the room for a moment, not really looking at anyone in particular. The slight dimple in his left cheek deepened as a grimace settled onto his mouth. He shook off Trayton's hand, but didn't get two steps closer to the door before Trayton was blocking his path. "You could lose your teaching position."

Everyone in the room was quiet, apart from Maddox, who'd found some saltbread slices to munch on. Darius dropped his attention to the floor, as if mulling over the possible repercussions of his actions. After a long moment, he met Trayton's eyes and nodded. "Well, we wouldn't want that, now would we?"

Trayton smiled and slapped his hand on Darius's shoulder twice before turning back to the room. As Darius exited, Trayton said, "You heard the man. On your feet, Barrons. You too, Healers."

Melanie was the first one on her feet, and it wasn't long before David, her Healer, was following her out the door. As the rest of the crowd busied itself and began filing outside, I stood and looked at Trayton, who seemed at peace with the entire situation. "Did I hear that right? Are we going on maneuvers outside the wall?"

"Yes, we are." He smiled brightly then, and I could see the excitement in his eyes. Barrons lived for the fight, and he was hoping that walking the perimeter in the dark of night might bring about the adrenaline rush he was looking for. It was beyond my understanding, but I deeply respected the reckless nature of that need to chase, that need to hunt.

Maddox shoved a saltbread slice in her mouth and chewed as she spoke, not caring that the occasional crumb would fly out of her mouth. "I'll walk you to the south gate and wait for you there 'til you get back. You excited?"

Excited—that was one way of putting it. I would have leaned more toward nauseated and gripped by fear. My stomach roiled at the idea of stepping outside of the wall again, knowing that Graplars lurked on the other side. But it wasn't like I had a choice. Trayton was counting on me, and if I wasn't there to heal him when he needed me to be, he might die. It sounded dramatic, but it was true. He was counting on me.

Maddox and Trayton chatted casually all the way to the south gate, but I didn't feel much like making small talk. I was too focused on the memory of those teeth and how they'd almost chomped down on me, the way they had chomped down on Avery. Avery—it felt like a lifetime ago that we'd raced to the Harvest Festival together. In fact, it felt like another lifetime altogether. I wondered what she'd think of me being enrolled at some school where I was expected to do as I was told, in support of a cause that I didn't truly understand. I wasn't sure what she'd say about any of it, that is, except for my being Bound to Trayton. She would have nudged me and wiggled her eyebrows and laughed so hard that it made me want to smack her.

I really missed Avery.

The south gate was looming up ahead of us as we made our way across the dark campus. No torches tonight, nothing, not so much as a speck of warmth or comfort, flickered in the night. Just a group of Barrons and Healers, none older than nineteen or so, heading toward a large metal door that would lead us to the outside world with no one to rely on for protection but ourselves. My hands were trembling, but I couldn't tell if it was from the intense fear that someone—me, Trayton, someone else—might be hurt or killed, or from the excited thrill that was tickling its way up my spine. If Trayton asked, I wouldn't give voice to that excitement. It seemed like something that would disappoint him, a Healer experiencing a rush right before heading out into the unknown wilds. So I kept my mouth shut and marveled at the size of the door as we approached. Tonight it seemed ten times bigger than the last time I'd seen it. The sky also seemed ten times darker. I was ready for this. More ready than I would ever admit to Trayton.

Maddox patted me on the back. "See you in a few hours. Hopefully in one piece."

Rolling my eyes at her comment, I turned back to the door and swallowed my nerves as I watched the gate guard check people out. It was standard procedure for any planned maneuver—the gate guard had a list of names and if you weren't on it, you didn't get outside the wall. I'd heard a young redheaded Barron explaining the whole thing to his new Healer in the dining hall, so seeing the process wasn't a surprise. It did, however, make me see the amount of control that Headmaster Quill had over the comings and goings of his student body.

Before I knew it, it was our turn, and Trayton was leading me up to the guard—the same guard who had given me access inside the gate the night I'd arrived here. His mouth was pursed as he looked over the list, but as he came to my name, the purse turned into a smile. "Kaya? I remember you. Taken on any Graplars lately?"

Chuckling, I shook my head. "Not since that night, and I'm hoping not to see any tonight either."

He scribbled something illegible beside my name and said, "I wouldn't worry about it too much. Things have been pretty quiet lately. Just stick with your Barron and you'll be fine."

Trayton cleared his throat, as if mistaking our friendly banter for flirtation, and wanting to make certain the guard had noticed him. "She certainly will."

The guard looked up at him and then back at the list. "Trayton? I didn't realize you'd been Bound yet. Congratulations."

A strange electricity was in the air, a sensation that hinted at jealousy—not for me; the guard wasn't even attracted to me, nor I to him. But something in his words hinted that he'd been waiting for a Healer for a long time. It had to be difficult being without a Healer and then seeing someone from a privileged family get their name moved up the list. I was tempted to explain that doing so hadn't been Trayton's idea at all, but his father's, but I kept my mouth shut. It was none of my business, and would likely only cause further tension to say anything. Trayton smiled, but it didn't quite reach his eyes—maybe because he knew that the congratulations were a bit of a dig at his privileged life. "Thanks. I'm very lucky."

The guard scribbled something beside Trayton's name then and the purse returned to his lips. Under his breath, he muttered, "I'm sure you are."

Trayton grimaced, but said nothing. The metal of the door scraped opened and I stepped through it, Trayton right beside me. As we passed through, my lungs filled with air that felt fresher than that of the academy. It had to be all in my head, but the ground seemed softer, the trees greener, the world around us more real. Maybe it was because I hadn't been outside of that wall in days, and being locked away somewhere can really fak with your perception of a place, but everything seemed better outside of the walls of Shadow Academy. Especially when I forced my mind to forget the fact that there was now nothing standing between the Graplars and myself but their appetite.

The door slammed shut behind us and an ominous,

metallic tone rang out into the forest. There was no going back. Not until we'd searched the immediate area for any sign of Graplars or King Darrek's soldiers. It was just us out here, and the katanas carried on the Barrons' backs.

The group had formed a semicircle just yards from the gate, and all eyes were on Darius as Trayton and I approached. Darius's hair fluttered slightly in the breeze. "We're going to divide into three teams. The first and largest will take the eastern path along the wall, checking for any weaknesses in the structure and usual signs of intruders. The second will take the western path, covering the area from the south gate to the north gate. The third and smallest group will drop farther down the hill to do some tracking. The young Graplar's mother can't be far off, and it's that group's job to find her."

Slowly, I inhaled through my nose and blew it out, trying to relax the growing tension in my muscles. I would have given anything at that moment not to be counted in that third group, and was hoping like hell I was just being paranoid. But the truth was, I could feel it coming. As Darius started barking orders, I sucked in my breath and held it.

"Marcus, Greg, Amy, Nancy, Hannibal, Rick, Sara, Allen, and Tyrone—you're on the first team. Get going, and keep your wits about you. We don't know how that young Graplar got there or why it was left behind, but it's possible the parents are going to come looking for it right where we found it."

A slow sigh escaped me. Maybe I'd been wrong about that third group. Maybe that was precisely where I wanted to be.

"Thomas, Patrick, Sharon, Brian, Melanie, Zane, you're the second group. Pay special attention to the area nearest the north gate. As you know, Graplars have recently been attacking that gate, and I don't want anyone getting injured in a moment of forgetfulness. Just because you're near Shadow Academy doesn't mean you're safe inside of it. Be careful."

Now I knew that being in the third group was probably the safest place I could be. The tension left me, and I waited for him to say Trayton's name.

"Trayton, Luke . . . you're with me."

As Darius turned away, ready to lead us down the hill, Trayton said something under his breath that sent my heart into my throat. He said, "I love the risky patrols."

Tugging feverishly on his sleeve, I whispered harshly, "Risky? Why is this risky?"

Darius glanced over his shoulder at Trayton, but he shook his head, as if to say that there would be no more outbursts from his Healer. I furrowed my brow, that silly fear of being eaten alive filling me once again, and followed them down the hill.

As we descended, the temperature quickly dropped, which struck me as odd. Normally, climbing down in elevation made the air warmer, not cooler. But with each step I took, more gooseflesh spread over my arms. Several hundred yards down the steep hill, Darius paused and tilted his head, listening. Trayton tapped me on the arm and when I looked at him, he pointed to my feet. His message was clear: Stay here. Don't move.

I nodded once, wondering what Darius had heard that had stopped him from his descent, but I knew better than to ask, or to say anything at all without being prompted. This was a quiet pursuit, and the last thing I wanted to do was to attract the attention of any Graplars who happened to be lurking nearby—particularly any Graplar parents who'd recently lost their young.

Trayton moved soundlessly to Darius's side and the two stood there for a moment, an unspoken conversation passing between them. I tried to meet Luke's Healer's eyes, to see if she was as scared as I was that we might encounter a Graplar, but she was too focused on Luke to take notice of anyone but him. Maybe that's how Healers were supposed to be—blind to their own fears, concentrating only on the well-being of their Barron. If that was the case, I felt sorry for Trayton. Because I was probably the worst Healer in the history of Tril.

After a few minutes, Darius's shoulders relaxed some, and he nodded to Trayton, who moved silently forward, raising his hand and stretching it ever so closely toward the handle of his katana. As his fingers curled around the handle, my lungs snapped closed to the air outside. They'd heard something, or seen something, and we were about to engage one of those horrible monsters that had attacked Kessler. My heart was racing and I flicked my gaze all around us, trying to get even a glimpse of what was to come. Instinctively, I lifted my left foot and took a step back, just one step, just trying to get a little distance between me and the unseen Graplar. When I brought my foot down, a distinct, hard snap echoed into the air. In the time it took me to gasp, Trayton and Luke had unsheathed their katanas and moved to surround Luke's Healer and me, their backs to us in a protective stance. Only Darius remained where he was, but it didn't take him more than a few seconds more to turn his eyes on me in a glare. "What part of *'don't move'* do you not understand?"

I opened my mouth to answer, but no answer came.

Luke returned his katana to its saya, looking irritated. Trayton slowly raised his blade and sheathed it, a look of disappointment on his face. I wasn't sure whether he was disappointed in me for having broken a twig under my foot in a moment of panic, or disappointed that we weren't being attacked by some unseen foe. Darius sighed and gestured up the hill with his chin. "Take her back to the academy, Trayton. Luke and I have got this."

Looking from Darius to Trayton, I said, "I don't need to go back. I can do this."

Trayton replied as if he hadn't even heard me—something that sent an angry chill up my spine. "Are you sure?"

Darius shrugged. "We haven't seen any fresh tracks, so I'm fairly certain the cub just wandered in from the east. Besides, if we need you, we know where to find you."

The corners of Trayton's mouth came down in a frown as his disappointment deepened. He certainly didn't want to head back to the school and potentially miss out on any Graplar-fighting action. I didn't want to go back either—not because Darius was sending me back—but it didn't look like there was room to argue. Trayton forced a smile at me. "Well. Let's call it an early night then."

He was trying to be pleasant. He was trying to be nice. He was acting as if I hadn't just completely ruined his good time. But I could see through the facade. The walk back to the south gate was a long and quiet one. I almost apologized several times along the way, but I couldn't shake the truth of it from my drooping shoulders and weary mind. It wasn't my fault that Trayton had been sent home early, like some misbehaving child. Darius had done this, and no one else.

As we approached the south gate, I dared to speak, hoping I wouldn't add to the tension in the air. "So it seems pretty clear that Darius despises me."

Trayton slowed his steps, glancing at me, but didn't

negate what I'd said. "Don't say that. Darius is just . . ."

"A total dek?"

Laughter bubbled out of him, breaking the tension between us. "Don't say that either."

I slowed to a stop, tugging his sleeve until he'd stopped walking too. "So what is it?"

Trayton stretched out his arm and brushed a stray hair from my eyes with his fingertips. It was such a simple motion, such a common gesture, but it made my heart skip a beat. "It's just that Darius is extremely particular whom he trusts on patrol and whom he doesn't. He doesn't trust you yet because he doesn't know you. That's all. I swear he doesn't hate you. And he's not a total dek."

He moved up the hill then, waiting patiently as I caught up to him. My head was full of a single thought— one that kept my mouth shut. All I could think about was the fact that Trayton was wrong about Darius. He was wrong on both counts.

Ten

"There are two sets of Protocol, which must be blended in order to act as the glue that holds our society together."

I folded my arms in front of me in an effort to warm my skin from the strange chill that was in the air. After a moment, I realized that the chill wasn't coming from the air. It was coming from Mr. Groff, my Protocol teacher.

"The first set, often referred to as common Protocol, are the rules given to you by those who raised you—generally, your parents. These rules encompass what is and isn't acceptable in a social environment, and the intricacies of engagement between those who are Skilled and those who are Unskilled. They govern what is expected of a Barron and Healer in order to maintain the balance and order to which Trillians have become accustomed. These well-established and time-honored rules have made it easier for people to live and work together.

The second set of Protocol consists of how we run our military forces and the way those forces interact with one another. Just as an Unskilled person is, for lack of a better turn of phrase, subservient to a Skilled person, a Healer is in a subservient position to a Barron. And with any position—both the supportive and the high-ranking—come certain rules, certain Protocol, that must be followed to keep order and maintain a happy and prosperous society."

He scanned the classroom slowly, his intense gaze scrutinizing each of his students. By the time his eyes met mine, I could feel the prickle of gooseflesh breaking out over my arms. Something about him made the tiny hairs on the back of my neck stand on end. This man loved Protocol. This man lived to support the very cause that my parents had run away from. I could smell it on him, coming off in metallic-tasting waves that sent my stomach roiling. He seemed to pause in his scrutiny, lingering on me momentarily, before plucking a small, red leather book from his desk and holding it up for everyone to see. When his eyes left mine, I released a quiet sigh of relief. "Protocol, ladies and gentleman, is precisely what you have come here to learn. Please turn to page fifty-eight of the class handbook."

The last thing I wanted to do was follow this man's instructions on anything, but I dutifully reached inside my satchel and withdrew the small book, thumbing my way carefully through it until I saw the number fifty-eight in bold, black print on the lower right corner of the page. I folded the cover back, opening the book, and read the chapter title, which screamed at me from the sinewy parchment. PROTOCOL.

"I'll give you all a moment to read the first paragraph before we proceed. You should note that—" The door opened and Mr. Groff's head snapped up with an intolerant glare, his words falling to the floor, forgotten.

As Trayton entered the classroom, several first-year students—both Healers and Barrons, much to my surprise, as most classes were just for Barrons or just for Healers—whispered to one another through cupped hands. A few, mostly female, blushed in awe. I merely sat in shock, as I had no idea why Trayton would be interrupting a Protocol class. It seemed a bit ironic to me that a rule-following Barron would break Protocol in a Protocol class, but maybe I was just looking for something to think about that would take me away from that bold word on the page. Trayton passed so closely to my table that I could have reached out and touched him, but I didn't dare move a finger. With a nod, he held a slip of parchment out for Mr. Groff. "My apologies for the interruption, Mr. Groff, but I was only just transferred to this class, on the recommendation of Headmaster Quill. He said you'd understand once you read his note."

Mr. Groff snatched the note from his hand with an impatient tug, but as his eyes moved over the words written on it, his mood softened. "Take your seat next to Kaya, Trayton, and turn to page fifty-eight. We are reviewing common Protocol."

Trayton turned, without looking at me for even a second, and walked around my chair, taking his seat to my left. He pulled a red book from his satchel and opened it to the correct page. I turned my head slightly, eyeing him with interest. What was he doing here? Surely Trayton had already taken a course in Protocol. He was taking advanced courses. There was no way he belonged in a first-year class.

The corner of his mouth lifted in a small, knowing smile and he met my eyes, his voice a soft whisper. "What?"

Shaking my head, I resisted a smile and turned my attention back to that bold word on the page. Beneath it was a paragraph about duty, and about what duties we had, as Skilled people, to protect the Unskilled from things that they were better off not knowing. Thinking back to my days in Kessler, to the villagers I knew and loved, I couldn't imagine any of them as ill-equipped to deal with the reality of war and Graplars and Skilled traits the way that the book described. The author or authors—no one took credit on the cover or beginning pages of the tome—had clearly never spent any extended time around the Unskilled, or else they might have known that the Unskilled were a lot more similar to the Skilled than they were comfortable admitting. A bit more relaxed, maybe. And more focused on tilling the soil and creating items for everyday use than fighting and maintaining the ridiculous decorum known as Protocol.

Tearing my thoughts away from Kessler, I stole another glance at Trayton before turning my attention to Mr. Groff at the front of the class. He stood with his legs slightly apart, his spine tall and stiff, his hands clasped behind his back. Even though his demeanor seemed calm, I got the impression that he was not a Barron who had taken lightly to retirement and a teaching position. I got the feeling, in fact, that he went out kicking and screaming, biting and clawing, doing whatever he could to remain in the war. It frightened me to know that someone could be that way, could be so blind to a cause and so in love with the rules imposed on them. Even my parents, who had been ever loyal to the cause until the day they'd agreed to elope, would have feared this man. Loyalty to anything in such an absolute manner was dangerous. *He* was dangerous, and I couldn't wait to get out of his stuffy, oppressive classroom and breathe in the clean air. "As I was saying, you should note that the first paragraph best sums up what we have come to understand as the societal need for Protocol."

Scanning the page, I found words that filled my heart with dread. Things like duty and honor, and not once did I see anything at all about freedom. I went back and read the paragraph he'd instructed us to read, but doing so just made my head ache. This was going to be a long class—a long school year, a long life—and nothing I could say or do would remove me permanently from Mr. Groff's Protocol class. Except for graduation, that is.

But at least Trayton was there to keep me company.

Once class had blissfully come to an end, Trayton slowly walked with me to the door, both of us relishing in this semi-alone moment. "What are you doing here?"

"What? In a class I took last year?" His grin was infectious. "Headmaster Quill thought it might do me a bit of good to freshen my memory on the subject matter. He also thought it might help you."

Leave it to Headmaster Quill to know what would be good for me. My mood deflated some, but I pushed the dark cloud away. Nothing was going to ruin this stolen, all-too-rare time alone. "Well, whatever the reason, I'm glad you're here. What did you think of the subject matter the second time around?"

"Groff's a good teacher. He taught me Protocol when I first came here. Of course, I knew him years before that. He and my father are good friends." Something sour crossed his face then, and it had absolutely nothing to do with Mr. Groff.

Hesitation held my words back, but only briefly. "You don't like your father much, do you?"

A shadow passed over him then—one filled with doubt and an immense sadness that I couldn't comprehend. "Does anyone understand their father?"

"I do. I love mine very much. Enough to come here,

just to protect him and my mother." A familiar lump formed in my throat at the thought of them. What were they doing now? Had they told anyone in Kessler where I had gone? Were they safe? Or, moments after I'd gone, had armed Barrons burst through the door and taken them into custody? Or worse.

His shadows lifted under the strength of curiosity. "Protect them? From what?"

"From the Zettai Council."

He shook his head, as if I had no idea what I was talking about. "They don't need protection from the Zettai Council. The Zettai Council is in place to protect people."

My jaw clenched and the threat of tears made my nose tingle. Turning toward the door, where I knew that Maddox would be waiting, I whispered over my shoulder, hoping that Trayton would hear, and that he wouldn't follow. "Do you believe everything Quill tells you?"

He might have followed, but I didn't know. As soon as I pushed open the door and spotted Maddox, I was gone.

CHAPTER

Eleven

Maddox may have been small, but she was strangely intimidating in the crowded hall on the way to the dining hall—especially when breakfast was at stake. Boys much larger than her stepped to the side, making room, and I followed along, marveling at their reaction. The looks on their faces said that they weren't being polite or treating her a certain way because she was female—it was something else, something oozing from Maddox's pores that said if they messed with her, she was going to cause them pain. And even though I had yet to see Maddox cause anyone so much as a moment of pain, I believed the looks on their faces as much as they seemed to feel it. An angry fire burned at the center of Maddox. It was something that everyone believed, but no one dared give name to, for fear the flames might envelop them. As we walked toward the dining hall doors, I found myself enormously grateful that Maddox was on my side.

The room was packed with Barrons and Healers, all hungry for the usual breakfast and socialization that the dining hall had to offer each morning. I scanned the room, grateful not to see Darius, but just as my heart had settled into a calmer rhythm, I spied Trayton sitting at our usual table. Only this time, Melanie was sitting on his lap.

Maddox and I exchanged questioning glances as we approached. I wasn't about to avoid the situation, and truth be told, Trayton wasn't technically my boyfriend or anything. He was just a guy . . . who I happened to be Bound to by blood, ritual, and a hint of forever.

As we approached the table, Maddox's mouth got away from her, as it had a tendency to do. "So do you two need extra napkins, or will your make-out session be less moist than I anticipate?"

She pulled out my chair and I sat down, catching Trayton's eye. The shame in his expression was instant. Gently—too gently for my comfort—he pushed Melanie from his lap and turned to face me. "It's not what it looks like. I swear. We're just friends."

Maddox snorted over my shoulder, and Melanie stood to Trayton's right, folding her arms in front of her, looking indignant. When I didn't say anything, he looked over his shoulder at her and said, "*Just* friends. Nothing more."

Melanie turned and stomped off then, shoving her Healer out of the way as he approached with her tray of food, inciting an eyeroll exchange between Maddox and me.

After she'd gone, Maddox's voice dripped with irritation. "It's a nice day out. We could always have a picnic if the scenery in here bothers you, Kaya."

When I looked back at Trayton, he mouthed the words "don't go." Then he placed his hand on mine and said aloud, "Please."

His eyes were large and full of apologies that I didn't know if I could trust, but what the situation boiled down to was this: Melanie had already proven to be highly aggressive in her pursuit of Trayton, and Trayton had assured me that there was nothing going on between them. For the moment, that was enough. It had to be.

"Maddox, can you get me some breakfast, please? I think I'll eat inside today." I could sense the "but" on the tip of her tongue, but Maddox didn't give voice to it. Instead, she stalked off in the direction of the food line, leaving Trayton and me alone at the table.

He kept his hand on mine, and I let him. After all, I wasn't nearly as upset by seeing Melanie trying to sink her claws into him as Maddox seemed to be. It bothered me, yes, but technically, Trayton and I had never had the please-don't-cuddle-with-other-people conversation. I wasn't even certain I was entitled to that conversation. We were Bound, yes, and I very much enjoyed his company, but did that give me the right to tell him who he could touch in certain ways and who he couldn't?

He gave my hand a squeeze, tearing me from my thoughts, but before he spoke, he sighed, running his free hand through his hair in a way that made it seem like whatever he was about to say wasn't easy. "Kaya, I have to tell you something. It's stupid, but . . ."

My nerves twitched a little, and I really hoped that this wasn't any sort of confession to do with Melanie. "What is it?"

"We're Bound."

Um, duh. "That much I know."

"And being Bound, I feel a real connection with you. Actually, I felt a connection with you even before the binding ceremony. But I feel really stupid having to ask you this." He held my gaze, his voice soft and eager. "Please don't feel like you have to say yes. I'm just curious, and if it's not the case, it's perfectly all right. I just need to know. Being Bound certainly doesn't assure a romantic relationship, but . . . I like you. And if you like me, I think maybe we should set some ground rules. Don't you?"

My heart felt instantly lighter. "I think that's a great idea. And just so you know, I like you too."

He smiled with ease. It would have been so fitting for him to sigh in relief at that moment, but he didn't. His shoulders, however, did release much of their tension. "I'm going to do everything I can to stay away from

Melanie. I don't know exactly what's gotten into her, but lately, she's become even more aggressive than usual."

I hated how happy I was to hear those words come out of his mouth. I hated how jealous I was of a girl who had absolutely nothing to do with my life. "You don't have to stop being friends with her for my sake."

"It's more about what that friendship is doing to me. I enjoy Melanie's company, but I think she identifies our friendship as something that it is not, no matter how often I tell her that we're just friends, or how many times I push her away. Granted, I shouldn't let things go as far as they sometimes do, but Melanie is . . . persuasive." He dropped his gaze to the table momentarily. "I'm incredibly sorry about earlier. It won't happen again. I promise you that."

And I believed him. No matter what Maddox might have to say about the matter. For once, it was me who a boy liked. For once, it was my heart beating for someone. Not Avery's. Not anyone's but mine. And I never wanted that feeling to go away. "Apology accepted. So . . . we're kind of a couple now?"

When he smiled, that small dimple showed on his cheek. "It looks that way. If you'll have me, that is."

The grin on my face made my cheeks ache.

Maddox returned with a tray of food, and breakfast commenced. I tried to keep the chatter less on the mushy side, to alleviate Maddox's apparent nausea, but it was difficult. Once the tray had been cleared away, Maddox looked relieved. "Botanical Medicine time, Princess."

As I stood, Trayton caught my hand in his, his eyes sparkling. He didn't need to say anything. I could see it in his expression. He cared for me. And I cared for him. Giving his hand a squeeze before letting go, I followed Maddox dutifully out the doors and outside. The sun was shining brightly.

We crossed campus, and I did my best to not even glance in the direction of the training area as we passed by. Within minutes, I was taking my seat in Botanical Medicine at a table that was piled with bundles of herbs, a mortar and pestle, and piles of obviously well-read books. In the seat to my left was a bookish girl who looked a bit jumpy. To my right was a boy with a cleft chin who looked kind of cocky. At the front of the class stood a woman with an hourglass shape. She had curly, strawberry blond hair and sparkling emerald eyes. And, most importantly, waves of niceness rolled off of her. I could tell that this class was going to be a brief reprieve in my time here at Shadow Academy. "Come in, Healers, come in. And welcome to Botanical Medicine. I am Instructor Harnett and today we will learn all about roses and their significance in the Healing arts."

My interest was certainly piqued. I'd wondered why a school that focused on training individuals for war would have such lavish, expansive rose gardens, but I'd assumed there was a purpose, some method to their madness.

"Now, when I say the Healing arts, I am referring to the act of healing the wounded without the aid of bonded touch, which is something that you share with the Barron to whom you are Bound or Soulbound. But make no mistake—the Healing arts can also apply to aiding your Barron, if you are Bound. As most of you realize, being Bound isn't as strong as being Soulbound. You may be able to heal with touch, you may not. Nothing is certain. But what is certain is that roses are key in many healing potions, and that's what we'll be discussing today."

Instructor Harnett picked up a bundle of roses and sniffed them deeply, closing her eyes for a moment. "Roses fulfill many needs. Rose hips act as a vitamin supplement and offer anti-inflammatory benefits, while infusions created from rose petals offer cures to headaches, dizziness, mouth sores, and uterine cramps. Properly prepared, they also ease the pain of toothaches, earaches, and sore throats. Rose oil is also a key ingredient in fighting against the bacteria in Graplar saliva."

That was certainly good to know. It was also good to know that my gardening efforts weren't being wasted on something that just stood there looking pretty and occasionally jabbing someone.

"Now, as you may or may not be aware, the art of Healing is divided into two factions: the botanical aspect and the natural aspect. Botanically, Healers are able to aid in the healing of Barrons and other Healers with the aid of various herbs, salves, oils, and other plant-based medicines. Naturally, Healers are able to heal those that they are either Bound or Soulbound to with touch. Of course, healing naturally is a much easier and much simpler task, but as there are so few Healers compared to the number of Barrons in existence, it's vital that we understand the botanical method of healing. Not everyone has a Bound or Soulbound Healer, so it falls on our shoulders as Healers to assist all Barrons." Instructor Harnett smiled at the class. It was an honest smile. One that told me that she understood that being a Healer was more of a duty than a blessing. "Now, if you'll all please take notes, I'll walk you through the basics of how to create rose oil."

Most of the class let out a collective groan, but I didn't. For the first time since entering the south gate, I found myself mildly interested in what Shadow Academy had to offer. I opened my notebook and poised my pen on the page, eager to hear what Instructor Harnett had to say.

CHAPTER

Twelve

Instructor Baak was circling me and my fellow Healing 101 classmates like some kind of panicked vulture, so worried that one of us—and I think we all knew which one—was going to positively ruin the day. The sun was a pleasant warmth on my shoulders, and I smiled up into it. Beside me, Trayton was smiling. I couldn't see it, but I could sense it. He'd been smiling ever since we found out he'd be joining me on this little field trip. At first, I was terrified when Instructor Baak told us we were venturing outside school walls. But knowing that Trayton was joining me—he and a sizable group of well-trained Barrons—settled my stomach a bit. Even though butterflies were dancing inside of it.

"Please line up in an orderly fashion: Healers on the right, Barrons to the left. We'll proceed through the gate as quickly and orderly as we can, but remember that it will take time considering the size of our group. A Master Healer and three guards are awaiting you outside the wall. I will follow you, along with three more guards, for your safety." Her eyes fell on me briefly, and I stepped in line beside Trayton, forgetting about the sunshine momentarily. The smile stretching across my lips was genuine, and when Trayton laced his fingers with mine, my smile stretched on into eternity. He gave my hand a little squeeze, sending a small flutter through my heart.

About ten groups of Barrons and Healers stretched out in front of us, with another ten or twelve pairings behind us. As we all shuffled forward, happy chatter erupted through the crowd. Clearly I wasn't the only one who was excited about seeing my Barron. Someone behind me laughed, and I gave Trayton's hand a squeeze. It was a good day. A much needed one. And it wasn't often, I was certain, that such an optimistic vibe rippled its way through the stone walls surrounding Shadow Academy. For a moment—one that I was certain would be all too brief—I was hopeful, positive, and happy. Three things that I hadn't experienced much of since leaving my parents behind in Kessler.

Raden was standing at the gate with a clipboard, running through names. He seemed very distracted by the entire ordeal, and I could only imagine the security risks involved for taking so many ill-trained Healers outside. Couldn't we stage this battlefield inside the wall? After all, it was supposed to be a mock-up of post-battle trauma and how we should handle the situation. Did we really need to be in actual danger? Yes. Apparently, according to Instructor Baak, we did.

"Next!" Raden barked, and we shuffled forward. Trayton parted his lips to speak, but apparently, Raden already knew our names. "Next!"

A bizarre mixture of thrill and dread rushed through my veins as we crossed over the threshold, not knowing what the day might hold. I'd half expected the woods outside to be filled with shadows and haunting sounds, but instead I was met with the twittering of songbirds and generous sunshine filtering in through the leaves above. Several yards outside the gate, our group gathered, awaiting further instructions.

Once everyone was outside and our Barron guards were standing sentinel around us, Instructor Baak instructed several Healers to pass out bandages and other medical supplies. As they did so, she said, "Now, despite the beautiful day, a terrible battle has just taken place here, leaving your Barron terribly injured. Inside each of the medical kits, you will find a slip of paper indicating how your Barron was injured. You have twenty minutes to locate any additional supplies and treat the wound. Your time begins now."

A Healer boy that normally sat in the back of our class handed me a small box then, and I flipped open the lid. Inside were bandages, a small jar of ointment, scissors, and three small bundles of herbs. Stuck to the inside of the lid was a piece of paper. As I unfolded it,

Trayton sank to the ground dramatically, peering up at me with a smirk. "So what's wrong with me?"

Nudging him with my toe and chuckling, I read the note aloud. "Your Barron has suffered a shallow Graplar bite to the left pectoral."

"Ooh. Sounds painful." His eyes were sparkling. "How on Tril will you fix me?"

I took a seat beside him on the forest floor, mulling over my options and trying hard to ignore the irresistible flirtatiousness that was coming off Trayton in waves. Two of the herb bundles were fairly easy to identify. One was Sprigweed and the other Cragbark. But neither would be of much help when it came to a Graplar bite, and I had no clue what the third bundle even was. It smelled vaguely fruity and felt like silk on my skin, but I had no idea what its healing properties might be. Biting the inside of my cheek in deep thought, I sighed. "I'm not sure I can. You might not survive this."

Trayton propped himself up on his elbow and surveyed my medical kit, a frown on his face. "Damn. It was a good life. I was hoping to continue living it."

Laughter rolled out of me, and I gave him a light shove. "Stop it! I'm trying to fix you."

"Maybe you should start by cleaning my wound?" He raised an eyebrow at me, a dangerous twinkle in his eye.

I rolled my eyes. "Just take your shirt off."

"I can't. I'm injured."

When our eyes met, we both laughed so hard that Instructor Baak shot us a glare, killing our revelry. Clearing my throat, I said, "Seriously. I have like ten minutes left to fix you."

"You're the boss."

Ten minutes later, Trayton was wrapped haphazardly in bandages and slathered in gooey ointment. Instructor Baak surveyed my handiwork and uttered one word that should have hurt to hear, but didn't, for some reason. "Fail."

As she walked away, Trayton frowned. "Fak. I died."

Laughter ripped out of me so hard and so fast that tears spilled down my cheeks.

Hours later, Trayton and I were sitting in the dining hall, munching on freshly baked oat cookies and telling Maddox about our misadventures in healing. Maddox wasn't nearly as amused as either of us had been, but I guess it was one of those things where you really had to be there in order to truly appreciate the humor. She sighed, rolling her eyes. "I don't see what's so funny about killing your Barron."

"I didn't kill him. Not exactly."

Trayton smirked. "To be fair, you didn't exactly save me, either."

I gave his arm a light smack. "Whose side are you on anyway?"

"Mistroot." Both Trayton and I looked up when Maddox spoke, confusion filling our eyes. Maddox rolled her eyes again, as if the reasons behind her drastic subject change were obvious. "The herb you couldn't identify? It's Mistroot."

Trayton nodded. "Oh yeah. The fruity smell? A dead giveaway."

My jaw nearly hit the table as it dropped. "You both know this? And Trayton, you couldn't tell me it was Mistroot when you were lying out there dying of a Graplar bite?"

He shrugged and plucked another cookie from the tray on the table in front of us. "Life or death aside, that would have been cheating."

Maddox and I locked eyes then and burst out laughing. Trayton stared oblivious, having no clue why his staunch adherence to the rules would seem so absurd. Once I recovered, I picked up the tray and carried it toward the trash bin. I must have misgauged a step, because my tray hit someone and clattered to the floor, sending small plates, cookie crumbs, and glasses half full of milk to the floor and all over the front of the person I'd run into. I stared dumbfounded at the crumbs and milk as they clung to the front of his shirt and dribbled down. When I raised my chin, daring to look Darius in the eyes, I wasn't at all surprised to see that his face was turning red with fury. But even then, when he screamed at me, I jolted. "Extra duties!"

He turned to stomp off in a huff and I stepped in front of him, blocking his path. The crowd around me fell into a hush. But I was tired of Darius punishing me without reason. "Why? It was an accident, Darius!"

He was gritting his teeth, and when he spoke again, it was in a low growl. "There are no accidents."

I glared, but it had no effect on him whatsoever. He turned and walked around me, exiting the dining hall. From behind me, Maddox placed a concerned hand on my shoulder, but I shook her off. Whatever this animosity was, wherever it had come from, it was between Darius and me, and only he and I could settle it.

CHAPTER

Thirteen

The heels of my palms stung from the tiny bits of thorns that were wedged under the skin, and all I really wanted to do was find Darius and punch him in his stupid face. But Maddox had other plans. "Let's go get some powdered sugar rings to munch on."

"Maddox," I sighed, not wanting doughnuts at all, but too exhausted to resist her whims. "Okay, but let's not take long. Extra duties really took it out of me."

"Don't worry, Princess. We'll be in and out. I swear." She nodded and smiled, and for one, brief, idiotic moment, I believed her sincerity.

Three hours later, after Maddox had gorged herself on dining hall pastries and I'd insisted on getting to bed early, I lay there under my covers, eyes wide open, every inch of my nerves on edge. I just couldn't shake every mean thing that Darius had ever said to me, every dirty look, every unkind prickle that emanated from him to me. Finally, I whipped the covers from me and headed into the parlor, hoping that Maddox hadn't dozed off in a post-doughnut coma. Luckily, she was sitting on the chaise, a book in her hand. She looked up at me, only mildly surprised by my mid-night presence. "Hey. Sugar ring?"

My left eyebrow twitched, but only slightly. "No thanks."

She shrugged and popped the last powdered sugar ring into her mouth. As she was chewing, she said, "Couldn't sleep?"

Shaking my head, I plopped down next to her. "I'm just so irritated."

She flashed me a knowing look. "Darius, right?"

When I groaned, she said, "Why don't you just go over to his cabin, pound on the door, and demand to know what the hell his problem is, once and for all?"

"I can't. He's a teacher, remember?" Biting my bottom lip, I refused to give voice to the real reason that I was hesitant to confront Darius. The truth was, I was a little afraid of him.

Maddox shook her head. "Get over there and stand up for yourself already. After all, if you don't, who will?"

Her words, her meaning, her undeniable rightness sank into my pores then. There was no one else. Not Maddox, not Trayton, not my parents. There was only me. I had to stand up to Darius, or he'd never stop treating me this way.

At first, I didn't say anything in response to Maddox. But then I looked down at my hands—hands that were shaking with such anger and frustration, and I knew that she was absolutely right. I had to confront Darius, and now, not later, or he would go on picking on me for the rest of my time at Shadow Academy. "Okay, let's go."

Maddox raised an eyebrow and held up her book. "You're on your own. I just hit a good part."

My jaw hit the floor. "Maddox, I can't go out there alone! What about the Graplars?"

"I don't know if you noticed when you got here," she said with a smirk, "but the whole school is surrounded by a big fakkin' wall."

I considered this for a moment, and debated whether or not Maddox had completely lost her mind, but the odds seemed in her favor. I really didn't think that she'd let me get eaten by one of those horrible beasts, no matter how terrible a guard she was. Maddox liked me. And I liked her, trusted her. So with a deep breath, I stood up again and cast her a wary glance. "And if the headmaster catches me out past curfew and without my guard?"

Maddox shook her head slowly, sucking powdered sugar from her fingers, her eyes locked on her book the entire time. "Not a chance. He and a bunch of the Elder Barrons are at some big dinner celebration at Trayton's parents' place twenty miles from here. Pretty much if you want to sneak around campus and get away with it, tonight's the perfect night for it."

Insult filled me and I spit out, "I don't want to sneak around with Darius."

Maddox raised a sharp eyebrow at me. "I never said with Darius. Wow, guilty conscience much? Are you going to confront him or not?"

"Yes." My heart rattled nervously in my chest. "Yes, I am."

As I opened the door to the hall, my heart thundered inside my chest. I never fancied myself as much of a rule breaker. That had always been Avery's style, not mine. I was always the one coaxing her away from sneaking around with the Bowery boys or staying out past curfew. She was the one who'd talked me into "borrowing" her father's cart one evening, and if it weren't for her disrespect of authority, I'd never know what really went on in the guard shack at the edge of town after hours. Avery was the rule breaker, not me.

But Avery wasn't around anymore. So maybe now it was my job to break a few rules. Especially if I had good reason to.

A small part of me—okay, a large part, admittedly—was afraid what would happen if I got caught sneaking out alone after hours. What would happen to my parents? What would happen to Maddox? Would Trayton get in trouble? My mind filled with worried thoughts.

By the time I'd gotten down the hall, down the stairs, and out the door, I'd half convinced myself that the headmaster would be waiting for me with an army of guards, ready to whisk me away to parts unknown. To my agonized relief, he wasn't. The courtyard was completely empty, the grounds utterly silent. Above, a thousand stars twinkled their encouragement. So I moved forward, swearing that it would be the first and last time that I broke the rules, and that after tonight, I'd do everything I could to fit in here at Shadow Academy.

It's funny the things you tell yourself when you're scared you'll get caught doing something you're not supposed to.

Halfway across the cobblestone courtyard, I looked up at the cottage and my stomach shriveled into a deflated balloon. Darius's window was dark.

My steps slowed to a stop and I bit my bottom lip, staring at the window, debating my options. I could go back to my room and sort this out later—or even just forget it. Wasn't it a pretty stupid idea to confront a maniac like Darius anyway? And for what? A few snide remarks and dirty looks? So the guy didn't like me—so what? Why did it even seem to matter?

"It's after curfew."

I turned my head toward his voice, but Darius was already stepping out of the shadows and onto the cobblestone. How long had he been standing there? Snorting my irritation with him, I said, "Planning on giving me more extra duties?"

Without even flinching—maybe he was made of

stone, incapable of feeling a dig—he said, "What are you doing here?"

"I wanted to ask you a question." I waited for his response, but he said nothing. His eyes carried a strange sort of expectation in them, as if he'd been waiting for this conversation since the day we met. I took a deep, slow breath before speaking. "What's your problem, Darius? Why do you hate me so much?"

Disappointment crossed his features, followed immediately by annoyance. "My problem is no business of yours."

Cursing under my breath, I mentally kicked myself. Why was I surprised? Did I think we'd shake hands and end up fast friends because I snuck out to confront him? What did I really expect from a dek like Darius?

He turned toward his cottage then, his footfalls soundless on the cobblestone. Then, unexpectedly, his steps slowed. Without turning back to me, almost as an afterthought, he said into the night, "And I never claimed to hate you."

Shock filled me and I was responding before I could even think of the words to say. "So why do you act the way you do?"

"I also never claimed to like you. You should go back to your . . ." The venom was back in his voice as he threw a glance at me over his left shoulder, but it didn't last. "Wait. Do you hear that?"

Darius turned around in a slow circle then, surveying the darkness, scrutinizing every inch of shadow around us. I looked as well, but saw nothing, heard nothing. Maybe Darius was still on paranoid pins and needles from his recent hunting party. "I don't hear anything."

He frowned, his eyes still scanning. "Maybe it's nothing. Still . . . you should get back to the dorms. It's not safe for a Healer to be out alone. Especially at night. Even inside this wall."

Cocking my head to the side, I wondered how Darius could speak with such sincerity about something Maddox had said the complete opposite of just minutes before. Then I pivoted on my heel, turning back to my dorm building, and froze.

The shape of the enormous, hulking beast was apparent even in the darkness. Its broad head lowered and moved in close, the stench of its breath closing in around me. Its black, beady eyes seemed lifeless—an empty void of hunt, kill, devour—but I knew too well the life contained within. Graplars were fast, limber, instinctive, and powerful. I didn't make any quick movements, recalling what Darius had said to me the first time we'd met—what my father had said just moments before a Graplar had taken Avery's life—but turned my head slightly, inciting a low growl from the beast. But when my eyes fell on Darius, all hope of a repeat escape vanished.

Darius was also holding very still. Because a second

Graplar was standing directly in front of him.

My heart shot into my throat, choking back my words for a moment. Then, with a slow, deep breath, I dared a whisper. "What do we do?"

Darius was eyeing the beast, that light once more in his eyes—visible even in the darkness—filling his entire presence with excitement. I didn't share his enthusiasm. He parted his lips to speak and the Graplar blew out a snort, as if warning him that speaking wouldn't be wise and loud speaking wouldn't be tolerated. After a moment more of silence, he said, "I hope you can handle a sword. Otherwise this might be the last charming conversation we ever have."

It took all my willpower not to laugh, and most of that was probably nervous laughter. I knew he was being sarcastic, but part of me couldn't help but wonder if Darius were hoping that we might actually have future conversations, despite the fact that he seemed to utterly despise me. I was admittedly curious as to what those conversations might be. If we survived, that is.

Slowly, so slowly that I could barely tell that he was moving at all, Darius reached over his right shoulder and slipped the katana from its sheath. The metal sang quietly, as if the sword knew that any loud sounds would attract the attention of the Graplar, as if it were telling Darius that it was ready for action. "Now," Darius whispered—his words no more than a breath on the wind— "I'm going to toss this blade to you. If you like breathing and wish to continue doing so, you're going to cut that thing's head off as quickly as you can, or at least keep it at bay until I can finish this big boy off."

My heart was racing so loudly that I almost couldn't hear what he was saying. Did he want me to fight off a Graplar? Seriously? I must have been hearing things. "You want me to what? And . . . how are you going to kill it without a sword?"

My voice squeaked and the Graplar in front of me moved closer, baring its slimy teeth and emitting a low, guttural growl. It was a warning. I was sure of it.

A small line creased Darius's forehead. "Let me worry about that. You just try not to die until I can come help you. Now catch this thing on three. Ready? One. Two. Three!"

He whipped the blade overhand through the air, and I dove after it as it tumbled. The metal gleamed as it turned over and over again, high above my head. It was aimed perfectly for me to catch it as it fell. All I had to do was to stretch out my hand and grasp it. But then a thought entered my mind, worming its way deep within the part of my brain that makes me do really stupid things. What if I reached out and caught the wrong end of the sword? The sharp metal of the blade could slice straight through me. I'd lose a finger. Maybe many fingers. I pulled back at the last second, just as the katana was in reach, in a momentary panic. The blade clattered onto the cobblestone below, voicing its complaints loudly. I was hoping the Graplars wouldn't notice. But they did.

The Graplar in front of Darius lowered its head and lurched toward me, but Darius jumped up at the last moment and stomped down hard on its head. It whined and shook its enormous skull, slightly dazed. As the Graplar in front of me was moving forward, I shot a glance at the blade, but it was too far out of reach for me to grab. Taking a cue from Darius, I raised my foot up too. How hard could it be? Darius had just stomped on it and it was momentarily incapacitated. I could manage that much. Just as I was bringing my foot down, the Graplar lifted its head, pulling my leg upward in a quick jerk. I lost my balance, falling backward, and before I could recover, the beast shot its head forward, opening its massive jaws, and sank its teeth into my thigh. Screams tore out of my throat and into the night. I twisted my head around, but from where I was lying, I couldn't see Darius. For all I knew, he might be dead, and I might be this monster's dinner. I pounded on its skull with my fists, but it refused to let go, its sharp teeth sinking deeper and deeper into my flesh, pain lighting up my entire leg. Drawing back my fist, I aimed for its eye, and when I connected, it snorted and squealed and backed off.

Blood gushed down my leg, and I had to force my thoughts away from the damage the monster had caused. I stretched out my hand and grabbed the katana, gripping the handle so tightly that my knuckles turned white. Before I could even scramble into a squatting position, the Graplar lunged for me and I brought the sword up hard. The blade stuck into its throat, but just barely. With a horrific gurgling sound, the beast backed off, pawing at the blade, trying desperately to knock it free.

Scrambling to stand, my leg screamed with pain that sent my head into a whirlwind. I struggled to keep my wits about me, and focused through the pain, raising my good leg up. I brought my foot down hard on its skull, kicking it into the cobblestone with a crack. Then, my heart racing with terror, I grabbed the handle of the katana and jerked it upward, hoping like hell the thin blade would be powerful enough to slice through its neck. I didn't have to cut the head completely off, just damage the beast enough that it wouldn't be able to come after me again. But to my utter shock, the metal slipped easily through muscle, bones, tissue. The Graplar's head rolled wetly away from its body, which landed in a dead heap. I staggered backward, my hands trembling.

Darius took the katana from my hand and flicked the weapon forward, flinging blood from it before returning it to the sheath on his back. He looked over my handiwork and smiled. "Not bad. For a Healer."

His words didn't sting. Mostly because I could hear the tone of respect within them. Imagine that—Darius.

Respecting me. If I didn't know any better, I'd have thought it was all a dream. But the pain in my leg was enough to remind me that I was absolutely wide awake.

Behind him, the water in the fountain trickled down from one level to the next. As I watched, dazed, the water turned from clear to dark red. Floating grotesquely in the bottom of the fountain was the other Graplar's head. Its corpse was lying beside the fountain. A gasp escaped me. "How did you manage to cut its head off without a katana?"

Impossibly, Darius's smile broadened. But it soon wilted as he cast his eyes down at my leg. "You've been bitten."

He met my eyes and I saw what I'd thought to be impossible in his gaze—concern. It was intermingled with something else, but I couldn't quite identify it. "We'd better get you to the hospital wing. A Graplar bite can prove fatal if not properly treated."

"No, wait." I shook my head and the world around me shifted. Suddenly I was feeling very warm. Unusually warm. And dizzy. "If the headmaster finds out I was out after curfew, alone, and during a Graplar attack, he'll have my head on a platter, not to mention Maddox's."

I was certain that he'd insist we head straight to the hospital—after all, that was Protocol, now wasn't it?— but he surprised me by nodding, his eyes on my wound the entire time. "My cottage, then. Quickly. Wait quietly until I have a chance to debrief this to Raden, who will arrange cleanup and a report to Quill. If anyone finds out you're there . . ."

He didn't have to finish his sentence. I knew what he meant. If anyone found out I was in Darius's quarters—a teacher, an Unskilled, and after hours, unescorted—we were both dead. He turned and started a quick pace toward the south gate, and I called after him, because it couldn't wait. Because I owed him at least this. "Thank you."

He paused in his steps just long enough to offer me a nod before hurrying to find Raden.

My vision wavered a bit as I lifted my injured leg, but I forced myself to keep going, keep moving. I had to get out of sight quickly, before anyone saw me. It was a miracle that no one had. But I could only move so fast. I limped along the cobblestone to the narrow stairs that led up to Darius's quarters. Placing my good foot on the first step, I pulled my wounded limb along, fighting back tears. It was strange, but I couldn't shake the sensation that the injury was becoming more painful as time moved on. An eternity later, I pushed open Darius's door and practically fell inside.

Darius's quarters were simple, and if I didn't already know that he lived here full time, I might have mistaken them for a temporary place—somewhere that someone who was just passing through might sleep. There were no pictures on the wall, no books on the bedside table, no clothing on the floor, no personal effects of any kind. Just a simple, crisply made bed near the window, a small nightstand holding a single candle, and a wardrobe across the room.

I made my way to the bed and collapsed, groaning. The bite from the Graplar was beginning to burn me alive from the inside out. Lying back on the bed, I hoped like hell that Darius wouldn't be gone for too much longer.

At long last—I had no idea how much time had passed—the door swung open and Darius entered, closing it behind him once again, sealing us both inside. Alone. Together. He turned to face me, and then moved his gaze down my body—a little more slowly than I thought was necessary. When he spoke, his voice sounded vaguely husky. Or maybe it was just my imagination making it so. "Those leggings will have to come off."

My eyes must have bugged out of my head, and I sat up, my pain briefly breaking. "Like hell they do!"

He stared at me blankly, as if he had no idea why I was making such a ruckus over taking my pants off in front of him. I stood my ground, but it felt like the ground was moving. Steadying myself against the wall, I said, "The leggings stay on."

Sighing, Darius's expression turned impatient once again. "Look, I can't treat that bite properly while your clothes are in the way. So either take them off and let me help you or limp your way to the hospital wing and let the Master Healers give it a shot."

My wound throbbed, as if in protest. Only I didn't think it was protesting me. "Give it a shot? You act like they don't know what they're doing."

He shrugged. "They don't. Not entirely. Not when it comes to Graplar bites. I suspect that's largely because they've never been bitten before."

"And you have?" I wasn't sure why I'd asked. Of course he'd been bitten. He was a warrior. Even warriors get bitten.

"More times than I care to count. And I've treated every wound myself, healing twice as fast as those treated by Master Healers, and with far less scarring." Meeting my eyes again, he said, "Are you going to take your pants off or what?"

I snorted. "Turn around."

Rolling his eyes slightly, he turned around, but not because of my desire for privacy. Instead, he started rummaging through a small cupboard for various herbs and creams. Crushing three of the herbs together with a mortar and pestle, he added two different creams—one a sickly yellow color, the other bright white—and scooped most the concoction into a small, lidded jar. The rest he carried over to me. Luckily, I'd managed to sit on the bed and cover up all the important bits with the blanket. Darius's blanket. It was baby soft against my skin.

On his way across the room, he picked up a desk chair and placed it directly in front of me. Once he sat on it, he reached for the blanket. I drew back, hesitant. Maybe it was the poison coursing through my blood, but I was feeling more than a little paranoid at the moment. With a comforting glance, Darius reached out and moved the blanket just an inch higher, so he could get a good look at my wound. I swore to myself that I wouldn't look at it, but couldn't resist the urge. Though the Graplar had just barely nipped me, I could make out its teeth marks in my skin. The gash spread across the top of my thigh, its edges an ugly burgundy, pus already oozing from within. I swooned, and Darius spoke sharply, but not without concern. "Don't give into it. If you let the fever take you, the venom will work its magic even faster. Stay focused. Stay with me."

It was almost an impossible thing to do, to stay focused, to stay in the here and now when my world was spinning and turning upside down, but I held on, nodding my promise to him, hoping that he really knew what he was doing. As if the pain wasn't bad enough, a slight burning sensation had started at the center of the bite, spreading quickly to its outer edges and continuing down my leg. As it moved, it tightened, squeezing me in its grasp.

"Kaya. Look at me."

I obliged, but it was hard to see him. The edges of my world were quickly blurring.

His voice was calm and hushed, but kind. Kind like I had never heard it before. "This is going to hurt like hell, but I promise you that before I even finish applying the salve, you'll start feeling better, okay?"

I may have nodded—it was hard to tell what I was doing, other than being wrapped so tightly in that horrible, dizzying, burning pain. Pain that brightened considerably in a white heat when Darius first dabbed a glob of salve onto my open wound. Crying out, I pulled away, but he caught my arm with his free hand and held me still. "Just a few moments. You'll feel right as rain. I swear."

He dabbed on a bit more of the mixture as gently as he could, then began to smear it lightly over the bite. Tears coated my cheeks, but I couldn't find my voice. The pain was so intense, it seemed there was no escape from it. I couldn't see Darius anymore, and when he spoke, I couldn't make out what he was saying. My body was starting to shake, and I got the feeling I was falling without end in sight.

Then, slowly, my world came into focus once again. The pain was still there, but bearable, eased by the cooling sensation of Darius's magical mixture. I dried my tears on my sleeve, then focused my eyes on Darius, who was moving his fingers over my injury with the care and grace of a surgeon. "I'll stitch it closed, but not yet. Let's get the infection out first. Could take a few days. Feeling any better?"

"Much." I nodded, my voice hoarse—had I been screaming? My throat was burning.

He moved his fingers from the pestle back to my bite, dabbing tiny amounts of the salve onto the edges of the wound that hadn't yet been treated. My pain faded away and a strange silence settled between us. It wasn't awkward. Just . . . strange.

Beyond the scent of the salve, I could smell something else. Something that reminded me of wild, wooded places. With surprise, I realized that the scent was coming from my host. Not a shock—Darius seemed to live for the outdoors. It was a pleasant smell, and reminded me of home, of walks in the forest and camping near the river. I sighed, relaxing back on the bed. Darius glanced up at me and I managed a small smile. My throat was raw when I said, "You remind me of home."

His fingers slowed as they dipped into the pestle once again, his eyes still on mine. "In what way?"

Shrugging, I said, "You smell like the woods. Like wind and rain. It's . . . nice."

"Kaya . . ." His tone was something I barely comprehended. It was soft and wondering, unlike the man I knew Darius to be. He kept his eyes on his work, his tone even and focused. "If you feel the need to come talk to me, at least come during the day when it's somewhat safer, okay?"

I couldn't help but notice that he didn't say that I shouldn't come, only that I should be more careful about it. Did that mean he'd hoped I come see him eventually? And just what was that about, anyway? He hated me. Didn't he?

Darius sat the now empty pestle on the floor and examined his handiwork. As he did so, I dared a question. "So what's it like, being the only Unskilled allowed on academy grounds?"

"It's not so bad." He shrugged and sat back in his chair, the most relaxed that I had ever seen him. "A little lonely, maybe. But I have to keep a respectable distance from the troops. It's hard enough to earn their respect as an Unskilled. Even harder to keep that respect when they could excuse it with a label."

"Sounds . . ." Only one word came to mind to describe his fate. A word that sank my heart like a stone in empathy. " . . . awful."

"There are worse things." He shrugged again, this time with just one shoulder, but there was something different about his movements this time. He'd meant for his actions to be taken as noncommittal, but I could see the tension in his body, the haunted, angry look in his eye. Darius was hurting, and I'd have bet that he would never tell anyone why.

When he lifted his eyes to meet mine, I felt a spark of electricity. It was brief, but very, very real. Suddenly I was incredibly aware of his hand on my thigh, of the way he smelled, and the warmth coming off of his skin. Darius's eyes moved slowly downward, lingering on my lips before returning to my gaze. He was so close, I could feel his breath on my cheek.

"I . . ." He began to speak, but paused, as if stopping himself from saying something that he shouldn't. As he spoke again, he removed his hand from my leg, but slowly. Reluctantly. "I should really treat my wound before it gets infected."

He moved across the room and opened a door there, stepping inside. After a moment, I heard water running. I sat there, half naked, waiting somewhat awkwardly, not knowing what to do exactly. The medication that he'd put on my injury smelled pleasant, filling my nose with hints of rose oil and something else. I sniffed it and called to Darius, "So what's this ointment made out of, anyway?"

Darius snickered from the other room. "Trust me. You don't want to know. In fact, you're probably better off not knowing."

I sniffed the cream again and shrugged. Maybe he was right. Maybe I was better off not knowing. "Have you shared this recipe with the Master Healers?"

"You honestly think they'd be open to learning new tricks from an Unskilled?" He sighed quietly, as if punctuating his statement. He had a valid point. For the most part, the Skilled grossly underestimated the intelligence levels of the Unskilled. "You should try to put some weight on that leg, Kaya. Walk around a bit, get the blood pumping. It'll help speed up the healing process."

The very thought of standing up made my knees feel weak and my legs tremble. But Darius seemed pretty confident in his caretaking abilities and medical knowledge, so I wasn't about to argue with him. The faster I could heal, the faster I could walk without limping. Ever so carefully slipping my ruined leggings on up over my legs and easing them over my bandaged wound, I tossed the blanket to the side and braced myself for what I was certain was going to be an immense amount of pain.

Placing weight on my injured leg, I stood, ready to scream. But nothing happened. I took one step, then another. Apart from my muscles feeling a bit stiff, there was no pain at all. Darius was a miracle worker. I tried working the stiffness out by stretching, but it wasn't happening, so I took Darius's advice and began pacing the room. As I passed by the slightly open door that Darius had entered, I hesitated, biting my lip gently, berating myself for even being tempted to peek inside. But the part of my brain that's responsible for the really stupid things that I do on occasion edged me forward, until I was looking at Darius standing in front of his bathroom mirror.

Shirtless.

His silver hair just barely touched the nape of his neck. His broad shoulders came down in a V to his slender waist. His lean chest was completely bare. The man was beautiful. And flawless. My heart rate picked up in a steady rhythm at the sight of him. He was reaching over his left shoulder with his right hand, turning so that he could see the bite on his back a bit better. He was dabbing cream on gently, completely unaware that I'd even approached.

Allowing myself another moment of secret glances, and promising myself that after just a few more seconds, I'd move stiffly back to my place on the bed, I dropped my eyes back to his chest as he relaxed his arm and dabbed his fingertips back into the jar on the counter. And there, on his left pectoral, I saw something that made me suck in my breath in shock. At the sound of my gasp, Darius shot his eyes to my image in the mirror. The kindness, the gentleness that had been in his eyes just a moment before was gone, replaced by absolute fury. His face reddened, his muscles flexed, and he roared, "GET OUT!"

He turned and shoved me through the room toward the door. As he pushed me outside, he tossed the jar of salve with me. It tumbled down the stairs as I was forced to exit. Once I was outside, Darius slammed the door. His anger may have successfully removed me from his quarters, but there was something that it wouldn't change, something that I had seen on Darius's chest, something that had shocked and amazed me into utter silence.

Darius had a Trace.

Which meant that he wasn't an Unskilled at all. He was a Barron. And he'd been lying about it to everyone. But why?

The image of that small red crescent on his golden bronze skin was locked in the forefront of my mind as I leaned my forehead against the cool wood of the door. From the other side, I could hear him breathing. "Darius, I'm sorry."

What I was sorry for, I wasn't certain. For peeking in on him when I shouldn't have, maybe. For discovering his secret, no. But I had to say something. He was upset, and it was all because of me.

The door rattled sharply, and I could only guess that he'd punched it out of frustration. I jumped back, and then narrowed a glare at the door. "Fine. Be that way."

Making my way down the stairs, I moved through the still-dark courtyard to the dorms, marveling that the Graplar corpses and blood had already been cleaned up and cleared away. As I snuck inside and up the stairs, I fumed. It wasn't my fault that he had a secret. It wasn't my fault that he was a Barron. But he was mad at me. Why?

By the time I slipped into bed, my brain was overrun with conflicting thoughts. Half of them focused on the look in Darius's eyes as he screamed at me to leave. The other half couldn't forget the feeling of his breath on my cheek.

fourteen

The ceiling turned from black to pink to gold, but still I stared at it, mulling over anything that had nothing to do with Darius. Filling my thoughts in particular was my botched interaction with the Graplar. My parents had been right all along about their descriptions—the ones that everyone in Kessler had passed on to one another as fairy tales. Graplars were huge, awful, ruthless monsters that could only be stopped by people with amazing strength, cunning, and skill—three things that I didn't possess, but desperately wanted to. My father had taught me how to hold a katana, yes, but he'd never taken the time to teach me the art of wielding the delicate, dangerous weapon. Maybe he thought it was beyond my understanding. Or maybe he thought—hoped, even—that I'd never have use for that kind of knowledge. But he'd likely never imagined that I would end up attending Shadow Academy, or ever be exposed to Graplars at all. I didn't blame him for not taking his lessons further with me, only wished that he had recognized in me my need to learn, and both my desire and my ability to take care of myself. Maybe he thought he was protecting me, in a way. Or maybe he thought he'd given me just enough information to be dangerous. Either way, I wanted to learn more, wanted to be able to face down a Graplar with both the confidence and skill required to take the thing out. But how was I supposed to learn how to fight and kill a Graplar in a school where Healers weren't allowed to train?

The pillow sank under my head as I relaxed back into it with a single name captured at the front of my mind. Maddox. Maddox would train me. She didn't exactly care about all the rules and Protocol and the division between Healers and Barrons. And she had absolutely zero respect for the prim and pampered life of a traditional Healer. Besides, she was my friend. She'd help me. She'd teach me everything I'd need to know about killing Graplars.

Confident in my decision to ask Maddox to train me in secret, against the headmaster's wishes, I closed my eyes and allowed myself to slip into a deep slumber.

A burning sensation woke me hours later and I sat up in bed with a yelp. The colors all around me had blended into a sick stew and I could barely see, but I reached for the jar of salve on my nightstand anyway. Misjudging the distance, I tumbled over the edge. It felt like I fell for hours. The fever had me now. I knew that much. After a moment, a day, a year—I had no idea how long it had been—I heard Maddox's voice in the distance. There were no words, just concerned tones, and I wasn't sure that I could explain to her what had happened to me. After a long time, the darkness found me, and I was grateful for it. I slept. Or maybe I died. But at least the pain had stopped for the moment.

When I awoke, I looked around. Maddox had brought me to the hospital wing. Sighing in relief, I looked down at my bandaged thigh. It burned like hell, but the pain was far more tolerable than it had been. Two jars sat on the silver tray next to my bed. One was full of gray goop. One was full of white cream. I wasn't certain which the Master Healer had been applying to my wound, but my leg was feeling a bit better—though not at all as well as it had in Darius's cabin. I laid there for a long while, thinking about the Graplars that had attacked, and wondering if Maddox would be as open to training me as I hoped.

The afternoon sun was stretching out across my bed. Sitting up, I stretched myself into full wakefulness, only stopping when the door to my hospital room opened and the Master Healer stepped inside. She was carrying a tray with her. On top of it was a clear jar filled with more of the gray goop, as well as a pitcher of water and a roll of fresh bandages. She set the tray on the small table, nudging aside the jar of white salve that looked suspiciously like the one Darius had given me. A quiet sigh of relief escaped my lungs. Explaining just why and how a Barron had concocted a potion for my wound—a Barron who wasn't known to be a Barron, at that—was a bit more conversation than I was prepared to have at the moment.

"You're looking well this morning, Kaya. How are you feeling?" Her voice was pleasant, but her face seemed pinched, almost angry. It was difficult to judge her emotions.

"Much better. My leg still stings, but I think I can stand." I pulled back the covers, revealing my bandaged thigh. After a moment, she nodded happily.

"Wonderful! It's healing much faster than normally. If you can stand, I'd say you could return to classes later today. By the way, how exactly did you get bitten? Were you on patrol or something?"

Chewing the inside of my cheek for a bit, I said, "I can't really talk about it. You understand. Headmaster's orders."

After a moment, she nodded again, as if she understood completely. "Why don't you put some weight on that leg?"

I scooted to the edge of the bed and carefully put weight on my leg. After I stood—my pain moderately manageable and my muscles only a little stiff—I took a few steps toward the door, then turned around and returned to the bed. The Master Healer nodded. "I'll alert your guard to escort you back to the dorms. Take lunch and then report to your third period."

With that, she disappeared out the door, tray in hand, and I was left with a pile of my freshly cleaned clothes. After changing from the hospital gown into my torn leggings and tunic, I picked up the jar of white cream and waited for Maddox. Luckily, she'd spent the night waiting just outside, and within minutes, I was checked out of the care of the hospital's Master Healer, given fresh bandages (along with gray goop that I swore I would never use), and on my way to the dorm. Maddox and I made small talk all the way back, but I knew what was coming once we got inside my room and closed the door. The latch had no sooner clicked than she turned to me. "What the hell happened last night? Did you go outside the wall? Because those things are really dangerous, Kaya. You could have been killed. You're lucky you weren't. But now Trayton's asking all sorts of questions that I don't have answers to, and you better believe there's going to be an inquest with the headmaster after a Healer shows up in the hospital wing with a Graplar bite. This is serious, Kaya. Do you know how much trouble we're in? What happened?"

I waited until she was done rambling before saying anything. I got the feeling Maddox's head would have exploded if she'd gone on any further in her complaints. I said, "I went to talk to Darius and while we were in the courtyard, two Graplars attacked us."

"*Inside* the wall?" After I nodded, she said, "They don't get inside the wall. How did that happen? The wall's huge and heavily guarded. Not to mention several feet thick."

Shrugging, I offered my only thought on the matter. "Maybe they dropped down from the treetops. I don't know."

Maddox folded her arms in front of her, like she was the parent and I was the child—an idea that would have made me laugh if I hadn't spent the night in a bed in the hospital wing. "Okay, first, Graplars can only get about ten feet up a tree, no matter how high it is. And second, they're not smart enough to realize that anything could possibly be on the other side of a wall. Not a single Graplar has ever gotten into Shadow Academy in a hundred years. So that's not possible."

"Look, I don't know what to tell you, Maddox, but two giant, ugly Graplars attacked us in the courtyard last night and one of them bit me. Luckily, Darius knew how to treat the wound, but I guess it got infected after I fell asleep." An image flashed in my mind then—the image of Darius's shirtless, muscular shoulders. Immediate guilt filled me. "Please don't tell Trayton I went to see Darius."

Maddox wrinkled her nose. "Why would it matter? Besides, you went out without me—I have to tell him *something* about why I wasn't there."

Plucking a pillow from my bed, I whapped her in the

shoulder, and raised my voice. "I went out without you because you told me to! And I quote . . . 'I don't know if you noticed when you got here, but the whole school is surrounded by a big fakkin' wall.'!"

Maddox's eyes went wide with guilty realization. Then, her body slumping, she sighed. "Okay. So we won't mention anything about Darius's involvement. But what do we tell the headmaster about the Graplar bite?"

"We tell him a variation of the truth. We were on our way back to the dorm when two Graplars attacked us in the courtyard. You killed them, but not before one bit me, and after you hurried me back to the dorms, Darius found the corpses and reported the attack to the guards at the south gate." Maddox was shaking her head dramatically before I could even finish my sentence, ir- ritating me beyond belief. "*What*, Maddox? You have a better plan?"

Her words burst out of her so loudly, I couldn't help but wonder if anyone lurking in the hall could hear. "That won't work. He'll never believe I killed a Graplar, let alone two!"

"Why *not*?"

"Because I was never trained to fight, Kaya." Her words, though soft, pierced my heart. We were fakked. Absolutely fakked. Shrugging, she continued. "Sure, I supposedly have skills ingrained in my DNA that will help me naturally on the battlefield, but I grew up away from all the fighting and monsters, Kaya. I have no idea what to do with a katana or how to kill a Graplar. Why do you think I'm your guard and not standing out at one of the gates? They can't expect me to be able to handle something like that, and they have every right to stick me in a cushy Healer guard position. I'd just fak things up for everyone out there. Guarding you is . . . well . . . it's easier than fighting."

My heart deflated then, and sank like a stone in a pond. Not only wouldn't our lie work, but it was the least of my problems. Now I was left with no one to train me to fight, to defend myself against a Graplar, should another one or two or twelve happen to find their way through the gate again—or worse, should I face the battlefield at Trayton's side. And without that training, I was as good as dead. Something else—without learning how to stand on my own, the head-master would win, and I just couldn't stomach the idea of it, and couldn't stop picturing his pudgy, smug face shaking his head over my corpse. "Fak."

Maddox seemed to mull it over for a minute, searching for a bright side. "Look, it's not so bad. We'll just tell the headmaster that Darius rescued us. Besides, I'm sure Darius will want all the glory anyway."

"It's not that." Sinking back into my pillows, I sighed, lowering my voice. "I was really hoping you would train me."

Maddox raised an eyebrow at me. "In the art of escorting Healers from class to class?"

"No," I sighed, feeling the dream die before it ever crossed my lips. "In the art of fighting. I want to train, Maddox."

"But Healers aren't allowed to train."

"Which is exactly why I want to do it." I set my jaw, determined. "Why should I be stuck on the sidelines playing damsel-in-distress, when I could be on the battlefield, kicking Graplar butt and taking care of myself?"

I didn't give voice to the other reason—that I needed to protect the villagers that I loved so much, the way I hadn't been able to protect Avery. In fact, I couldn't bring myself to tell Maddox anything about Avery at all. That was another life, one just for me.

A proud smile danced on her lips.

"But without you . . ." the words caught in my throat for a moment. "No one will train me. It's not exactly something I can post on the dining hall board. HEALER SEEKING BARRON TO TRAIN IN THE ART OF COMBAT: MUST BE SKILLED, PUNCTUAL, AND KEEP COMPLETE SECRET FROM THE HEADMASTER. PUNCH AND PIE WILL BE SERVED."

Maddox cracked a smile. "You never mentioned punch and pie."

Groaning, I hit her with my pillow again. "Focus, Maddox. What am I going to do now?"

She grew quiet for a long time, and after a while, she moved to the door, opening it an inch just to make sure that no one was listening in. Satisfied, she closed the door again and looked at me. "I do know someone who might be willing to train you in secret. He's good. Really good. And I know for a fact he gets a bit of a thrill over bending the rules, so it might work. Only . . ."

"Only what?"

"Only you might not want to work with him."

"With who?"

"Darius."

Several foul words raced through my mind. Of course it was Darius. It had to be Darius. It couldn't be any of the rest of the thousand or so Barrons on campus. That would be too easy. Mulling over what I knew of Darius—his attitude, his hatred of me, his strange secret—I sighed, totally uncertain that being trained by Darius was the right choice for me, even though it seemed to be the only option available if I wanted to learn how to defend myself. "Let me think about it."

After changing into leggings without holes, my stomach rumbled loudly and so Maddox escorted me to the dining hall for lunch. Miraculously, I'd only missed two classes due to my late-night outing, but even that tiny blip hadn't been missed on the social radar. All around me as I entered the dining hall, there were whispers and curious glances, and I knew that Maddox was right. There were going to be questions, and we had better have some good answers to offer.

And I had to keep Darius's secret. I didn't know why I wanted to keep his secret, only that it seemed important to do so. It was important enough to him, after all. I wondered if anyone else knew his secret, or if I was the only one. Why would he choose to hide the fact that he was a Barron, anyway? It wasn't like Barrons had a hard life. They were revered in Skilled society, and rewarded at every turn if they followed Protocol to the letter. It was a strange thing to run from, but I was willing to hold my tongue. He had to have his reasons, and it wasn't my place to expose his secret.

We had barely stepped through the doors when Trayton was at my side. "I'm so sorry I haven't been to see you. I was overseeing repairs on the north gate this morning and, for some reason, wasn't alerted to your injuries. But the moment I heard I came running. Are you okay?"

"I'm fine, but you're sweet to ask." I smiled at him, his eyes so full of concern. There was no doubting his anger toward Maddox for failing to watch over me. He wouldn't even look at her, wouldn't acknowledge her in any way. The air around us was full of an unspoken tension. One that made my skin jump.

Maddox disappeared to the food line and once she did, Trayton seemed to relax. He led me to a table in the corner and I took a seat, ready for the question I knew he was going to ask. He met my eyes and kept his tone hushed, wanting this conversation to be a bit more private than it was. "What happened last night, Kaya?

People are saying you were bitten by a Graplar. Are you okay?"

Nodding, I stretched my hand across the table and covered his with mine, hoping to comfort his obvious concern. "I insisted on going for a walk, so Maddox came with me, even though she said it was a bad idea to be out after hours. And on our way back, two Graplars attacked. We only just managed to escape. Luckily, Darius heard the noise from his cottage and took care of them. If he hadn't come along, Maddox and I might not be around this morning."

It was a lie, yes. But a necessary one. I only hoped that Darius would go along with my ruse. Glancing over Trayton's shoulder, I spied Darius's silver hair across the room. He moved to an empty table, tray of food in hand, and sat, not looking at me even once. Not that I'd expected him to. I had, however, expected his demeanor to be a bit different. Maybe somewhat softer, gentler, but I had no real reason to expect that sort of change in him. So he'd shown some semblance of kindness to me once. So he'd had a moment of gentleness in stark contrast to his usual attitude. That was no reason at all for me to expect him to be forever changed. So why did I?

Trayton's eyebrows came together and he turned around, trying to glimpse whatever it was that had me momentarily distracted. I squeezed his hand, bringing his attention back to me, not wanting him to realize that I had been looking at Darius. Not wanting to admit to him or to myself that I had been hoping that Darius would notice me.

My stomach shrank, cramping slightly with nerves. Why was I feeling differently about Darius at all anyway? He was still the same person that had given me grief from the moment I reached academy grounds. He was still the same teacher that had given me extra duties for no discernible reason. A couple of bandages and a softer tone (not to mention an amazingly perfect chest, my memory reminded me) wasn't going to change who he was. Besides, I had no business thinking anything at all about any boy who wasn't Trayton. We were Bound. And that meant dedication. To each other. To the cause against King Darrek. To everything that wasn't about me peeking in on Darius and his lean, shirtless frame.

I focused my eyes on Trayton, taking in his lovely eyes, and the slender lines of his cheeks. He was gorgeous, and so thoughtful and sweet. How could I even think about another guy when the one I had—with the headmaster's blessing, at that—was utterly perfect? Selfish. That's what I was being. And maybe a bit rebellious too. Was I thinking about Darius because the headmaster approved of Trayton and I wanted to thumb my nose at the leader of our school? Maybe. But then I thought of the way that Darius had looked at me in his cabin the night before. There had been an electricity in the room—something I couldn't quite identify or explain. It hung in my thoughts now the way it had hung in the air between us then. I couldn't help but wonder why.

But I had no business thinking about Darius and the spark that I'd swore I felt. Only Trayton was my business now.

Taking my hand squeeze as a show of affection rather than distraction, Trayton relaxed visibly, a small smile appearing on his lips. "I'm sorry I wasn't there to protect you, but I'm glad that Darius was."

I could feel my lips pressing harder together in tension. It wasn't Trayton's fault—he'd been raised in a world where Healers were supposed to be protected by their Barrons. But the fact that he'd implied that I couldn't have taken care of myself sent an angry chill up my spine.

Maddox returned with a full tray of food—enough for me and Trayton and several small armies—and as soon as she sat the tray down, she threw me a questioning glance, as if to ask if everything was okay between Trayton and me. I shook it off, promising her with a look that we'd discuss it later, and reached for a slice of crispy bacon.

"You look well. Better than I thought you would after such a rough night."

Darius's voice stopped the bacon halfway to my open mouth. I froze with panic. Maddox and I hadn't yet had a chance to discuss with him the details of our plan, and here he was, blabbing to me about what had happened the night before. And besides that, he was being nice!

I turned my head to give him a look of what-do-you-think-you're-doing-exactly, but when my eyes found him, he wasn't looking at me at all. He was looking at Trayton. Mentally smacking myself—something that was becoming the norm for me lately—I relaxed in my seat, realizing that Darius was, of course, referring to the repairs at the north gate. Of course he wasn't talking to me. Why would he? I was no one. Just a stupid Healer who'd gotten mixed up with a monster in front of his living quarters.

Trayton pulled his hand back from mine as he spoke, as if it weren't manly to hold a girl's hand when speaking to one's instructor. It didn't bother me. Not really. Okay, not a lot. But some. "At least I got out of it without bruises."

The smirk on his face said that Darius hadn't escaped the task completely unharmed. Not that there was any evidence of that now that I could see. Darius grinned, and I bet that no one but Trayton would be allowed to taunt Darius in this way. Not without Darius taking them to task, anyway. "I imagine it's hard to get bruised when you're busy watching other people doing all the actual work, Barron. Or should I call you Supervisor?"

Trayton's laughter was loud and real. It was obvious that he and Darius enjoyed each other's company. I could tell the two shared more than a few inside jokes, and even though I was sitting directly between them, I couldn't help but feel distinctly apart from the conversation. I wondered if it was because I was a Healer. Or maybe because I was a girl.

"It appears I owe you my deepest gratitude, Darius. Kaya said that you came to her rescue last night." With every word that left Trayton's lips, I sank down another inch in my seat. This was it: the moment where Trayton would discover that I had lied to him, and the moment where Darius would learn that I had entangled him in my lies.

To my immense surprise, Darius didn't miss a beat. He smiled kindly at Trayton and offered a nod. "My pleasure. Still can't figure out how the damn beasts got inside the wall. Any theories?"

His pleasure? He was going along with my ruse, and even being pleasant about it. But why? At the moment, I didn't care why. I only cared that my moment of terror had passed in a single blink.

Trayton shook his head. "Not a clue. The wall's solid. We did a perimeter sweep before coming back inside this morning. Unless they somehow managed to get over the wall."

Darius shook his head too. "We keep the trees cut back enough that even if they could manage the height, they couldn't cross the distance. No way are they coming over the wall."

"Maybe someone let them in through one of the gates." My softly spoken words immediately drew the bemused attention of both Trayton and Darius.

Trayton bit into some buttered toast to hide his smirk, but Darius propped his foot up on the chair next to me and met my eyes. "That would mean a lack of loyalty on the part of forty Barrons at the same exact moment, Kaya. It's not an impossible idea, but extremely unlikely. Forty Barrons—skilled men and women—stand guard every night, watching the north and south gates. Ten stand inside each gate, and ten more guard each gate from outside. These Barrons are our best and brightest, our most skilled. I know. I personally chose them for their duties. If they banded together and decided to let two Graplars inside . . . well, I would be amazed by such blatant betrayal, yes, but also surprised by their immense stupidity."

"Stupidity?"

He nodded. "Why let in just two? When you could let in an entire army, thousands of Graplars, tens of thousands of soldiers? Why just send in two beasts? It makes no sense. Not to me."

It didn't make much sense to me either. But then, not very much did these days. Like the way that Darius was acting.

Maddox piped up, "Darius, can I talk to you for a second?"

With that still-troubled look on his brow, he turned and met with Maddox just feet away, where Maddox whispered feverishly. I didn't have the ability to read lips, but didn't need it. I knew what Maddox was saying. She was asking him if he would train me to fight and defend myself. Darius listened to her and after a moment, patted her roughly on the shoulder. He cast a glance back at our table before exiting the room, and in that moment I'd hoped more than anything that he was up for teaching me everything that he could. I wanted to learn. I needed to learn. Because while it was comforting to know that I was surrounded by a thousand skilled warriors whose job it was to protect Healers like myself, it wasn't enough. I and I alone was responsible for my well-being, and there was no way I wanted to play the weak and helpless Healer the next time Graplars got inside the wall. And after my bumbled attempt and horrible injury this time, I wanted nothing more than to develop my own talents. Just in case.

Trayton's hand, soft and warm, closed over mine, bringing me out of my thoughts and back to the present. When my eyes found his, something strange and startling occurred to me. My life, as of the moment that the Graplars had appeared in the courtyard, had become split. Two worlds coexisting within one life. On one hand, I was Kaya: reluctant student to Instructor Baak, Bound Healer to Trayton. On the other, I was Kaya: the Healer who wanted to fight, the girl who couldn't resist stealing glances at Darius when Trayton wasn't looking. What kind of person did that make me? I felt terribly guilty for letting my eyes linger on Darius whenever he was near—not to mention irritated at myself for doing so. Trayton was tender, caring, thoughtful, and gorgeous, and I was fortunate enough to be Bound to him. He was sweet to me, and I wanted to be sweet to him. We were meant to have a life together, to share a bond that might someday mean children and a home far away from the trials of war. But first, I had to stop looking at Darius in the way that made my imagination dredge up the night I'd seen him shirtless. After all, he was just a boy. And not a particularly nice one at that.

If I wanted to learn how to defend myself, my options were limited. But just because Darius might teach me didn't mean that I was cheating on Trayton. Did it?

My eyes widened hopefully. Trayton! Why hadn't I thought of him?

He smiled and once again, I was taken by how smooth and lovely his lips were. "You look oddly happy for a girl who was very nearly devoured whole last night. Care to clue me in?"

Giving his hand a squeeze, I leaned in close, keeping my voice low. "Would you tell me about katanas?"

Immediately, his eyes darted to Maddox, who didn't seem to be paying us much attention at the moment. He hesitated before answering, and when he spoke at last, I was certain he was going to refuse my request. "I . . . I'm not sure what it is that you're asking me for exactly. I could tell you about them, but any more would be—"

My shoulders sank in hopelessness, cutting off his words. He didn't have to finish speaking. I knew what he'd been about to say. Protocol. It would be against Protocol for a Barron to teach a Healer how to utilize weaponry. "Any more would be giving me at least the basics in how to defend myself. In case you're not around."

We watched one another for a long time, a heavy silence hanging between us.

At last, Trayton sighed, as if he'd been defeated. "Can you meet me in the armory tonight? After dark?"

It was difficult to resist a grin. Why I hadn't thought of just asking Trayton before never occurred to me. He was skilled, talented, well trained, and what's more, he liked me. I could think of no one better to teach me. "I'll be there."

His smile was genuine, but a bit guarded. I wondered if he was worried that we'd be caught. Not that there was anything to catch. Not really. I hadn't asked Trayton to teach me—not yet. I'd only asked him to *tell me* about katanas, which, as far as I knew, wasn't against Protocol or any of the rules that the headmaster was here to enforce. Bending the rules wasn't the same as breaking them, though I intended to do that as well. I'd break their rules to save myself from both the indignity of having to wait for someone else to rescue me and from the danger of not knowing how to stand against a Graplar if no one was around to save me.

Maddox interrupted my thoughts. "Class starts soon, Princess. We should walk."

I started to stand, but Trayton held fast onto my hand, his eyes on mine. "Kaya . . ."

He almost said no. I could see it in his crystalline eyes, the *no* burning there on the edge of his irises. He almost changed his mind about meeting me in the armory and showing me what a katana was and what it could do. But he didn't. He just spoke my name, his tone full of doubt and fear and wonder that maybe what he was about to do wasn't exactly the right thing, that maybe he was too close to breaking Protocol—something that meant a great deal to him. Trayton, after all, wasn't just a rule follower. He was a rule enforcer. An admirable trait, for certain, but one that I desperately hoped he could set aside for just one night. And then maybe just one more.

I met his gaze, but said nothing, hoping that Trayton wouldn't utter so much as a whisper of his doubts. To my amazement, he didn't. Instead, he squeezed my hand as he raised it to his lips, then brushed a feather-light kiss against my skin.

But it was more than a kiss. It was more than the first time that Trayton's lips had pressed against my skin, no matter how lightly. It was a promise. He would show me how to wield a katana. He would explain the parts of the weapon to me. He would bend this rule for tonight, and that was all I could hope for.

Squeezing his hand, I released my light grip and so

did he. Then I stood, following Maddox out the door. She had a distant look in her eye, one that made me wonder exactly what she'd been talking to Darius about. "What's going on, Maddox? You seem distracted."

Maddox nodded, steering me toward the building that was home to Mr. Ross's classroom. "I started to ask Darius if he'd train you, but he interrupted me to give me some bad news. Apparently, several Elder Barrons have decided that many guards would do better on the battlefield rather than guarding Healers inside the confines of schools, despite the fact that they lack Bound or Soulbound Healers. So they're making a list of guards who will be moving to the front. No one knows yet. Darius was seriously going out of his way to warn me."

My hand found my mouth in shock and my feet came to a sudden halt. "You're going to war? But Maddox, you aren't trained! And you have no Healer!"

As if I were telling her anything she didn't know already.

Foregoing her usual snark, and playing it off with casual indifference—which I could tell was just barely covering her panic in a thin glaze—she said, "Darius said if he can keep my name off that list, he will. I trust him. I'm just . . . concerned."

I was concerned too. Fak that, I was worried. The very idea of Maddox facing down Graplars and soldiers and some horrible, seemingly invincible king seriously frightened me. I liked Maddox. She was probably the best friend I had ever had. Which was weird, considering how obnoxious she could be.

Resisting the urge to hug her—something told me that Maddox, no matter how much she was hurting, wouldn't exactly be very receptive to anything vaguely sensitive—I started walking with her again, and tried to find the right words, words that might lessen her stress level some. "Why don't we ask him to train both of us?"

Maddox sighed. "And give them more reason to send me outside the wall? No, thank you. I'm clinging to my Healer duties as long as I can."

And that's when it hit me. Not only was Maddox afraid to die. She was afraid to fight at all, afraid to train, for whatever reason. Making the decision not to push the issue any further, I said, "It'll be okay, Maddox. If you trust Darius, I trust Darius."

Apparently, I'd chosen well, because she smiled at me through the shadows of her troubled expression. Once we made it to Mr. Ross's room, I dared a change of subject. "I was thinking of asking Trayton to train me. You know. Instead of Darius."

She cast me a sidelong glance that said that that was a pretty terrible idea, but apparently she wasn't in the mood to berate me for choosing poorly, because she said, "Trayton is Darius's best student. But . . . why not just learn from the best?"

I shrugged in response, resisting the urge to say so much more. I couldn't tell Maddox about the way my stomach jumped whenever I pictured Darius shirtless. Hell, I hadn't even told her I'd seen him shirtless. And there's was no way I could find the words to say what it had felt like, what it had meant to me when Darius had let his guard down and shown me just a brief glimpse, a tender moment of fragility. Because the truth was, it had meant more to me than I would dare give voice to. I couldn't admit those things to myself, let alone Maddox.

But at least one thing was settled: tonight, after boring Healer classes and my usual extra duties in the rose garden (this time thanks to my outpouring of laughter when Instructor Baak referred to Healers as nature's way of blessing Barrons with long life), I was going to spend some time with Trayton, learning about katanas, and maybe, if I was lucky, forgetting about the look in Darius's eyes when he'd spoken of his loneliness.

*O*nce the last rosebushes had been mulched, I hurried back to the dorms with Maddox, made myself presentable, and headed to the dining hall to grab some dinner before they closed down for the evening. I hadn't seen Trayton since this morning at breakfast and was hoping to see him at dinner, but when my eyes swept the hall, all I found was disappointment.

Maddox filled a tray with food, and I took my now usual seat at the corner table. To my surprise, I had company. Company that I'd not been expecting.

Melanie forced a smile. "Well, well, if it's not the walking bandage. I heard your encounter with a Graplar went as expected, ending with you cowering in a corner."

My defenses went up in a flash, and I opened my mouth to tell her just what had happened—that not only had there been two Graplars, but that I'd not only assisted in taking them out, I'd also beheaded one entirely on my own. Even with my bumbling, that was an impressive feat. But then I remembered the story that we'd told everyone, and closed my mouth again. But only for a second. "What do you want, Melanie?"

Her smile struck me as somewhat sadistic and absolutely surreptitious. She crossed her long legs and I could sense several pairs of eyes falling on them all around me. There was no doubting Melanie was beautiful. But skin could only get you so far. "I came to ask a favor of you."

Everything inside of me, every cell of my being screamed "NO!" before I parted my lips to speak, but curiosity got the best of me. "A favor? What favor?"

She seemed to gauge me for a moment before speaking. "There are changes coming to Shadow Academy. To all the schools, really. And I want your assistance to make those changes a bit easier on my Healer. You do want to help a fellow Healer, right?"

"Why should I make things easier on your Healer, and exactly what are you talking about?" Maddox had mentioned certain changes that had apparently been set in motion, but was that what Melanie talking about? Putting guards on the battlefield would hardly affect her Healer. Or were the changes she was talking about something completely separate from that?

"I'd like you to tell the headmaster that you've made a terrible mistake and that you believe that my Healer,

David, would make a far better Healer to Trayton than you. Then I'd like you to request to be my Healer."

It only took me a second to hear what she'd said, and a second more for my laughter to come pouring out of me. Melanie? My Barron? I didn't think so. "Why on Tril would you think I'd be even remotely interested in the idea of switching, especially considering that no Bound Healer and Barron have ever switched before?"

"That's not true. Two have switched throughout history, though it's nothing that the Elder Barrons will discuss. Mistakes are made on occasion. And with the right assurance and insistence, it can be done. As for why . . . well, let's just say that a little bird witnessed a certain Healer limping into a certain teacher's quarters the other night. And how would that look to the headmaster?"

My heart froze solid. I didn't know what to say, what to do, to deter Melanie from her path of thinking. The truth was that seeing me waltz into Darius's cabin, limping and bleeding or not, wouldn't look harmless at all to any of the authoritative figures on campus. Darius could be fired, or worse. And whatever punishment they doled out for me couldn't possibly compare to the threat that the headmaster had given me when I'd first learned of his existence: my parents could be made to suffer for my insubordination. Would they be killed because I'd entered a teacher's quarters unchaperoned? Maybe. I doubted it, but not enough to laugh off Melanie's threat. "Who told you that?"

"David did. He was on his way back to the dorms and saw you limping up the steps to Darius's quarters. Curious, isn't it, that you'd choose a teacher's bedroom over the hospital wing."

"It's not what it looked like." It wasn't, but I knew that even if Melanie believed me, she wouldn't admit it. Not when she thought she could get something out of it. Regarding her smirk, I said, "Besides, you can't prove it."

Her smile turned sinister and dark. "I don't need to prove it. I just need to whisper it in Trayton's ear."

For a moment, my heart stopped. Would Trayton really believe her over me? Maybe. The very notion that she would tell him about where I'd been that night was enough to raise the alarms inside of me, at any rate. "Why would you want me as your Healer?"

"I don't. But I do want David as Trayton's Healer. We have an . . . understanding, shall we say."

And that's when the pieces clicked neatly into place. With David as Trayton's Healer, it would still be a challenge to get Trayton to break the rules of no Barrons coupling, but with me as Trayton's Healer, it would be impossible. All this because she wanted my Barron to be her boyfriend, despite the fact that Trayton would never agree to go against Protocol like that. Melanie would destroy lives to acquire anything that she couldn't rightfully have. She was completely delusional. I shook my head. "The headmaster will never agree to it."

"See to it that he does. Or I'll tell Trayton what David saw . . . with a few added details of my imagination, of course." She winked at me and left the table. My stomach turned over, sour and full of tension. By the time Maddox returned with a tray full of food, I wasn't the least bit hungry anymore.

I debriefed Maddox over some spicy chicken and a salad, and as I spoke, she looked more and more furious with every word that crossed my lips. By the time I'd caught her up on all things Melanie, I thought her head was going to explode.

"That girl is insane! You aren't actually considering it, are you?"

Flashing Maddox my best what-are-you-stupid look, I said, "Of course not. But what am I going to do? It's not like it sounds innocent, even without Melanie's imaginary details about what happened."

After I was finished eating, Maddox dropped off my tray and started walking me back to the dorms for the night. As we moved out the door, she said, "What *did* happen, anyway? You've been kinda quiet about the details. I mean, I'm not saying that any of it is my business, but . . . what happened that night between you and Darius? Because it's clear that something did."

Stopping just outside my door, I considered exactly how much to tell Maddox. It wasn't that I didn't trust her. It was that I wasn't exactly comfortable revealing what had transpired that night. I turned to Maddox.

"Darius saved my life. We talked—just talked—and I learned something about him. Something I'll never tell anyone else. So this is the last time I'll speak of it. He helped me, Maddox, and I owe him my silence for that."

She eyed me for a bit, and I could tell that she was itching to know what secret I was keeping. But to her credit, she didn't ask. She merely shrugged. "Good enough for me. Now what are we going to do about Melanie?"

Biting my bottom lip, I shook my head. I had no idea what to do and was completely out of options. One way or another, Melanie was going to get her way. Unless I thought of something fast. But nothing came to mind.

A light filled Maddox's eyes and my heart lifted for a moment. "Of course there's the obvious. You could always tell Trayton yourself. That would take the wind out of her sails."

My heart's upward journey didn't last. I couldn't tell Trayton. He'd be furious. I looked at Maddox and was about to give voice to my doubts, but she shoved me inside the suite and whispered, "Better he hears the truth from you rather than lies from someone else."

As I walked into my bedroom and caught a glimpse of the fresh roses that Trayton had sent over that morning, I knew that Maddox was right. I had to tell Trayton what had happened the night I was bitten. But I didn't have to tell him everything.

After a long, hot bath and a lot of silent personal

debate, I dressed in a fresh uniform. Maddox knocked on my door and we headed out to the armory. We were barely out the door when she grabbed me by the sleeve. "Listen. If I disappear for a while, just carry on like I'm right there, okay?"

I shot her a questioning glance. "Why? Where will you be?"

"I'm going to talk to Darius, see if he's heard anything more about the rule change." She looked at me as she opened the door to the outside and winced, as if expecting me to smack her—which I was totally debating doing as she spoke her next words. "And ask him if he'll train you."

A sigh escaped me. "Maddox, I told you, I'm going to ask Trayton to train me."

The look in her eye said that she already knew what Trayton's response would be. But even so, I was still asking him. Trayton liked me, and I had an idea that Maddox didn't know how much. But I did. Every time Trayton looked at me, I could feel how much he liked me, how much I liked him. Every time he touched me, no matter how brief or casual, an electric charge passed between us. Trayton cared about me. Of course he would want to help me.

She shook her head as we crossed the cobblestone of the courtyard. "Don't ask him, Kaya. If you ask him to teach you how to fight, he'll go to the headmaster. It's Protocol whenever someone tries to engage in rule breaking. Let alone conspiracy. Trayton will inform the headmaster and you'll be punished, maybe even assigned a new Guard. I'm telling you—it's a bad idea."

"He wouldn't do that." Even as I spoke the words, I didn't know them to be true. What Maddox was saying was very possible. After all, there was a reason that the headmaster viewed Trayton as his golden boy. But as much as the idea frightened me, angered me, I had to take my chances, and trust that Trayton would keep my confidence. "I'm asking him, Maddox. If I don't ask him, I'm saying that I don't trust him. And I do."

"I'm still asking Darius." She glanced my way. "Just in case."

I followed Maddox across the cobblestone of the courtyard toward Darius's cottage. Just as I was about to ask where the armory was—it hadn't been part of my initial tour of the campus or my wanderings up until now—she led me around to the back of the building and gestured to a plank wood door with large rusted metal hinges. Balling up her fist, Maddox pounded on the wood twice, eliciting Trayton's response from inside. "Enter and be known."

Maddox wordlessly tugged open the door and gestured for me to go inside. Everything about her posture, the look on her face, everything, said that she was absolutely convinced that I was making a huge mistake. I was only hoping she was wrong.

The room beyond the well-worn door had a dirt floor

and walls made of the same plank wood as the door, lined with several hundred wooden-peg racks, which were completely filled with hundreds of sheathed katana swords. At the far end of the room, sitting perched atop a wooden stool, oiling a blade, was Trayton. He looked up as we entered, and though I thought I spied some of that uncertainty from earlier in his gaze, his smile blossomed and erased all signs of doubt. "I was just preparing this for storage. You're timing couldn't be better."

He flicked his eyes to Maddox, and it seemed a question was poised on his tongue, but Maddox beat him to the punch. "Remember when I said you'd owe me for that little alone time stunt at the library, Trayton? Well, you're about to pay up. I need you to keep an eye on Kaya for me for a while. I have an errand to run, and she can't come with me."

Trayton looked surprised, but nodded happily. "Of course."

Maddox paused at the door, as if doubt were creeping its way into her thoughts. She was about to leave my Barron and me completely alone together. Was she making the right decision? It was like I could read her thoughts scribbled out across her forehead.

Her wordless pause proved fruitless, and Maddox moved back out the door, closing it behind her. Trayton and I were left to fend for ourselves. Alone.

"So . . . why do you want to learn about katanas?" His

voice was hushed, almost gruff sounding in the small room.

The oil lamps around the room cast a low, warm light, giving an even more intimate feeling to the moment, and I stepped closer, my eyes on the sword in his hand, yes, but more on his hands themselves. His skin was smooth, tan, and supple, and though I knew why I was here—to convince him to teach me how to fight—all I wanted to do at the moment was run my fingertips along the back of his hand. Resisting the urge, just for the moment, I said, "I'm curious. There's no crime in that, right?"

The corner of his mouth lifted in a smile. "No. No harm at all."

Slipping the blade into the leather sheath, he stood and held the katana out in front of him, chest height, between us. "Your parents are Barrons, so I won't bore you with the details of sword care. I'm betting you know about oiling a blade and storing them properly. But what else did they teach you, I wonder?"

Shrugging, my eyes fell to the katana, an anxious feeling fluttering in my chest. It was an invitation, although a subtle one. Maybe asking Trayton to train me would be the smartest decision I could make. Maybe Maddox was wrong. "Surprisingly little. I can oil a blade, even hold a katana correctly, but I was never taught the specifics. I never learned the parts of a katana, and certainly never learned how to wield a blade in proper battle form. My father sparred with me, but I think it was more to amuse himself than to teach me how to fight."

For a moment, I thought that maybe hearing this would change Trayton's mind completely about our evening together, but instead, he breathed his next words, and hearing his tone sent a hot shiver through my core. "Then let's start with the basics, shall we?"

"The sheath that a katana is stored in is referred to as a saya. It serves two purposes. One, to protect the blade from damage. And two, to protect the flesh from injury. The blade . . ." He withdrew the sword from its sheath again, slowly. The metal gleamed in the low light. As he continued his description, his voice quieted, as if in respect for the weapon in his hands. ". . . is incredibly sharp. The metal is forged from the black sands of Kaito, where it's believed that Graplars originate from. Because of that, this metal can slice through the beasts with ease—both soft tissue and bone—unlike any other metal on Tril. A katana created at Starlight Academy can easily be deadly to anyone, including the one who wields it, so it must be treated with immense respect."

Going back and forth through my mind about the most delicate way possible to ask him to hand me the sword, I met his eyes. "May I?"

It took him a moment to answer, but when he did, he smiled slightly. "Please."

I wrapped my fingers around the handle, taking the katana from him. It felt surprisingly light in my grip.

"Your hands are too close to one another." He moved behind me, sliding my hands into the proper position. His breath was hot on my neck, and I was acutely aware of how close he was standing to me. "Your dominant hand should be placed directly under the guard, while your other hand should be placed low on the pommel. Grip it, but don't squeeze it. The weapon should act as an extension of you, part of you."

It was hard to focus on why I had come here, and not focus on Trayton's nearness. His arms were still around me, his hands over mine. Ever so slowly, he slid his hands back, giving me full control over the weapon.

Ready to seize my opportunity, I said, "How do I attack properly?"

"The katana is a slicing weapon, not a stabbing weapon. If you were moving to attack, you'd place your feet shoulder-width apart . . ." Gently, he nudged my feet apart with his. His lips brushed my ear softly, his words but a whisper. ". . . twist your wrists slightly . . ."

His hands returned to mine, guiding them in a slow slash. Goose bumps had risen on my skin, and the sensation of his breath wasn't helping to settle them any. ". . . and follow through, snapping at the end."

We brought the blade down together, and I marveled at the way the steps molded into one fluid act. Of course I'd seen it in action, but even sparring with my father hadn't shown me the intricate details that went into a simple cut. "It's like a dance."

"Yes. That's exactly what it's like." He took the katana from me and I turned slowly to face him, so close that we were almost touching, and I was very nearly enveloped by him.

He moved in and I knew that he was about to kiss me. But I couldn't let him. Not yet. Not before I'd done what I'd come here to do. Placing my hand on his chest—I could feel his heart racing within—I stopped him and said, "Will you train me to fight, Trayton?"

A hard line formed on his brow. It was indicative of betrayal, and anger. Hastily, he stepped back, sheathing the sword once again. "Kaya, you know I can't train you. No one can. It's against Protocol."

"Fak Protocol!" I threw my arms up in frustration. I hated that word and it haunted my every move. "I have a right to defend myself, Trayton. How can you expect me to stand on the sidelines and wait for someone to rescue me?"

His eyes snapped to mine. "Don't you trust me to save you? That's my job, Kaya, my duty. And one I hold as the highest importance. How can you go against eons of tradition without even giving a thought to the honor of your position as a Healer?"

My heart sank. That was it, then. Maddox was right. I shouldn't have asked him to train me. What was I thinking? Had Trayton given any indication at all that he was a rule bender? No. But stubborn stupidity had pushed me forward, and now he was going to report my request to the headmaster. Who knew what that would mean for my parents' well-being?

He shook his head, placing the katana on one of the racks on the wall. There were hundreds of swords. So many I couldn't have counted them all in the time it would take Trayton to shove me out the door. "I knew showing you anything about katanas was a bad idea. You're too curious, Kaya. That's dangerous."

A dark cloud settled over my mood. If my curiosity, if my burning need for knowledge was dangerous, then what did that make me exactly? Before he had the chance to label me any further, I turned on my heel and headed straight for the door.

"Where are you going?"

"To find Maddox." I gripped the door handle and was about to pull it open, when Trayton's hand pushed the door closed again.

When I looked at him, his eyes were a mixture of emotions. On one hand, he seemed intensely upset with me. On the other, he looked concerned. Against my will, my eyes dropped until they were focusing on his smooth, slender lips. By the time they found his eyes again, he'd stepped back and gestured to the door, tearing his gaze away from me.

Yanking open the door, I stepped out into the night and let the wood slam behind me. At first, Maddox was nowhere to be found, but then she came walking around the corner of the building, a pleased smile on her face. As she spoke, the corner of her mouth lifted in a smirk. "Good news, Princess. Wait, why do you look so flushed?"

Turning east, I led the way around the building and back toward the dorms. "Trust me. It's not because of the reasons you're thinking. We didn't even kiss. I'm mad at him."

"He said no to training you, eh? Told ya so." She hurried to catch up, careful to keep her voice low. Even so, it felt like sound carried exceptionally well at night. I kept a watchful eye out for anyone who might be listening, but saw no one. "Trayton's not exactly a rebel, Kaya. I mean, come on, the guy actually respects the headmaster. What did you expect?"

"Not now, Maddox." The last thing I needed to be reminded of was my failure at recognizing the obvious. "So what's the good news, anyway?"

"You have a teacher. Training begins tomorrow morning. Before the dew falls."

Minor relief flooded me. At least I had a teacher now. If Trayton didn't follow Protocol and report me, that is. I raised an eyebrow as we crossed the cobblestone. "Why so early?"

Shrugging, Maddox said, "Darius doesn't want to take any chances of being found out. We'll meet him here, you'll suit up, and he'll take you outside the wall to a small training area that no one uses anymore."

My steps slowed. Mostly due to lingering fear of what

lurked outside that wall. "*Outside* the wall? What about Graplars?"

"I don't know. Graplars are pretty much nocturnal, so you shouldn't have much to worry about." We neared the building and she opened the door, ushering me inside. It must have been getting dangerously close to curfew.

"But isn't it still dark before the dew falls?" My voice squeaked slightly.

But my guard didn't stick around to hear it. She was already halfway up the stairs, on her way to my room.

"Maddox?" I whispered harshly, demanding an answer—an answer she was refusing to give. "Maddox, isn't it still dark that early?"

She opened my door, shaking her head and rolling her eyes, like I was complaining about the most minute details. "Don't worry so much. You'll have Darius with you. You'll be fine. Probably."

I could have strangled her. "Probably?"

The sound of footfalls on the stairs behind me filled my ears, and I turned my head toward them. Trayton, barely breathing heavy at all, shot a look at Maddox, who was standing half inside my room, half in the hall. "A moment, please."

Rolling her eyes again, Maddox disappeared inside, leaving us alone in the hall. What did he want with me? To tell me he was reporting my actions? To remind me that I was just a lowly Healer? To tell me that he wished that he'd been Bound to anyone but me, maybe someone who respected the rules the way that he did? I didn't want to hear it.

His words came soft and caring—not at all what I'd expected. "I only said no because I care deeply about you, Kaya. I just want you to be safe and protected at all costs. I want to protect you, and if you start protecting yourself, what does that mean for me?"

"It means that you trust me to take care of myself."

"That's not all it means. It means that I have no purpose in your life." His eyes, so dark, shimmered. He was hurting, torn between what he'd been taught was right and his Healer's request. He wanted no more than to please me, but couldn't do that without breaking the rules that he so desperately needed to uphold.

I shook my head, sorry that he was torn. But not at all sorry for wanting to develop fighting skills. "Trayton, you'll always have purpose in my life."

"If we lived in another time, in another place, for what it's worth, I would teach you everything that I know about how to survive." His shoulders slumped in defeat. "But we don't. We're bound to certain rules, like them or not. And without rules, our society would crumble."

"I understand, Trayton. I do. But don't you ever question whether the Zettai Council actually knows what they're talking about when they devise these rules? How do they know better than you or me? Who put them in charge of every little detail? Will we ever get the chance to govern our own lives?" With a heavy heart, I turned to my door, more than ready to call it a night.

Gently, but firmly, Trayton grabbed me by the arm and pulled me back to him. "Can you forgive me for not indulging you?"

I shook my head. "There's nothing to forgive."

Then he leaned in and kissed me, his lips so soft and tender, his fingers trembling on my arm. I surrendered to the sweetness of his kiss, allowing myself a moment to just be a girl, and my heart soared.

Sixteen

f you'll turn to page fifty-one in your Protocol handbook, you'll see some examples of what we've been discussing today in class." By "discussing," of course, Mr. Groff was referring to the things he'd been barking at us that were generally accepted as social norms. Like the fact that when Barrons were socializing in a group, it was expected that their Healers would not join the group unless all Barrons were in agreement that it was an appropriate moment for their interaction. My head was starting to throb due to the subject matter. He stood at the front of the class, his muscles tensed, as if he were on high alert. I'd realized three classes ago that this was simply his way of standing, his way of being. The idea exhausted me completely.

Flipping through the handbook, I came upon a list of certain social cues that Healers were supposed to be aware of. I shook my head in aggravation, and when

Trayton raised a questioning eyebrow in my direction, I threw my hands up some, hoping he would understand just why I was so annoyed. But Trayton wasn't the only one to notice my irritation. Mr. Groff snapped his head in my direction. "Kaya, do you have a problem with today's lesson?"

What amazed me, what truly surprised me, was that it seemed as though no one but me had a problem with what was being taught. I glanced around the class, looking for support, but found none, just a few uncomfortable wriggles. When I turned my head back to Mr. Groff, I inhaled slowly in an attempt to stay calm. "I have an enormous problem sharing the viewpoint that Healers are subservient to Barrons, yes. We're people, after all, not cattle."

Silence followed my words, but it wasn't the usual silence of a classroom. It was heavy, and far more oppressive. I was convinced that Mr. Groff was at most going to rip my eyes out of my skull, and at least was going to give me extra duties for the rest of my life. I didn't regret sharing my views, but I knew that I'd pay for doing so. Whatever. It was worth it. After all, if you can't be true to yourself, what else have you got? So I sat back in my chair, watching him, waiting for his head to implode.

Only it didn't.

He looked me over, his stern gaze piercing my calm facade, and when he spoke, it was with a strange sense of appreciation. "Perhaps you don't yet fully appreciate the delicate function of Protocol. But I suspect you soon will. Now . . . if you will all turn to page fifty-six, we can continue today's lesson."

As students all around me flipped pages at our teacher's command, I felt my irritation give way to anger. "Actually, Mr. Groff, I do appreciate the history and reasons for Protocol. I just don't understand the need for current application."

Mr. Groff breathed in deeply through his nose, causing his nostrils to flare. "Over time, society has developed a need for order. Protocol helps us to maintain that order."

He turned away from me then, as if dismissing my next words, but I insisted on being heard. I raised my voice, just a little, just enough to make certain they'd reach his ears effectively. "I think people are capable of maintaining order without a strict set of rules. I think you underestimate them."

Turning back, he smirked at my challenge. "Then clearly you've not seen what happens when rules don't exist to support people. Chaos. Complete and total chaos."

I leaned forward, resting my elbows on the table in front of me, the one that Trayton and I shared. "And exactly how much chaos have you witnessed from here in your cozy classroom?"

Trayton tensed beside me. The rest of the class drew a collective gasp, as if I'd bounded into forbidden territory, which is precisely where I wanted to be.

Slowly, Mr. Groff approached my table and leaned on it with his palms. He leaned close to me, so close that I could count the pores on the tip of his nose, and growled, "You will find your loyalty to this cause, Miss Oshiro, if I have to beat it into your skull."

I bit back, "Loyalty to any cause doesn't have to be forced on people, *Mister* Groff."

The left corner of his lip twitched slightly. His eyes narrowed into slants. "You will report to the rose gardens for extra duties after class."

I leaned forward, until we were almost nose to nose, and I kept my voice low enough that my next words were for him and him alone, though Trayton was close enough that I knew that he could hear every syllable. "I'll be happy to. And every time I remove a prick from my skin, I'll think of you."

Mr. Groff's face turned bright red, his words bellowing out of him as he pointed at the door. "Get out of my classroom, you insignificant Healer!"

Pushing back my chair, I stood and walked out of the room, letting the door slam behind me. I felt right. I felt justified. And as far as I was concerned, that moment was worth a hundred hours of extra duties, a million thorns, a thousand scrapes. Some pains were worth it.

CHAPTER

Seventeen

The sun hadn't even thought about stirring before Maddox was knocking quietly on my door the next morning—or what could technically be referred to as morning, anyway. Shoving my head under the fluff of my down pillow, I willed her to go away, but it didn't seem to be working. She yanked the pillow away, tossing it on the floor, and reached for my covers with a threatening tone. "Get up and get dressed, or Darius will be training you in your underwear."

That got my attention. Mostly because it confused me. I was wearing my sleeping clothes, so just what exactly did Maddox plan to do to get me out of bed, strip me down and shove me out the door? Knowing Maddox, it wasn't out of the realm of possibilities. As I begrudgingly sat up in bed, I muttered, "Fine. I'm up."

She tossed a wad of clothing at me and grumped, "Don't forget. You asked for this."

After a very quick, very cold bath, I hurried into my clothes, and Maddox led me out the door and across the courtyard. I thought about Trayton the entire way. How his lips had felt against mine, but more so, how much it hurt that he'd refused to arm me with the knowledge that I'd need to defend myself in a war that I hadn't even volunteered for. Comforting myself as well as I could with the knowledge that I'd have that training despite Trayton's reluctance to break a few rules, I followed Maddox around the cottage once again to the shabby wooden door. She knocked, just as she had last night. Only this time, there came no answer.

Not in the form of words anyway.

Darius opened the door, his eyes falling on Maddox, then me. At first, the look in his eyes was one of surprise, but it quickly grew into irritation. He closed the door again, but had apparently underestimated Maddox's reflexes. She shoved her foot in the door, stopping it from closing all the way. "Come on, Darius. You promised."

"I never promised this."

"You promised me you'd train a Healer how to fight. Does it really matter that much that it's Kaya?"

As if her insinuation had to be immediately refuted, he yanked the door open again and met my gaze. "Maddox will bring you here every morning at four. Don't be late. If you're not here by four, I won't train you anymore."

I shook my head, all business now. There was nothing I was willing to do to fak this up. Darius was my last chance at learning how to take down a Graplar. My only chance. "That's not a problem. Anything else?"

His eyes oozed a stern coldness that chilled me to the bone. There was no arguing with Darius. I immediately felt a bit sorry for the students he taught. "You will obey my every order, without question. Training will be difficult, painful, and at times, agonizing, but you will not quit until you are worthy of being called a warrior. If you can't agree to these terms, then walk away now, because once we start training, I won't let you quit."

Straightening my shoulders, refusing to show him any weakness, I said, "I'm ready for whatever you can throw at me."

"No, you're not." He flicked an unforgiving glance at my guard. "Maddox, stay here. Out of sight. We'll be back at dawn."

Darius was wearing a katana on his back, but he picked up one more, along with a bag, and thrust them into my arms. His voice was a monotone growl, not revealing so much as a hint as to what he was feeling. "You play, you pay. Carry your own equipment."

I didn't have time to speak before he turned around and moved out the door, didn't have time to assure him that I had planned on carrying my own equipment and that I was fully capable of handling myself. He was there one moment and gone the next. Throwing a glance at Maddox, I hurried out the door after him before he could leave me behind for good. Something told me that if Darius could find a reason not to train me, he'd use it and damn my need to learn. He had been excited about the idea of training a Healer, about teaching a Healer to fight against the rules of the academy. Until he discovered that I was that Healer, it seemed. I caught up with him about twenty yards from the cabin, moving along the wall at a steady pace for a Barron, a fast pace for me. As we approached the south gate, his steps slowed. He whispered to me without looking at me or even turning his head my way. "Put your face mask on. Don't speak. Don't move. Wait here."

I did as I was told, slipping my mask on and freezing myself to the spot. As Darius moved closer to the gate, the quiet darkness enveloped him. Moments later, a hand was on my biceps. I jumped, a yelp readying itself inside my throat, but then Darius whispered again. "Come with me. The gate will only be unattended for about a minute. We have to hurry if we want to avoid being caught."

I nodded and Darius led me to the gate, opening it just wide enough for us to slip outside. Keeping my eyes on the wall, I watched for the on-duty gate guards, but saw none, and instantly wondered how Darius had pulled off this magical feat. It wasn't like Barrons to abandon their post. Not without a damn good reason, anyway.

We walked down the hill for some time, and then Darius turned and led us east. He seemed to relax once we were out of sight of the academy wall, and honestly, I did too. There was something unnerving about that enormous, ominous wall. Not to mention the fact that ten skilled Barrons should have been posted outside the south gate, and that who knows how many more Barrons would be doing perimeter sweeps on a regular basis. The farther we got away from the school, away from that wall, the better, and it was clear that we shared that belief, at least.

Darius came to a stop in a small clearing. The forest floor had been emptied of all rocks, twigs, and undergrowth, and the ground looked unnaturally smooth. I didn't speak, didn't comment on my observations. I got the feeling that Darius wouldn't appreciate my deciding when it was a good time to betray his order of silence. If I was going to do this—and I was determined that I was—I was going to do it right. And if that meant adhering to Darius's orders without comment, doubt, or question, then so be it.

After a moment spent surveying the area, Darius said, "I cleaned it up last night. Took a lot less work than I figured it would. It amazed me that an old training area would still be in such good shape."

I nodded as if I had any idea at all what he was talking about. But in my mind, I was thinking about something completely different. "How old are you?"

"Seventeen." At my surprised eyebrow raise, he smirked. "What? You expected me to be older?"

I shrugged. "Well . . . yeah. You're an instructor, after all."

It was his turn to shrug. "Let's just say I was a fast study."

I looked around the clearing with a frown. It just seemed so . . . exposed. "Why don't Barrons train here anymore?"

"Several years ago, the Graplars in this part of Kokoro became pretty unbearable. So they had to move everything inside. It's not safe out here. Especially for new troops."

Casting a nervous glance around, always on the lookout for free-roaming Graplars, I said, "Can I ask why exactly you've decided to train me here?"

"No one will see us here. No one will ask questions. It'll be just you, me, and the blades." He straightened his shoulders, stretching slightly, and inhaled deeply through the nose. It was easy to see how much he enjoyed being free of the academy's walls. On that, we could definitely relate. "I'll have to work on a more efficient way of getting you outside the wall every morning. Telling Raden to gather the south gate guards to warn them about a potential weakness in the wall's western side won't work twice."

Tilting my head, I cast a nervous glance up the hill. I couldn't see the wall from here, but the idea that it might have defense issues sent a nervous chill up my spine. "There's a weakness in the wall?"

"Of course not, but I had to tell them something. They wouldn't have let you outside the gate without permission from the headmaster. Not even if you're with me. Besides, even if they did, there would be questions. Questions on where I was taking a student Healer and why. It's too complicated." As if answering a question that he'd silently asked himself, he said, "The training mask might work to hide your identity. If they don't speak to you. But we'll need a good story. I'll work on it."

"This . . ." He slipped a katana from its sheath on his back—the metal singing in the quiet woods—and held it out in front of him. ". . . is a katana, the pre-ferred weapon of Barrons everywhere. It's lightweight, easy to maneuver with a bit of finesse, and if used correctly, deadly. I'm not going to teach you how to swing a sword. I'm not going to teach you how to utilize a blade. I'm going to teach you how to kill. To survive, you must be fast. You must be vigilant. And above all, you must be scared."

I hadn't expected him to say that. What I'd expected was for him to talk about honor and bravery, not fear. Flashing him a questioning look, I parted my lips to speak, but he answered before I could.

"Bravery gets you into trouble. Bravery leads you into battle. But if you really want to survive that battle, you must first know what it is to fear death."

The way that Darius was speaking to me, the way that he was teaching me, was completely different than how Trayton had approached the subject of weaponry. Whereas Trayton had been gentle and informative, Darius was straightforward and didn't shy away from the uglier aspects of fighting. I appreciated both approaches, for very different reasons. With my eyes on the katana, I said, "My parents are both Barrons. My father showed me a bit when I was younger. We used to spar."

"That is playacting. A father would never put his daughter in true danger. By the end of your training, I will be coming for your life. It's the only way you'll learn to truly defend yourself against an enemy." He cocked an eyebrow. "Are you ready for that?"

My heart pounded within my chest. "I will be."

Flipping the weapon around, he held it out to me, handle side first. "Show me how you hold a katana."

Wrapping my fingers around the sword handle, I took the blade from Darius and held it like Trayton had showed me to, building on what my father had showed me.

"Like this?" I hadn't meant for there to be a question at the end of my sentence, but there it was, brought on by the knowledge that someday, maybe soon, Darius was going to try to kill me—and he'd succeed if I didn't train as hard as I could.

Furrowing his brow, Darius shook his head. "Spread your hands farther apart. A broader grip means more control."

I spread my hands some and looked at him, seeking his approval. With a nod, he said, "We will begin with proper fighting stance. You have an advantage over many Barrons, as you're female. Girls tend to be smaller, leaner, and with practice, can move in ways that are delicate and fierce, just like the weapon in your hand. Now spread your legs apart and lower your center of gravity."

Sliding my right leg over a few inches, I squatted down some and awaited further instructions. Darius walked around me in a circle, scrutinizing my stance. With a chuckle, he said, "What are you doing, sitting down? Straighten your back. And spread your legs farther."

I straightened my back, but apparently didn't move fast enough for Darius's tastes, as he kicked the inside of my foot with his toe until it was a few more inches away from my other foot. From behind me, he said, "Better. Now hold up the blade at a forty-five-degree angle. Keep your grip firm, but gentle. Work with the weapon, not against it. It's an extension of you, not a foreign object to struggle with."

His last words reminded me of Trayton, of what Trayton had said about katanas. It was almost verbatim. I couldn't help but wonder if Trayton had merely repeated what Darius had taught him in class. I held the sword up, angled it slightly, and remained as still as possible. A long, silent moment passed before Darius spoke again. "Now raise your arms, keep that angle, and bring the katana down in a long slash. Remember, the katana is a slicing weapon. Not a stabbing weapon. Be smooth. Be fluid."

As instructed, I brought the blade up, my shoulders already burning from holding it aloft for so long. The blade sang as it cut through the night air, and I stopped short before I got it too close to the ground. Darius moved in front of me, his silver hair bright even in the darkness. I imagined it was a disadvantage for him on the battlefield. He must have stood out. He withdrew the katana on his back from its sheath and held it in front of him in proper form. "Snap the end of your stroke. Otherwise your cut falls weak. Snap it forward and it ends with strength. Like this."

He whipped the blade forward effortlessly, snapping his wrist forward, stopping his blade work with a short angular cut. I copied him several times. By the fifth time, I felt like I had it, but my arms were screaming in pain. Despite Darius's assurance that a katana was a lightweight weapon, it grew heavier and heavier every moment it was in my hands. After another three strokes, Darius nodded. "Good enough. For now. Now let's work on those arms."

Lowering the sword, I blinked at him. "What's wrong with my arms?"

"You have no muscle. Strength is lurking under the surface, but without utilizing the muscles there, you'll never be able to wield a weapon in the long term of a battle." He took the katana from me, returning it to its sheath. "Push-ups. Now."

"How many?"

"As many as it takes."

"To do what exactly?"

"To make your arms shake. To make you feel so weak that you can no longer stand to hold up your own weight. Then you can stop for the day and we'll go back to proper form."

At first, I nearly laughed, but I swallowed that laughter when I realized that Darius wasn't joking. He fully intended to make me do push-ups until I fell over from exhaustion. And though I was sorely tempted to tell him where he could stick his push-ups, the fact was that Darius was right.

He held out a hand and I placed the katana in it before dropping to the ground in a push-up stance. Darius counted off as I lowered myself to the ground and lifted myself up. As I hoisted myself up again, I could feel Darius's foot on my butt, pressing down. "Keep your body perfectly straight. At a forty-five-degree angle, just like the blade."

I lowered myself again, my shoulders and chest and back burning, and he counted off another. After a while, the numbers that he was saying didn't matter anymore. I listened to the rhythm of my movements, punctuated by his voice, and fought off a cramp in my right shoulder blade. But I kept doing the push-ups. Down, breathe, up again. Over and over again, until Darius wasn't counting anymore. My biceps trembled with exhaustion after a while, but I swore to myself that I would not fall, would not show such an incredible sign of weakness. I was better than that. But fak, my right shoulder blade was cramping and my nose tingled with the threat of tears. My body hurt in places I hadn't even known existed, and it would never, ever stop. Not until the sun came up.

Blissfully, the light began to change just as I felt my arms turning into jelly. Darius spoke again, his voice nonchalant, as if I hadn't just worked myself like a dog to fulfill his training requirements for the day. "We should head back. Put your face mask on."

I collapsed on the ground, coughing and panting, trying not to die from exhaustion. Darius would have none of it. He thrust the bag I'd carried to the clearing at me. "Hurry up. Much later and someone will notice your absence."

From my place on the ground, I tried hard not to whine my complaints, but I wasn't at all certain I was pulling it off. "Who's going to notice? Maddox? I'm not due to class for another hour."

"I suspect Trayton will notice his Healer's gone missing if you don't show up for breakfast."

From inside the bag, I pulled a face mask and a Barron's training uniform. "The mask will help, but what about my clothes?"

"Change."

I looked around, suddenly feeling very exposed. "You mean here? In the woods?"

A sarcastic smirk danced on his lips. "Wouldn't be the first time you've been pantless in my presence. I sense a growing trend here."

Rolling my eyes, I pulled the training uniform from the bag. "In your dreams. Now turn around."

Once he'd turned his back to me, I took another look around to be sure we were alone. Shaking the uniform out of its folds, I could tell it was going to be a little big on me, but it wasn't too far off from my size, and I could easily put a few stitches in to make it fit me right. I hurried out of my clothes and slipped into the uniform, my skin cooling quickly in the outside air. As I pulled the new leggings on, I glanced at Darius, who was dutifully remaining turned away from me, respecting my privacy. My thoughts turned back to the night the Graplars attacked us, the night I discovered that Darius was a Barron. Biting my bottom lip for a moment in contemplation, I finally asked, "Darius . . . when are we going to talk about your secret?"

He tilted his head to the side slightly, but didn't turn around. "What do you mean?"

I pulled the new shirt over my head and said, "The fact that you're a Barron and telling everyone at Shadow Academy that you're Unskilled."

Without asking if I was dressed or not, he turned to

face me. "It's . . . complicated. I really don't want to talk about it."

"Why not?" I pulled my shoes back on and shoved my clothes inside the small bag.

When I stood and looked at him, he seemed to pale before my eyes. "Because my Healer died three years ago at the second battle at Wood's Cross. It's a rather painful memory, and I'd rather not discuss it."

An image filled my mind, jolting me. It was the image of a small red crescent against Darius's bronze skin. "But . . . your Trace is red. That means your Soulbound Healer is alive."

"I don't know what you think you saw, but my Trace is black." He slipped his shirt over his head, and I struggled to keep my attention on his Trace.

He was right. It was black.

I shook my head, not understanding. I could have sworn it had been red. "I'm so sorry. I thought—"

"Let's just get back to the academy." He picked up the spare katana and headed up the hill without another word. I watched him take several steps before I followed, slipping my face mask on.

What kind of person insists on dredging up the past when someone else says they'd rather not talk about it? My curiosity had clearly brought to mind an experience he'd rather forget. Guilt weighed my steps all the way back to the armory.

As he was reaching for the door, I hoped my bumbled

apology would ease any tension I might have caused. "Darius? I really am sorry. I shouldn't have brought it up. It's none of my business anyway. But . . . I have to ask you something."

He looked at me, and I could tell that he'd built a wall around his emotions. There was no feeling in his eyes, no reaction at all. Just impatience and the urge to get this conversation over with.

I shuffled my feet a bit before speaking. "How does no one here know that you're a Barron?"

"Because I trained at Starlight Academy, and the two schools only ever interact in full-scale battles. So no one here knows what I am, and no one there knows what happened to me."

"Oh." I had a million more questions, but something told me if I started asking them, Darius wasn't going to be very giving with answers.

As if in response to my thoughts, he nodded wordlessly, and opened the door. As I stepped inside, he turned to me, the subtle hint of a smile on his lips. "Wear the outfit you're wearing right now tomorrow, so you don't have to keep getting naked in front of me, okay?"

As positively obnoxious as Darius was, he had an intriguing charm about him that I admired. I smiled as my new instructor walked away, relieved I hadn't completely fakked everything up.

I entered the armory with answers to a question that had been bugging me since the day that we had met.

Darius was a dek much of the time because he was hurting from the loss of his Healer. And he was hiding away from the world under a guise of secrecy because of whatever had happened at the battle of Wood's Cross. Of course he was. Who wouldn't? When I learned I'd lost my Barron, I was heartbroken, and I hadn't even known him. Clearly Darius had cared very much for his Healer, and had been left deeply scarred by his or her demise.

Darius disappeared around the corner, leaving me alone to greet Maddox. She was seated on a stool as I entered, looking more bored than I'd ever seen her. I tried to hide my smile, but the look in Maddox's eyes said that I was the worst liar in Tril. Furrowing her brow, she said, "What's this now? What happened?"

Stepping inside the armory, I closed the door behind me, sealing us away from the world outside for the moment. "It was amazing, Maddox! I learned how to hold a katana properly, and how to swing it. And I did so many push-ups, I almost passed out!"

She looked as if she were questioning my sanity level, so I tried desperately to stop my smile from turning into a grin. And failed.

She raised a sharp eyebrow. "You almost passed out and you're happy about it?"

"Oddly, yes."

"Will we be back here tomorrow?"

I didn't even have to think about my reply. "Definitely. And every day, until Darius deems me fit for a Graplar encounter."

"You really hate those things, don't you?"

"It's not that." At that moment, an image flashed through my mind. An image of teeth and blood. My leg began to throb, right where I'd been bitten. "I mean, it's not *just* that. Maybe it doesn't bother you, or maybe you just never really took notice, but Maddox . . . it really kills me that Healers are expected to stand around and wait to be rescued. It really troubles me that we're not viewed as equals with Barrons."

Maddox shrugged, hopping down off her stool. "I noticed. I just don't see the point in rallying against something we can't change. And I've never heard a Healer be so bothered by it before you, Kaya."

We made our way outside again, where the cool evening air was giving way to the warmth of morning. Waves of guilt lapped at my heels. "Maddox . . . are you sorry I got you mixed up in this?"

"Are you kidding?" She snorted, relieving that guilt— or at least lessening it some. "In case you haven't noticed, the headmaster is a total dek."

Eighteen

"Again." Darius brought his blade across his body and I did the same, stopping just short of the metal hitting in midair. My shoulders felt like they were on fire, and my back had cramped twice already. "On your own now. Go until I say stop."

I brought my blade up again and then down in a hard slash. Darius circled me slowly, his eyes burning holes in my every fault. "Bend your knees. Straighten your back."

I did as instructed, trying hard to ignore the threat of another cramp—this one in my side. He barked, "Again. Swing harder. You're not getting it."

Using all of my strength, I swung the katana forward, snapping it into position. As I ended the slash, the muscles in my side cramped hard and I cried out, dropping my weapon to the ground and clutching my side. As I stood there, doubled over in pain, Darius said, "Give me fifty push-ups and you're done for the day. Unless, of course, you can't hack it."

Dropping to my knees, I gritted my teeth against the pain and pressed my palms into the soft ground, stretching out my legs behind me. I dipped down, counting off the first push-up, and swore that I wouldn't let a little pain frighten me away from the training I desperately wanted. Just forty-nine more push-ups and I could go have breakfast with Trayton.

As I left the dining hall later that morning, I felt a bit lighter, though my muscles were terribly sore. Dining with Trayton was fun, even if every word I said was followed by the knowledge that Melanie had yet to enact her hateful plan, and every other word out of Trayton's mouth was something about how I should be behaving in Mr. Groff's class. Still . . . Trayton's smile gave me reason to trudge forth to my Botanical Medicine class, despite the fact that all I really wanted to do was lie down in a hole somewhere and pretend the outside world didn't exist anymore.

But once inside Instructor Harnett's class, I found my second wind. "Today, Healers, we will discuss the remedy for aching muscles."

Relaxing some, and thanking whatever omnipotent force had sent Instructor Harnett to teach at Shadow Academy, I flipped open my notebook and prepared to take detailed notes. Instructor Harnett smiled pleasantly and began her lecture by writing several ingredients on the board. "Now, something that I want you to remember at all times is that a Healer's life is just as important as a Barron's. Perhaps more so. After all, if King Darrek had his way and rid the world of Healers, where would our dear Barrons be without us there to heal them and tend to their wounds? Your life is valuable. To your Barron, to your fellow Healers, and to you. Despite what other instructors might say."

The obvious dig at Instructor Baak instantly raised my respect for Instructor Harnett by two clicks. But the classroom door opened, interrupting my inner celebration.

Instructor Baak stepped inside, her hair wild and the whites of her eyes showing in a manner that made me question her sanity. It also made me wonder if she'd been eavesdropping through the door for some crazy, possibly paranoid reason. She crossed the classroom to Instructor Harnett, her long finger pointed and shaking in a chastising manner. "How dare you! How *dare* you. You can't do that. You can't spread lies and insult fellow faculty members. It's against Protocol!"

Instructor Harnett folded her arms in front of her and spoke calmly, as if she were used to these kinds of outbursts. "To what section of Protocol are you referring exactly?"

Instructor Baak's face turned purple. I was beginning

to wonder if she'd stopped breathing. "Lies! You've lied to these students!"

"About what, Shara?" Instructor Harnett eyed her closely for a moment, and when Instructor Baak could only respond with sputtering, she said, "Perhaps you should take this up with Headmaster Quill."

"I will!" She spun around, leaving the classroom just as quickly as she'd come, slamming the door behind her.

After taking a cleansing breath, Instructor Harnett smiled pleasantly. "Now that we have that out of the way, Healers, let's discuss how to ease muscular pain."

I didn't think that I could possibly like Instructor Harnett more than I did at the onset of that class. But I was thrilled beyond belief to be proven wrong.

Nineteen

A scream woke me that night, permeating my dreams and twisting them into something that I feared would stay with me, but when I opened my eyes, the images were gone, and I lay there, wondering whether or not the scream had been real. Then I heard it again, just outside my window. Jumping out of bed, I flung open the window and looked down. Maddox was standing in the courtyard, a haunted expression on her face. Just as I was about to ask her what all the screaming was about, she screamed again at the hulking mass that was moving ever closer to her in the shadows. Without thinking, I stepped onto the ledge and jumped, tucking and rolling as I fell on the soft grass below. My left hip screamed from the fall, and I knew I'd be bruised, but I had to get to Maddox, had to help her in whatever way I could.

Something dark and fast whipped by my right side

and I turned my head toward it. As I did, it moved by my left. Swift shadows that I knew had to be made of substance. Maddox flew through the air toward me, landing in a heap. The crackle of the torches was drowned out by a horrible screech—one that I recognized instantly. Another Graplar had gotten inside the wall.

Instantly, I opened my mouth to call for help, to yell in hopes that someone in the dorms would hear me, but I snapped it closed again. I couldn't scream, couldn't cry out. Sounds would only attract the Graplars. The smartest thing I could do was stay still and silent and try to figure this out on my own. I could count about fifty paces to the armory, and it would take another twenty paces to get around to the armory door. Which meant that it might as well have been on the other side of Tril. Which meant that I was without a katana. Which meant that we were dead meat.

Maddox moaned from where she lay on the ground. As slowly as possible, not wanting to attract the Graplar's attention, I inched over to where she lay and squatted beside her. Blood was pouring from the bite wound on her neck, coloring the ground an inky black in the moonlight. I ripped a large rectangle of fabric from my sleeping clothes and pressed in into the wound, trying to stop the blood from coming. Maddox was hurt badly and needed immediate medical attention. And without a Healer Bound to her, I wasn't sure she could survive this—not even with the Master Healer's assistance. But

I had to try, had to get Maddox to the hospital wing as quickly as possible.

A figure was moving from torch to torch, dousing them, and when my eyes focused in the darkness, I was relieved to see both a face I knew well and a katana on his back, but I couldn't believe that no one from the dorms had heard the commotion. "Raden! Hurry, there's a Graplar inside the wall!"

He looked about and found me quickly. When he ran over to where I was holding Maddox, he didn't miss a beat. "What direction? How many?"

"Just one that I saw. It ran west, but it bit Maddox."

His eyes scanned the darkness. "It won't go far. They prefer to feed rather than injure. Stay here and stay still and quiet. I'll get it."

He took off at a sprint, but I could barely make out the sound of his footfalls. Tears rolled down my cheeks and dripped from my chin to Maddox's hair. After a long silence, a horrific screech filled my ears, ringing through me. Raden returned a moment later, a triumphant look in his eyes, and scooped Maddox into his arms. As we hurried to the hospital wing, I swore that I would figure out how the Graplars were getting into the school, and I swore silently to Maddox that I would stop it from happening ever again.

Twenty

I awoke the next morning in a chair beside Maddox's hospital bed, my head lying on her blanket. Maddox's neck was covered with a thick white bandage, her face pale. When she saw me stir, her eyes brightened. I glanced around the room, happy to find that we were completely alone. "Maddox, how are you? Do you need anything?"

She started to shake her head, but then winced at the pain the action had caused her. "I'm fine. Really."

"What were you doing outside? I thought you were confined to the parlor at night."

"It's stupid." She sighed, but I could tell she was holding back her movements. She must have been in a great deal of pain. "I heard the dining hall was open late and serving fruit pastries."

I threw her a disbelieving look. "That is stupid. How's your neck feel anyway?"

"Sore." For a moment, the Maddox that I knew was gone, replaced by someone who seemed softer, more fragile. She looked at me, and lowered her voice to a mere whisper. "I'm so scared, Kaya."

I flicked a glance at her bandage, uselessly hoping to get a look at her wound and see how it was healing. "You don't need to be scared, Maddox. Raden killed the Graplar that bit you."

"That's not it. I mean, that's part of it."

"So what's the rest of it? What are you afraid of?"

Her eyes looked haunted, as I had never seen them before. The sight of them frightened me. "I don't have a Healer, Kaya. And I'll probably never have a Healer. And I have no idea what I'm doing with a katana. I'm scared that I'm going to die. Maybe not now. But the next time I encounter one of those things."

My voice caught in my throat as I shook my head again. "You can't think like that, Maddox."

Maddox sat up in bed, her expression hopeless. "Why not? It's true, isn't it? All of it's true."

It was hard to imagine what it was like to live in a world full of people who knew that they could be healed by the touch of a hand, but that you couldn't. I reached out and squeezed her hand. "When you get better, I'll teach you everything I know about how to kill Graplars."

A small ray of hope returned to her eyes then, and I was grateful to see it, grateful to see a glimpse of the girl that I'd come to care about. But guilt came crashing down hard all around me. I should have offered to show her what I'd learned before. If I had, she might not be lying in bed, injured right now. "Thanks."

Hours later, at the Master Healer's insistence, I finally exited Maddox's room in the hospital wing. Maddox didn't need me there. Her wounds had looked far worse than they actually were, and now she was well medicated and cleanly bandaged. The Graplar's bite had been treated to the best of the Master Healer's ability, and when the Master Healer wasn't looking, I'd retreated it with some of Darius's amazing healing cream. After that, it was a matter of waiting. All I had really been doing for the past three hours was holding Maddox's hand and apologizing for something which I had absolutely no control over. So, with needless guilt weighing down my every step, I let go of Maddox's hand and moved into the hallway.

Trayton was waiting for me in the hall—for that, I was truly grateful. Despite the fact that he hadn't been in the courtyard when I'd needed him. He stood as I approached and cupped his hand over mine, intertwining our fingers. His eyes were locked on mine, as if he were trying to gauge my well-being. "How is she?"

My heart was so heavy I could barely speak. "They say she'll be back in action in two or three days."

"Are you okay?"

"I'm fine. But where were you?"

A flash of guilt crossed his face. "It's not always easy to hear through the dorm walls. Believe me, if I had kn—"

I cut off his sentence with a look and sighed. "This is exactly why Healers should know how to fight, Trayton. If I'd had a katana in my hands, I could have protected her."

Shaking his head, he did his best to sound reassuring —and failed miserably. "Don't beat yourself up wondering what might have been. And don't forget that Maddox is a Barron. Even if she's not trained in the art of fighting, she has a natural ability that far surpasses anything that even a well-trained Healer could accomplish."

I shot him a look. "And why wasn't she trained exactly? She is a Barron, after all."

Trayton looked past me down the hall. When he met my eyes again, he lowered his voice, as if what he was about to say were a secret. "The headmaster thought that if she had training, she might eventually use it in an effort to leave the academy."

Disgust filled me. "So instead of teaching her a skill to defend herself and risking her running away, he'd rather keep her ignorant and ensure she stays here? That's ridiculous."

"It may seem ridiculous, but it's for her own good." He shrugged, and then went back to looking down the hall toward Maddox's door. "Besides, like I said, Maddox has a natural ability. With or without training, she could defend herself in a dire situation, I'm sure."

The urge to argue with him was undeniable. I don't know who'd been put in charge of deciding who had a natural ability to do what, but Maddox seemed far more like an Unskilled than she did a Barron. I could have taken down that Graplar ten times quicker than Maddox could—even if she had been armed. But there was no use in arguing with him. Trayton had grown up believing that Healers were Healers and Barrons were Barrons, and that's just the way it is. Opening his mind would take more than a five-minute conversation in the hospital wing.

My thoughts drifted to the wall, and I wondered about possible weaknesses in it. Darius had assured me that the wall was solid, and that Graplars could not possibly get through or over it. But what if he was wrong? What other way could Graplars possibly be getting inside? "Do they have blueprints of the surrounding wall at the library?"

Trayton narrowed his eyes a bit in suspicion. "Of course."

"Good."

"Can I ask why?"

As we moved down the hall, I answered, "Because I want to know how Graplars are getting inside the wall, and I think that's a good place to start. Don't you?"

"The blueprints aren't going to show you anything that you don't already know or haven't already seen.

Besides, don't you think Headmaster Quill has patrols searching every inch of that wall even now?" He held the door open for me, and as we crossed the campus I mulled over what he was saying.

"The outside of it or the inside?"

"What? Where the patrols are searching?" At my nod, he replied, "The outer perimeter, of course."

I straightened my shoulders, certain I'd found the answer to our dilemma. No one was searching the inner perimeter, so clearly, the problem had to be there. It wouldn't be the first time that Barrons' arrogance had been their downfall. "Then I'll start my own search inside."

"Tomorrow." Trayton smiled, as if he were trying to pacify me. "You need your rest tonight."

As we passed the courtyard, I glanced up. Darius's window was dark.

I couldn't help but wonder where he'd gone.

Twenty-one

So of course the Outer Rim has been designated the most dangerous area in all of Tril, running through all three continents—that is, Kokoro, Haruko, and Kaito—in an oval shape." Mr. Ross breathed in, his breath wet and nasally, before continuing his lecture. I was leaning my cheek on the heel of my palm, trying desperately to keep my eyes open. "It is highly suspected that this ring of danger is due to the elevation of each of those areas. Graplars, as we all know, thrive best in high elevations, and all along the naturally formed Outer Rim are the highest peaks throughout Tril. Sadly, this area is also home to many Skilled villages. Tens of thousands of lives have been lost on this front, and so the Outer Rim has become the most active part of the battleground and our fight against Darrek. If you'll turn to page—"

The door opened abruptly and someone moved inside. Whoever it was, I was blissfully thankful that their presence had silenced Mr. Ross for the moment—even though I knew that silence would be painfully short. I could feel the breeze of their swift movement on my arms as they stepped past me to the front of the class, but didn't bother looking to see who it was. I was too close to sleep and the blissful dreams that would take me away from Mr. Ross's boring history lessons. Who cared about the history of the war against Darrek anyway? The point was, we were fighting him. For reasons that had yet to be explained to me. It was yawn inducing. Almost coma inflicting.

Just as I was starting to feel myself slipping away into a nice nap, a hand—warm and strong—closed over my biceps and squeezed, as if to shake me from my stupor. I opened my eyes and looked up to find Darius staring down at me. Under his breath, he said, "Come on. Let's go."

Confused, I blinked at Mr. Ross, who nodded and gestured to the door. So with his permission, I gathered my books into my satchel and made my way out the door. I followed Darius in wondering silence for several yards, until we were out of earshot of any of my fellow students, before I hurried to his side and whispered, "What's going on? Where are you taking me? How did you get me out of class?"

He didn't even look at me as he replied. "You're welcome for that, by the way. Probably the dullest lecture I've ever had the misfortune of overhearing in my life."

As we rounded the corner of his cabin, Darius said, "Wait here, but stay out of sight. If someone sees an unguarded Healer milling about, we're fakked. We're going on a little field trip, and we'll need supplies. I'll be back in a minute."

Leaning with my back against the wall, I kept my head down and tried to act casual. Darius seemed to do nothing without express and distinct purpose—aside from irritate me, which I suspected was solely for his amusement—so I trusted that this, too, had its purpose. Several long, grueling, worry-filled moments later, Darius returned with two rucksacks, stuffed full of the supplies that he'd said we'd need. As we moved west, toward the south gate, I dared a question. "Where exactly are we going?"

He didn't pause in his steps, didn't change his breathing or even so much as blink when he replied, "We're going to the Outer Rim."

I very nearly stumbled, but managed to keep my feet moving forward. Everything that I had heard about the Outer Rim said that it was very much a place that you wanted to avoid—and if you couldn't avoid it, you really wanted to surround yourself with many talented Barrons. It was the most dangerous area of Tril, full of more Graplars and soldiers from Darrek's army than anyone cared to think about. Grabbing Darius by the sleeve, I tugged in a near panic. "Are you crazy? We could die out there!"

Turning his head toward me, he paused briefly, his demeanor calm and cool. "We could die in here too, or have you forgotten?"

His eyes dropped to my thigh and I released my grip. When he moved forward, I followed. He had a point. Nowhere was safe. Still, that didn't mean I understood his apparent death wish. As we approached the gate, Darius muttered, "If Raden asks, you're gathering moss sprigs for the Master Healer."

The south gate was relatively quiet, but as we approached, Raden had his list of names of people who were allowed outside at the ready. He smiled at me in recognition, but furrowed his brow as he looked over the list. "Darius, I have you here, but I'm afraid Kaya's not on the list."

Darius looked bored and disinterested, and Raden's eyes turned to me. Shrugging, and trying to ignore the way my heart was racing, I said, "I'm gathering moss sprigs for the Master Healer."

Raden chuckled then and made a note on his list. "That explains it. Darius's favorite task. Be careful out there, you two. See you tomorrow."

Darius strode forward, still looking bored, and I followed. We were steps from the now open gate when Raden grabbed the handle of the second katana that Darius was wearing—my katana. His brow furrowed with suspicion. "What's this then? You're bringing a spare weapon? Expecting trouble while on a simple herb-gathering mission, Darius?"

We were caught. Raden knew that something was up, that we were headed outside the wall for nefarious reasons, and he was going to report us for sure. I tried not to look panicked, but wasn't certain I was pulling off cool and confident, as my heart was practically jumping out of my chest.

Darius shrugged Raden's hand away casually. "The blade's a bit pitted. I was working on cleaning it when I got wind of this little trip, so I figured I'd bring it along. It was either this or stare at tree bark while she picks weeds."

Raden's laughter followed us out the gate and was only cut off by the clank of metal as it closed behind us. Once we were down the hill several yards, I hurried to Darius's side. "We'll be gone overnight?"

"Yes. It takes that long to get where we're going. Fortunately for us, moss sprigs only grow in one area of Tril. So the story's believable enough."

"So . . . what exactly are we doing? Hunting Graplars?"

"No. We're actually going to practice your stealth as we make our way to the Outer Rim. But that's not the real reason I'm taking you there." He stopped moving and pointed to my rucksack. "You might want to change. If we do get attacked, the training uniform is so much easier to maneuver in than the Healer uniform."

He turned around and as I changed, a question burned its way out of me. "What's the real reason you're taking me there?"

He turned his head to the side just as I was tying the sash of my top into a knot. "Because you're learning how to fight, but you have no idea *why* we fight. You lack reason. You lack purpose. Every time you bring that blade down, you have to mean it, and you don't yet."

The image of Avery's blood on my father's shirt flashed in my mind briefly, and I clenched my jaw defiantly, shoving my Healer uniform into the bag before slipping it over my shoulders. "I have my own reasons. I don't need yours."

Darius gauged me for a moment, and for a second, I was sure he was going to say something other than what he did. "Yes, you do."

As quietly as possible, we moved through the woods and down the mountainside. Neither of us spoke, and I tried like hell to control my breathing so we wouldn't attract any unwanted visitors to our day hike. After two hours of walking, Darius glanced at me, but I shook my head, unwilling to admit that I was exhausted already and needed a break. An hour more and I gave his sleeve a breathless tug. He nodded, turning his head, checking carefully that it was a relatively safe area to stop briefly. When he gave another nod, I let out an exhausted sigh and sat on a fallen log, opening my rucksack in search of food. There were three brown sacks inside: one containing some type of dried, seasoned meat; one containing different types of dried fruit; and one containing a small baguette and some cheese. I bit into the cheese, chasing it with a bit of bread, and my stomach gurgled its gratitude. I chewed on a few more bits of the bread before giving the dried meat a try. It was somewhat spicy, but oddly tender for jerky. Darius watched the area around us as I ate, always on alert. We didn't speak—I knew better than to talk without him giving me the go-ahead out here. We were far away from the school now, even farther than Kessler, and well on our way to the Outer Rim. This was dangerous territory, and completely unfamiliar to me. Once I'd finished my snack, I tucked the rest of the food away, and slipped my rucksack back on, its weight feeling heavier than it had when Darius had first handed it to me. There was a long road ahead of us, and I knew that that pack was going to get heavier with every step. But I didn't complain—mostly because I knew that complaining would do nothing but irritate Darius.

At his signal, we continued silently south for several hours, until the sun was setting just over the trees. Though I could still spy it, the forest had already become incredibly dark—something that seemed to put Darius's nerves even more on edge than they had been. We moved swiftly through the growing night, and soon our downward trek became an upward climb. We were almost there—I could feel it in my bones. But just as I was catching my second (or, to be honest, my fifth) wind, Darius stopped in his tracks and listened. My muscles tensed, but when he removed his rucksack and dropped it on the ground, I relaxed a little. It was time to camp. "Tomorrow morning, I'll show you Kingsland."

"Won't Maddox or Trayton be suspicious that I'm gone?"

"Maddox already knows. I told her this morning when I stopped by to see her and give her some salve for her bite."

Silently, I wondered if he'd noticed that I'd used some of his medicinal mixture on Maddox already. I was betting that he had. Darius wasn't the kind of person who didn't notice the tiny details.

"And Trayton . . ." He nodded then. Not to anything I had said, but perhaps something in his thoughts. "He'll believe me."

I didn't question how he knew that, just trusted the sincerity on his face. Something told me that he and Trayton had been through a lot together. They trusted each another.

I strained my memory, but couldn't recall ever having heard of the village he'd mentioned before. "Kingsland? Should I have heard of it?"

"I would hope so." His jaw clenched momentarily, and his eyes gave way to a haunted, sad expression—a hole in his armor that I had not been prepared to see. "It lies just north of Wood's Cross."

My heart froze its rhythm, and then sank. Of all the places that Darius would take me, it would have to be the place that haunted my parents still, the place that had robbed from them their dearest loves until they became a couple. Rolling out my sleeping blankets, I lay quietly as Darius circled the area, peering through the darkness to the treetops. I didn't know if he planned on sleeping, and soon, I surprised myself that I could.

When I awoke the following morning, my back was stiff, and my hair was moist with fallen dew. Darius sat atop a large nearby boulder, ever alert. Without even glancing in my direction, he said, "Eat something. We only have about an hour before we have to head back to Shadow Academy. It's all the time we can afford before suspicions arise that we might not actually be on an herb-gathering expedition."

Without speaking, I rolled up my sleeping blankets and placed them inside my rucksack. I chewed a bit of jerky, but I wasn't sure my queasy stomach could handle much more than that. We were going to Wood's Cross today—a place I'd hoped I'd never see, a place that was now the eternal resting ground for several thousand Barrons and Healers. Many believed it to be a cursed area. Even my parents, who believed there was a rational explanation for just about everything, didn't like to talk about Wood's Cross, or even to speculate on some of the strange things that had happened there. No one—not even the academy scholars, as far as I had heard—could even give a logical reason why the two largest, most damaging battles in the war against Darrek had taken place in exactly the same place, just twenty years apart. It was a haunted place, and no one in their right mind dared to visit it of their own accord.

So of course we were going there.

Darius hadn't said that. He'd said that we were going to Kingsland. But what he'd meant was that we were going through Kingsland, to Wood's Cross. He wanted me to have a reason to fight, and no matter what I might have said to refuse, he was convinced that Wood's Cross would give me that reason. He might have been right, but if he was, I didn't want to find out. The truth was, it scared me. No place that had shaken under so much war or soaked up so much blood could be safe. Energies remained—especially negative energies—and all that I had heard about Wood's Cross told me that it was a nasty, frightening place to be.

"Darius . . . why do you think that the two biggest battles of this war have taken place in exactly the same spot?" I was hesitant to ask him, but curious about what his response might be. He might tell me to fak off or something, but I had to ask. My curiosity couldn't be contained.

He didn't answer at first, and just as I was beginning

to think he never would, he said, "Darrek's looking for something. Something that only appears once every two decades."

There was no question in his reply, and the certainty in his tone only drew me in further. "You seem so sure."

"I am sure."

"How?"

"I've seen him."

I wanted to push for details, but something in the way that his mouth was set told me not to. Quietly, I packed up the remainder of my supplies and slipped my rucksack on before retrieving my katana from beside Darius. He stood listening quietly to the woods before leading me over the next ridge. Nestled at the bottom of the ridge, in an overgrown valley, were the remnants of a small village.

It was difficult to see from the top of the ridge, but as we descended into the valley, through overgrown vines and brush, several buildings came into view. They weren't exactly buildings anymore, being partially burned and ravaged by war, partially reclaimed by nature. The remaining walls were crumbling, but I could still make out soot from where they'd been burned. By the time we reached what had been the main street through town, I could see how Kingsland had once been laid out. The main street had been comprised of eight large buildings—likely a grocer, tailor, blacksmith, and other important establishments. Fanning out around those in a southward direction were two hundred or more small buildings. Houses. Which families had called home.

Darius moved down the street and I followed, my feet feeling unsure on the brush-covered ground. I lost my footing once, but managed to steady myself relatively quickly. Darius paused and looked at me over his shoulder. "Watch your step. The ground still holds weapons from both battles here. The greenery grew over it, but it takes metal a long time to be fully reclaimed by Tril. So the ground is a bit uneven in spots."

"I'll be careful." I nodded and when he continued, I followed. All along the main street, we passed ravaged buildings, mounds of refuse that were now small hills, torches that vines had grown up and around, making them look like very small trees. When we reached the other end of town, Darius stopped and turned back with a solemnity that I had never seen before. "Six hundred and thirty-two people called Kingsland home. They were Unskilled, not a part of this war at all. Each died a horrible, terrified death, having no idea why they were dying. And the sick truth is that we could have saved them, could have saved them all. But the Zettai Council voted that it was more important to protect the secrecy of Skilled society than to save six hundred people from a horrible fate."

My heart seized momentarily. I had witnessed the selfishness of the Zettai Council firsthand in every panicked glance that I had ever seen in my parents' eyes, but still I had no idea the lengths to which they would go to hide the fact that Barrons and Healers existed from those they had labeled the Unskilled—as if they were unworthy of any title but one that showed their sub-servience. The Zettai Council had refused to view the villagers of Kingsland as people, as anything other than a threat, and so they'd sentenced them to death. The fact sank in my stomach like a sour stone.

Darius's voice softened in respect for the dead—dead which might have been lingering in the place that we were standing. I didn't know if I truly believed in spirits or the afterlife, but I did know better than to disrespect those who had fallen—especially in the place that they had fallen. So as Darius spoke, I listened to him, keep-ing my eyes on the remnants of town sprawl for any sign of threat, living or not. "The men, the women, the elderly—they were bad enough. But Kingsland was home to two hundred and twenty-nine children, Kaya. And because children aren't deemed a threat, they were killed last. They watched as Graplars and Darrek's soldiers entered the town and murdered their loved ones. They watched as strangers, Barrons and Healers, entered town and fought against those who'd stolen their families away. Then, as King Darrek entered town, the Graplars were turned on the children. So while everyone suffered, it was the children who suffered more than anyone."

Sorrow wrapped around me like vines, twisting and pulling until they threatened to rip me apart. Children.

How sick was it to destroy adult lives, let alone the lives of children? Lives that had only just begun. Lives filled with so much promise and hope, wiped away with the murderous carelessness of two warring parties. It left a sick sensation in my veins.

"Who's at fault for their suffering? Most would say Darrek. But the Zettai Council had a hand in their pain, I assure you." His jaw tightened and he turned to face me, his eyes fierce. "Every time I reach for my sword, I hear a child cry. And every time I kill a Graplar, I think of the people who let those children suffer. Skilled, Unskilled—those are just labels. Children are innocent, and they need our protection. The ghosts of them haunt me every night, and I will not stop until I am purged of this pain, this guilt. They are why I fight."

Suddenly, I knew why Darius had brought me here. Because he had his reasons for fighting. He had his draw to the battlefield, his cause to defend. And he wanted me to have mine as well.

Closing my eyes briefly, I pictured the streets of Kessler—the Kessler I knew before Avery was murdered. The townsfolk wore friendly, unguarded smiles. The shopkeepers waved as people walked by. The children ran through the streets, laughter trailing behind them in ripples. They were my reason for coming here, for staying here—the villagers of Kessler. And I would be damned before I would let what happened to the villagers of Kingsland happen to the people of Kessler.

Opening my moist eyes, I nodded to Darius. I got it. He'd driven his message home. With a nod in understanding, he set his jaw and said, "Now we're going to Wood's Cross."

I shook my head. There was no reason to go to Wood's Cross now. I had my cause. I didn't need to visit that horrible place. "What? Why?"

A shadow seemed to eclipse him as he turned and headed farther out of town, he said, "Because now that you know what you're fighting for, you need to know what you're fighting against."

Dutifully, I followed him out of town and through a wooded glen, though every fiber of my being was pulling at me, pleading with me to stay, to turn back, to get the hell away from that horrible place before I ever even got there. I moved forward, trusting Darius to have good reason for this trip, even though my hands were trembling at the thought of visiting Wood's Cross.

The glen grew darker as we moved through it, and as we climbed over a small ridge, a strangling sensation wrapped around my throat. I swallowed hard, trying to resist it, but it seemed to be my body's natural response to the area. I knew that we had entered Wood's Cross without having been told. It was a sickness hanging in the air, a darkness that permeated everything around it. Looking down the hill, I could make out the crossroads of what had once been two major roads. Greenery had grown over much of the area, and it didn't look much different than other areas that we had traveled through to arrive in Kingsland, apart from the large, worn wooden sign at the crossroads that read "Wood's Cross." It amazed me that the simple structure still stood after two major battles had ravaged the area, but there it was, haunting the crossroads, standing sentinel over the area that had tasted so much blood. We descended the hill and Darius led me to the exact center of the crossroads. With every step, my throat felt more and more constricted. By the time we reached the sign, my heart was fluttering in an unexplainable panic. Darius had his eyes on me the entire time. "You feel it, don't you? They say that Healers can sense it more easily—the darkness, the utter evil of this place."

Unable to speak, I nodded, wanting nothing more than to run, to flee this place and get back to Shadow Academy. Even Kingsland would have been a welcome distraction from the strange dread of Wood's Cross.

"Remember this feeling. Because it is everything that oozes from the pores of King Darrek. And if we allow it to permeate the rest of Tril, what happened to Kingsland will be a picnic in comparison to the hell awaiting us. Remember it, and use it in your fight." He held my gaze for a moment and then led me back up the ridge. With every step, I felt lighter, my throat less constricted. By the time we'd returned to Kingsland, I could breathe again, but the sick horridness of Wood's Cross was still with me. I couldn't explain why it was so awful. I just knew that I never, ever wanted to return to that place.

I barely noticed the village as we crossed back through it. But as we climbed the ridge on the other side, where we had slept the night before, my heart seized. Standing just over the ridge was a group of six Graplars, sniffing our campsite with interest.

They hadn't noticed us, but rather than double back, Darius led me around them, pointing back at my feet in a reminder to use stealth. I shifted my weight to the balls of my feet and stepped as lightly as I could, carefully navigating my way over fallen branches and twigs. It felt as if every heartbeat rang out into the forest, sounding like a gong.

As we were rounding a large oak, the largest Graplar raised its head toward us. I froze, as did Darius. That moment, with the beast's beady eyes locked on where we were standing, dragged on for an eternity before the hulking creature sneezed and meandered off into the woods. Releasing a quiet sigh of relief, I again followed Darius's lead. It took hours to return to the familiar area around Shadow Academy, but we didn't speak. Maybe we were both tired. Maybe we had both been affected by the journey to Wood's Cross. Maybe we were terrified that our voices might attract more vigilant Graplars. I didn't know. And I certainly hadn't been expecting to feel a sensation of relief at seeing the wall around the academy. But I did.

My relief, however, was short-lived. I tugged Darius's

sleeve in a near-panic. "Darius, the herbs! We were sup-posed to be gathering—"

"Moss sprigs? I know." He dug in his satchel for a moment before producing a swatch of leather that had been rolled up and tied closed. I took the package, dumbfounded as to when he'd gathered the herbs, but guessing it was while I lay sleeping last night. A strange gratitude filled me, and I was surprised at its presence. I was grateful that Darius had brought me on this strange field trip, grateful that he'd reminded me that I already had a reason to fight, and that it wasn't just the ghost of Avery—that it was the still-living people that I cared about. And more than that, I was glad that he'd shown me Wood's Cross. Because evil like that was likely just a drop of what Darrek contained, and it could not be allowed to permeate our world, no matter what. Avery had been my reason for coming here, but now I had reason to fight, and reason to learn. Reason, it seemed, to give it my all here at Shadow Academy.

As Darius knocked on the giant metal door, I said, "Thank you."

He nodded over his shoulder at me just as the small window opened, revealing Raden's eyes on the other side.

Twenty-two

"Maddox, slow down!" I shouted after her, but she just rolled her eyes at me over her left shoulder as she exited my dorm room. Ever since we'd left the hospital wing, she'd been scurrying about all day, like some kind of wild toothboar. It was almost as if she had to prove just how healthy she really was, despite having been bitten by a Graplar just a few days before.

I had waited all day for Trayton to appear, but there was no sign of him anywhere. Maddox and I were headed out of the dorm for, of all places, the rose gardens. But just as Maddox had finally slowed her pacing a bit so I could catch up, Melanie passed in the hall with a smirk on her face. "By the way, Kaya, Trayton looks ravishing today. Or . . . haven't *you* seen him?"

She put an emphasis on the word 'you' that I didn't much appreciate, but I walked by her, pretending that I hadn't heard a word she'd uttered. As I did so, she stopped me with a hand on my shoulder and leaned in close, her smile twisted and threatening. "Tell him, Kaya. Tonight. Or I will."

I shook off her hand, flashed her a hard glare, and followed Maddox down the hall and down the stairs. By the time we reached the outside, my stomach was in knots.

Melanie was going to tell Trayton about my having been in Darius's cabin, if I didn't tell him first. She'd left me just the way she liked me, with no choice, in a no-win situation. My shoulders sank with defeat.

"There you are!" Trayton ran over to me from across the courtyard, a big smile on his face. His feet barely made a sound on the cobblestone, and when he reached me, he wasn't even out of breath. "I've been looking for you all day. Did you miss me?"

It was easy to smile around Trayton, but my smile still felt false, forced somehow. "Of course I did."

"How was your trip? I heard you and Darius were picking weeds in the Outer Rim."

Shrugging, I said, "It was pretty boring and uneventful, considering all the warnings we hear about the area. What about you? What did you do while I was away?"

Trayton smiled. "I'm just glad that Darius was with you. I would have gone, but apparently the orders came in while I was busy fortifying the north wall. But you were safe with him. He's probably the only person besides myself I'd trust to guard you outside the wall. Do anything interesting since you've been back?"

It struck me then just how many interesting things I did when Trayton wasn't around. An image flashed in my mind—one of katana blades slicing through the air—but I pushed it away. "Oh. You know. Nothing much. Studied some weeds. Terked off Instructor Baak."

Trayton chuckled, so trusting. I was his Healer, after all. Why would I lie to him? "The usual, huh?"

"Yeah." I bit my bottom lip, my stomach roiling some in tension. "The usual."

What I wanted to do was to tell him everything, that I had been training with Darius in secrecy this whole time, that I had been in his cabin not so long ago, that Melanie was a terrible person and trying to blackmail me. But what I did was smile and hold my breath and wait for Maddox to announce that we had to get going or Mr. Gareth would wonder where I was. As if on cue, Maddox said, "We should really get going, Kaya."

I could have hugged her, and probably would have.

If I'd wanted a slug in the arm, that is.

Twenty-three

Slipping my training mask over my face, I took a deep breath and let it out slowly. I hadn't been training with Darius for long, but that didn't diminish my fears. Darius, it turned out, wasn't a guy to hold back for a girl . . . or a Healer . . . or anyone at all. When he came at me with his katana, he came at me full force, stopping just short of lopping my head from my shoulders. He'd explained how most Barrons train in levels. The first year of training they'd wield a wooden bokken, and only after that would they move to an actual blade. But Darius wasn't a first year instructor, so he had no easy access to the bokkens. Taking one would have alerted the first year instructor that something was up, so it was best, Darius insisted, that I learn with an actual katana from the start. Besides, it earned me a glint of respect in his eyes.

Sure, he hadn't said that, but I could see a glimmer of

pride in his gaze whenever I'd swing the blade forward at just the right angle and snap it into place crisply.

I was improving, but the practice wasn't easy. My legs were covered in countless bruises, and two days ago, I tripped as Darius was taking a swipe at me, catching my arm on his blade. It wasn't a deep cut, but it hurt like hell and had bled all over the sleeve of my training uniform. Maddox helped me wash it out in the sink, and I stitched up the hole. Something about the repair job made me smile. The cut reminded me of my training, and I was immensely proud of myself for sticking it out even this far. A week might not have been much, but Darius said I was picking up the skills pretty quickly— especially for being a Healer, which I took as a compliment.

Now my mask was on and I moved across the school grounds without Maddox, my footfalls as silent as I could manage. Darius said I sounded like a drunken Graplar tromping through the woods more than I did a Barron—his charming way, I was guessing, of saying that we needed to work on my stealth.

The south gate was busier than usual, but I approached it as I had every morning that week, and looked around for my instructor. Darius patted a fellow Barron roughly on the back and turned my way. "You're late," he grumbled, as he did every morning. "Again."

I wasn't late. And the first few times he'd accused me of being late, it had infuriated me. But on the third

go-round, I realized he was just being Darius, just egging me on, for no reason at all that I could understand.
I'd let it roll off of me ever since then, and accepted that
it was just his strange way of greeting me.

We moved out the gate, Darius in front, as always,
and walked down the hill, quickly making our way
to the abandoned training area. When we got there,
I removed my mask and hung it from a low-hanging
branch. Adjusting my hair, pulling it tight back in the
leather thong, I noticed Darius was looking at me. I
raised an eyebrow, wondering what I was doing wrong
now. "What is it?"

Darius shook his head, a small smirk lifting the
corner of his mouth. "Nothing. Now if you're done
primping, we can practice some offensive maneuvers.
Or do you need to put on a skirt first?"

Rolling my eyes, I stepped into the center of the
training ring, my katana on my back. The weapon felt
lighter after a week of training, and I found myself
growing more comfortable with the sensation of it in
my hands as the days went by. Every morning began the
same way: three hours of training with Darius, a quick
breakfast, then off to Instructor Baak's ridiculous Healing 101 class to learn just why good Healers should sit
on the sidelines and let their Barrons do all the work.
And every evening ended the same way: extra duties in
the rose garden after terking off Instructor Baak. Luckily, Trayton had taken to keeping me company there,

and we were getting to know one another pretty well. I never mentioned my training. I knew how he'd react to it, and there was no way I was going to endanger my family or my instructor, simply because I couldn't keep my mouth shut.

Darius unsheathed his katana and stepped into the ring. "The thing about fighting Graplars is that most moves you'll use will be defensive. You want to wear them out, and keep their mouths busy until the right target presents itself at the right time—that target being its throat. A katana can definitely take down a Graplar, but almost never in a single cut. Decapitating a person is one thing—taking the head off a Graplar is quite another. The trick is getting to a right angle on the beast so that the neck is exposed. Best course of action is to evade a charge and cut through the knee, then pivot as the Graplar stumbles and take the head. Or you can hit the creature under the chin with a rising cut in order to raise its head and expose its throat for a horizontal cut. But be quick and firm about it—don't let the beast suffer. We kill to protect our fellow man. Not to be cruel."

That excited light entered his eyes as he spoke and, once again, I could sense his deep respect for Graplars, though I couldn't understand it. As far as I had seen, Graplars were stupid, drooling monsters that deserved to have their heads lopped off. But what Darius saw when he looked at them was something else entirely. He actually admired the creatures. I got the feeling that if there were any way to protect Barrons and Healers from King Darrek's advances without harming a single Graplar, Darius would do it in a heartbeat.

It really made you wonder about his social life.

"Never forget. You must move swiftly like the wind, stay as silent as the forest, attack as fierce as the fire, and be undefeatable like the mountain. Now," he said, his eyes becoming serious, his lips thinning into a line, "attack me."

Holding the katana in front of me, with my right hand directly beneath the guard, I placed my other hand about three inches down on the pommel. I kept my center of gravity low and my eyes on Darius, who barely moved with each breath he took. Then I stepped forward, raising my blade up and swinging it through the air at the perfect angle, its metal singing, my arm pulling the weapon through the air, ready to cleave Darius's shoulder in two.

But the idea of hurting him put hesitation into my blow, and Darius knew it—I could see it in his eyes. He moved forward, light on his feet, and pulled his blade up against mine. The sound of metal on metal rang through the air. And the next thing I knew, he brought his foot up and kicked me in the stomach, sending me flying. I landed in the underbrush several feet back, the air knocked from my lungs, a terrible ache at my core. Pain rocketed through my spine as I landed on my backside, but all I could think about was getting to my katana—wherever it was—and getting back in that ring.

Darius stood over me, a katana in each hand. He wasn't smirking, but I could tell that he was fighting not to. "You"—he said as he held my katana out to me and smiled—"lost."

Yanking my weapon from his hand, I stood again and headed for the ring, brushing a mess of stray hairs from my eyes. "Let's go again."

"No."

Spinning on my heel, I met his eyes. "What? Why not? We're here to train, so let's train."

He shook his head slowly, sheathing his katana once more. "You're not in the right frame of mind. You have to be clearheaded to attack successfully. Right now your head is clouded with anger. We'll continue our lessons tomorrow."

He turned away from me then, and within my veins, my blood began to boil. Before I gave it much thought, I ran after him, raising my katana in an attack. Darius, as if expecting this move, brought his sword back, blocking my blow in a clang of metal. He stopped, holding there, as if awaiting my next move, but I hesitated. Twisting around, he forced my katana away. His eyes were bright and fierce, and my heart was rattling with fury. The blade of his sword was pointing down, and as he backed away, he maintained his grip on it, as if he were ready for action. He looked at me pointedly and I could tell that his patience was wearing thin. His tone meant business. "We're done."

"No, we're not!" I whipped my sword around and brought it up, then down toward his head in another attack.

Darius countered by bringing his katana up just in time. Our bodies were intimately close, my skin on fire with anger. I wanted to fight, wanted to train harder, faster, longer, until I got it right. He moved his right elbow hard in, catching me in the mouth. Pain exploded on the side of my face, and blood trickled from my lip, only infuriating me more.

I slashed my sword at his neck, not aiming to kill, just to wound, just to stop him from controlling my actions. The way the headmaster controlled them. The way Protocol controlled them. Darius raised his sword again in a block, his face flushing with color as he struggled to control his own rising anger. No sooner had he thrown me off than I came at him again, this time from the side. With his blade singing through the air, he stopped my advances again, but just in the way that I was hoping. As my blade fell from his block, I swung the katana around, so hard and so fast that I could barely see the metal swinging through the air. Darius ducked to the side just in time. Recovering quickly, he spun around, nailing me in the side. I stumbled forward, but as I planted my foot to recover, I spun around, sword raised. And that was when I noticed that Darius was swinging his katana too, right for my head.

Our blades stopped short just of one another's necks, our chests heaving. We could have killed one another.

Without another word, Darius dropped his weapon to the side and moved up the hill. Only when he'd crested the hill did he return his katana to its saya. Guilt seizing me, I called after him. "I'll see you tomorrow."

But I didn't know if I'd see him tomorrow at all. Or ever again. I'd crossed a boundary that I knew not to cross. I'd attacked him against his instruction. And we'd ended in a draw.

Slowly, I gathered my things and made my way to the gate. Alone.

The sun was already setting by the time I entered the rose gardens that evening. It had been a long day, but uneventful, apart from my usual inability to keep my mouth shut around Instructor Baak whenever she was talking about the glory of being a Barron and the duty of being a Healer. I was pretty sure she was suffering from delusion, because she was crazy to think there was anything wrong with being a Healer. We could heal Barrons with our medicinal skills, and heal Barrons we were Bound to with a single touch of our hand. All of that was pretty amazing in my book. And glorious. So I kind of told her to fak off. Which didn't really matter anyway.

We both knew I was going to have extra duties for one reason or another.

Trayton had missed Protocol class to run some errand for Headmaster Quill, but he was waiting for me near the toolshed now, with a smile on his lips. "What was today's gem?"

"I told her to fak off."

"Charming."

"I try."

We exchanged smiles before Trayton said, "Mr. Gareth wants you to start on the far north side applying plant food. He said it's getting cooler, so we need to make certain the plants are ready for a change in weather."

It amazed me how quickly it had transitioned from *I* to *we*, with Trayton spending almost as many hours tending the rose gardens as I did. Not that he ever had extra duties. He just came to keep me company and, I suspected, to lighten my load a bit. Little did he realize that I'd grown to enjoy my time among the roses. It was hard work, but paying off with every bloom. Besides, it was quiet there. Not to mention blissfully Melanie and Instructor Baak free. But if Trayton preferred to while away his hours at my side in the dirt, who was I to argue?

"Not a problem. Help me carry supplies?"

"Of course."

We loaded up the wheelbarrow with large containers of plant food and, once it was full, Trayton pushed it to the far end of the garden. "How was your day, anyway? Staying out of trouble? I didn't see you at lunch."

"That's because Darius took a few of us out to patrol the perimeter outside the wall."

At the mention of Darius's name, I held my breath a bit. Truth was, Darius had been on my mind all day, and I was desperately hoping for a chance to apologize for attacking him the way I did. "Don't you get scared out there?"

He set the wheelbarrow down next to a particularly large rosebush and began unloading a few of the containers. After removing the lid from one, he handed it to me and opened the next. The plant food smelled a bit too much like rotten vegetables. "To be truthful, it is pretty frightening at times. But not like the Outer Rim. Now there's a scary place. Graplars are relatively thick in numbers along the Outer Rim. And something about the way they move out there says that it's their territory. They seem tougher. Larger. More in control. Patrolling the wall's perimeter? Much easier."

Crouching by the base of the first rosebush, I dug my hand into the container and scooped out a handful of plant food. I tried my best to sprinkle it on, but the consistency was a bit moist and clumpy for that, so I ended up flinging big globs of the smelly stuff at the base of the plant.

Nobody ever said I was delicate.

In my mind, I wasn't mulching rosebushes, but instead creeping quietly from tree to tree, hiding from the Graplars as Darius and I left the Outer Rim. My heart thumped loudly at the memory. "So why go to the Outer Rim at all? Why patrol an area that's overrun by Graplars?"

Trayton gathered a handful of plant food in his hand and gingerly tossed it around the base of the second rosebush, as if he'd done it a million times before. "It's important. If we can keep them out past the Outer Rim, it lessens the chances they'll get close enough to assault the gates."

So far, Darius and I had been lucky enough to avoid any Graplars during our training sessions. But that didn't mean I didn't have nightmares about them sneaking up on us while we were training. "Which gate is the most vulnerable? I mean, which one stands a bigger chance of Graplars overrunning the area around it?"

"The north gate. That's why we use the south gate as much as possible. It's just safer." He knelt in the earth beside me and got to work feeding the next plant, but I could tell that something was on his mind. After he'd finished what he was doing, he sat back and met my eyes. "Listen. I want to talk to you about the other day. About your curiosity when it comes to katanas."

I reached back into my container and flung some more goo on the base of the next plant. Some of it landed on the roses themselves, and I had to admit I had a pretty terrible aim. But the plant food was only a minor distraction from Trayton. "And if I told you that my curiosity had been contained . . . ?"

He smiled, but there was no joy in it. "We'd both know that was a lie."

It surprised me how well he knew me already. And what's more, he was right.

"There's nothing wrong with being curious."

"You're right. There's not." He held my gaze for a moment. After screwing the lid back on his container, he dropped it inside the wheelbarrow with a thud. "Actually, I'm pretty grateful for your seeming inability to follow the rules."

I raised a suspicious eyebrow at him. "You are?"

"Absolutely." He stood, brushing the remaining plant food from his hands so he could move the wheelbarrow farther down the row. "Because if you didn't tell Instructor Baak off every day in class, I wouldn't know so much about the care and cultivation of rosebushes."

As he helped me up, we both chuckled, and I playfully smacked his shoulder with my plant food–covered hand. It was after we'd moved down the row and started on the next plants that I remembered Melanie's threat. "Actually, Trayton, I have something I need to talk to you about too."

"Would this be anything to do with Darius?" My heart shot into my throat. He reached for the container of plant food and met my gaze, shrugging. "Melanie told me that you were alone with him in the courtyard the night those Graplars attacked. She said some other things, but I wanted to get your side before I jumped to any conclusions."

"Melanie is . . ." A particularly nasty adjective flitted through my mind, but I kept it to myself. ". . . trying to blackmail me into switching places with her Healer."

His eyes widened. "She left that part out. Why would she do that?"

"I'm not sure I follow the logic in it, but I know it has something to do with how much she likes you."

"There is an enormous difference between the word *like* and the word *covet*." A dark, brooding light filled his eyes then. One that made me wonder about his and Melanie's history. But it passed just as quickly as it had come. "So what about being alone with Darius? Where was Maddox?"

For the moment, I went with the truth, knowing that I could only reveal so much of it. "I snuck out without Maddox to confront Darius. He's been such a dek to me since the day I got here. I wanted to know why."

"And did you find out?"

Slightly irritated that I hadn't, I flung a particularly large glob of plant food onto the base of the rosebush in front of me. "No."

Trayton wore a small smile. "Want to know a secret about him?"

He didn't know the half of it. Darius, it turned out, was full of secrets. "What's that?"

Trayton leaned closer, cupping his hand to his mouth, as if we were sharing some grand secret. As he whispered, it tickled my ear. "Darius is like that to everyone."

Laughing, I nudged him away with my shoulder. "Not to you."

"He was for a long time."

"What happened?" I couldn't imagine a time when Darius wasn't so . . . well . . . grouchy. Maybe he'd been nicer before I'd come to Shadow Academy. But it seemed like his attitude was simply part of his genetic makeup.

"I don't know." He turned to face me, his eyes full of wonder. "It was like one day he just started trusting me. Ever since then, we've been all right. I stay out of his business and he stays off my case."

I wiped my hands off on my leggings, my thoughts a million miles away. "Do you trust him?"

"Completely." He sighed heavily and sat the container down between us, as if he tired of feeding the stupid roses. "I just wish he didn't seem so drawn to Graplars."

CHAPTER

Twenty-four

Of course, twenty years to the day after the battle at Wood's Cross, a second large-scale battle would take place in the exact location—known as the second battle at Wood's Cross—though no one can seem to identify exactly why two identical battles would take place in the same exact spot two full decades apart. In fact, both Shadow Academy and Starlight Academy are still recovering from the echoes of that battle, which ended just three years ago." Mr. Ross scribbled the titles of each battle on the board as he spoke. With each word, I sank further in my seat, not wanting to hear about the battle that had stolen my parents' Soulbound Healers away, or about a repeat of that kind of horror. I would have napped all through history, but my body was too tense. I blamed the subject matter.

"There are theories, of course—that Darrek is searching for something at Wood's Cross, that Wood's Cross naturally draws evil to its center, etcetera—but none have been proven. In fact, King Darrek himself may not have any cause to fight with such fury in that location. Perhaps this is a case of fate, and nothing more."

Stories of fate and locations of immense evil, and *this* was what passed for education around here? I'd learned more about the second battle at Wood's Cross from my brief field trip with Darius than I would in ten years of Mr. Ross's lectures. I blew out a snort, drawing the eyes of several classmates and Mr. Ross. "Something you'd like to add, Kaya?"

Dropping my eyes to the tabletop in front of me, I said, "I have nothing to say."

"Are you sure? After all, your father, Patrick, was the leading general at the initial battle at Wood's Cross. Perhaps he shared some tales with you about what took place?"

All eyes were on me now, but my eyes were on Mr. Ross, and I was wondering if what he'd said were true. My father was in charge of the raid? He'd never mentioned it, had only barely mentioned Wood's Cross. I had no idea he'd been such an important, integral part of the fight. Quieted by my awe, I shook my head, vowing to ask my father about it the next time I saw him . . . if I ever did. "No. Nothing. Please . . . go on."

It was the first day I made it through History class without falling into a coma. But that alertness only barely followed me from one class to the next.

Hours later, as I sat in Instructor Baak's classroom fighting a spontaneous nap, she walked back and forth in front of the class. Her hands were clasped behind her back, her spine rigid. She looked a bit like an evil dictator. Strangely enough, it suited her. "Today you will write a five-hundred-word essay on what you would sacrifice in order to support your Barron. Would you give up time? Sleep? Would you sacrifice your very life in order to save that of your Bound or Soulbound Barron? Just how far are you willing to go, how loyal are you to the cause?"

At the mention of sleep, I rested my cheek against my upturned palm and let my eyes droop. It was difficult enough facing Mr. Ross's lecture in a conscious state. I couldn't be expected to roll through Instructor Baak's blathering without at least a short break.

"Every single person in this classroom is related to someone who served in the war. How many of them were Healers who lost their lives? Kaya." I jumped slightly at the sound of my name, and only just barely resisted the urge to yawn. She stopped pacing and faced me, her nose stuck slightly in the air. "As I understand it, your parents served in the first battle at Wood's Cross, yes? Which is the Healer, your mother or father?"

It was a natural presumption for her to make, but that

didn't mean that it hadn't stung a bit. Glancing to my left and right before answering, my voice came out softly, as if I was embarrassed, even though I had nothing to be embarrassed about. "My parents are both Barrons."

Instructor Baak pursed her lips, as if the very idea of two Barrons coupling had sent a wave of nausea over her. "And their Healers?"

"Their Healers both died in that battle."

She snorted. "A prime example of Healer sacrifice. Your parents should be proud. As I am proud—my own daughter perished in the second battle of Wood's Cross."

I shook my head, unsure of what I should take away from her insinuation that anyone dying for any reason could be a good thing. "I'm so sorry for your loss."

"Why? I'm not angry. I'm not bitter. My heart isn't completely broken." Her eyes were wide and crazy looking again, the way they'd been that day in Instructor Harnett's class. And something else—Instructor Baak was lying. It was written all over her face. She was still mourning the loss of her daughter, but it seemed like she was pushing that pain away, just for appearance sake. For a moment, I felt immensely sorry for her.

Then the sadness left her eyes, replaced quickly by something ugly. On its edges burned anger, but I wasn't convinced that it was aimed entirely at me. She leaned closer and narrowed her eyes at me in a glare. "What will *you* give when the time comes? Will you die for your Barron? I doubt it."

Before I could say anything—not that I had anything to say to that—she snorted again and went back to pacing. I returned my cheek to my upturned palm and waited for class to be dismissed. Only this time, I didn't fight the yawn.

Twenty-five

The next morning, I slipped my mask on over my face and walked around the building toward the south gate. There weren't many guards out this morning, but my attention wasn't focused on them anyway. It was on the distinct, undeniable absence of my instructor. My nerves bundled into a tightly coiled ball at the pit of my stomach. I scanned the area around the gate, but he wasn't there. Then, just as I was about to turn around and head back to the dorms, a hand fell on my shoulder. I jumped slightly, but relaxed immediately, knowing it had to be Darius.

But when I turned around, I saw that it wasn't. It was Raden. "You're the one getting extra training from Darius, right?"

I nodded, but didn't speak. Mostly because I couldn't. That ever-present fear that I'd get caught tickled the base of my spine.

Raden frowned, as if he were about to deliver some bad news and didn't want to be put in the middle of anything, but was forced to. "He showed up earlier, told me to tell you he's canceling today's session. Maybe tomorrow too. Maybe for good, he hasn't decided."

My heart sank. With sagging shoulders, I started to turn away, but paused, turning briefly back to Raden. "Thanks."

As I walked away, he called after me. "From what I hear, you don't need those sessions anyway, Barron."

Walking away, I couldn't shake Darius from my thoughts. Where was he? Had our draw really been such a big deal to him that he'd actually walked away from training me? Wasn't I supposed to develop enough skill to match my instructor? If I was doing what I'd set out to do, what Darius had set out for me to do, then what was the problem exactly? Why would it end with him walking away without another word and not a congratulatory handshake? I didn't get it.

Or maybe I did. Maybe my assumption that Darius hated me had been a hundred percent correct after all. And maybe my attacking him had just solidified his reasons for disliking me. My stomach was in knots as I crossed the campus, slipping back behind Darius's cottage to the armory where Maddox was waiting. As I opened the door, she looked up, confusion filling her features. "What happened?"

Slipping my mask off, I shook my head. A terrible

disappointment had seeped into every fiber of my being. It seemed silly, moping about something that I had no control over. But I was, and couldn't help the way that I was feeling. "Darius didn't show. Raden said that he mentioned canceling. Maybe for good."

Maddox frowned. "Did he say why?"

"He didn't have to." I sucked in a breath and let the confession come pouring out of me. It was a bit of a relief just to say the words aloud, but in no way eased my tension completely. "Yesterday, we were facing off and it ended in a draw."

Her jaw almost hit the floor. As I changed clothes, she tried to speak several times, but in the end, just grabbed me by the arm and tugged me out the door. Of course she was shocked that I'd matched Darius in a fight—who wouldn't be? I certainly didn't think that it was possible, especially this early on in my training. And I never thought that doing so would be enough to end our training sessions. Of course, it was possible that that wasn't the reason at all. Maybe it was because I'd lost my temper. Maybe it was because I'd totally disrespected my instructor by attacking him. And maybe my unexpected attack had simply surprised him, and that's the only reason we were in a draw. Or maybe he let me come to a draw, because he felt sorry for me. I had no idea, and might not ever know.

All I did know was that my feet felt heavy as we snuck back to the dorms, and that my chest felt tight as I got dressed in my school uniform and made my way down to the dining hall.

The hall was busy as usual, and Trayton waved us over to our table in the corner. Maddox disappeared to the food line and I pushed my way through the crowd, stopping only when I noticed the familiar face seated next to Trayton. I slid into my seat across from Trayton and he stood, brushing his hand over mine before giving it a squeeze. "Morning, Kaya. I hope you don't mind the company. Darius has something he wants to talk to me about."

"Of course I don't mind." I managed a smile at Darius, who simply nodded at me. There was no emotion there, no reaction to me at all but for the nod. I didn't know what he was up to exactly, but something about the timing of this little chat felt off. Glancing over at the food line, I tried to find Maddox, but she was nowhere that I could see. Great. I was going to have to face this on my own.

"As I said, Trayton, I could certainly use your advice on something. You see, I've taken to giving extra training lessons to a Barron who desperately needs them." As Darius spoke, the corner of his mouth lifted slightly in a smirk. Darius was about to say something that both of us might come to regret. My chest tightened, but in a whole new way. "But I've reached a point where I'm not at all certain whether or not I should continue my efforts to better her skills."

Trayton sat back in his chair, listening intently. "It's not like you to give up on someone, Darius."

"Not normally, no. But this student is kind of a dek." He sat back then, cocking an eyebrow, and there was no doubt at all that he was talking about me.

Trayton chuckled. "What makes her such a dek?"

"She's stubborn, hardheaded, thinks she knows better than me."

"Not good traits for a Barron, but are you sure that's the problem? Maybe she has a thing for you. It wouldn't be the first time a student fell for you." Trayton shrugged. His tone was matter of fact. It shouldn't have surprised me that girls often fell for Darius, but for some reason, it did. Maybe because everyone else at the school thought that he was an Unskilled, and that label put him beneath them somehow. Or maybe for some other reason entirely.

"That may be the case . . ." He didn't look at me, but I could tell that he was tempted to. I pretended to look for Maddox. Attracted to Darius? Oh heavens no. Not me. Not even a little bit. Forcing my thoughts away from the shirtless image of him, I cleared my throat. Darius propped his feet up on the table. "But the larger problem is that she lost her temper yesterday and attacked me full on, unprovoked."

Maddox returned to the table then, tray full of food in her hands. As she set it on the table, she said, "Who attacked you?"

"A student."

Maddox shook her head and shrugged, irritation burning on the edges of her frown. "Drop 'em and report 'em to the headmaster."

I had to resist the urge to kick Maddox. Hard. Leaning forward, casually plucking a grape from the food tray, I said, "The question is *why* she attacked you. Did you give her any reason?"

Darius grew quiet with contemplation. After mulling my question over for a bit, he shook his head adamantly. "None at all. We were running through some offensive maneuvers and she lost her temper when I took her down."

"That calls for regrouping." Trayton looked at me and offered an explanation in answer to my questioning glance. "Stepping away from the fight. Keeping a cool head is essential in a battle, so it's a big part of training, and probably the most difficult thing to learn."

Darius reached out and brushed a smudge of dirt from his left boot. When he spoke, it was directly to me, though no one else at the table was aware of that fact. "So the question remains . . . what to do? Do I end our training sessions outside the classroom, or do I continue?"

The table went quiet for a bit. Maddox shot me a glance that said that she only just realized that Darius had been talking about me. Trayton chewed on a strip of crispy bacon before responding. "That depends, Darius, on whether or not you see potential in her for success."

Darius returned his feet to the floor. He didn't speak for a long time, and in his silence, he allowed his eyes to find mine for the briefest of moments.

"Her skills at times surprise me." His voice had soft-ened some, and he dropped his gaze to the table between us. When he spoke again, my heart jumped a little. "Yes. The potential is there."

I cleared my throat, hoping that Darius understood that I was apologizing. "Everyone deserves a second chance."

With that, Darius stood, popped a grape into his mouth, and turned to walk away. Before he'd taken two steps, he said, "I suppose they do."

CHAPTER

Twenty-six

The next morning, I approached the south gate. The grass was dewy under my feet, making my steps sound soft and wet. My breath came out in puffs of fog. The temperature was dropping a little more every day, Summer tripping steadily into Fall. Looking over the Barrons standing near the gate, I sighed. Darius was nowhere in sight.

But then I spied him, coming out of the guard shack. After noticing me, he came over, all business. "You're late. Again."

Behind my mask, I smiled. I was glad to see him too.

"Glad I caught you. I was worried I'd have to search the woods. Not that I'd know which way to look." Trayton's voice came from behind me. I immediately stiffened.

What was he doing here? Did he know that I was the one Darius had been talking about at breakfast yesterday? I was caught. Oh fak, I was caught and there was nothing I could do about it. But then, I thought, maybe it wasn't a bad thing. After all, Trayton's tone seemed completely calm. Maybe he was okay with the idea of me training after all.

Darius smiled. First at me, then behind me at Trayton—which told me that Trayton likely had no idea that I was me at all. And with the face mask, he wouldn't. Not unless I spoke. "We would have waited. But not for long. Let's get out there and back before the dining hall opens for breakfast. I'm hungry enough as it is."

Trayton moved around to my right side and offered me a nod. "Name's Trayton."

Darius spoke before I could utter a squeak that would undo every bit of secrecy my face mask offered. "This is Tabitha. Now if you ladies are done with the small talk, let's focus on some quiet practice this morning, shall we?"

Trayton bowed his head respectfully and led the way to the south gate. I looked at Darius, whose smile simply grew as he extended his arm in front of him, as if to say "ladies first." With a scowl, I followed after Trayton, my curiosity driven to the brink. Why was Trayton here? What was the point of this? And did Darius have any idea what it would mean if Trayton learned that I had been training behind his back? My relationship with Trayton would be in jeopardy. He'd have to follow Protocol and turn me over to the headmaster. And my parents . . .

I swallowed hard. My steps slowed, but still I followed Trayton out the gate and down the hill, with Darius close behind me. The air felt heavy. I wasn't certain whether that was because of the thick layer of condensation hanging in it, or the worry in my heart that Darius might betray my confidence at any moment. But I moved through it, counting my paces until we reached the secret training area. It felt wrong, being here with someone who wasn't Darius. Like an intruder had invaded our space.

Trayton slipped his training mask on and removed his katana from the sheath on his back. Darius poised himself between us, all echoes of his previous smile completely removed. He was all business now. "I've asked Trayton to face off with you today, Tabitha. He's my finest student, and if you can best him, I'll know that that little stunt you pulled yesterday wasn't just a fluke. I'll also know where to take the next training steps. So if you'll step into the ring, Trayton will be on the offensive to start. Take the fight where it leads, and finish strong. Hesitation is your weakness."

Trayton moved immediately into a fighting stance. With a nervous breath, I struck my pose, ready to face him. My heart was rattling inside my chest, and my legs were shaking. Facing Darius was one thing, but facing down the man that I was Bound to—that was another thing entirely. What if I seriously injured him? Not only would that be an awful experience for Trayton, but I'd have no choice but to expose myself and heal him. If I didn't, Trayton might die. And if I did . . . what would become of my parents?

With a million possible scenarios whipping through my mind, I readied myself for Trayton's attack. Trayton raised up his katana in an attack, swiping it forward faster and more crisply than I was currently capable of. His attack struck me as familiar, and as I blocked it and turned, it occurred to me that I had encountered it before. Trayton fought like Darius.

As I turned, I brought my sword around and slid my left foot out, lowering my body closer to the ground. I brought the blade hard toward his shins, but at the last possible moment, Trayton jumped over my blade. Part of me was relieved. I didn't want to injure Trayton, but then again, I didn't want to get hurt by him either.

The moment he hit the ground, he spun and swung forward, aiming his katana right for my neck. I ducked to the side in a near panic. My heart raced so fast that it felt like a single, long beat inside my chest. The horrified realization that Trayton was aiming to kill swept over me, and I had to fight from crying out.

If I did that, if I so much as uttered a peep, it was all over. My training, my time with Darius. Everything.

My jawline felt warm and wet. I reached up, feeling the blood on my neck. Trayton had just nicked my ear, but there was no time to examine it. He swung again, this time straight at my head, and I brought up my katana in a block, my instincts taking over. The sound of metal on metal rang through my ears as our katanas met in the air between us. Our blades still together, he pressed down hard with his sword and I braced my weapon, my shoulders burning, knowing it was just a matter of time before he broke through my defenses. Behind Trayton, I could see Darius. His foot was propped up on a rock, one hand stroking his chin as he watched our interaction. I could read the expression in his eyes.

He looked pleased.

Disgust filled me, coupled with rage. My lungs burned as my breathing came hard and heavy, but I pushed back, and was surprised to find that I could hold Trayton's advances at bay. He stood a foot over me at least, but here I was, holding him off, keeping him from breaking through. By the look of the tension in Trayton's body, he was surprised too—even though he was under the impression that he was fighting a Barron, an equal. Not some lowly Healer. Especially not *his* Healer.

As if the thin thread that was holding his patience together had snapped, Trayton pivoted the weight on his weapon, slamming the handle of his katana into my shoulder. Pain rocked through me and I fell back. Regaining my balance, I swept his leg and he went down. With Darius's smug expression locked in the forefront of my mind, I pulled my weapon through the air in a crosscut with all the strength I could muster. Pulling back at the last second, my blade stopped at Trayton's neck.

He whipped off his mask, his eyes furious and dark. My heart slowed, sinking some inside my chest. I could have killed him. I could have taken Trayton's life in a moment of fury against my teacher.

Wordlessly, I slid my katana into its sheath on my back and held out a hand. When he took it, after a moment's hesitation, I helped him stand. We stood there, catching our breath, until Trayton wiped the blood from his neck. "You're a hell of a combatant, Barron."

"That she is." Darius entered the circle then and excused Trayton with a nod. Trayton picked up his mask and retreated up the hill. Several minutes passed before either of us moved or spoke.

He'd complimented me, yes, but Darius had also done the unforgivable. When I was sure that we were alone, and that Trayton was completely out of earshot, I whipped off my mask and tossed it to the ground. I shoved Darius as hard as I could, fury welling up from within me. "What the fak was that about?"

Darius barely moved from my assault. His words were eerily calm, as if he'd been expecting my reaction. "It was just part of the training."

I didn't have to look far to see the lie in his eyes. Snatching my mask from the ground, I shoved it on and ran up the hill toward the gate. If this was what he deemed just an everyday part of training, then he could forget it. No amount of training could be worth exposing me to Trayton and endangering the lives of my parents. I was done. I was finished. With Darius, with training, with everything.

After my final class of the day, and after a long day spent avoiding Trayton and nursing my shoulder, I walked into my room, shutting the door between Maddox and me, hoping to spend some time alone thinking. I also wanted to rub my injured shoulder with rose oil, and coax the muscles there into a less painful state.

On the small table near the door was a fresh vase of red roses, with a note.

"Meet me at the library tonight after dusk. –Yours, T"

Maybe I should have been happy about the regular appearance of fresh flowers in my room. Any normal girl might have been thrilled about the love notes and attention. But even though I smiled each time I saw them, inside I felt like I was doing so because that was how I was supposed to react. Not that the flowers and notes weren't perfectly nice, but I wanted more than roses and poetry. I wanted respect.

I bit my bottom lip in contemplation. On one hand, I really wanted to be left alone, really wanted to confront Darius about what he'd done. On the other, I longed to spend some quiet time with Trayton, to be alone and normal and forget about Graplars. My nightmares had all but ceased, and I was really looking forward to some sound rest, but how could I resist an evening at the library with Trayton? I couldn't. So with a deep breath, I opened the parlor door and showed Maddox my most charming smile. Instantly, she snorted. "Whatever, Princess. Let's go."

Not long after, we were walking up to the library. The entire walk, I thought about my mother and how much I missed her. Maddox was great, but she wasn't exactly the kind of friend you could cry to. Maddox was a solution-finder, a fixer, not someone who'd let you sob into their shoulder because a boy was mean to you. Every day I waited for a letter from my parents, some sign that they were alive and well. I'd written to them weekly, but there was no guarantee that the school messengers were actually delivering my notes, or that Headmaster Quill had even allowed them to carry my scribblings off Shadow Academy grounds. The very thought made me feel incredibly lonely.

Trayton was waiting for us just outside the library. His smile was earnest—so unlike the one I'd offered Maddox to get her to take me to the library when I should have been studying for a quiz on herbal remedies. His smile spread the closer I got to him. "You're not an easy girl to run into."

Trying my best not to let my guilt show at having avoided him all day, I smiled back. "A girl can never be too easy to find. Gives boys ideas about them."

He opened the door and we moved inside. As we moved up the stairs, I flashed Trayton a questioning glance. What were we doing at the library? We certainly couldn't sneak into the secret room he'd shown me. Not with Maddox there—she'd done Trayton enough favors. But Trayton didn't answer my look with anything but one that said that I should just wait and see what he had planned.

As we reached the top of the stairs, Trayton turned to Maddox. "Twenty minutes."

Maddox shook her head. "This time's gonna cost you some trinks, Barron."

Trayton faked a gasp and dropped three coins in her open palm. "Maddox! I'm shocked. Bribery?"

Maddox shrugged and sank into one of the chairs in the loft. "It's a living. Twenty minutes. No more."

As Trayton opened the secret door, I couldn't help but smirk. "Breaking the rules, Barron? I thought you had to follow Protocol."

Trayton grinned. "Section three, paragraph twenty-two of the Protocol handbook states that newly Bound Barrons and Healers are allowed up to three hours of private time together in the first year in order to ex-change details of one another's history."

"Ahh. A loophole." With a chuckle, I stepped inside and we moved up the stairs together. Trayton's hand was warm in mine, and I struggled between mixed emotions as we touched. The guilt over not being honest about training. The fear over having faced him in combat. The thrill over holding his hand in a dark, secret place that was ours to share. We moved into the small attic space. Once we were seated, I looked up at the stars, which were twinkling down at me from the crystalline ceiling. "What was it like," I wondered aloud, "growing up the way you did."

He shrugged and put his arm around my shoulders. As I nuzzled into him, he said, "Nothing out of the ordinary, I suppose. My father was always away, fighting in the war, and my mother was always taking trips to the front to be on call in case he needed her. I grew up with a variety of nannies until I turned thirteen—that's when I came to Shadow Academy to study. What about you?"

I couldn't imagine what it must have been like to grow up without your parents around. With nannies talking care of you until you were old enough to be shipped off to some school. Picturing my parents doing something like that to me was an impossibility. "I grew up on the outskirts of a small Unskilled town. Every day my father hunted or fished, and every night my mother would sew or knit by the fireplace. I read tons of books, played in the brook by our house, and went to school with people my own age."

Trayton's attention was on me, as if every word that I'd uttered sounded to him like a fairy tale. "That sounds amazing."

Sighing, I said, "It was. Until I received a letter from the headmaster, saying I had to come here."

He tilted his head then, so that we were eye to eye. His words were a whisper. "Has it been so terrible, life at Shadow Academy?"

"I just miss my freedom." Lifting my face, I found myself almost breathless at Trayton's close proximity. "But if I'd never come here, I never would have met you."

Then he leaned in and pressed his lips against mine. Our mouths melted together. Trayton pulled me closer and I winced as pain tore through my shoulder—pain that I'd almost forgotten, pain that he'd unwittingly been the cause of. We parted instantly and he furrowed his brow. "Are you all right?"

Rubbing at the muscles in my shoulder, I said, "I'm fine. Just pulled something while I was working in the rose gardens, I guess."

The look in his eye said that he believed me. But I had to fight the urge to tell him that he shouldn't.

CHAPTER

Twenty-seven

The gate door opened and in front of me, Barrons filed out. I filed out with them, disguised as one of them and so nervous that I'd be found out that my hands were shaking. Darius had run through their maneuvers with me that morning, but I just knew I was going to step with the wrong foot at the wrong time, or something else so simple that it would give me away. Inside the wall, the Healers waited, along with several Master Healers. Headmaster Quill had decided that these maneuvers were so close to the school that it didn't make much sense to risk the Healers' lives by sending them out where Graplars had been spotted. He was probably right, but seeing the Healers left behind made me nervous for so many of the Barrons. It also made me think about how Trayton might be feeling. He hadn't seen me waiting with the other Healers and had to question where I was. He had to wonder what I was doing that was more important than waiting here to assist him, if he needed my help. I wondered if he felt afraid at all, or if he simply felt angry that I wasn't here to see him off. I couldn't see where he was standing, whether he was in front of me in the group somewhere or behind, but I could spy a flash of silver hair to my right and when I turned my head, Darius nodded at me, his jaw stern, his eyes sparkling, ready for the fight to come. A light breeze moved his hair and I wondered again why he never wore a face mask, or why no one insisted that he did. Whatever his reasons, I was certain that Darius would defend them to the end.

As I crossed through the door, a scent danced on the breeze, a foul odor that could only mean that death was near. Together, the Barrons and I turned and moved to the south, over the crest of a large hill, and then down into the valley on the other side. Their feet were sound-less on the forest floor, but mine found every dead leaf, every twig. If any Graplars were in the vicinity, they'd know our location by my tromping. I was trying to keep quiet, but doing so made me fall behind, and the last thing I wanted while on maneuvers was to have a large distance between myself and Darius. He was, as much as I was loathe admitting it, my best defense if I got into any trouble I couldn't handle.

My katana felt oddly heavy on my back, as if the saya were weighted, or perhaps pulling on me to stay still, to keep as far away from the world outside the wall as I possibly could. I moved forward, staying close to Darius, and when he broke into a run, I followed, keeping his pace, even though running that fast made my lungs burn and my thighs ache. He moved ahead of me without so much as a change in his breathing, and I was grateful when his steps finally slowed and I could catch up. He and several other Barrons were standing at the apex of a small ridge, looking down on the other side. By the time I reached him, the smell had overwhelmed my senses. Something—or someone—was dead.

I didn't want to see what or who was lying at the bottom of that ridge, but the Barrons were looking, so I had to look too. Planting the toes of my shoes in the earth, I climbed the ridge. But when I reached Darius's side, determined to cast my eyes on the scene that had them all so alert, Darius grabbed me by the arm and turned me away from it. As we walked away, back down the hill, he muttered under his breath, "Another Healer. Definitely a Graplar. You don't have to look at the body in order to convince them you're a Barron."

Shaking his hand from my shoulder and glancing around to be certain no one would hear me speak, I said, "What if I wanted to look? What if I wanted to see it?"

Darius looked me over for a long moment. Then he stepped back and looked back at the ridge. He waited, silently, but we both knew that I didn't want to see the body. It wasn't that I couldn't handle it, but I knew that once I saw it, I could never unsee it. After a long time, he turned from the ridge and began moving south again. My shoulders sagging, I followed.

Barrons spread out through the woods around us, but none were ahead of Darius as he moved with certainty around this tree and that. Once we crested another small hill, we were joined by six others. Silently, alertly, we moved deeper and deeper in the forest as a team, and once we worked our way across a small creek, I saw where Darius was leading us. An enormous oak tree stood on the other side of the creek, its trunk marred with large claw marks, some of them fresh. Darius pointed at the tree. "It watches."

He dropped his arm, gesturing to the creek that we had just crossed. "It drinks."

The Barron to my left removed his mask, shaking his head. I was surprised to see that it was Trayton. He looked back over his shoulder, in the direction we had come from, and I could tell by the look in his eyes that he was thinking about the body of the Healer that they'd found. Under his breath, he spoke, his voice eerily calm. "It feeds."

They were talking about a Graplar that had apparently made camp just outside the school walls. Not on the Outer Rim, but here, here where we were supposed to be relatively safe. My heart rattled inside my chest, and I couldn't help but wonder whether it was around now, maybe watching us from the treetops, maybe hungering to rip the meat from our bones.

I tilted my head back, scanning the trees, but saw nothing lurking above us. By the time I'd brought my attention back to my immediate surroundings, Darius was crouched and looking furtively over some markings in the soil. In a moment of alarm, he jerked his head up and looked back past the creek, in the direction we'd come from. A moment later, a sound filled my ears. A horrible screeching that I knew all too well.

As if they were one body, the group of Barrons darted over the creek and back up the hill. They moved quickly, their footfalls silent on the forest floor. My thighs burned as I tried to keep up, but I fell behind, my lungs aching, sweat pouring down my brow. When I finally caught up to them, the scene before me made my heart seize momentarily inside my chest.

A large group of Graplars were facing off with several Barrons at the north gate, metal slicing through air, then flesh. Teeth biting, chewing. It was horrendous to see, but two Graplars were doing the unthinkable. They threw their bodies against the gate, and when the metal refused to break under the pound of their scaly flesh, they'd back up and do it again. The beast on the left had hit the door so hard that the skin on top of its skull had split open. Blood poured from the wound, but it backed up and flung itself forward once again. The sound of flesh against metal resounded through the forest. Only a scream tore my attention away. A Graplar to my left had sunk its teeth into a Barron's shoulder and was thrashing its head back and forth, refusing to free its prey. Instinctively, I reached back, freeing my katana and ran to assist.

The voice at the back of my mind told me to keep running, to get the hell out of here and let someone who was more qualified handle this, that I couldn't possibly help this Barron anyway, but I told it to shut up and ran at the Graplar with my sword at the ready. I'd asked for this. I'd begged Darius to let me come along. And now I was going to kill the monster. I was going to save that Barron. If I had to die to do it. And fear wasn't going to stop me.

Slashing through the air, I brought my katana down hard, cutting straight through the beast's right eye. The thing let out an angry howl, opening its jaws wide. The rows and rows of teeth parted, releasing the trapped Barron at last. He stumbled, then fell on the ground, clutching his wounded shoulder. Blood poured from the bite. His face flushed, and I thought for sure he was going to pass out cold right there, but to my shock, he remained standing.

The Graplar shook its massive head and, recovering from my blow, it narrowed its black, soulless eyes at me. I had thought, prior to that moment, that Graplars were incapable of emotion, that they were simply mindless, heartless killing machines, bent on chewing people to bits for the sheer pleasure of it. But at that moment, staring into the dark abyss of its gaze, I learned that Graplars were absolutely capable of feeling emotion, and that this one was incredibly terked off. At me.

Without thinking—because if I took even a second to do that, I might have screamed—I raised my blade as fast as I could and brought it down again, but this time, the Graplar ducked my advances and charged forward, knocking me on my back. My lungs clenched closed as the wind was knocked out of me. My chest was frozen in a state of panic. I couldn't breathe, couldn't move. And I couldn't see the Graplar.

Scrambling to my feet, I tried to catch my breath, but before I could, I was hit in the side by the creature's massive bulk. My back hit the ground again, and the Graplar gnashed its teeth forward. Thinking fast, I brought up my blade just in time. It bit down on the metal just inches from my face. I thought that it might back off then, because the katana was cutting into the corners of its mouth, blood dribbling down the blade, down my arm and onto my chest. But the beast narrowed its eyes even more and pushed toward me, forcing the blade deeper into its own flesh. It didn't care. It only cared that its actions would bring its hungry jaws closer to me.

My heart was racing. What more could I do to stop the beast? What more could I do to save my own life?

I pushed hard with the katana, sinking the edge of the blade in deeper still, hoping to lop off its head, but I couldn't get enough leverage on the blade, and drool was dripping from its jaws in anticipation of its next meal. Then, over the Graplar's shoulder, I spied the Barron who I had saved. The tip of the katana's sharp blade was sticking out of the side of its hungry mouth, and with precision, the Barron grabbed the tip with his hand. The metal sliced slowly into his flesh and blood poured out of him. He barely winced, and I was reminded of my parents and their enormous resistance to pain. He pulled the blade back, deeper into the beast's mouth. The katana cut through the Graplar's head cleanly, and with a gurgle, its giant body stumbled to the left before collapsing lifeless on the ground.

Before I could thank the Barron, he was gone.

I hurried to stand, flinging the Graplar's blood from my blade before I turned to survey the battlefield. My heart was racing inside my chest, a steady stream of beats, pumping blood through my body. The thud of that blood rushing through me pounded in my ears, but not enough to drown out the sounds of fighting as they fell flat all around me. Most of the Graplars were dead, but the ones that weren't had run off to parts unknown. Surveying the Barrons around the battlefield, it didn't look like any lives were lost. Just a few scrapes and cuts, maybe a bite or two. All in all, we were wildly successful in our efforts. Pride filled me, replacing the adrenaline. I allowed myself a small smile as I looked around. We did this—the Barrons and I—we stopped the Graplars from getting inside the wall.

A hand closed over my face mask and ripped it away, flinging it onto the ground. I spun from whoever had grabbed it, but his other hand closed over my arm, as if to tell me that I wouldn't be going anywhere. I shoved at him then, and only then did I notice that he'd removed his mask as well. Trayton's eyes burned with a betrayal that shot straight through me. My jaw fell open, but no words would come. A low whisper made its way through the group, one that I tried desperately to ignore. And the entire time, Trayton's eyes, now moist with anger, were on me, refusing to look away.

Twenty-eight

The waiting area outside the headmaster's office was completely silent, apart from the sound of my heart drumming in my ears. Maddox was standing just to my left, fidgeting like she was dying to blurt out something inappropriate, but was managing not to do so, for my sake. Trayton sat to my right, sharing the bench I was seated on, but we couldn't have been further apart. My mouth was stubbornly closed, the tension in the air so thick, and I refused to utter even a single word to him after he'd reported me to Headmaster Quill. He was a traitor, and I wanted nothing to do with him.

By the look on his face, the feeling was mutual. He stared ahead, miles away from me, and even further away from the kisses we'd shared. Across from me sat Darius, who was leaning forward, his elbows resting on his knees, his eyes cast downward. The air grew increasingly heavy with tension as the seconds crawled by. At long last, the door to the headmaster's office opened and he stuck his pudgy head out the door. "Maddox. Inside. Now."

She glanced at me first and my heart followed her through that door. When it closed behind her, all I could do was bring my legs up and hug my knees to my chest in worry. What would happen to Maddox? Would she be sent away? I'd do anything to keep her here, but what could I do? It was Trayton's fault that she was here. One word from him to Headmaster Quill that I'd broken Protocol in a big way, and my guard had been called in for punishment as well.

The shouting began just a moment after the door had closed behind her. Raised voices—both Maddox's and Headmaster Quill's—shook the walls, but very little of what they were shouting could be deciphered from the side of the door that I was on. Not long after the argument ceased, the door whipped open and Maddox exited, her face flushed red with fury, her eyes piercing. She moved in front of me and I put my legs down, searching her face for any sign that everything would be all right. "I've been replaced as your guard, and he's forbidden me from speaking to you ever again, but if he thinks the powers that be are going to tear me away from my best friend, he's got another think coming, Kaya. Oh . . . and I've been permanently reassigned . . . to guard the north gate."

At this, even Darius straightened in alarm.

"But, Maddox . . ." I whispered, my heart heavy. "You aren't trained. And the north gate is the one most attacked by Graplars."

Maddox nodded, her anger giving way to tears. "I'll stop by tonight after your classes to see how your meeting went, okay?"

The door swung open again, and before the headmaster could wedge his pudgy head out the door, Maddox turned and disappeared down the hall and out of sight. "Darius. You're next."

Darius stood and entered the door with no sign of emotion at all. If anything, he moved with an air of confidence that I didn't understand. I also didn't understand why he'd stepped forward on the battlefield and admitted to Trayton that it was his fault I was there at all. I hadn't agreed with him—it was Darius who had trained me, but it was my choice to fight—but no one was listening to me.

Once the door had closed behind Darius, I dared a glance at Trayton, who remained stone-faced beside me. What was he thinking? That I had lied to him, betrayed his trust? Maybe he wasn't thinking about me at all. After a long silence, Trayton glanced my way, his eyes full of accusation. "Your shoulder? It wasn't injured gardening, was it? It was you that day outside the wall."

"If you'll recall, I did ask you to teach me. You said no. So I found someone who would."

"Yeah. My best friend." The scowl on his face deepened.

I sank into my seat. There was no need to respond.

From within the headmaster's office came muttered voices—not shouting as it had been with Maddox. After a moment, the door opened again. Surprisingly, Headmaster Quill peeked out from behind the heavy wood. "If you two would join us for a moment, I believe we can put this matter to rest."

Without another glance at Trayton, I stood and moved toward the door. My footfalls sounded heavy on the marble floor, their echoes filling the formerly silent room. As I pulled the door open and moved over the threshold, the air changed from cold and empty of emotion to stifling hot and filled to the brim with annoyance and irritation. Headmaster Quill gestured to the two unoccupied chairs in front of his desk. Darius was seated in the third, staring straight ahead, devoid of any emotion. Apparently, he had taken a page from Trayton's book.

After I sat down, Headmaster Quill took his seat behind the desk and eyed both Trayton and me wordlessly. Finally, he spoke. "There has been a complication, Kaya. A complication caused by your unforgivable actions and it demands a suitable punishment."

He looked at me, pausing, as if waiting for me to agree with him. I wouldn't. I wasn't about to agree to anything.

He cleared his throat before continuing. "You convinced your guard Maddox to acquire the teaching services of Darius, knowing that Healers are not allowed to train. It is your blatant disregard for the rules that has brought you here today. You should thank Trayton—he knows what's good for you. He knows the difference between right and wrong. You could take a page out of his book."

I sank deeper into my seat, fuming. Talking back would only get me into more trouble, and would likely only hurt Maddox more. So I said nothing, and waited for the chubby dictator to finish his rambling.

"Healers do not train to fight, Kaya. If I so much as glimpse you practicing whatever maneuvers that Darius has taught you, it will be your parents who are made to suffer for your insubordination. Am I making myself clear?" His threat shot through me and I sat motionless, the image of my parents' faces locked in the forefront of my mind.

My word came out in a whisper. "Abundantly."

"And Darius . . ." Headmaster Quill's attention turned on him then, though his tone turned much kinder. "I think it would be a good idea if you were transferred to Darkmoon Academy. They have need of an advanced level instructor, and I think you may fit the bill. A move certainly is warranted and may in fact be necessary."

"It's not, Headmaster." As Darius spoke, his voice cracked slightly. When he spoke again, his tone's usual strength had returned. But I had already seen behind the curtain. "A move is not necessary. But I would like to request a month's leave of absence in order to get my head together and put this behind me. Behind all of us."

The headmaster considered this briefly before nodding. "I think that would be wise. Consider your request granted. Trayton will cover your classes, with Raden's assistance, while you're away."

Darius barely let him finish his reply before he interjected, "If it's all right, I'd prefer to leave immediately."

Headmaster Quill merely nodded. He scribbled a note on one of the papers on the desk in front of him before turning eyes back to our little group. "Kaya, you'll serve extra duties for the next month."

I shrugged, uncaring.

"You're dismissed. All of you."

As we exited, Darius remained behind with the headmaster. Trayton held open the door for me, but refused to meet my eyes. I passed by him so closely that I could feel the heat radiating from his skin, could see his Trace peeking out from behind his dark hair. The urge to apologize was immediate and intense, but passed as quickly as it had come. After all, I wasn't in the wrong. I had merely wanted the ability to defend myself on the battlefield—nothing more. It wasn't like I was merely sneaking away to spend time with another boy for no reason.

As I turned my head away, I was tempted to stop moving, stop walking past him and say something—anything—to acknowledge him in some small way, the way that he was ceasing to acknowledge me. But in the end, I did continue walking, and stepped out into the hall, where a boy was standing. Sandy blond hair, caramel brown eyes, light freckles dusting his nose and cheeks. He looked nice enough, though he didn't smile. "Pleased to meet you, Kaya. My name is Edmond. I'll be your guard from here on out. Now if you'll follow me, I'll make sure you get some lunch before heading back to your room to study."

Immediately, my eyebrow rose up in an arch. Study? I didn't recall anything at all about saying I'd planned to study. Not that I was opposed to it or anything. Studying was important. But the last thing I wanted to do after facing down Graplars and terking off Trayton was study the proper way to administer a tonic.

With another glance at Trayton, who'd already moved halfway down the hall, I followed Edmond toward the dining hall, missing Maddox already. It worried me that she was guarding the north gate now, especially after what had happened there this morning. Picturing her, I imagined she was likely clearing away the dead Graplars. Their breath was so rancid that I could only imagine the smell of Graplar corpses. With visions of rotting blue flesh locked in the forefront of my imagination, I moved into the dining hall, the need for food squashed by an onset of nausea.

Edmond walked me to an empty table at the center of the room and pulled out my chair for me. With a polite nod, Edmond left me alone at my new table and went in the direction of the food line. Slumping in my seat,

I looked around, completely convinced that I'd see no one of consequence. No one I wanted to see, anyway.

Two tables over, however, I spied black hair and pale skin. It hurt that Trayton was sitting somewhere other than with me, but what really stung was the company that he was keeping. Melanie tossed her hair over her shoulder in an annoyingly feminine way, her laughter rolling through the dining hall, like poison in my ears. Neither looked my way. I slumped further down in my seat, hoping that I'd do the impossible and disappear. Or at least that they wouldn't notice me at all.

What was this? I knew he was hurt—mad, even—but was that really cause to start hanging out with Melanie? Especially after I'd told him of her twisted plans to get them together?

As I waited for Edmond to return, I tore my thoughts away from Trayton and his motives for hanging out with Melanie, turning them instead to the Graplars, and just how they'd been getting inside the wall. Everyone seemed to think that Graplars were so incredibly stupid, just big, hulking masses of muscle with little brains. But if that was the case, how were they getting inside? And doing so in such a way that completely hid how they were accomplishing it? It was mind-boggling. Unless . . .

I sat up in my chair, gently biting the inside of my cheek in deep thought. Unless someone was helping them get inside.

But who? A guard? A Healer? An instructor? My eyes flicked to Melanie.

She certainly was devious enough. But why? She had no reason to help Darrek, did she? She did hate Healers though, so I made a mental note to keep her on my list of potential suspects. There was also Instructor Baak, who seemed crazy enough to do just about anything. Mr. Groff loved Protocol too much, so he was off the list—unless being a total dek was enough of a reason to accuse someone of this kind of treachery. And Headmaster Quill was certainly evil enough, but did that put him in league with Darrek?

I chewed my bottom lip in contemplation. I'd just have to keep a eye on everyone, it seemed.

CHAPTER

Twenty-nine

My bed was covered in various piles of notes from each of my classes, but I wasn't reading any of them. Guilt about lying to Trayton all this time was robbing me of the ability to really focus on anything else. Edmond had dutifully been insisting that I attend class and eat right for almost a week now, and I had smiled politely through it all. It was only as I lay in bed at night that my true feelings surfaced. Darius was gone—off to wherever he needed to go in order to escape the trouble he'd gotten me into. It was his fault, after all. If he'd never pitted Trayton against me, Trayton never would have recognized me on the battlefield, I was sure of it.

And Trayton was here, but not really here at all. I had barely seen him since that day in the headmaster's office, and hadn't spoken to him at all. Whispers in the hall said that he and Melanie had been spending an inordinate amount of time together, and I was beginning to wonder if the rumors were true. Or if it was my place at all to say anything about how much time Trayton spends with anyone else in secrecy.

The familiar squeak of the window being opened drew my attention. Maddox slipped inside, closing the glass behind her. "Again with the dramatic moping? You've been like this every night this week."

Flicking my eyes to the parlor door, I shushed her with a wave of the hand. "Quiet! Edmond might hear you!"

Maddox rolled her eyes. "Does he ever come in without knocking? Of course not, apart from an emergency situation, that would be against Protocol."

I flipped through a paperback copy of *The Art of Healing* and sighed. "You hardly ever knocked."

"Well, that's the difference between Edmond and me. I don't give a fak about Protocol." She grinned and gingerly jumped onto the bed beside me, sending notes flying. "Have you talked to Trayton yet?"

My heart sank further into the dark depths inside of me. "Little difficult to talk to him if I can't even manage to run into him."

Maddox raised an eyebrow. "You sleep one room away from the guy, Kaya. It can't be that hard to get him alone. Not if you really wanted to."

"Are you saying I'm avoiding him? Why would I avoid him?" My tone was two decibels past irritated, and I was beginning not to care if Edmond heard us or not.

"Because you worry that you hurt his feelings by sneaking around with a hot commodity like Darius and bonding in a way that you and Trayton never have. There's an intimacy that goes hand in hand with training, after all." As my jaw fell to the floor, Maddox shrugged. "Sorry. But you did ask."

Flopping back into my pillows, I groaned. She was right. Completely, annoyingly right. Not about the intimacy with Darius—I couldn't even think about what she might be implying when she said that—but how was I suppose to approach Trayton to talk about what had happened, to defend my actions, when I'd known all along that it was wrong to lie to him about what I was doing every morning? I felt enormously guilty.

And twice as guilty for kind of enjoying my time with Darius. Not just the training, but his presence.

My stomach churned. No way. I hated Darius, and had every reason to.

Trayton and I were Bound, which meant that we shared a bond that would last an eternity. I had to get Darius and training and lies out of my head, had to fix whatever was broken between Trayton and me, and move forward. Like Darius was doing, wherever he was.

"Come on." Maddox tugged my arm until I was reluctantly standing. "You might want to grab a sweater or something. It's chilly out tonight."

As I slipped my arms into the sleeves of the softest

sweater I owned—one that my mother had knitted me out of purple sheepsilk, I said, "Where are we going?"

"*We* aren't going anywhere. *You're* going to talk to Trayton and straighten this whole thing out. Think of it this way, if he's going to hate you for doing what you did, he should at least listen to your reasons. I know for a fact that Trayton's at a party right now. You head into his room and wait for him to come back. I'll go to the party and coax him to call it a night. Then you corner him in his room, talk it all out, and there you go."

"You're forgetting one thing, Maddox. How am I going to get past Edmond? He'll never let me into Trayton's room, and even if he did, he'd never leave us alone together."

She pushed me toward the parlor door, and then changed direction, nudging me to what I thought was the wall. "Minor setback. But not one I hadn't thought of. I'll distract him while you sneak by the window."

"Window?!" Freezing in my tracks, I shot her a look filled with amazement. "Maddox, I'm not tiptoeing along the ledge outside just to talk to Trayton. Are you crazy?"

"Do you like him?"

"Of course I do."

Maddox folded her arms in front of her and gave me a look that spoke volumes. "Do you love him?"

At first, I couldn't reply. I liked Trayton, yes. And just seeing him was enough to make my heart flutter. But love? I wasn't sure. Avery was the one who had given her heart to every boy who handed her flowers, not me. So I didn't know if I loved Trayton. But I did know that it was breaking my heart that he wasn't speaking to me.

Maddox must have seen the answer on my face, because she jabbed a thumb at the window and said, "Then get out there, and figure it out. I'll go distract Edmond."

A million questions filled my mind. What if I fell? What if I somehow managed to sneak into Trayton's room and he still wouldn't talk to me?

"Kaya . . ." Flipping the latch, Maddox pushed the window open. A light breeze brushed my skin, and I was glad I'd put on the sweater. Because one way or another, Maddox was pushing me out the window. "Don't make me volunteer you for private tutoring with Instructor Baak."

Stepping over the windowsill and onto the four-inch-wide ledge, I forced my eyes to focus on the darkness, counting each brick as my fingers moved along them. I inched my way toward Trayton's window, until my back was no longer touching window space, but brick. Before closing the window, Maddox said, "Don't fall. And if you do fall, aim for the grass. Tuck and roll."

Rolling my eyes at her eternal wisdom, I kept my focus on my heels as they moved along the ledge, breathing slowly in and out, and hoping like hell I didn't die. It seemed like an eternity before I neared the parlor window. From inside, I heard girlish giggles that probably belonged to Maddox, but sounded unbelievably foreign.

Maddox didn't flirt. I wasn't even all that convinced that Maddox was interested in boys. But she was proving to be incredibly loyal.

A slight breeze rushed along the building, sending goose bumps up my arms, but I pushed forward, inch by treacherous inch, until I came at last to Trayton's window. The terrifying thought gripped me that it might be locked from the inside, but when I pushed on the glass, the window slid open with ease. It didn't even squeak.

Stepping over the threshold, I rubbed some warmth back into my arms and looked around. It was the first time I'd ever seen Trayton's room, and though I felt a bit wrong about having snuck in, it was nice to be close to him again, in some manner of speaking. A fresh pile of laundry was occupying the chair by his desk, which was covered with books—mostly manuals on different fighting stances, but some on the history of weaponry. His floor was clean and clear of any kind of mess, unlike mine, and his bed was made. It felt strange to be inside his room without permission, and I had to fight the urge to scramble back out the window and abandon Maddox's grand plan.

After a while, I sat on his bed. The room smelled spicy, warm, and very much like Trayton.

Along the headboard of his bed was a row of thick candles, and I imagined Trayton lying there, reading up on war materials, his cozy pillow stuffed neatly under his head. The image was completely endearing, and at once I missed his company more than I had all week. My body sank into the soft mattress, and I lay back, counting the minutes, wondering all the while what I was going to say to Trayton when he walked through that door.

The bed was so soft, so welcoming, that I didn't realize that I had fallen asleep until I heard the door close with a determination that suggested that Trayton had immediately noticed my presence.

I sat up, resisting the urge to stretch, and met his eyes. Words formed in my mind and faded away again, so quickly that I didn't have time to snatch them from the air and hold them out as an offering to his good will. His body was full of tension, and the look on his face said that he wasn't exactly happy to see me. He growled, "What are you doing here?"

A strange relief shot through me that he hadn't emphasized the word *you*, like he'd been hoping to find someone else waiting for him in his bed. As quickly as I could manage, I found my voice. "I wanted to talk to you. To see you."

He paused briefly before sighing, and I couldn't tell how mad he really was that I'd snuck into his room without permission. "Well, you've seen me. What do you have to say?"

"You've been avoiding me all week."

"With good reason."

Score one for Trayton. Suddenly, my skin grew incredibly warm, and I slipped the sweater from my arms. Was it really that hot in here, or was there something about guilt that made a person feel like they'd caught fire? I chose my next words carefully. "Don't you even want to know why I was training?"

He removed his shoes with a casual flair, as if this conversation was already finished, and he had already won. Not that anyone should be winning. "Because you're drawn to Darius and share his recklessness."

"Recklessness? Is that how you see me, Trayton? Because if so, you need to take a closer look." My voice had risen, and I didn't care if anyone heard. I was tired of being discounted, just because I was a Healer. "I just want the same thing that you have—the knowledge and training to protect my family and friends."

He pointed a finger at me, his eyes dark and serious, his voice a low growl. "It's not your place to defend anyone."

"And it's not your place to tell me what my place is!" I stood quickly, my jaw so tight it was aching. It wasn't fair, the way he was treating me. It wasn't right that Trayton wanted me to submit myself to rules that I heartily disagreed with, despite my fervent objections. "I've been told repeatedly that I'm supposed to stand on the sidelines of a battle and wait for someone else to rescue me. But I'm not just a lowly Healer, Trayton, I'm a person, and I deserve the right to know how to stand up for myself, just in case you aren't there to save me."

"I will be there. Every time."

"Did it ever occur to you that I've been training for a reason? What if you weren't there to rescue me? What if Graplars got into the school and you weren't by my side at that exact moment? I have a right to defend myself."

Trayton shook his head. "Maybe it would be different if you'd been defending yourself, but we both know that you were outside the wall, fighting Graplars with complete disregard for the rules. Rules that are in place to protect us, Kaya."

"Rules that are meant to control us, you mean." I was seething. "You worry too much about rules, Trayton. Too much about people's perception of you."

He seemed to take a moment then to let my words fill his ears, and to really consider what it was that I was saying. "Kaya . . . I would have taught you. If you would've insisted, I would have—"

"No, you wouldn't have." My tone wasn't accusing in the least. It was matter-of-fact. Because we'd already been down that road, and Trayton had adamantly said no to the idea of teaching me how to fight. I met his eyes, hoping that we could somehow come to an understanding. I was wrong, yes. But I was wrong for a damn good reason. "We both know that. And none of the knowledge and skill that I learned from my lessons with Darius could have been acquired without a little deceit. I'm sorry that I lied, Trayton, but I had little choice."

He sat on the edge of the bed, his shoulders sagging.

After a moment, I joined him. He looked at me, all anger gone, and said, "When I saw you on the battlefield, covered in blood, not knowing if any of it was yours or not, my heart shattered. You shouldn't have been there without telling me. And learning you've been sneaking off with Darius to train in secret . . ."

Suddenly my throat felt incredibly dry. "I wanted you to train me, remember? But you said no."

"So you run to my best friend to get training? That's how you handle 'no'? By sneaking around behind my back with someone that I trust? That's fakked up, Kaya." He turned his head as if to look at me then, but his eyes didn't quite make the journey. "That's really fakked up. How are we supposed to have a relationship if you can't trust me? If I can't trust you?"

I shrugged. "Who else was I supposed to ask? Maddox doesn't know how to fight, and Darius is the best. Besides, he said yes. The choice seemed pretty obvious at the time. All I care about now is that my Barron can't trust me to take care of myself, and that you refuse to support my decisions or support my deepest desire. It hurts me, Trayton."

He dropped his gaze to the ground between our feet, looking so sad and defeated that I very nearly felt bad for him. "I'm sorry. I'll try to be more understanding. But you have to promise me that you'll fulfill these urges in a way that won't endanger lives. Namely, yours. I don't know what I'd do without you, Kaya. My world would be shattered if I lost you. Please be careful."

Toeing my way into delicate territory, I kept my voice low, hoping that my accusation wouldn't destroy the quiet manner in which he was sitting. "Are you sure you even want to be in a relationship with me? It seems you're spending a lot of time with Melanie."

He didn't move at first, didn't speak. Then he pushed himself back and lay down on the bed, pinching the bridge of his nose and squeezing his eyes tight. "Do you love him, Kaya?"

Groaning, I resisted the urge to smack some sense into Trayton with a pillow. "Who, Darius? No! It wasn't about sneaking around or cheating on you, Trayton. It was about learning how to defend myself. How could you think that?"

He reached over and ran his hand over my hair, his fingers gently intertwining with it. His eyes moved to mine in the near darkness. "Do you love me?"

I swallowed hard. It would have been easy to say yes, but I wasn't certain that that was what Trayton wanted. It seemed he'd be more satisfied with the truth. "I don't know. I think so. Maybe."

His eyes searched mine for a moment, perhaps for a small flame of hope. In that moment, I wished very much that I had been able to say yes.

"I love you so much it hurts." His hand slipped from

my hair to my cheek. He loved me. Trayton loved me. And he'd said it like he'd been saying it his entire life. It came easily, like a breath.

Before nervousness or fear could whisper in my ear, I leaned closer to Trayton, feeling his breath on my skin. Our lips melted in a kiss that made my heart race. A heat began at my core and washed through me, cooled only by the light dance of his fingertips across my skin. His hands moved up my arms, over my shoulders, and tangled in my hair, and my breath was stolen away. I wanted more of this, this feeling, and I never wanted it to end. I kissed him harder and he pulled me to him, down with him onto the bed. Our bodies were touching from head to toe, and we were melting into one another, into the mattress. His right hand slid slowly back down my body, pausing at my waist to pull me into him. The shock and thrill of his action pulled me out of the moment and back into reality. It took every ounce of will that I possessed to pull back away from that kiss and look into his eyes, to tell him silently that I wasn't ready for things to go any further. Disappointment filled his features, and for a moment, neither of us moved. I rolled over and he snuggled up behind me, arms around me.

As we drifted off to sleep together, three things occupied my mind. One, I was going to have to sneak out of Trayton's room before breakfast unless I wanted to catch hell from Edmond. Two, I still hadn't forgiven Trayton for exposing me on the battlefield and turning me in to Headmaster Quill, endangering my parents' lives. And three, I was going to do everything I could to steer clear of Darius after he returned.

If he returned.

Edmond trailed behind me, content to follow as I moved along the wall, searching for any signs of distress. But no stones were loose that I could see or reach, and no sign that Graplars had somehow managed to climb their way inside. It baffled me that no one seemed able to discover exactly how the damn things were getting inside the wall. There were no holes, no signs of entry at all. Maybe the Graplars were changing, acting in a way that they hadn't before. Maybe they'd somehow learned how to climb giant stone walls. There had to be answers somewhere. The question was, where?

My stomach rumbled, but I hoped that Edmond couldn't hear it, or he'd make me break for lunch. It was bad enough that he'd forced me to stop for breakfast on my way out the door. Between classes, I planned to search the inside perimeter of the wall. So long as Edmond didn't keep bothering me with pesky things like the need for food.

As if he'd heard my stomach's complaints, Edmond said, "We should head to the dining hall and get you some lunch. And since you forgot your Botanical Medicine book, we should stop by and pick that up too."

I strode forward along the wall, scanning it for any sign of weakness. "I'm not hungry, and I'll grab the book later. Besides, I'm not done searching yet."

Edmond's hand closed over my shoulder, and he turned me toward him. "You need to eat and you have a test tomorrow."

Wrenching my shoulder away, completely irritated by his interruption, I said, "I don't feel like eating, Edmond. What I really feel like doing is figuring out how Graplars keep getting inside. But if it'll shut you up for an hour, then take me to get the stupid book and I'll grab a quick lunch afterward. But then I'm searching this wall, and you have to promise to help me. Deal?"

After a long, silent consideration—in which I was sure he was weighing the outcome of my untimely death by starvation—Edmond nodded.

We crossed campus, heading west without another word. Once we reached Instructor Harnett's class, I moved inside alone, as always. Sitting on my chair was the rogue schoolbook. I plucked it up and turned back to the door, my thoughts still very much focused on the Graplars' point of entry.

Then something heavy smacked hard against my head, sending a jolt of pain through my body. I tumbled away into a darkness without end.

CHAPTER

Thirty-one

*M*y head was throbbing and something warm was lying on the back of my neck. I suspected it was blood, but when I attempted to touch it, my wrist caught, bound behind my back with something that felt like twine. When I opened my eyes, my vision wavered. It took a moment to focus. But when it did, I realized that I was outside, lying on the edges of the rose gardens. Instructor Baak was standing over me, madness lighting up her eyes. Light glinted off the jagged blade of the dagger in her hand. At first, confusion filled me, but then that confusion mingled with my upset and I pulled at my hands, trying to wrench them free from their binds. The twine tore into my skin, burning me, bruising me, but I couldn't break free.

Instructor Baak shook her head, her grin spreading across the lower half of her face. "There's no use, Kaya. That twine, if you'd paid attention in class, is made of knotbush and virtually unbreakable without a sharp blade."

"Let me go."

"I won't set you free, child, can never set you free. Because with you, I can lure him here, and without you, my heart goes on breaking forever."

I had no idea what she was talking about, but it sounded like she was in love with someone—someone that I had access to. Trayton? Darius? "You think tying me up will bring him here?"

"I know it will." She pulled back the top of her shirt, revealing a large amber pendant on a silver chain around her neck. She ran a hand lovingly over the stone, and something inside of it glinted in a strange, luminescent blue. The blue dimmed as Instructor Baak withdrew her fingers, and I couldn't help but think that the thing inside the stone was alive somehow. "The Graplar King gifted me with this a year ago today. Do you know where this amulet was mined, Kaya? Of course not. No one does. None but the most loyal. The amulet—all of Darrek's Graplar-controlling amulets—were mined in the caves beneath his fortress, in the place where he first discovered the creatures' existence. Sound reverberates through the stones, making it possible to communicate and command the creatures. It's quite fascinating, really."

I said nothing. The utter shock that Instructor Baak had been at all involved with King Darrek's mysterious motives coiled around me, making it difficult to breath easily.

"Darrek may be no better than the monsters he commands, Kaya, but who's to say that Barrons are any better than him? With this amulet, I can control Graplars. They won't harm anyone who holds it—Darrek promised me that and he was true to his word. Unlike the Elder Barrons, who promised me that my daughter would be fine on the Outer Rim." Her expression darkened and her knuckles paled as she gripped the handle of the dagger tighter. She was no longer the bothersome teacher that I faced every day in Healing 101, but a madwoman. Her face set permanently in a horrifying grin.

"They lied. Oh, how the lies spewed from their lips. Then the second battle at Wood's Cross happened, and my daughter was killed." Her grin, at last, relented. "She should have been protected. Her Barron should have saved her. But he was selfish, like all Barrons. He let her die and went unpunished. But his time for punishment has come. Do you know anything at all about fogmoss, Kaya? Of course not. I'd bet you're a terrible Botanical Medicine student." That jibe stung, as I actually really enjoyed my Botanical Medicine class. But try as I might, I couldn't recall having learned anything at all about something called fogmoss from Instructor Harnett, but I lay silent, pulling at the knotbush, trying to wiggle free. "Fogmoss is a forbidden herb here on campus—on any campus, really—because it brews a tea that renders the drinker your willing servant. They will do anything that you ask and remember only what you tell them to remember. Which is precisely how I've been letting Graplars inside the wall."

My jaw dropped. "You're sick. People have been hurt, have died! Those things are so awful. How could you?"

She smiled, her eyes dazed. "It was easy enough to get the gate guards to drink the potion. Guards are frequently gifted with drink and food while on night duty, and I am a trusted instructor. So I gave them the tea to drink, instructed them to assist me, and then blurred their memories about how the Graplars ever got in. It took practice, to make certain I had the potion right. Fortunately, I did. And why not take out a few people while I'm at it, and maybe infect the school with a little healthy fear? Maybe he'd be afraid they were coming for him. And I definitely want him to know what fear is."

Clearly, this was about vengeance. Vengeance against the boy who'd let her daughter perish in that horrible battle. She closed her eyes briefly, and when she opened them again, all that remained of the Instructor Baak I knew withered away into dust. "I let hundreds of Graplars inside the gates just a few minutes ago. And I instructed the creatures to kill them all. Darrek was right. It's the only way to stop this terrible war. Every Healer, every Barron that fights against him must die. Let's end it. Let's just end it, and be done with this pain."

At last I had my answer at how the Graplars were getting in. But how was I supposed to warn anyone, when I was tied up? I pulled at my binds to no avail, and pushed myself backward, scooting along the ground until my shoulders met with the log that Mr. Gareth had placed near the gardens as a bench. In the distance, the screams began.

Everyone at Shadow Academy was going to die. No amount of Barron skill could possibly hold the monsters at bay. No amount of healing could fix the wounds that they would cause. Everyone was going to die, and it was at the hand of a woman whose loyalties had shifted, all because she felt that her daughter had been wronged.

Ever so casually, Instructor Baak approached the log and sat down, running her fingers over my hair, as if she was petting me. I don't know where she was at that moment, but it wasn't with me in the rose gardens. Instructor Baak was somewhere else, long ago. "You're such a pretty girl, Katelyn. You deserve better than this, better than what Darius has given you."

Pulling away from her touch, I shook my head. "It was an accident, Instructor Baak. Darius was just trying to take down King Darrek. He didn't mean for anything to happen to your daughter."

Her eyes turned toward me, but she wasn't seeing me. She was seeing Katelyn. She was speaking to her dead child, and stroking her dead child's hair. "Fourteen was too young to go to battle, Katelyn. Too young, and not experienced enough. I told you not to go. Mother knows best. You could have hidden away, but you insisted on going. Not your fault. I raised you right. But you couldn't protect that boy. And he wouldn't protect you. I was right all along about him. He chose glory over duty. And look how they rewarded him."

Her fingers tangled in my hair as she ran them through, yanking at my roots painfully. I wriggled away, but she refused to let go, lost in her delusion. "Your soul will soon be free, my love. Darrek's Graplars can punish those that praised Darius for his failings. He returned to Shadow Academy just an hour ago. And now he'll come for you, to save you as he should have saved you then. And when he does, I'll pierce his heart and set you free."

In the distance, the sounds of war filled the campus. Shrill screams reached my ears, sending gooseflesh over my entire body. Graplars' growls echoed throughout Shadow Academy. Death was in the air.

I laid helpless on the ground, my hands bound, my back against a log, a madwoman's hands tangled in my hair. All I could do was listen as Instructor Baak's terrible plan unfolded before me. No one would rescue me, no one could. And I prayed that Instructor Baak was wrong and that Darius would stay far away from Shadow Academy, or else his life would be forfeit as well. I struggled against my bonds, but they were too tight, too strong. I just hoped that Instructor Baak would kill me before the Graplars could. I couldn't imagine a more painful death.

"Kaya!" Trayton hurried closer, the look on his face one of immense relief.

As he drew closer, one of Instructor Baak's hands closed over my mouth. "Shh," she whispered. "There now. It'll all be over soon, Katelyn."

Trayton's chest rose and fell in heavy breaths, as if he'd been running for quite some time. "I've been searching the grounds for you. Figures I'd find you here. Are you all right? Graplars have overrun the—"

His eyes fell on Instructor Baak's hand in my hair, and confusion washed over him. When his attention dropped to her hand on my mouth, he reached back, his fingers lightly grasping the handle of the katana on his back, his eyes dark and mistrusting. "Instructor Baak?"

Her hand loosened on my hair then, and the hand over my mouth retreated. For a moment, the woman that I'd come to know seemed to reappear. She stood slowly, carefully, as if she'd found herself again. Relief filled me, settling my heart's rhythm. Shaking her head, she said, "Trayton. My word. I don't know what came over me. Kaya, I am so sorry. I never meant to—"

Then she lunged forward, raising the jagged blade high into the air. I stared in disbelief as time slowed, her dagger shining in the moonlight, Trayton's katana almost glowing as he withdrew it from its saya. He didn't bring the sword forward. It was as if he was frozen in disbelief. The dagger came down, plunging into his neck. I wrenched forward, but there was nothing I could do. Blood spurted from the wound as she pulled the dagger out again, several droplets spattering my cheek. The katana tumbled to the ground, landing softly in the grass at Trayton's feet. Trayton clutched his neck and crumpled soundlessly to the ground.

Thirty-two

*T*ime rolled forward, picking up speed as it went, until everything was moving the way that it was supposed to once more. Trayton lay on the ground, coughing against the pain of his injury, blood seeping from the corner of his mouth and pouring from between his fingers. Scrambling forward, I rolled, hoping to heal him, to save him, but Instructor Baak pointed her bloodied dagger at my eye. "Back, girl. There will be no healing this boy. They all have to die. It's the only way to put Katelyn to rest and bring this war to an end."

My hand was inches from Trayton's neck, but it might as well have been miles. There was no doubt in my mind that if I edged so much as a millimeter closer, she was going to stab me. She was going to kill us both, and then kill everyone else on campus. "You're a monster! This war is Darrek's doing! And Katelyn's death was a tragedy, but she died doing what Healers do, supporting her

Barron. You preach about that duty every day in class."

"It's a duty that was above my daughter!" Her eyes glossed over again, as if she were having a difficult time staying in the present. "You should have been a Barron, Katelyn. I wish you had been a Barron."

"Killing innocent people won't lay Katelyn's soul to rest, Instructor Baak. And what makes you think it's at unrest, anyway? Katelyn is dead, and I'm sure she wouldn't want her mother murdering people." Slowly, I scooted backward, back to the log, an idea fixed firmly in my mind. To my great relief, she didn't seem to care if I moved away, only if I moved toward Trayton, who was paling fast, his grip on his bleeding neck weakening. "Killing people isn't going to bring your daughter back."

"You know nothing of my daughter!" She sobbed, large tears rolling from her crazy, widened eyes.

Pressing my back against the log, I pushed myself to standing and stepped toward her, ready, hoping that my plan would work. Narrowing my eyes in a furious slant, I hissed, "I'm ashamed of you, mother!"

"NO!" She howled. "You're not my daughter! You're not my Katelyn! He killed her! Darius killed her! You're not her!"

Her face red, her maddened grin turned into a maddened snarl, she whipped her free hand forward, backhanding me. Pain exploded in my cheek. It ached through my jaw and echoed through my skull. I fell, forcing my body to fall at just the right angle, and when

I hit the ground, something in my left knee popped. Ignoring the pain, I slipped my binds over the katana's blade, slicing neatly through them. Then, as fast as I could move, I pressed my left hand to Trayton's neck and lifted the katana with my right.

As I raised the sword, Instructor Baak brought her dagger down. She was fast. Too fast. I wouldn't be able to block it in time. But maybe, just maybe, Trayton would heal in time to avenge my death. Beneath my fingers, he continued to bleed. There was no tingling in the palm of my hand, no sensation of power as I pressed my skin to his. There was just blood, and the overwhelming feeling that I was losing him.

My heart beat hard and fast, as if trying to get its last workings in before the dagger entered. Time had slowed again, and I watched the blade edge nearer and nearer to my chest. I brought the katana up and sliced into her arm, cutting deeply. But it wouldn't be enough to stop her. The sound of metal slicing bone grated in my ears, and her blood poured out, drenching us both.

A hand closed over Instructor Baak's injured arm and twisted it back, sending her flying. She landed several yards away, with shrill cries that hurt my ears. Darius met my eyes with so many questions that I didn't know which to answer first. Then he looked at Trayton and his expression darkened with concern. In his eyes were the words that I didn't want to hear: *He's dying, Kaya. If we don't get him to the hospital wing immediately, he's dead.*

A sob choked me and I dropped the katana to the ground, pressing both of my hands to Trayton's wound in desperation. But still, the sensation that I had experienced in our Binding ceremony escaped me. I was failing him and had no idea how to make him well again. "Don't leave me, Trayton! Please don't leave me. Heal. Just heal!"

Darius closed a hand over my shoulder. At first I thought he was comforting me, but as his fingers pressed, I realized he was trying to silently gain my attention. Sniffling, I turned my head, and my heart stopped.

Two Graplars were standing to either side of Instructor Baak, who was giggling madly. Her laughter pierced the air, sending a sharp chill up my spine. Her grin had returned, broad as ever, and if a miracle didn't present itself soon, the three of us were as good as dead.

Stroking the amulet around her neck, Instructor Baak purred to the savage beasts at her command. "Kill the girl quickly, but leave the boy to me."

My hand found the katana again before I could even think to do so. Slowly, I stood, forgetting about stopping Trayton's bleeding for the moment. The Graplar to her left lunged forward, toward me. Darius turned to confront it, gripping the handle of his katana in determination. Behind him, Instructor Baak edged her way closer, raising her dagger high. I shouted Darius's name, but he was already turning toward her, already countering her move with one of his own. He raised his blade and made contact. Once again the sound of metal on bone filled the air. Once again blood flew. But it was Instructor Baak's blood. Her hand tumbled through the air, still gripping the dagger.

Instructor Baak didn't make a sound.

The Graplar moved forward and I readied my blade. Lurching toward me, its foul breath filled the air, making me gag. But I gripped the handle, ready for the beast's assault.

"Stop!"

Instructor Baak raced forward, her eyes once again clouded, her handless arm gushing blood, and flung herself between me and the Graplar, her eyes wide and terrified. "Leave her be. Leave my Katelyn be!"

The Graplar froze, unable to resist the whims of the amulet's keeper. I didn't know what to say, what to do. I also didn't know how long this madness would carry on in my favor.

Darius slowly returned his katana to his saya. I wanted to scream at him not to trust her, not to believe that this was the end of her violent desire for justice, but my voice froze in my throat. Darius fell on his knees in front of Instructor Baak, his brow heavy. "I'm sorry, Instructor Baak. I never meant for anything to happen to Katelyn. I should have protected her. And I'll never forgive myself."

I took a step toward Instructor Baak. She was facing away from me, her eyes on Darius. Both looked pained beyond belief. Tears welled in Darius's eyes. "Please. End it. Set her soul free. But spare the others. Katelyn's death was no fault but my own."

Instructor Baak's eyes filled with hatred as she looked down at Darius. Her grip on the amulet tightened, and I knew the next words that left her mouth would cause Darius's demise.

I reached out to snatch the necklace from her neck, but she yanked it away before I could. Cursing at us, she ran off into the growing darkness with more strength than I thought was possible in her current state. Instinctively, I moved to go after her, but then felt Darius's hand on my arm. The look in his eyes was more serious than I had ever witnessed. Darius stood, hoisting Trayton into his arms. "We have to get him to the Master Healer, Kaya."

Trayton's skin was a deathly pale. His arms hung limp, his eyes were closed. If I had to guess, I might have thought him to be dead already. But I clung to the hope that Darius was right to believe there was a chance at saving his life.

With a determined nod, I gripped the katana tightly in my hands and led the way. Instructor Baak would have to be dealt with later.

Thirty-three

We made our way through the darkness to the hospital wing, which was packed with people—many moaning, some screaming in pain. Darius laid Trayton on an empty gurney and was checking his pulse when I grabbed the shoulder of a passing Master Healer. "We need help. My Barron is—"

"We'll get to you in a minute." He turned as if to rush down the hall.

My skin flushed, almost burning. "No! You don't understand, he's dying!"

It was only then, when Darius's hands closed over mine, that I realized that I was holding Trayton's katana up in a threatening manner. He slipped the blade from my trembling hands and met my eyes with complete understanding. Then he looked back to the terrified Master Healer and said, "She's very upset, as you can understand. But she's also right. Trayton is in dire straits. Please."

"Trayton?" As if his name was well known—and it likely was, due to his father's fame—the Master Healer forgot all about me and hurried to Trayton's side. After just a moment, Trayton was rushed away, and Darius directed me to a bench in the hall. I sat down, tears welling from my eyes, and when Darius sat beside me, I cried into his shoulder, soaking his bloodstained shirt. After a while, I shoved him from me, so overcome with the bitter mixture of grief and rage. "Where were you? You could have saved him!"

His shoulders sank, as if weighed down by guilt. "You're right. I should have been here. I traveled to Haruko, not far from Darkmoon Academy. I like it there. It's where I go to clear my head sometimes. But the moment I overheard two of Darrek's drunken guards in this pub I frequent discussing a teacher at Shadow Academy who was loyal to Darrek's cause, I hurried back."

My eyes ached from crying. "You shouldn't have left in the first place."

He said nothing. Mostly because there was nothing to say.

My Soulbound Barron had died. Now I was about to lose my Bound Barron too. The pain was overwhelming. Before this moment I had never truly understood what my father had meant by the term "soulbroken." But I did now. My heart ached. My insides felt hollowed out. I was hurting, and there was no end in sight for my pain.

After minutes, maybe hours, with my throat raw from crying, I finally asked the question that had been burning through my soul since I'd laid a hand on Trayton's wound. "Why couldn't I heal him, Darius? What did I do wrong?"

Tightening his arm around my shoulders, he breathed into my hair. "You did nothing wrong. Being Bound isn't as strong as being Soulbound. It's not as reliable. More serious injuries are questionable. You may be able to heal them. You may not. But you tried. And that means everything in the world to Trayton right now."

I dried my tears and sat up, tugging his sleeve. I was still mad at Darius, still so angry that he'd ever exposed me to Trayton's watchful eye. But for the time being, I needed him. "Come on."

Darius looked at me with one eyebrow raised. "Where are we going?"

I stood and picked up the katana, determination replacing my immense sorrow for the time being. "We're going to find Instructor Baak and get that amulet."

Thirty-four

Darius and I moved across the campus, sticking as close to buildings as we could. Graplars ran by, their giant, muscular forms pounding the ground all around us. Some glistened with sweat from the effort of their assault on the school's occupants. Others were dripping with blood. But it was those who seemed to grin as they passed us that bothered me the most. I didn't know for sure whether or not Graplars were capable of emotion, but their lips stretched so wide to reveal their teeth in a horrifying grin. The absolutely worst part of it was that between the rows of razor-sharp teeth were bits of chewed meat—meat that had likely been a person just moments ago.

The Graplars screeched as they continued their assault, their voracious appetites refusing to cease. A particularly large beast bit into a girl as it crossed the cobblestone of the courtyard, carrying off a snack for later. A still-screaming, still-very-much-alive snack. But who knew for how long? Horrified, I moved forward to engage the beast, but Darius stopped me with his fingers on my shoulder. When I looked at him, his eyes had narrowed, his mood darkened. "Stop. This one's mine."

An angry heat filled me. Once more I was being told what not to do. Once more I was being pushed to the side. I gripped the katana in my hand and ran forward, toward the beast.

Darius had broken into a run two seconds before I had, and he was already engaging the Graplar. He slashed at its front legs, and it reared up in response, growling, but refusing to release its prey. The poor girl screamed, her blood running freely into the creature's mouth, drizzling onto the cobblestone below. As the Graplar whipped its head to the side, she fell back, her eyes wide with terror. For a moment, our eyes connected, and then the beast moved its head once more, shaking her like a lifeless doll.

I couldn't see the girl's face at that moment. All I could see were things my imagination had conjured up about the night my life had changed forever. Avery's terrified eyes, Avery's screaming mouth, Avery's blood spattering onto my father's shirt as the Graplar tore her to bits.

Before I even realized what I was doing, I'd jumped up, bringing my sword down on the Graplar's neck. Its head flopped forward, still connected to its body by just a thin layer of tissue. The jaws opened and the girl was free. She lay on the ground, sobbing. I stood in front of the monster that had almost taken her life and watched as its body staggered to the left before landing in a lifeless heap. I flicked its blood from my blade just as Darius came to stand beside me. "In case you didn't hear me, I said that this one was mine."

My jaw ached from being clenched so tightly. "After today, I never want to see you again, Darius."

He paused, but only briefly. "Why?"

Glaring at him, I said, "Because bringing Trayton in to spar with me was wrong. Because you endangered my parents' lives with your stupid move. Why him? Why Trayton? Why not any other Barron?"

"Because you care about him. If you can stand against even an ally, that means your training has reached a certain admirable level. Plus, he distracts you. And we both know that you struggle with distractions." He eyed me for a moment before continuing. His tone was even, almost completely devoid of emotion. In the background, the girl's sobs were quieting, but slowly. Her injuries were terrible, maybe deadly. I didn't know.

Darius shrugged. "But you did well. The lesson went better than I'd hoped. So what's the problem?"

A Barron that I didn't recognize ran by, and I stopped him with a hand to his chest. "Wait. Take this girl to the hospital wing."

With a nod, he scooped her into his arms as gently

as possible and ran off, without argument. I turned back to Darius.

"The problem is that you risked my parents' lives with that stunt. And you did it without consulting me at all." I took a deep breath and let it out slowly, still very angry, but not wanting to lose my temper. "I want an apology. Strike that. I deserve an apology."

He was silent for the longest time, as if taking everything that I had said into consideration and mulling it over. A chorus of death surrounded us. Then he parted his lips and said, "No."

"What?" My eyes flashed with fury "What do you mean *no*?"

He turned from me then and began making his way out of the courtyard. I moved quickly, quietly, on the balls of my feet, lifting my katana as silently as I was able. At the last moment, he freed his weapon and spun around, our blades meeting in midair. The clang of metal rang through my ears. "You owe me an apology, Darius."

He pushed back with his blade, but I dug my heel into the ground, gritting my teeth against his strength. To my surprise, my stance held for longer than I thought it would, but then Darius reached the end of his patience and shoved me back. I stumbled backward, but when I recovered my footing, I swept his left leg and Darius lost his balance. Bringing my katana around fast, I counted on his Barron reflexes to deliver and they did. He jumped back, straight into the fountain, and I stopped my blade against his throat. He swallowed and the metal nicked him, blood drawing a thin line down his neck. Holding my weapon steady, I leaned closer and said, "I said I want an apology. You owe me at least that much. I have kept your secret, after all. Despite what you've done. The least that you can do is apologize."

His gaze, full of surprise at my skill, softened then and fell to my blade, then rose to my mouth. As the words passed over his lips in a whisper, a chill tickled up my spine, and he raised his eyes to meet mine. "I'm sorry, Kaya."

A loud screech jolted me, and before I realized, I'd dropped my sword to waist height in distracted fear. In seconds, Darius had his katana poised, ready for action. I whipped my head around, searching the immediate area for any sign of a Graplar. I saw nothing near us, but the sounds of the beasts moving through academy grounds filled my ears. Then I heard another sound. The voice of Instructor Baak in the distance, her words accompanied by mad laughter. "Kill them all! Kill them all!"

Darius took off, pausing briefly to throw a wordless glance over his shoulder at me. I broke into a run. We had to get to Instructor Baak, had to get that amulet away from her and stop this attack before any more people died.

She was standing at the center of the Barrons' training area, arms raised, eyes so wide that there was no questioning her sanity level anymore. Her arm had been tightly bandaged, but I was still shocked to see her conscious. She'd lost so much blood. Maybe, I wondered, she knew something about herbs that Instructor Harnett hadn't taught me.

As Graplars clashed with students all around her, she twirled in slow circles to the music in her head. I'd never thought anything would frighten me more than a Graplar. But seeing Instructor Baak lose her mind completely, watching as her madness took over any ounce of reason that she'd once had . . . it terrified me.

Darius ran at her, but just before he could make contact, a Graplar dove into him, knocking him to the side. Instructor Baak cackled with glee. Fury ignited my movement—fury that a crazy, selfish woman like Instructor Baak was standing here laughing, alive, while poor, giving Trayton was lying in the hospital wing, dying. I moved carefully around the edges of the training area, my eyes on the amulet—the cause of this whole mess.

The training area was filled with Barrons, Healers, and Graplars, with Instructor Baak reigning over the chaos from the center. Her eyes were alight with madness, and though several of the creatures nearly hit her as they ran by, she seemed completely oblivious to the danger she was in. It was as if she were in another time, another place, one where she and her beloved Katelyn were at peace. I crept around the perimeter of the area until I could see Instructor Baak's back clearly. But between us stood three Graplars, and a handful of Barrons who would only prove to be in my way.

Breaking into a run, my heart slamming in my chest, I jumped up and planted my foot onto the first Graplar's head as it bent down. Pushing off, I jumped toward the second, but slipped on its scaly skin and fell to the ground. My ankle twisted some, but I hurried to stand before the beast could lunge at me, snapping its shimmering teeth in a bite. One of the Barrons engaged the beast and I hurried behind its massive form, using it as a hiding place as I crept toward Instructor Baak.

The amulet glimmered from its place on the thin chain around her neck, beckoning to me. Taunting me.

Another Barron stepped in front of me in a protective stance, katana raised at the Graplar between Instructor Baak and me. "Get out of here. It's not safe!"

But I couldn't leave, couldn't run. I was the only one who had any idea how to stop this horror, and I wasn't about to stop until I grasped that amulet in my hand. I shoved the Barron to the side. The movement caught the Graplar's attention and it dove after the Barron, but there was no time for me to assist him.

I crept up on Instructor Baak and stretched my hand out, grasping for the chain on her neck.

Instructor Baak whipped around, clawing at me with her remaining hand. Her shrieks filled the air. Her fingernails dug into my face and hands. I pulled back, my katana falling to the ground. The silver chain strained, then snapped free. The amulet glowed brightly in my hand. The howl of a madwoman filled my ears.

Free of the Graplar who'd tossed him to the side, Darius grabbed Instructor Baak and pulled her back, holding her away from me as gently as he could. It amazed me to see that kindness in him, and I wondered what she had been like before Katelyn had been killed. I held the amulet up, hoping that it would work for me the way it had for her. "Graplars, cease your attack, gather the rest of your kind, use the gates to get outside the wall, and stay there."

At first, the two hulking beasts nearest to us simply snorted. Then, slowly, the one on the right turned and ran toward the more populated area of the school. I only hoped that it was actually leaving. The beast on the left toed the ground, as if it were too stupid or stubborn to comply. I was about to repeat my command, when Instructor Baak elbowed Darius hard and spun away. He reached out for her, but missed and she grabbed the amulet from my hand. She held the amulet up, cackling wildly. "Take me to my daughter! Take me to Katelyn!"

She brought the amulet down, smashing it on a rock. I didn't know why—maybe because that's what King Darrek would have wanted her to do, maybe because doing so would prevent us from controlling Graplars in the future. I had no idea what her motives might have been. I simply watched in shock as bits of amber flew through the air, catching on her clothes.

The remaining Graplar obliged her final order and lunged forward, biting into her throat. It dragged her off toward the rose gardens and sounds reached my ears that I hoped I would soon forget, but knew that I never would. Biting sounds. Chewing sounds. Instructor Baak was dead. Reunited at last with her beloved Katelyn.

Darius turned his head away the moment the Graplar had bitten into Instructor Baak, his features paling. My breaths came quick and shallow. I didn't know what to say. After a moment, he picked up my katana and handed it to me before turning toward the south gate. The weapon felt strangely heavy in my hand. "Where are you going?"

"You sent them outside." He looked over his shoulder at me, his expression blank. I wondered if that was because watching Instructor Baak perish had been painful for him. "But they won't go without taking food with them."

With a deep breath, I chased him through campus and out the gate. I might not have been able to save Trayton, but I refused to let any more people die. As I ran after Darius, Trayton filled my thoughts. He'd hate what I was doing, that I was running willingly out onto the battlefield again. But I had to do it. Had to do what I could to help those in need.

Darius was fast, but I was vigilant and didn't fall behind once. We ran through the forest, jumping over rocks and fallen branches, dodging trees and prickly undergrowth. The sound of the battle hit my ears long before I could see it. The smell came shortly after. It smelled like fear. It smelled like blood.

Once we'd crested another hill, a strange electricity was in the air. Dozens of Barrons were outside the gate, in the forest, katanas in hand. Beyond them were dozens more, deeply entrenched in battle with over fifty Graplars. The beasts lunged and bit. Screams and squeals from both sides echoed throughout the forest, shooting through me.

With a glance at me, Darius withdrew his katana and bolted down the hill. As he descended on the battle, he leaped into the air, bringing his blade down on one of the beasts' necks. The Graplar howled, tossing him back. But Darius recovered quickly and spun around, slashing at its legs, bringing the monster down. As it fell, he pulled his sword up sharply, slicing its head clean off. Blood spurted from its headless neck as it fell forward and landed in a heap on the leaf-covered ground.

To my amazement, Darius sheathed his sword. Then, jumping up once more, he grabbed onto the corner of another Graplar's mouth with his hands, swinging himself around the beast's head. Using his weight, he pulled the Graplar's head down, smashing it on a large, pointed boulder. The monster's neck hit hard and the stone acted as a blade, slicing its skull from its body. Darius paused once it was dead and looked back at me with a grin, as if to say that that was how he'd killed the beast with the fountain. But he didn't pause for long. I watched, mesmerized, as Darius ran farther into the battleground. He was a machine, with one distinct purpose: kill them all.

Reaching back, I drew my katana and moved down the hill, my heart racing. Something large and heavy slammed into my side as I descended the hill and I went flying, landing in leaves moist with blood. My grip tightened on my katana as I fell. I scrambled to stand, and came eye to eye with a hungry Graplar, its mouth foaming, its gaze intent. Fighting the urge to bolt, I eyed it down, waiting for it to make the first move. It snorted, as if to say that it knew what I was thinking, and for a moment, I wondered if it did.

It leaped into the air and descended on me. In a moment of panic, I hesitated and the beast took me down, standing over me as I lay on the forest floor. It lunged forward, its mouth open, its horrible teeth shining with drool. Regaining my senses, I brought my sword around, catching the metal inside the thing's mouth. It bit down and the razor-sharp blade sliced into its jaws. Yelping, it scrambled backward, freeing me. I stood and ran at it, jumping into the air and onto its back. Its scaly skin felt smooth on my hands as I straddled its neck. I'd expected the beast to feel cold to the touch, but it was warm, almost hot. Reaching around its head as it tried to fling me away, I gripped the handle of my katana and pulled, yanking the blade hard toward me. The blade slid easily through the Graplar's mouth, through its skull, slicing most of its head off. Its impulses hadn't told the Graplar that it was dead, because the thing lurched forward in a spasm, tossing me from its shoulders. The mostly headless beast staggered, and finally fell to the forest floor.

Flicking my wrist hard, I cleaned my blade the way that Darius had shown me, by flinging the blood from the metal, and looked around, ready to go again. But to my utter relief—relief mingled with disappointment— most of the Graplars had been either killed already or chased away, reminding me that I wasn't a Barron, that I lacked their speed. In the time it had taken me to kill just one Graplar, they had taken care of the rest. Slightly disappointed in myself, I turned around, taking in the carnage of the battlefield. Injured Barrons lay all around the ground. Lifting my spirits was the fact that very few of the Graplars that had attacked had survived.

I searched the grounds for Darius, but couldn't find him among those who were helping carry the wounded inside the now-open gate. It was possible he'd already gone inside, or was patrolling in search of any more Graplars, but the heavy feeling in my chest told me to keep looking. He was here somewhere. I just had to find him. I moved around the battlegrounds, stepping carefully over the injured and the dead, looking for the telltale sign of Darius's shocking silver hair. I'd all but given up when a hand closed around my ankle. When I looked down, I realized why I hadn't seen his silver locks.

Darius was covered in blood.

A deep gash crossed his forehead, flooding his hairline with crimson as he easily bled. His face was ashen.

My bottom lip shook as I knelt beside him. Darius was dying, and he had no Healer to heal him. No amount of herbs and salves could fix this. Tears welled in my eyes and poured down my cheeks. He was dying and I could do nothing to stop it.

But I had to try.

Swallowing my sobs, I pressed my palms tightly against his wound, trying to stop the bleeding. Blood flowed between my fingers, like water through a broken dam. Darius was broken. Forever broken, and I would never be able to tell him how much I appreciated his teachings, and the risk he'd taken to share his knowledge with me.

My words came out in terrified whispers. "Hold on, Darius. You have to hold on. Please."

My efforts were useless. No one and nothing could help him now. Darius was paling faster than ever, and the blood was slowly ceasing its flow. I pressed hard on his wound, crying out, begging in whispers for Darius to stay with me, knowing that he'd never be able to fulfill my request. My hands were warm and tingling from the rush of adrenaline I was experiencing. Then, nothing.

The bleeding stopped, and I swallowed my tears, certain that it was over at last.

Darius's trembling hand closed over my wrist. Shocked, I looked down and met his eyes. How could this be? His coloring was improving. His eyes were open. He was drenched in blood, but looked, for the most part, healthy enough to stand.

My eyes fell on the hand that still cupped Darius's wounded head. As I pulled it away slowly, my heart picked up its rhythm in a panicky race. Then it all but stopped.

Darius's wound had healed. It had healed at my touch. There wasn't even so much as a scar remaining. He was perfectly healthy, brought back from the brink of death by a single touch. My touch. Which meant something that I could barely comprehend, something that sent my mind into a dizzying spiral of emotions.

Darius and I were Soulbound.

But how could that be? His Soulbound Healer was dead. His Trace was black. I knew. I'd seen it. And no Barron can be Soulbound to two Healers. It was impossible.

I searched Darius's eyes for the shock and wonder and utter confusion that I was feeling, but found only embarrassment and sorrow.

He knew.

Darius knew that we were Soulbound. And he didn't tell me.

With a shaking hand, I reached down and slowly pulled the fabric of his shirt away, revealing a red Trace on his chest.

Red.

Because we were Soulbound.

Red, like I'd sworn it had been that night in his cabin. Not black, as I'd seen in the training area that day. Had he colored it to fool me?

He parted his bloodstained lips to speak, his voice gruff. "Kaya . . ."

There was movement just a few feet in front of us, and I looked up to find Trayton. His mask was in his hands, his neck wrapped in a blood-soaked bandage. His katana was on his back, a look of shock on his face.

He'd seen everything, and had heard Darius speaking my name. With a trembling breath, I met Trayton's eyes.

None of us spoke.

THE ADVENTURE CONTINUES IN

LEGACY *of* **TRIL**

BOOK TWO:

Soulbroken